TELEVISION PRODUCTION

TELEVISION PRODUCTION

A Classroom Approach

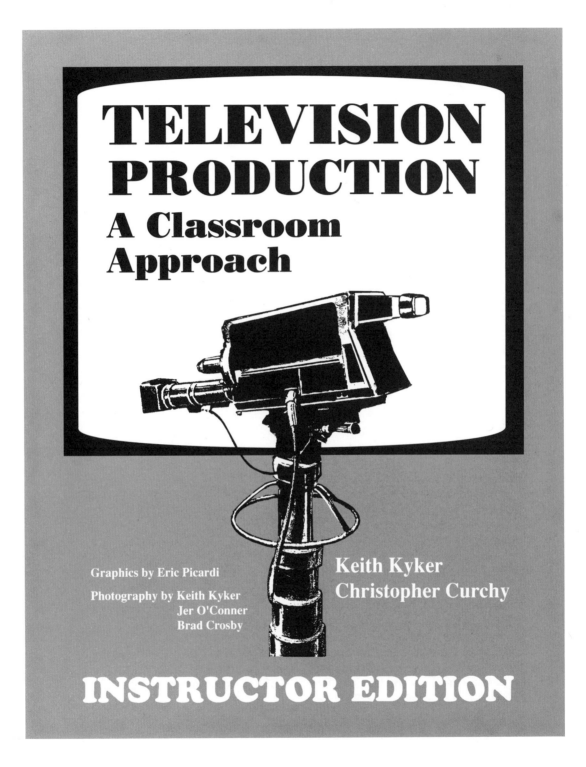

Graphics by Eric Picardi

Photography by Keith Kyker
Jer O'Conner
Brad Crosby

Keith Kyker
Christopher Curchy

INSTRUCTOR EDITION

1993
LIBRARIES UNLIMITED, INC.
Englewood, Colorado

To Shelba and Sarah
—K.K.

To my family and friends for surrendering their summer.
—C.C.

LIBRARIES UNLIMITED, INC.
P.O. Box 6633
Englewood, CO 80155-6633

Library of Congress Cataloging-in-Publication Data

Suggested cataloging:

Kyker, Keith.
Television production : a classroom approach / Keith Kyker and Christopher Curchy. -- Englewood, Colo.: Libraries Unlimited, 1993.
Includes bibliographical references and index.
xvi, 378 p. 22x28 cm. (Instructor Edition) ISBN 1-56308-101-6
iv, 121 p. 22x28 cm. (Student Edition, Book I) ISBN 1-56308-108-3
iv, 137 p. 22x28 cm. (Student Edition, Book II) ISBN 1-56308-161-X
27 min. (Video) ISBN 1-56308-107-5
1. Television production and direction. 2. Television equipment and supplies. I. Curchy, Christopher. II. Title.
PN1992.75 K9 1993
791.450232 (DDC 20)

CONTENTS

Chapter 1
INTERMEDIATE TELEVISION PRODUCTION *(continued)*

FOREWORD

Over the past three months I have flown to Europe eight times, and this Saturday I go once more! My continual contact abroad convinces me more than ever that our American students need a book such as Keith and Chris have created.

Why? Simply put, when it comes to visual literacy, to the production of sophisticated imagery, we come in a distant second to some of our international counterparts. The Kyker-Curchy team has addressed, at least in part, how to solve that problem—put video cameras in the hands of students! And keep doing it, and add to the minutes, hours, and days that our students view their world through the lens.

Only in that way will they begin to look beyond themselves and outward to their much larger world, a world that foments, festers, and fumes, a world that, with the help of this text, may very well result in another Spielberg, Lucas, or Stone. Who can tell?

I have known Chris Curchy and Keith Kyker for many years, initially as students in our Educational Media graduate programs, and later as friends, loyal helpers, and creative teachers of innumerable students.

I've seen the looks on their own students' faces as first one, then another, grasped more completely the potential of television as a communicative and creative art form. I've seen them mirror joy, despair, frustration, and excitement as each came face-to-face with the realities of good camera work, of the patience required to complete a simple edit, and of the happiness displayed upon winning an international award.

I can say, with unabashed pride, "these were my students once, and look what they've been able to accomplish!" Is there any better reward for having been their teacher?

Richard A. Cornell, Ed.D.
Area of Instructional Systems
University of Central Florida
Orlando, Florida

ACKNOWLEDGMENTS

The authors would like to thank the following individuals and organizations for their cooperation and support:

Vue-Com, Inc., of Orlando, Florida
Video Factory, Inc., of Orlando, Florida
Doug Binder of Universal Studios Florida, Orlando, Florida

Thanks to Dr. Richard Cornell of the University of Central Florida, whose flexibility motivated us to begin this project.

Thanks to the administration of Dr. Phillips High School, Orlando, Florida, especially Bill Spoone, Alice Joosens, and Rose Taylor, for their progressive, aggressive approach to scheduling our students over the last five years.

The authors would also like to thank the following television production instructors who completed and returned a survey that described their school's television production facilities and programs of instruction.

Beth E. Anthony
Lake Mary, Florida

R. J. Ashley
Stuart, Florida

Pamela Qualls Baker
Kissimmee, Florida

Chris Carey
Orlando, Florida

Michael W. Carter
Orlando, Florida

Desiree N. Clayton
Melbourne, Florida

Janice P. Deans
Pierson, Florida

Thomas Elledge
Glen St. Mary, Florida

Betty Flowers
Niceville, Florida

Wilson L. Gillett
Spring Hill, Florida

Laura Hagen
Clermont, Florida

Paul B. Harley
Crystal River, Florida

Thera Harris
Chipley, Florida

Steven A. Johnson
Live Oak, Florida

Janet LaVassaur
Largo, Florida

Sally Lemons
St. Cloud, Florida

Judy Power
Orlando, Florida

Jim Rishebarger
Melbourne, Florida

Michael A. Robbert
Gainesville, Florida

Joy Rodriguez
West Palm Beach, Florida

Thomas F. Scahill
Apopka, Florida

D. Charles Schomer
Sanford, Florida

Daniel Sell
Miami, Florida

Shelia Sorrells
Jacksonville, Florida

Cher Stempler
Altamonte Springs, Florida

Karen F. Todd
Orlando, Florida

James Warford
Ocala, Florida

Randy J. Weddle
Boca Raton, Florida

Julie D. West
Miami, Florida

Deborah B. Yowell
Tampa, Florida

Margie Zant
Ft. Walton Beach, Florida

The authors would especially like to thank the hundreds of students who have been enrolled in our television production classes over the years. This project would not have been possible without your excitement, enthusiasm, and willingness to learn.

The authors are especially grateful to the students who appear in the photographs displaying their video production talents. Thanks.

INTRODUCTION

USING THIS BOOK AND TEACHING TELEVISION PRODUCTION

Welcome to *Television Production: A Classroom Approach.* We've prepared this text to assist instructors interested in teaching television production skills. The book you are now holding is actually only one of three parts of our instructional package. A student version, recommended for each student in your class, is also available. We have also prepared a videotape of student projects, which will help you in the adoption of a program of studies for your schools.

Television Production is designed to serve as the primary text in your television production class, facilitating the needs of the student, the instructor, and the school.

The instructor edition serves as your guide through the program, covering everything from the first day of beginning television production class to video yearbook creation and news show production.

You'll find that each student lesson is divided into eight sections:

- **Objectives** are listed at the beginning of each lesson. These statements should be useful in planning classroom implementation of the text and preparing the students for the lesson content.

- **Vocabulary.** Each lesson includes definitions of new terms presented in the lesson text. Definitions are presented in straightforward, practical terms. You may want to include a weekly vocabulary quiz based on these important terms.

- The lesson **text** is presented in a readable, realistic format. By using school-oriented examples and illustrations, the text speaks directly to the student audience and encourages production-related ideas. Based on practical application as well as on theory, the text teaches the important skills of television production in concrete terms, citing equipment available in most high schools.

- **Review questions** based on the facts of the lesson text are included. By using their student texts, students can complete review questions after reading the lesson. Review questions also provide an excellent resource for instructor-produced tests.

- **Activities** designed to enrich the educational experience follow the review questions. While the review questions assure content mastery and reading comprehension, the activities can be used to stimulate class discussion and apply television production to the real world. Instructors should select the activities that best relate to their school's television production program.

- While most texts end at this point, we continue with a unique feature of this curriculum: the **project plan**. Each project reinforces the lesson content, giving the students a chance to sharpen their skills within a given framework. Early projects are described in precise detail, while later projects leave more room for student and instructor interpretation.

- A **project evaluation sheet** follows each project plan. The evaluation sheet targets the skills covered in the lesson and provides objective grading of a very subjective medium. Students can use the grading sheets from their texts and submit them at tape-grading time.

- The teacher edition also contains a **notes to the teacher** section for each project. This section offers specific suggestions, based on our years of experience, for the use of these projects in your class. Implementing the ideas in this section can provide a smooth, educational opportunity.

The supplemental videotape shows examples of each student project.

Philosophies

The development of this course of studies is based on five philosophies of television production instruction.

1. *Get the equipment in the hands of the students.*
   Most of the students entering your classes will be excited about television production. They may be aspiring reporters, camera operators, actors, or directors. Chances are they'll be mentally prepared to learn; early, positive experiences in television production can extend that excitement.

2. *Use video projects to teach new skills.*
   Each lesson in this text is followed by a student project. These projects are designed to reinforce the skills presented in the text section of the lesson. Completion of these projects will give your students a sense of accomplishment and tangible results, while avoiding boring competency tests.

3. *Start simple and progress.*
   The first video project in your class should *not* be a 10-minute drama or a documentary about the history of your city. The adage "You have to crawl before you can walk" is especially relevant to television production. Start with the beginning projects in this text, and progress to the more complex assignments.

4. *Give equal importance to technical and on-camera aspects of television production.*
   Unfortunately, many programs stagnate because the instructors do not apply this philosophy. These two areas, technical and talent, are interdependent and should be emphasized equally. Doing so may require additional training on your part, but the results will definitely outweigh any inconvenience. Also, beware of labeling any student "talent" or "technical." In an attempt to establish the order that so many teachers crave, many beginning television production instructors assign production jobs during the first week of school. A young lady who studied television production at her middle school recently entered our program. For her entire eighth-grade year, she had been the "art director" and "lighting director" for her school's news show. This involved changing the bulletin board paper behind the news

desk each week and turning on the fluorescent lights each morning. We found this young lady to have a high aptitude in the areas of character generator operation, audio control, and electronic news gathering (ENG) reporting. Being pigeonholed had stifled her obvious talent.

5. *As an instructor, continue your professional education.*
   Television production is a changing field. Fortunately there are many avenues for continuing your professional education. These include reading professional magazines and journals, attending county in-services, enrolling in college and vocational classes, and visiting your industrial video vendor.

Applying these philosophies can help you establish a thriving, balanced program of television production instruction.

Objectives

Have you thought about the true objectives of your program? Your program objectives should be based on the philosophies that *you* have decided to adopt. Establishing your program objectives now will help you avoid some early mistakes. Consult your administration and district-level television production supervisors for suggestions for appropriate program objectives. When someone asks "Why don't you videotape all of my volleyball games? You're the video person, aren't you?," it would be nice if you could say, "Because it doesn't fit the established needs of my program," instead of mumbling through some excuse that really isn't even necessary. Here are some objectives that we use in our television production program of instruction:

1. To provide quality academic instruction and training in television production.

2. To provide for schoolwide communication. This objective includes school news show production, student-body program production (e.g., registration update, awards assembly), and video yearbook production.

3. To develop a high level of video awareness. This objective includes teaching faculty members to use video equipment in the classroom and in extracurricular activities, with independence as a desired outcome. It also includes serving on media and technology committees and acting as a resource person for copyright questions.

After you have decided on the appropriate objectives for your program, put them in writing and get feedback from your administration, department chair, and media specialist. Once a formal set of objectives is established, have all relevant personnel sign the list of objectives and keep a copy on file. This will probably save headaches in the future, and help you avoid making snap judgments that may appear to some as favoritism.

Instructor's Job Description

Carefully examine your program objectives, and determine specific behaviors that you, as the instructor, must perform in order to meet those objectives. Here is a list of job responsibilities that we have devised in order to meet the objectives of our program.

1. Instruct television production classes as assigned.
2. Plan instructional units as outlined in the state curriculum guide.
3. Direct students in school news show production.
4. Direct students in video yearbook production.
5. Facilitate student entries in video contests.
6. Maintain, evaluate, and procure school equipment.
7. Maintain, evaluate, and procure consumable supplies (e.g., videotape, labels).
8. Maintain the television production budget.
9. Videotape significant school activities as requested by the school administration.
10. Produce video programs to inform students and faculty about administrative policies and procedures.
11. Offer faculty workshops on video-related topics.
12. Continue personal television production education.

Of course, you will want to make sure that this list includes all of the duties prescribed by your contract. Discuss your proposed list of job responsibilities with your principal. The final copy of this job description should be filed in the school office and kept on file in your cabinet as well.

Why do we recommend written program objectives and job descriptions? Are we paranoid? No. This is the voice of experience. If you have 100 faculty members at your school, each one will have a different impression of your job responsibilities. You will be a highly visible faculty member because of your involvement with high-profile school activities. Many faculty members may not realize that you teach 125 students each day. We have spoken to many television production instructors who are considering abdicating the position because they are overwhelmed by videotaping requests. Developing written program objectives and job descriptions can help you focus your energy on the true goal of your teaching effort—teaching students to communicate using the medium of television.

Good luck. We hope this text is helpful to you!

TELEVISION PRODUCTION FACILITIES AND EQUIPMENT

Your entire approach to television production instruction will be shaped, in part, by the amount and type of equipment with which you have been given to work. Some instructors will be working in complex studios designed to facilitate almost any type of television production imaginable. Other instructors will be working with one or two camcorders. The good news is that quality television production can be accomplished in either situation. In this section, we'll examine three different levels of television production equipment and discuss the essential components and applications of each. The levels are basic single-camera configuration, multiple-camera configuration, and television production studio configuration. We'll also examine equipment features, equipment selection criteria, and funding of equipment purchases.

Basic Single-Camera Configuration

Camcorders and Camera/Deck Systems

The basic single-camera configuration is used by schools that have one or two camcorders or camera/deck systems. The single-camera configuration can be used for videotaping any number of activities around campus, including interviews, sporting events, school assemblies, and simple school news shows.

The single-camera configuration consists of five elements: camcorder or camera/deck, power supply, tripod, microphone, and headset.

Two basic approaches are available for recording your video image: the camcorder and the camera/deck system. The two setups perform basically the same task. The camcorder, as you probably know, is a combination camera and videocassette recorder (figure I.1). When video was being developed for the consumer market, one of the main concerns was to save the user from having to make any necessary equipment connections. Thus, the camcorder was born—permanently connecting the camera to the VCR. Now, almost all portable consumer-oriented video recorders are camcorders. The camera/deck system (figure I.2) is still quite popular with some schools and in industrial settings. The camera/deck system performs the same basic functions as the camcorder, but the camera and video deck are separate units. The technician must connect the camera to the video deck to record on videotape.

Although the camcorder and camera/deck systems are both fine for recording the video image, there are some differences that need to be explored.

Fig. I.1. Camcorder.

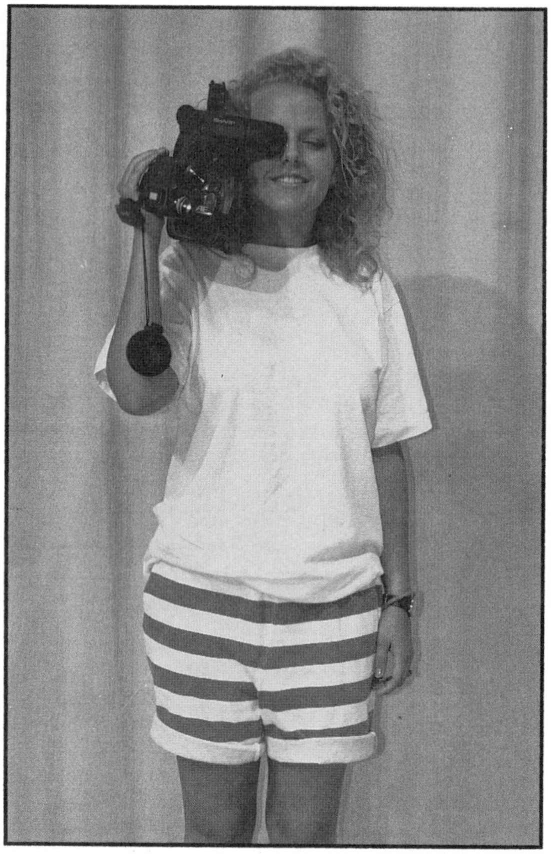

Fig. I.2. Camera/deck system.

- Camera/deck systems are usually much more expensive than camcorders. A good camera/deck system will cost about $3,000, while a camcorder can be purchased for about $1,000.
- The two-piece approach makes the camera/deck system heavier and bulkier to manage. Elementary or physically smaller middle school students find using the camera/deck system difficult. Most students can handle the size and weight of the camcorder.
- The camera/deck system is much more durable than the consumer camcorder. The camera/deck system is made to be used by professionals, not hobbyists.
- The camera/deck system is usually also easier to service. While most cameras and decks can be repaired at the local service center, many camcorders have to be sent to the factory for repair. Also, if a camcorder breaks, an entire system is down. If a video camera breaks, the matching video deck can be used in other ways until the broken camera is fixed.
- The camera/deck system accommodates accessories more readily than the camcorder. If your students are conducting interviews around campus, they will need to use a hand-held microphone. This mic can be quickly plugged into the camera or the deck. The camcorder may not be so accommodating. Also, most camera/deck systems have an amplified earphone jack so the videographer can make sure the microphone is functional. Many video decks can also be synchronized to other decks for pinpoint editing.

- Finally, the use of a video camera/deck system is conducive to learning a new skill. Take a survey on the first day of your television production class. Ask how many know how to use a camcorder. Most students already use one regularly. The two-piece system approach teaches a skill that can be used in the workplace. Its use also emphasizes the component characteristic of video production. Use of a camera/deck system helps the student understand the way the video system works.

In summary, the camcorder is less expensive and easier to use than a camera/deck system. The camera/deck system is more durable, easier to have serviced, accommodates accessories readily, and teaches a vocational skill.

To make matters more complicated, industrial-level camcorders are now emerging on the video scene. The industrial camcorder retains the size and ease-of-use aspects of the consumer camcorder, while maintaining the picture quality and durability of the camera/deck system. The industrial camcorder is priced about midway between the consumer camcorder and the camera/deck system, and represents a wise choice for school television production departments.

Power Supply

Portable video equipment can be powered by either alternating current (AC) found in wall taps or direct current (DC) found in batteries. If you are videotaping within a reasonable distance of a wall electrical plug, then AC is the way to go. Using AC instead of battery power means that you won't have to worry about the battery running out at a crucial point in your video program. Battery power is used when the camera is moving (e.g., along the sidelines of a football field) or when no electricity is readily available (e.g., interviewing students cleaning a city park). AC and DC perform the same function in the video process. The choice is usually dictated by the circumstances of your videotaping assignment.

Fig. I.3. Tripod.

Tripod

A tripod (figure I.3) provides steady, tireless camera support. (A discussion of the tripod use is included in part I, chapter 1.) The tripod is essential to the single-camera configuration. This simple investment can make your video production watchable and more professional.

Microphone

Most video cameras and camcorders have microphones installed on them. Unfortunately, those microphones are not designed to perform most of the tasks needed for video productions. (A discussion of microphone characteristics and use appears in part I, chapter 1.) Hand-held and tie-pin microphones can be purchased inexpensively. Audio contains at least half of the information of your video program. Make sure that you have the proper tools to accomplish the task.

Headset

Just as the camera operator uses the viewfinder on the camera to see what is being videotaped, he or she should always use a headset to hear what is being videotaped. Most portable stereo headsets are appropriate for this use, as are earphones available at most electronics stores.

Multiple-Camera Configuration

With the addition of a few more items of television production equipment, a school can construct a small studio using portable equipment. Schools on a limited budget use the multiple-camera configuration as a ministudio for production of school news shows and talk shows (see part I, chapter 1). Schools with complete television production studios often maintain the multiple-camera configuration to use for remote broadcasts of awards assemblies, pep rallies, and school plays.

In addition to the video cameras, power supplies, tripods, microphones, and headsets used in the single-camera configuration, the following items of equipment are needed. For a complete discussion of multiple-camera configuration connections, see part I, chapter 1.

Video Switcher

A video switcher allows the selection of a video source in video production. Two or more cameras can be connected to the switcher. By pushing a button or operating a fader bar, a video source is selected. Most small switchers will have between two and four video inputs.

Audio Mixer (Audio-Mixing Console)

All audio inputs should be connected to an audio mixer. The mixer will allow the selection of different sources (microphones, music sources). Microphones can also be mixed with music sources for a professional result.

Monitors

Because the technicians operating the switcher and audio mixer will be making the decisions, they need to see and hear the sources both before and after they are selected. This is done using audio and video monitors. Video monitors are like television sets. A video monitor is needed for each video input. Another video monitor—a line-out monitor—carries the final video picture. Audio monitors—headphones and speakers—are used by the audio technician. Most switchers and audio mixers have monitor connections available.

Videotape Recorder

With the multiple-camera configuration, the final audio and video signals are *not* recorded by the cameras or camcorders. The final program is recorded by a separate videotape recorder. The main switcher output and the main audio output are connected as inputs to the record VCR.

Source VCR

You may want to include a video "roll-in" in your program. For example, while interviewing the football coach on your weekly talk show, you can show videotape of a recent game. This tape is played on a source videotape recorder. The source VCR is usually connected as a separate source in your video switcher. But it can also be connected between the switcher and the record VCR (part I, chapter 1, lesson 5 shows you how to do this).

Music Sources

Music can be integrated by adding music sources—cassette or compact disc players. The music sources are connected to the audio mixer.

Television Production Studio Configuration

Some schools have a professional television production studio. A television production studio should include all of the equipment listed above, plus the following.

Character Generator

A character generator (CG) allows the technician to type graphics on the screen. The character generator is usually treated as an input into the video switcher.

Additional Source and Record Videotape Recorders

A television production studio should have several videotape recorders that can serve as sources for roll-in footage or record VCRs. Studios usually have VCRs in at least two different formats (for example, VHS, S-VHS, 3/4-inch U-Matic).

Time-Base Corrector

A time-base corrector (TBC) converts the inherently unstable signal generated by a videotape recorder into a rock-solid video signal that can be combined with the strong signal produced by video cameras. Some modern videotape recorders and switchers have built-in time-base correctors or employ technology that makes the TBC unnecessary.

Talent Audio and Video Monitors

A television production studio usually consists of two rooms—the studio and the control room—separated by a wall and soundproof glass. Audio and video monitors need to be provided for the talent during productions.

Intercom Systems (Headset and Wall-Mount)

Communication is important in television production. Every studio should have two intercom systems: a headset system for the director, floor director, and camera operators, and a wall-mount system with one station in the studio and another station in the control room. The headset system is used for the director to communicate on-air program direction to the camera operators ("Camera 1, pan right; camera 2, check your focus") and the floor director ("Cue talent in 5 ... in 4 ... in 3 ... in 2 ..."). The wall-mounted intercom is used when the director needs to speak with the entire crew, including talent, at the same time ("Good job, people. Take five!"). While the headset system can be quite expensive, a simple wall-mount system can be purchased very inexpensively from an electronics retailer.

Studio Lights

Studio television cameras require more light than standard camcorders. Studio lights provide that extra illumination.

Lighting instruments used in small television production studios usually fit into three categories: fresnel lights, scoop lights, and cyc lights. Fresnel lights are named after the fresnel lens on the front of the lighting instrument. A fresnel lens has a series of concentric circles that allows the light to be focused into a specific area, or flooded into a larger area. (An overhead projector stage is a fresnel lens.) Consequently, a fresnel can be used in the "spot" setting as a spotlight and in the "flood" setting as a floodlight. When unfocused, diffused lighting is needed to illuminate a general area, a scoop light can be used. A scoop, as the name indicates, is a single lightbulb in a reflective half-sphere. A scoop has no lens on which to focus the light. The third type of light is a cyc light. "Cyc" is an abbreviation for "cyclorama," which is the background curtain or scenery flat. Illuminating the cyclorama adds a perception of depth to the camera shot. Cyc lights are usually high-output quartz bulbs installed in reflective boxes. Some cyc lights are designed to hang from a ceiling grid and point down, while other cyc lights are designed to sit on the studio floor and face upwards. The cyc lights are always positioned behind the talent and in front of the cyclorama.

Gels and scrims can be affixed to the front of lights to change the color and diffuse the harshness of the lights. A gel is a colored sheet of plastic/gelatin that can withstand the high temperatures produced by studio lights. A scrim is a sheet of spun cotton, wire, and/or glass that fits in front of the lens to change harsh, directional light into softer, diffused light. Gels and scrims can help refine the illumination created by studio lighting instruments.

Studio Light Board and Dimmers

The light board can be compared to an audio mixer. A series of fader bars allows combination of several different studio lights. The dimmers are professionally installed controls for the lights.

Installations

Television production studios also require several installations to accommodate the television production process. These include a high ceiling from which the lights are hung; wide barn doors that allow scenery to be brought into the studio; a smooth, level floor for precise camera operation; a quiet air/heat system; and enough electricity to run all of the lights and production equipment. You can now understand why schools adding television production studios usually start from the ground up!

Equipment Features

Most of the features available on video equipment are discussed in later chapters and lessons. But because a consideration of their features is crucial to selection of television production equipment, we will discuss some of the most basic ones here.

Automatic Features/Manual Override

With the advancement of video technology, many of the functions that formerly required manual adjustment are now automatic. The three most obvious are camera white balance, camera iris control, and camera focus. A good video camera should include both the automatic functions and the manual overrides. Some consumer camcorders offer only the automatic functions and an "indoor/outdoor" choice for white balancing. To produce creative video programs, it is often necessary to manually control your camera's white balance, iris, and focus.

Tape Counters

How does the tape counter work on your favorite VCR? When it displays "3487," what does it mean? Some VCRs count the revolutions of the take-up reel; others count the revolutions of the supply reel. However, the best counter is a real-time counter, which counts the hours, minutes, and seconds of videotape. (To find out how this works, see part II, chapter 1, page II-1-14.) A real-time counter will be consistent from one VCR to another. Reel revolution counters are often inaccurate and show no real value. (One of the author's home VCR counter adds one number for every two take-up reel revolutions—confusing and worthless!) Knowing how long your segment lasts and its *exact* location on the tape is well worth a moderately higher price.

Size

Along with microprocessors to perform our white balancing and focusing, technology has allowed complicated video equipment to become quite small. Just as large, room-sized computers gave way to PCs, laptops, notebooks, and credit card-sized electronic dictionaries, television production equipment has gotten smaller and less expensive. But how small is too small? If you think about it, the research and development associated with the creation of a new item of television production equipment is a one-time cost. After the technology is developed, the biggest cost comes from the raw materials and cost of manufacturing; thus it is in a company's best interest to make video equipment as small and lightweight as possible. Although no electronic news gathering (ENG) videographer wants to return to the days of the 35-pound "portable" videotape recorder, it *is* possible to make television production equipment too small. The idea of a "palm-sized" character generator sounded good to one television production instructor. But when he saw the tiny keyboard and the metal toothpick used to depress the buttons, he quickly realized he had made a poor selection. The students never really learned to use it, and it now collects dust in a closet. Another school recently ordered an editing control unit packed with professional features at a very reasonable price. Although the price was good, the size—about that of a hockey puck—was a major drawback.

At this point, the reader who doesn't own a character generator or an editing control unit might be saying "I'll take it! I'd be satisfied with anything." This philosophy of accepting unsatisfactory equipment is one reason that so many television production departments are mired in mediocrity. The "palm-sized" character generator mentioned above sold for about $300. For another $500, you could purchase a good, *full-sized* industrial character generator. It is nice to have smaller videotape recorders, headphones, and monitors available but remember: It is possible for some equipment to be *too* small.

Ergonomics

How does the equipment *feel*? Is it easy to hold and operate? Does the camera fit the curve of your shoulder, or dig into your flesh after holding it for five minutes? Is the camera's viewfinder eyepiece adjustable? Is the portable VCR's strap padded? Does the tripod accept the camera readily, or is it a "knuckle-buster"? One of the most valuable features on any item of equipment is its degree of comfort when operating it.

Compatibility

If you aspire to work beyond the single-camera level of television production, all of your equipment needs to be compatible. Will your record VCR accept the signal from your audio mixer? Can your source VCR provide a signal for your switcher *and* a monitor? Can your hand-held microphones be used in the studio *and* in the field? These questions need to be answered before the equipment is purchased.

Equipment Selection Criteria

Now that you understand the features available on video equipment, you can begin to establish criteria for your equipment purchases. Some of those criteria are discussed below.

Features

The item of equipment should meet the standards discussed above—and the needs of your specific program.

Durability

Inspect the materials used in the equipment construction. Are the materials plastic or metal? Do the buttons continue to allow pressure after they have been pressed, possibly damaging the circuitry underneath? Is the cabinet assembled tightly with screws, or just glued together? Unfortunately, most items of equipment are dropped within their lifetime. Durable, well-constructed equipment can survive a certain amount of abuse and remain serviceable.

Service

Purchase only equipment that can be repaired locally within a few days. Some items that may seem like bargains at the time of purchase become liabilities when they need to be repaired. Many factory-authorized repair facilities can be found in larger cities. Smaller towns may find this criterion more challenging to meet; however, personal service from a local factory-authorized repair facility is well worth a one-hour drive to the nearest city. Any item shipped to a regional facility—or worse, to the factory overseas—will probably result in a lengthy delay in production activities. Plan for the worst *before* you buy.

Vendor Support

How does the seller view this transaction? Is this "just another camcorder" to the vendor? What happens if you need technical support and advice when you return to the school? Depending on your personal video expertise, you may need a great deal of support from your vendor. The salesperson should be able to tell you how to operate the item of equipment and how to interface it with your existing setup. A vendor can also keep you informed on the latest technological developments, as well as offer class sets of equipment specifications and catalogs. A vendor should be a valuable resource in your teaching endeavor. If your video dealer also sells microwave ovens and radar detectors, you may want to contact a colleague for the name of a vendor whose total focus is servicing small-format television production equipment.

Firsthand Demonstrations

Probably the most important criterion in selecting television production equipment is your direct experience with that equipment. There are many different ways to gain such experience. Any vendor who really wants to sell the equipment will let you work with it for a few hours. If the vendor won't allow you to work with the equipment before purchase, you're at the wrong place. Bring a student along, and see how he or she likes the item. Ask the vendor for the names of other schools and businesses that use the same equipment, and contact them to discuss the equipment's performance and reliability. Remember, a magazine advertisement or a flashy videotape cannot substitute for this direct experience. Advertisements never show the drawbacks of the equipment, and a videotape demonstration shows the equipment being operated by an expert from the factory. Even testimonial endorsements are often compensated. Needless to say, the people who bought the miniature character generator and the hockey-puck editing control unit didn't get a firsthand demonstration. Surprises are fine on birthdays, but the excitement from purchasing video equipment should come from watching your students use this new tool—not from the complexity of the instruction manual or the size of the box.

Funding Equipment Purchases

The television production facilities within a state, or even a district, can vary greatly. One school can have a professional studio while another school five miles away works with consumer camcorders. And many students working at small but functional studios in junior high school will "graduate" to a high school that has no program of television production studies at all! Although some districts are recognizing these variances and funding programs accordingly, many are content with installing television production studios in their new schools and allowing the older schools to fend for themselves.

However, fund-raising is not a consideration for only those schools who are impoverished when it comes to video equipment. Schools with established programs are constantly faced with repairing their older equipment or replacing it with the new technology that will maintain the program's value in career training. Large, established television production studios are not without funding needs. When a three-chip studio camera or an editing VCR breaks down, a large repair bill is sure to follow!

While many districts and schools provide funding for television production, many schools will want to supplement that funding with additional money. That money can come from donations, grants, and video sales and services.

Donations

Donations to television production programs can take many forms. You may be able to solicit cash donations from civic groups or school clubs. You will probably be more successful in your solicitation of donations if you can specify the need for the donation. For example, rather than requesting a general donation, tell the group members about an item of equipment that you would like to buy, and ask if they can help. Groups will be more likely to donate if they can visualize the result of their donations. PTAs and other parent groups can probably find $100 for a tripod (and a PTA member may also be able to get a wholesale price).

This brings us to another type of donation—the business donation. Local discount chains and drugstores may be able to donate a box of videotapes or a CD player. Even a donation of a few pairs of portable headphones will ease your budget pinch.

If you live near a broadcast or cable television station, contact their production department and ask about donations of used videotape and old equipment. Most television stations use a videotape only once or twice, which leads to a lot of used tape! One school received a telephone call from a local cable television station asking if the school could use a few used 3/4-inch U-Matic tapes. The instructor traveled to the station, expecting a box of 10 or 15 tapes. You can imagine his students' surprise when he returned with more than 200 slightly used professional-quality tapes. Because the school uses U-Matic tapes for its daily school news show, the one-time donation saved the school thousands of dollars. Another local production company donated two older U-Matic videotape recorders to the school because the company was eliminating the U-Matic phase of its business. A trip to the video repair shop for a much-needed cleaning yielded the school two fine videotape recorders with many miles left on them for less than $100.

Although equipment and videotape donations are impressive, many schools also receive *service* donations from local video businesses. These donations can take the form of editing time, graphics production, and audio mixing. Many schools may need professional-quality graphics only once or twice a year, and a good character generator may be out of their price range. Local television stations would probably be glad to help, and the students could benefit from the educational visit. Contact your local stations and production centers to see if they would be willing to make this "time" donation.

Grants

Many school programs can be funded with money received from agencies and organizations in the form of grants. In fact, many school districts have found it well worth the expense of establishing "grant offices" to help schools apply for grants. Schools have received grants to purchase video equipment through various programs, including dropout prevention and English as a second language (ESL) programs. Contact your school district office for a list of possible grants.

Video Sales and Services

Many schools are able to partially fund their programs by selling video projects or providing video services to the school and community. A successful video yearbook can raise thousands of dollars for the program. (Part III, chapter 1 features video yearbook production.) Community groups that don't have the funds to hire a professional production company may be eager to hire your students to produce an informational program. (This concept is further discussed in part I, chapter 2.) One school recently produced a 10-minute program for a local conservation group. The group made a generous donation to the school, and had the tape duplicated professionally to use in their conservation efforts. You can imagine the pride of the students as their names rolled in the credits at the end of a program seen throughout the state. Some groups within a school will donate equipment and supplies to the television production program in appreciation of the program's support of the club and the school. For example, a school student council presented the television production program with a box of blank videotapes in gratitude for assistance in producing a video program about the student council shown at a state student council convention. A few months later, the school awards committee purchased a wireless intercom system for the television production program for use during the live closed-circuit awards presentation (see appendix C). Naturally, the committee donated the intercom system to the television production department at the conclusion of the program.

Notice that the funding discussed in the preceding paragraphs does not include charging students or school groups for providing video services. Unfortunately, some schools actually try to fund their programs by soliciting "donations" directly from parents and students. There is a fine line between using the resources of your parents, school, and community and charging for an education. Crossing that line is neither beneficial, professional, nor appropriate in education. Use of the above funding methods should allow your program to grow and provide an outstanding educational opportunity for your students.

Conclusion

Whether your school has a professional television production facility, a ministudio, or a few camcorders, the acquisition of the necessary equipment used in television production is important. Careful selection of the equipment and vendor, coupled with creative funding, can make it possible for any school to have a working television production facility.

Part I
STUDENT EDITION, BOOK I

1 BEGINNING TELEVISION PRODUCTION

Lesson 1 Equipment Orientation

Objectives

After successfully completing this lesson, you will be able to:

- *name and describe the three main parts of the camera.*
- *explain the difference between a camcorder and a camera/deck system.*
- *name and describe the two types of imaging devices.*
- *explain the need for a tripod in video production.*
- *explain the principle and process of audio dubbing.*
- *describe the function of the macro lens and name real-world uses for it.*
- *operate a camcorder or camera/deck system on a tripod.*
- *frame and focus a subject using a macro lens.*
- *operate a fade control button.*
- *audio-dub over existing audio on a videotape.*

Vocabulary

Audio dub. The process of replacing the existing audio track(s) with new audio.

Camcorder. A combination video camera and video deck. Camcorders are often less expensive than camera/video deck systems, and are more commonly found in schools.

Charge-coupled device (CCD). A photo-sensitive microchip that serves as an imaging device for many video cameras/camcorders manufactured since 1988.

Imaging device. The part of a camcorder or video camera that transfers the light that enters the camera into electrical signals.

Lens. The curved glass on the front of the camcorder/video camera that selects part of the environment and produces a small image of it onto the imaging device for processing.

Macro lens. A separate lens, usually installed within the regular lens, that allows for videography of objects normally too small or too close to the lens to bring into focus.

Tripod. A three-legged camera mount used to stabilize camera operation and relieve fatigue.

Video camera. A piece of equipment consisting of a lens, viewfinder, imaging device, and internal electronics, that transfers light into electrical signals.

Video deck. A device that records the electrical signal generated by the video camera onto magnetic tape. The video deck usually performs playback, rewind, and fast-forward functions. Unlike a home VCR, a video deck does not include a tuner.

Viewfinder. A small monitor, usually monochrome (black and white), mounted on top of a video camera or camcorder that allows the camera operator to see the video signal being created by the camera.

Television has often been called "the magic box." When thinking about the amazing technology behind the process of television production, it's easy to see why most viewers think of the medium as magical. As quaint and traditional as this terminology may seem, it brings with it a major problem when teaching the skills of television production. If we see television technology as magical, then we see no way to control, manipulate, or change it. Many students have left television production classes bewildered and confused, not because of a low level of instruction but because they find it impossible to believe that the amazing, magical technology available on their television sets can be mastered by mere mortals.

Therefore, if we are to truly understand the elements of television production, we must stop thinking of the technology as unapproachable. Television production involves a series of machines. These machines perform the tasks for which they are created. To provide a simple analogy, a toaster is a machine that has been created to turn bread into toast. By the same (albeit, much more high-tech) token, a video camera converts light into electrical signals. Both the toaster and the video camera were created to perform certain, useful functions. Each has a series of adjustments that can be made to alter the end product. While most individuals can learn the technique behind making toast in a few minutes, operating television equipment takes longer to master. However, the idea remains the same: Learn what the equipment was designed to do, then learn what you can do to get the most out of the equipment.

The Camera

The video camera takes in light, and converts that light into an electrical signal. That signal is called video signal. This operation requires three basic elements of the camera: the lens, the viewfinder, and the imaging device (figure 1.1).

The *lens* gathers the light that the camera uses as its raw material. Video camera lenses used by schools usually range from 6 x 1 to 20 x 1. To understand what those numbers mean, we need to understand the concept of focal length. The lens performs according to its focal length—the length from the optical midpoint of the lens to the front of the camera imaging device. A long focal length indicates a powerful lens, one that can magnify and get close-ups of objects far away. A short focal length lens performs in the opposite way. We can get wide-angle shots with a short focal length. A still photographer at a baseball game would probably alternate between two lenses: a long lens, also known as telephoto, to get close-ups of the players on the field, and a short lens, also known as wide-angle, to get shots of the entire field. These are known as fixed focal-length lenses. That's why you

Fig. 1.1. Parts of the video camera.

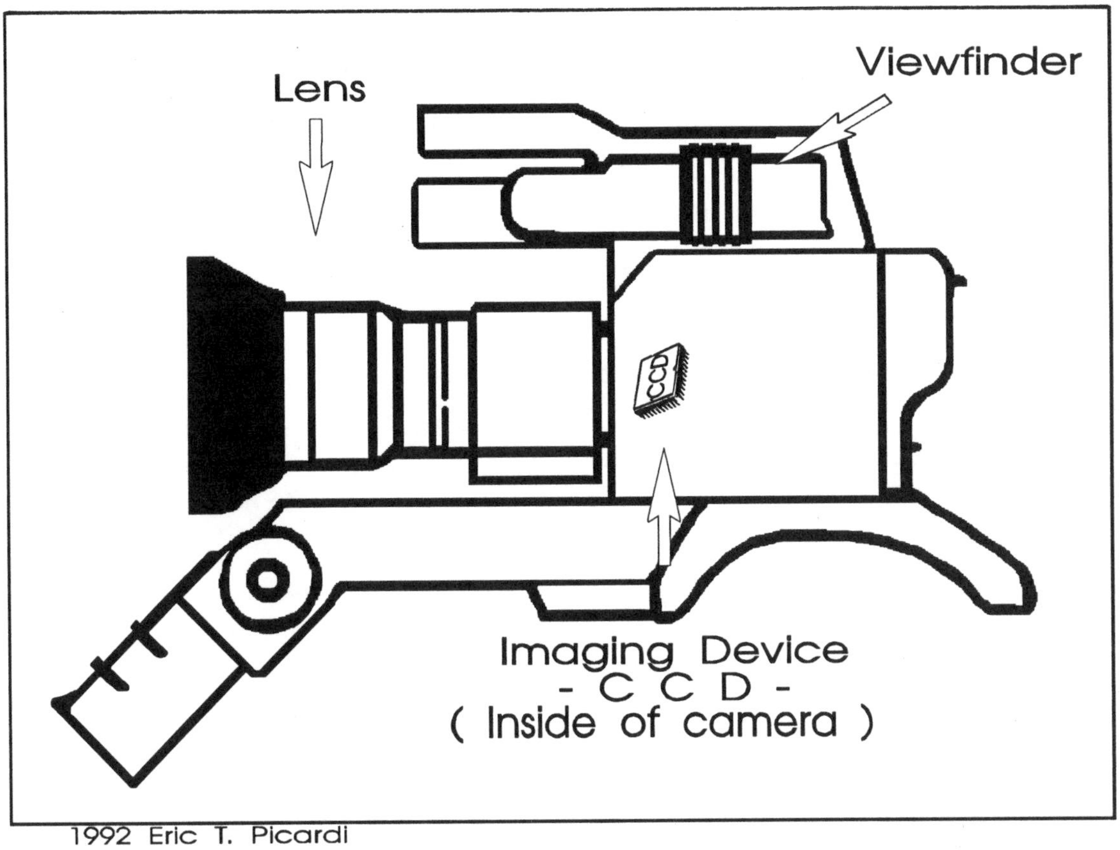

often see a still photographer with two or more cameras. Its quicker, albeit more expensive, to have two complete cameras than to constantly change lenses.

In order to avoid the multiple-camera/multiple-lens scenario, the *zoom*, or variable focal length lens, was developed. The zoom lens is actually a standard lens that houses another, movable lens inside. By twisting a dial or operating a camera control, a videographer can move that "lens within a lens" to adjust the focal length. Instead of changing the lens on a video camera or camcorder, the videographer simply adjusts his zoom lens.

Now we can get back to the numbers. The zoom lens is described as a ratio. Because many school camcorders have a 12 x 1 zoom lens, let's use that as an example. The second number in the ratio (1, in this case) describes the shortest focal length in millimeters (mm). A focal length of 1 millimeter approximates normal vision. (Remember, a short focal length indicates a wide-angle shot.) The first number (12) indicates the number of times the focal length can be increased. So, in our example, the lens has a *zoom range* of 1mm to 12mm. This lens could capture normal vision in its widest, "zoomed-out" setting and magnify 12 times normal vision. A zoom lens of 50 x 1 would have the same wide angle setting as the 12 x 1 lens, but would be able to "zoom-in" much closer, getting close-up shots at great distances.

Now, let's manipulate the second number. Let's say you've been given a video camera with a 12 x .5 zoom lens. The second number, .5 tells us that this lens will be able to capture wide-angle shots. A photographer could stand reasonably close to a large group and capture each group member in the picture. (School club photographers often use a fixed .5mm lens.) The second number says that the .5 setting can be multiplied 12 times. Twelve x .5mm = 6mm—not very long. Therefore the zoom range of this lens is .5mm to 6mm.

Here's another example. Your lens reads 15 x 8. How can we describe this lens? Looking at the second number, we know that the shortest focal length will be 8mm. This is *not* a wide setting, to say the least. How long can the lens get? 120mm. Wow! You'll be shooting close-ups from across the parking lot!

Don't expect the shape of your zoom lens to visibly change as you change the focal length. Remember, the zoom lens changes *within* the lens housing.

Be careful when using lenses with extremely long (more than 12mm) or extremely short (less than 1mm) focal lengths. The longer, more powerful the lens, the harder it is to steady. You will probably need to use a tripod when videotaping with a long lens. Even the slightest camera movement will shake your subject out of the picture.

Lenses with short focal lengths cause barrel distortion, that strange curving at the right and left sides of the picture. People standing at the extreme sides of the wide-angle shot may appear to be "leaning-in" on the videotape. A lens of 8 x 1 or 12 x 1 is usually sufficient for school video productions.

Most lenses have a macro lens installed within the lens. The macro lens allows the videographer to shoot extreme close-ups of small objects. A penny can be videotaped to fill the screen, or a giant eyeball can seem to leer at the viewer. With standard lenses, the minimum object distance is two to three feet, meaning that anything closer will not come into focus. With a standard 12 x 1 lens, an extreme close-up of a postage stamp will not come into focus, no matter how the focus ring is twisted. But a macro lens can easily perform this function! The lens should be put in the macro position for any videography under two to three feet.

The aperture is the opening in the lens that allows light to enter the camera body (figure 1.2). The lens is rarely "wide open." The size is often decreased by the lens iris, the mechanism that controls the aperture. In the light of a dozen candles at a sixth-grader's birthday party, the aperture is open quite wide. However, while videotaping on a sunny summer day, you can expect your iris to close the aperture down to the size of a pencil tip. Most video cameras and camcorders use lenses with automatic iris control, so the videographer generally doesn't have to worry about this. However, under certain circumstances, the videographer may want to override the automatic function, for example, if your subject is standing with the sun to her back. The automatic iris in the lens automatically keys onto the brightest part of the picture—the sun. Of course, your subject will now appear as a silhouette in a picture dominated by the bright, orange ball.

Fig. 1.2. Aperture of a lens.

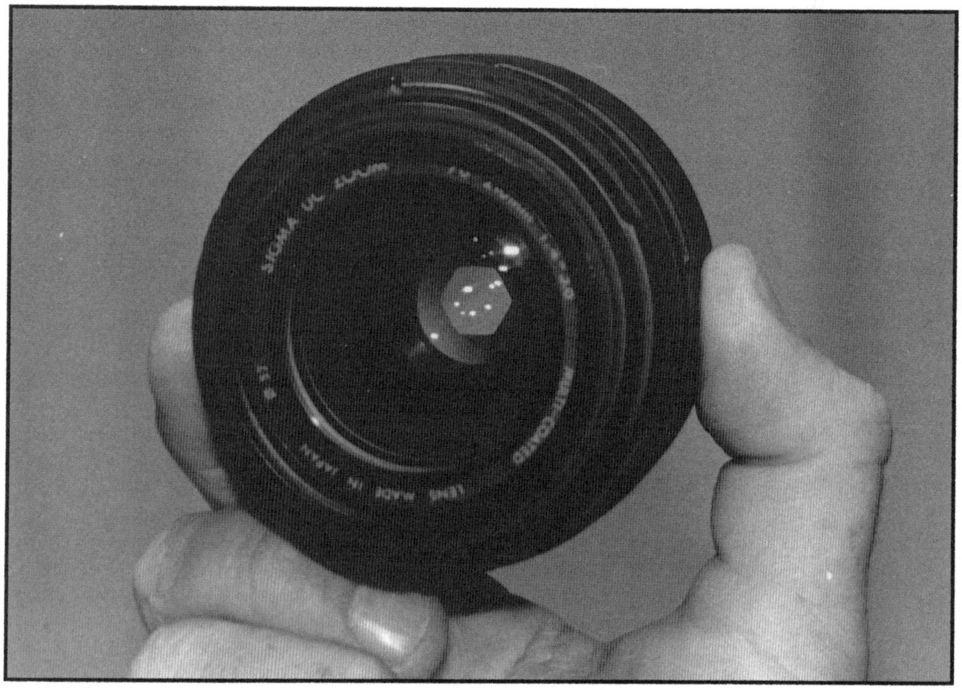

A *viewfinder* is a monochrome (black and white) monitor that displays the video picture that the camera is producing. Most viewfinders are actually of very high quality because the viewfinder screen is to close to the eye. As a comparison, briefly stand with your eye about three inches from a regular television screen while a video program is playing. See the difference? On the regular television screen, you probably see only a series of flashing dots. On the viewfinder, you see a complete, high-quality picture.

Most viewfinders are monochrome, however, some newer cameras feature color viewfinders. There is really very little advantage to having a color viewfinder, and it is basically a gimmick on consumer equipment. A viewfinder should be used to evaluate the picture composition, the shape of the items in a picture, and the amount of light in the picture. The presence of a color picture in the viewfinder distracts the camera operator from those objectives. If a video camera is in good condition and is properly white-balanced, the color trueness is not really a problem. If your cameras are already outfitted with color viewfinders, accept them and enjoy the luxury. However, a color viewfinder should not be considered a criterion for selecting a camera.

Many viewfinders display pertinent information about the camera or video deck's operation. By looking into the viewfinder, a videographer can often tell how much battery power is left, how much tape remains on the cassette, or if the proper amount of light is present, in addition to whether or not the video deck is actually recording. Because of space limitations, many of these functions are symbolically abbreviated. Consult your owner's manual for correct interpretation of these symbols.

Finally, when a video camera or camcorder won't operate correctly, check the viewfinder connection to the camera after determining that the camera is indeed getting power. Many embarrassed students have complained that their camcorders were broken, only to find that the viewfinder was disconnected.

The *imaging device,* along with the electronic connections inside the camera body, converts the light collected by the lens into the video signal. The imaging device, therefore, is located within the camera body directly behind the lens. There are two types of imaging devices in cameras used today: 1) tubes and 2) charge-coupled devices (CCD).

When video cameras were invented in the 1920s they used heavy vacuum tubes, called camera pickup tubes, as imaging devices. The tube is a cylinder of glass that allows electrons to respond in a vacuum. Early tubes, such as Image-Orthicon, were quite large (about the size of an arm) and could get hot during long periods of operation. Although modern technology has eliminated these problems, the pickup tube is not without disadvantages. Tubes are expensive to replace and need attention during production. It is not uncommon for the colors to become distorted during a shoot. Because tube performance is temperamental, matching the color and brightness on two-tube cameras becomes an all-day task.

Most cameras made since the mid-1980s use CCDs for imaging devices. A CCD is a microchip stemming from the technology that gave us microcomputers. The CCD usually measures from ½ inch to 1 inch square. The CCD is divided into thousands of tiny areas called pixels. Each pixel is capable of interpreting that part of the light that comes from the lens. As you can imagine, the more pixels on the CCD, the higher the resolution of the television picture. Once again, though, modern technology allows us to cram a large number of pixels onto a very small CCD. The size of the CCD can no longer be the only factor in the resolution of the picture.

Most video cameras used in schools have a single tube or a single CCD. More professional cameras often employ up to three imaging devices. Three-tube/CCD cameras are the norm at television stations. The result of multiple imaging devices is, of course, a better-quality picture. The disadvantage is increased purchase and maintenance cost and brighter light requirements. That is why it is common to see a professional videographer using a portable light during the day. His or her professional camera requires a great deal of light to produce such a high-quality video signal.

All of the elements that make up a video camera work together to make a useful tool for the videographer. A high-quality lens allows light to pass through bright and undistorted. A high-resolution imaging device produces a clean, clear video signal. And an accurate viewfinder gives the videographer a true representation of the video signal.

The Tripod

A tripod should be used for many of your video productions. Tripods are light, portable camera supports that are relatively inexpensive and easy to use. A tripod can be set up in seconds and left standing for hours. Tripods provide a steady camera picture and tireless service. Tripods are strongly recommended for all advanced projects.

When choosing a tripod, make sure that it is designed for video camera use. Most tripods have weight limits; do not exceed them. Spending $20 or $30 more on a true video tripod is much cheaper than a costly repair of a lens or CCD.

Audio Dub

Many camcorders and video decks have audio dub capability. To audio dub means to replace the old audio (sound) on a videotape with new audio. Even though most cameras/camcorders are stereo, most audio dubs erase and re-record both the left and right channels at once. A few of the more advanced models have split-channel capability. Audio dubbing is usually a matter of pressing the "audio-dub" button and the "play" button at the same time, much like you would push the "record" button and the "play" button of a tape recorder at the same time to record. However, the two functions must not be confused. When in the record function, the videotape recorder erases the video and audio channels and replaces the space on the tape with new video and audio signals. Even if no microphone is connected, the audio channel will be erased and replaced by a new signal; in this case no sound at all will be recorded. Let's suppose that you have videotaped several shots of your school and you wish to put the school song on the videotape. You currently have the school song on audiocassette. You can simply make a connection between the audio-out jack on the audiocassette deck and the audio-in jack on the videotape recorder. Then, by following the owner's manual, you can audio dub the school song onto the videotape, erasing any ambient sound you may have recorded at the time. If you accidentally press the "record" button instead of the "audio dub" button, you will erase the video and audio tracks. For a more convenient audio dub with less fidelity, you can use a microphone instead of the cord connection. Remember, the audio-dub function erases the existing audio and replaces it with new audio. The record function erases and replaces both video and audio, even if nothing is connected to the inputs.

The technology behind basic video production is actually quite simple to understand. As you continue your television production education, remember the concepts of television production that you have learned in this lesson.

Review Questions: Lesson 1

1. The video camera takes in [light] and converts it into [electrical/video energy].
2. What is the main problem with a powerful telephoto lens? [It is difficult to get a steady shot with a telephoto lens.]
3. What side effect is produced by a wide-angle lens? [The wide-angle lens often produces barrel distortion.]
4. What is the minimum camera-to-object distance for most lenses? [two to three feet]
5. What should be done when the camera-to-object distance is closer than the minimum? [The videographer should use a macro lens.]
6. What type of information can be found in the camera viewfinder? [Depending on the camera model, the viewfinder could include battery level, record indicator, counter, tape remaining, illumination, white-balance indicator, etc.]
7. What two benefits are provided by a tripod? [1. Provides a steady shot 2. Relieves fatigue]
8. Audio dubbing is replacing [old audio] with [new audio].
9. What happens if a videotape is audio dubbed, but no microphone is connected? [The old audio will be erased, and replaced by new audio. Nothing will be recorded because a microphone was not connected.]

Activities: Lesson 1

1. Ask a parent, grandparent, or community member about the differences between television now and television when he or she was young.

2. Using microforms at your local library or school media center, find a magazine article about television production from the 1940s or 1950s.

3. Visit a local television station and ask to see old photographs of the equipment that they used many years ago.

4. Set your camera's zoom lens on its most telephoto setting. Make some videotape as you walk around campus. How does the tape differ from the same scenes recorded with the lens on the wide-angle setting?

5. Brainstorm a list of 25 uses for a macro lens.

6. Try making some videotape without using the viewfinder on your camera or camcorder.

Student Project Plan: Macro-Lens Project

DESCRIPTION OF COMPLETED PROJECT

The finished project will be a 2-minute videotape program consisting of 8-10 15-second shots of still photographs and a soundtrack that augments the content. The program will fade in on a hand-drawn title card and fade out on the last picture. Twenty seconds of black should precede and follow the project on the videotape.

METHOD

1. Collect photographs that have a central theme.
2. Create a title card that reflects the content.
3. Videotape the photographs and the title card.
4. Audio dub the soundtrack.

EQUIPMENT

video camera and deck or camcorder

tripod

monitor/television set

audio-dub system

EVALUATION

The project will be worth 150 points:

photo selection	(25)
title card	(25)
camera work	(50)
fade-in and out	(25)
audio dub	(25)

Evaluation Sheet: Macro-Lens Project

NAME ____________________

Photo selection	(25)	________
Title card	(25)	________
Camera work	(50)	________
Fade-in and fade-out	(25)	________
Audio dub	(25)	________
Point total	(150)	________
Letter grade		A B C D Re-do

COMMENTS:

Lesson 2 Microphones for ENG Reporting and Videography

Objectives

After successfully completing this lesson, you will be able to:

- *identify and describe the different types of microphones available to the television production interviewer.*
- *identify and describe the different pickup patterns available on microphones.*
- *exhibit the correct use of hand-held and lavaliere microphones.*
- *plan for an on-camera interview.*
- *identify possible topics for on-camera interviews.*
- *conduct a 1-minute on-camera interview, following an established format.*
- *videotape a single-shot, 1-minute interview.*

Vocabulary

Condenser microphone. A microphone that generates audio signal by using air pressure to oscillate a diaphragm near a backplate. Condenser microphones require a power source.

Dynamic microphone. A microphone that generates audio signals by using air pressure to depress a magnetic coil.

Electronic News Gathering (ENG). The process of reporting timely events using basic videography equipment: a camera/deck system or camcorder, a microphone, earphones, and perhaps a light and tripod.

Hand-held microphone. A heavy-duty microphone designed to be used by an ENG reporter.

Impedance. Resistance to audio signal flow. Audio systems can be either high impedance (hi-Z) or low impedance (lo-Z).

Lavaliere microphone. A very small microphone (often called a tie-pin microphone).

Omnidirectional pattern. A microphone pickup pattern that allows the microphone to pick up sounds from every side of the microphone.

Shotgun microphone. A microphone with a very narrow unidirectional pickup pattern.

Unidirectional pattern. A microphone pickup pattern that picks up sound from only one side of the microphone. Also called the cardioid pattern.

Wireless microphone. A microphone system that uses radio frequency instead of a microphone cord as a means to transport the audio signal from the microphone to the audio input on a camera or an audio mixer.

Not much news happens in a television studio. Sure, every once in a while a celebrity makes a startling revelation on a talk show. But by and large news happens in the real world. If television reporters are to report the news, they must learn to make quality television in the real world, outside of the studio.

Electronic News Gathering (ENG)

No other part of a news program has the information, the drama, and the urgency of a reporter on the scene of a news event. This technique is known as electronic news gathering, or ENG. ENG is the process of reporting the news using the basic tools of the television trade: a camera/deck system or a camcorder, and a microphone. The tape rolls and the reporter and videographer try to convey the information and the atmosphere of the situation. The evening news is generally a series of ENG reports introduced by studio anchors.

ENG is different from electronic field production, or EFP. EFP involves taking more equipment into the field, in effect creating a small studio at the scene of the remote broadcast. Many top facilities have remote "trucks"—studios on wheels—that contain all of the equipment necessary for a complex EFP shoot. While EFP usually involves multiple camera setups, a switcher, graphics, and a great deal of planning, ENG is much more basic. An ENG team usually consists of a reporter and a videographer. Infrequently, a sound technician is added to record and monitor the audio. Sometimes the videographer is the only member of the ENG team, taping segments to be narrated by the anchor in the studio during the news program.

Because no producer or director is present, the ENG team must be self-reliant and self-directing. Successful ENG reporters must be knowledgeable in microphone technique in addition to their journalistic skills.

Microphones

In Lesson 1, the video camera was defined as a device that converts light into electrical energy. A microphone is a device that converts sound into electrical energy. The electrical energy produced by a microphone is called the audio signal. The audio signal is then fed into the microphone jack on the camera or the video deck to be recorded simultaneously with the video (figure 1.3).

Elementary physics tells us that anything that makes a sound vibrates, and that vibration in the air travels to our ears and is converted back into the sound. A microphone, like the human ear, can also receive and interpret those sound waves. The part of the microphone that actually performs this function is the element of the microphone. A microphone element can be compared to a video imaging device in terms of function.

Two types of microphones are generally used in school-based ENG reporting: the dynamic microphone and the condenser microphone.

Fig. 1.3. Audio hookup to videocassette recorder.

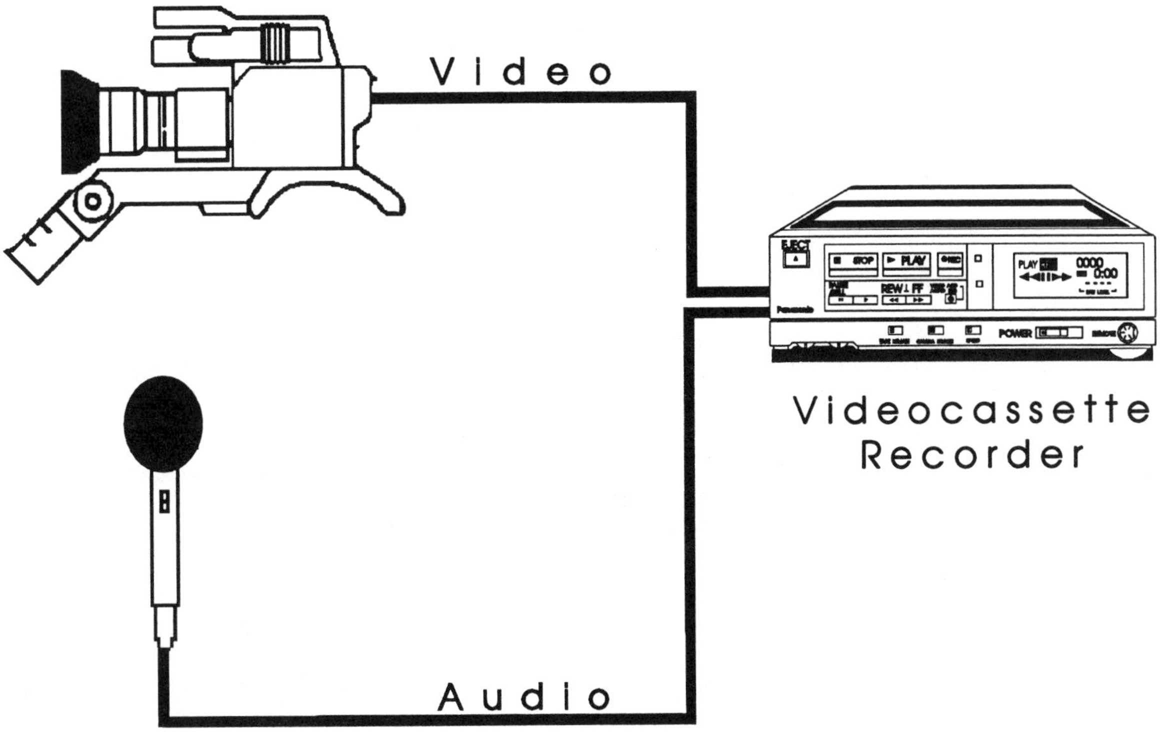

The *dynamic microphone* is the workhorse of school-based television production. Dynamic microphones are relatively inexpensive and quite durable. The dynamic microphone element consists of a diaphragm connected to a moving coil of wire. The sound waves collide with the diaphragm, causing the diaphragm to push against the coil. This push causes the coil to move up and down. It is this motion that produces the audio signal. Dynamic microphones offer moderate sound quality that falls well within the range of the needs of school-based television production. A dynamic microphone cannot, however, pick up the low bass and high treble sounds that we expect for high fidelity. Therefore, a dynamic microphone should be just fine for an interview with the assistant principal, but probably shouldn't be used to record the school orchestra.

The *condenser microphone* is higher in quality and is generally preferred by television professionals. A condenser microphone element consists of a diaphragm that vibrates in proximity to a backplate. It is this vibration that is converted into the audio signal. Condenser microphones give a good, flat response. The term "flat" in this case is good. A "flat" response means that the microphone responds well to high, medium, and low frequencies. If you were to draw a curve of the response, the curve would be flat on top, because the response is the same for all frequencies, or pitches (figure 1.4).

A condenser microphone needs its own power source to function. In most hand-held condenser microphones, the power supply comes from a battery within the microphone. Battery size can range from hearing-aid size to 9 volt, depending on the microphone. Because these condenser microphones provide their own power supplies, they are called electret condenser microphones. Some condenser microphones, especially those designed for television or music studios, get their power from the audio mixer. This power provided by the mixer is called "phantom power." Higher-quality audio mixers usually have a switch labeled "phantom power." With that switch in the "on" position, nonelectret condenser microphones, also known as "true" condenser microphones, will get their required power supply directly from the audio mixer. Condenser microphones are more expensive than dynamic microphones, but the investment is worth it, especially for schools with elaborate television production departments or videographers who regularly tape events that require high-fidelity audio.

Fig. 1.4. Curve of a microphone flat response.

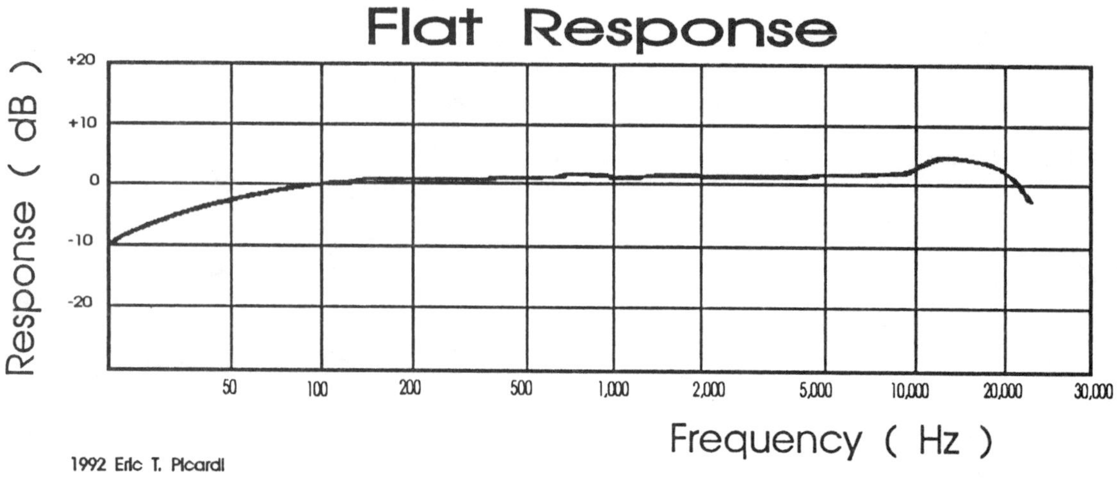

Microphone Pickup Patterns

Not all microphones process sound waves in the same way. Also, not all microphones receive sound from all areas of the environment. The area of the environment from which the microphone receives sound waves is called the microphone pickup pattern. Figure 1.5 illustrates the two major pickup patterns: the omnidirectional pattern and the unidirectional, or cardioid, pattern.

Fig. 1.5. Microphone pickup patterns.

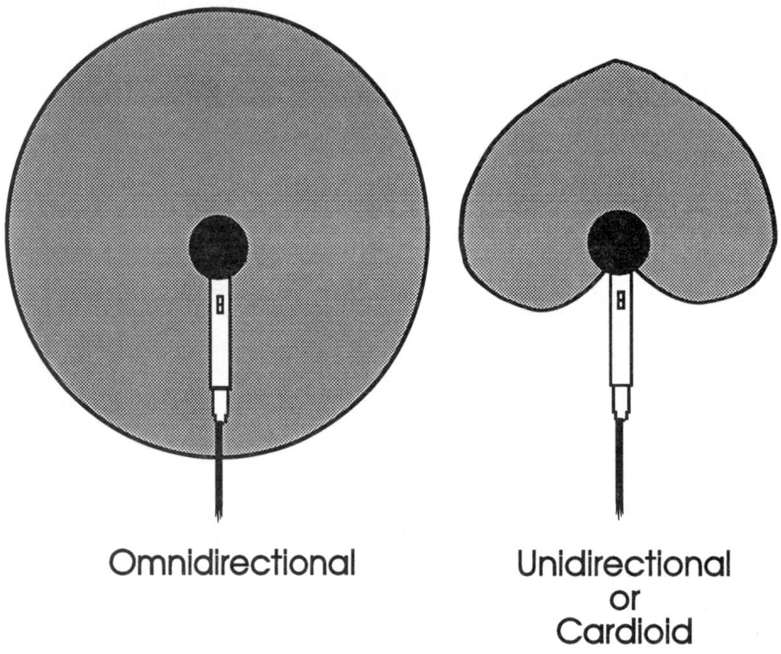

Omnidirectional microphones pick up sound from all directions, as the name implies. An omnidirectional microphone could be placed in the middle of a singing quartet standing in a circle. Each singer's voice would be recorded equally well. Omnidirectional microphones are great for collecting ambient, or environmental, sound. A videographer making a tape of the scenery at a park could use an omnidirectional microphone to simultaneously record the sounds of the babbling brook, the chirping birds, and the children playing catch on the playground. Omnidirectional microphones can also be used for interviews, as long as the ambient noise is at a minimum. But if an airplane flies overhead or a fire truck zooms by, say good-bye to the audio of the interview subject. The omnidirectional microphone will pick up evenly all sounds within its range.

The microphone most frequently used in interviews is the *unidirectional microphone.* A unidirectional microphone receives sound from the top much more than from the sides or back. The pattern is heart-shaped, with the microphone being in between the lobes of the heart shape, pointing toward the point. It is for this reason that the unidirectional microphone is often called a cardioid microphone. Cardioid microphones are used whenever a specific sound source needs to be recorded. Of course, when the sound source changes, the microphone direction must be changed. If an interviewer uses a cardioid microphone, she must change the direction of the microphone each time a different person speaks. A cardioid microphone can be called a "sound flashlight" because it must be pointed at the source of the sound. If our interviewer continuously pointed the cardioid microphone at herself throughout the interview, the comments of her guests would be barely audible.

Cardioid microphones can vary in their degree of pickup pattern narrowness. A cardioid microphone with an extremely narrow pickup pattern is called a shotgun microphone (figure 1.6). Shotgun microphones can be used when the source is a moderate distance from the audio technician. For example, let's say that your science teacher is demonstrating an experiment and you are videotaping the experiment for other classes to watch. You could mount a shotgun microphone to your camera or camcorder to record the teacher's description of the experiment. Terms used to describe very narrow pickup patterns have included super-cardioid, hyper-cardioid, and ultra-cardioid. Some more expensive microphones have a three-way switch that allows you to choose the narrowness of the pickup pattern. Testing the shotgun microphone beforehand can best describe the characteristics of your particular cardioid microphone.

Fig. 1.6. Shotgun microphone.

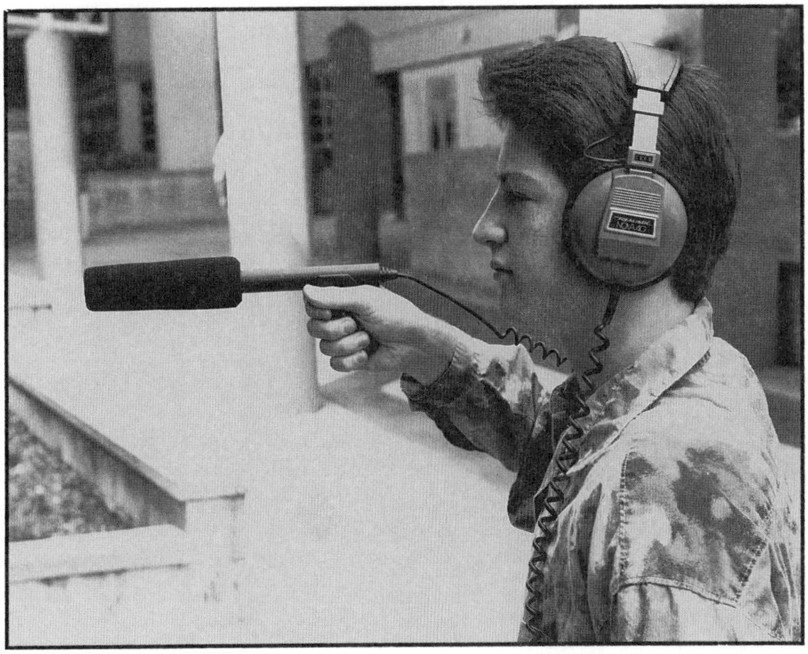

Using Omnidirectional and Unidirectional Microphones

As with the camera, the quality of the audio signal depends on the type of microphone you have and its proper use. A great microphone, used improperly, will produce a poor audio signal. The general rule is speak *across* the top of an omnidirectional microphone and *into* a unidirectional microphone.

Determining Which Microphone to Use

Each microphone fits into two of the four categories listed above. A microphone is either dynamic or condenser, and either omnidirectional or cardioid. Therefore, most microphones fit into one of the following four combination categories:

dynamic omnidirectional

dynamic cardioid

condenser omnidirectional

condenser cardioid.

Unfortunately, the size and shape of the microphone has nothing to do with its element or its pickup pattern. A dynamic omnidirectional microphone could be identical to a condenser cardioid microphone. But as you know, the microphones are very different. Consult the owner's manual before you use the microphone. Don't be fooled by appearance.

Microphones for Special Situations

Up to this point, we have specifically referred to hand-held or camera-mounted microphones. Two other types of microphones are available to school-based videographers: lavaliere microphones and wireless microphones.

Lavaliere microphones, commonly called "tie-pin" microphones, are very small and lightweight (figure 1.7). Since the inception of television, on-camera talent have wanted a microphone that could travel around the studio with them and still leave their hands free. Early television instructional

Fig. 1.7. Lavaliere, or tie-pin, microphone.

Fig. 1.8. Lavaliere battery pack.

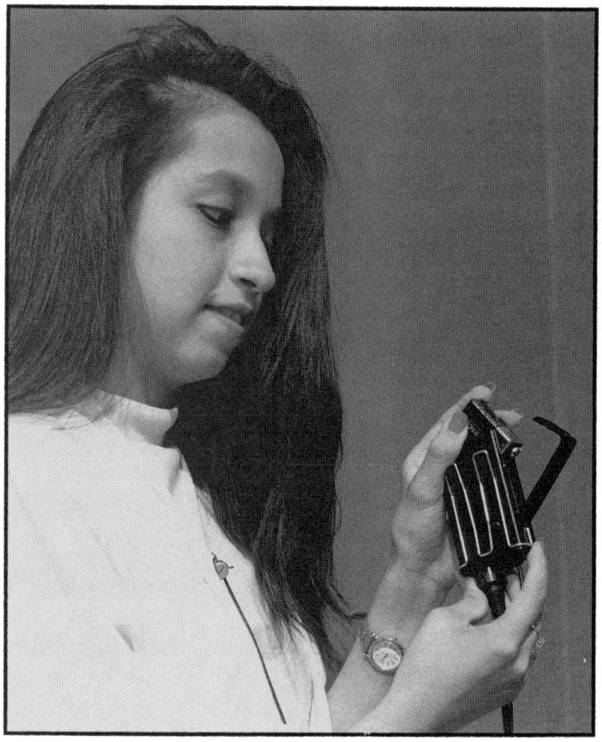

programs show a chef cooking in a kitchen with a hand-held microphone tied around his neck with a rope or chain; lavaliere microphones are a smaller version of this early technology. Now professional lavaliere microphones can be as small as a hat pin, and still deliver full-frequency response. Lavaliere microphones are surprisingly affordable to schools, costing about as much as a good hand-held dynamic microphone. However, a lavaliere is definitely a one-source microphone. Each person must have his or her own lavaliere. (This can get tricky when a camera has only one or two microphone input jacks.) Lavaliere microphones are usually condenser omnidirectional. Because the lavaliere is so small, a hearing aid battery is usually used for the power source. Some lavalieres run a thin cord from the microphone to a power supply about 2 inches square into which a 9-volt battery is inserted (figure 1.8). This battery pack can be attached to the belt or put in a pocket. Lavalieres can be very useful when hands-free performance is desired.

Wireless microphones are used in television production when running a line of microphone cable is impractical or impossible. Wireless microphones, as the name indicates, do not use microphone cable to connect the microphone to the video camera or audio mixer. Instead, a broadcasted FM signal is used. A wireless microphone system consists of three components: the microphone, the transmitter, and the receiving station (figure 1.9). The microphone can be either hand-held or lavaliere. The transmitter produces and broadcasts the FM radio signal, just like a small radio station. (Usually, the signal is well above the FM dial.) The transmitter for the hand-held wireless microphone is usually installed within the microphone itself. In the lavaliere wireless microphone, the transmitter is usually a small plastic box worn on the belt that is connected to the lavaliere microphone with a thin, lightweight cable. The receiving station is nothing more than a high-quality radio receiver tuned specifically to the frequency broadcasted by that particular wireless microphone. Some of the receiving stations can be tuned to different frequencies, but the majority affordable to school-based video facilities will have manufacturer pretuned receiving stations.

Fig. 1.9. A wireless microphone system.

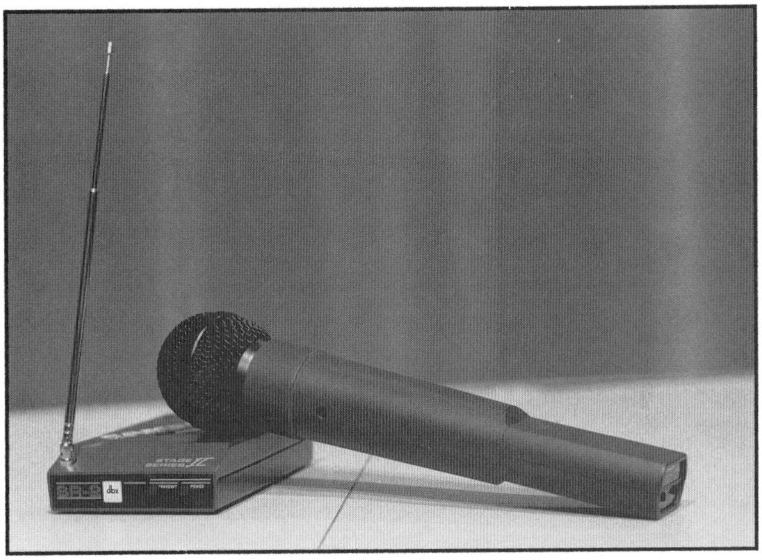

Wireless microphones are frequently used in talk shows and variety shows to allow the talent to move about without worrying about snagging or stumbling over the microphone cable. A singer could stand at midfield to sing the national anthem before a football game. The possibilities are endless. A broken microphone cable is indeed a frustrating experience. Let's say your school has arranged for a prominent member of the community to come to speak to all of the 10th graders who have gathered in the auditorium. Your assignment is to videotape the presentation so that the entire student body can watch it. In order to get a good long shot and a good close-up, you position your camera on a tripod about 10 rows, or 40 feet, from the stage. Your microphone is positioned at the lectern next to the microphone for the public address system. If you have a wireless microphone, you simply plug the receiving station into the microphone jack on your camera (figure 1.10). If you are using a traditional microphone, you must string a microphone cable through the rows and connect it to the camera. For safety's sake, the cable must be taped to the floor, but still you run the risk of damaging the cable as 400 sophomores trample through. The wireless system is obviously more convenient in this situation.

Fig. 1.10. Wireless microphone connection.

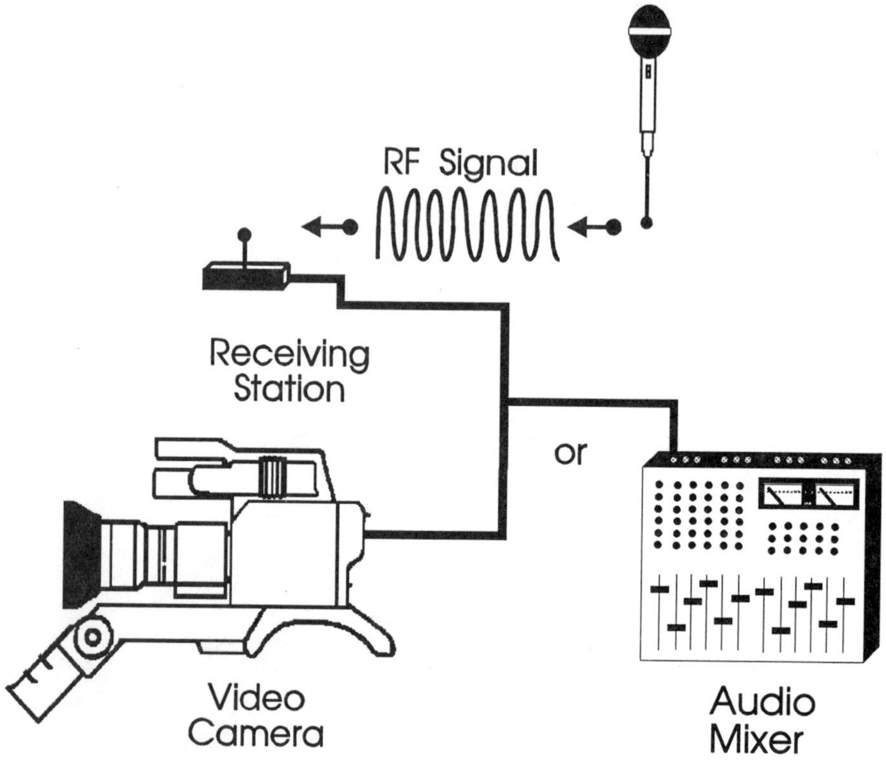

Wireless microphone systems are not without their disadvantages. The most obvious is cost. A medium-quality wireless microphone system costs about $300. That's a lot of videotape! In order to function properly, a wireless microphone should have a direct line of sight with the receiving station. Trees, brick walls, and fences have been associated with poor wireless performance. Adverse weather conditions can also hamper use. A proximity of high-voltage equipment, such as theater lights, can also distort the sound.

Obviously, investing in an expensive system requires careful thought. The range, or transmitting distance, is a significant consideration. Recently, a small consumer video-oriented business offered a wireless microphone system for only $49.95. Unfortunately, the range of transmission was only 35 feet! That much microphone cable can be purchased for about $10. More professional systems offer ranges from 500-1,000 feet. But remember, the environment is everything. High voltage in the area can cut range by more than 50 percent. The frequency is also an important consideration. Wireless microphone frequencies can vary from 48 mHz (megahertz) to 200 mHz. Generally speaking, the higher the frequency the better. Forty-nine mHz is generally used for toy walkie-talkies. Purchasing that $49.95 model would give you a tinny, poor-quality sound. About 170 mHz is the professional range. Make sure that your wireless microphone will give you a professional sound.

Other wireless microphone criteria include the presence of cross-frequencies, and the quality of the microphone itself. A wireless microphone receiver cannot discriminate between the intended signal and any other signals of the same frequency in the area. Here's an example: A principal is using a lavaliere microphone that broadcasts at 49 mHz while giving a speech to the student body. The auditorium technical crew is operating the lights and raising and lowering the curtain. They are using wireless walkie-talkies that also use a frequency of 49 mHz. Imagine the embarrassment when the cue "Dim the lights" comes over the public address system! The wireless microphone receiving station has received both the principal's signal and the technical crew's communications.

Most wireless microphone companies offer a number of different frequencies, or "channels," for purchase. For example, let's say you are responsible for mixing the music for a quartet of singers. Should they all use the same frequencies for their wireless microphones? That's up to you, and there are advantages and disadvantages to each choice. If they each use the same channel, you could use one receiving station to receive all four singers. This is fine, unless one singer is singing too loudly, and another is singing too softly. With one frequency, you could not adjust the volume within the frequency. In this case, the choice might be to go with four separate microphone channels. However, this can get very expensive.

It would be nice if all wireless microphone systems included high-quality microphones. But, unfortunately, they don't. When considering the use of a wireless system, evaluate the microphone as if you were selecting it on its own merit. Range and frequency mean nothing if the microphone itself is of poor quality.

Wireless microphones are certainly impressive and convenient, but they aren't a panacea. Their use often raises more questions than answers, and their merits and demerits should be carefully considered before purchase.

Microphone Use

Ideally, the correct microphone placement is 6 to 8 inches from the source (figure 1.11). This placement allows for the recording of a source, and not just a general area. When an area is miked, background noise often plays a prominent role. Whenever possible, the audio technician should try to record the source of the sound.

Fig. 1.11. Correct microphone placement.

Hand-held microphones should be held at about chest level, unless a great deal of ambient noise is present. The noisier the area, the closer the microphone should be to the mouth. For example, if a student is reporting from a quiet park, the 6- to 8-inch rule applies. If, however, a segment is recorded during a noisy pep rally, the microphone should be held closer to the lips.

A windscreen is recommended for all outdoor microphone uses. Many professionals use windscreens all the time to enhance and standardize the microphone appearance. A windscreen is simply a piece of foam rubber shaped to fit over the head of the microphone. The windscreen effectively muffles any rumble or whistle caused by breezes, while allowing the desired sound to pass through undistorted. Windscreens are more important for omnidirectional microphones. Because the omnidirectional collects sound from all areas, it is more likely to catch the direction of the wind. Windscreens can be purchased at most audio and electronics supply stores. A simple generic windscreen can be purchased for less than $2. Windscreens custom-made to the size of your microphone will cost more. However, the investment pays for itself on the first windy day.

Experience is the key to effective microphone use. Even microphones of the same make and model may perform differently in the field. Knowing the particulars of each microphone in your collection can help maintain high quality throughout your video production.

Microphone Impedance

A microphone for use in a school can be either high or low impedance. The term *impedance* refers to the amount of resistance to the audio signal flow. High-impedance (Hi-Z) microphones are used in consumer and some professional situations. Low-impedance (Lo-Z) microphones are used in professional and broadcast situations. A distinction must be made because the two systems are not compatible.

High-impedance microphones can be used only with high-impedance systems, including camera jacks and audio mixers. The maximum cable length for high-impedance systems is about 35 feet. After that, the signal becomes weak and distorted. High-impedance systems generally do not sound as clear as low-impedance systems.

Low-impedance microphone systems are used in professional and broadcast productions. Cable length can go up to 1,000 feet, and the quality is generally clearer.

Most schools will use high-impedance systems. Because low-impedance systems are more professional, they usually cost more. Some schools with elaborate television facilities will have low-impedance systems in their studios, but these studio microphones may not be compatible with the cameras used for ENG work.

Microphones can be changed from high to low or low to high impedance by using an impedance adaptor. Impedance adaptors are available from most electronics and audio stores and cost around $20. Some microphones have switchable impedance for use with either impedance system.

High-impedance microphones usually have ¼-inch "headphone-type" jacks as connectors, while low-impedance systems usually use three-pronged XLR connectors. The operative word here is "usually." While the rule makes common sense, it is not always applied. Of course, any electrician can change the connector for a nominal charge.

Audio is certainly a critical part of ENG reporting. With a correct knowledge of microphone types and their uses, an ENG team can venture into the "real world" to bring the news to everyone.

Review Questions: Lesson 2

1. Define the following terms:

   ENG [*E*lectronic *N*ews *G*athering]
   EFP [*E*lectronic *F*ield *P*roduction]

2. What is the difference between ENG and EFP? [ENG refers to a videographer and perhaps a reporter gathering news with simple portable audio and video equipment. In EFP, complex studiolike equipment is taken into the field to produce an entire program.]

3. A microphone converts sound waves into [electrical energy or audio signals].

4. Which type of microphone requires a power source? [A condenser microphone.]

5. Where does "phantom power" come from? [Phantom power is provided by the audio mixer.]

6. A microphone with a very narrow pickup pattern is called a [shotgun microphone].

7. What situations can have a negative effect on the range of a wireless microphone system? [The following situations have been known to adversely affect wireless microphone systems: trees, walls, fences, adverse weather, and proximity of high voltage wires.]

8. What is the correct placement for a hand-held microphone? [Six to 8 inches from the source.]

Activities: Lesson 2

1. Call a local television station or production facility and ask for a tour of an EFP truck. Report to the class.

2. Ask the local television station about the requirements for the positions of ENG reporter and videographer.

3. Videotape several ENG reports from your local newscast. What types of microphones do they use?

4. Compare television news coverage of events to the newspaper stories on the same events. How are they similar? How are they different?

5. Ask parents, grandparents, or community members how television ENG coverage has changed through the years.

6. Research the history of microphones. What types of microphones (other than condenser and dynamic) have been used in the past?

Student Project Plan: Interview Project

DESCRIPTION OF COMPLETED PROJECT

The finished project will be a 1-minute interview with anyone who comes to this school on a daily basis. The video will consist of a two-shot/bust shot, and the audio will be the actual interview.

METHOD

1. Students select the job they want: interviewer or videographer.
2. Students select a partner and form a team.
3. Team selects a person to interview.
4. Interview is scheduled with guest.
5. Interview is videotaped.
6. Team views and critiques videotape.
7. Videotapes are shown to the class and evaluated by the teacher.

EQUIPMENT

camcorder or camera/deck system
hand-held microphone
headphones

EVALUATION

The project will be worth 150 points:

Interviewer:

microphone technique	(20)
quality of questions	(20)
camera presence (eye contact, posture, etc.)	(20)
format/script	(15)

Videographer:

proper shot	(20)
steady shot	(20)
15 seconds before and after	(20)
background/location	(15)

General Impression (75)—same for each team member

Sample Format/Script: Interview Project

(Total time—1 minute)

Hello. Our guest today on ____________________ (show (series) name) is ____________________ (name of guest).

____________________ (name of guest) is ____________________ (why you are interviewing this guest).

Questions and answers.

Thank you, ____________________ (name of guest). For ____________________ (show (series) name),

I'm ____________________ (interviewer's name).

Hello. Our guest today on "Meet the Panthers" is Coach Tom Carlsen. Coach Carlsen is our head football coach here at Dr. Phillips High School.

Questions and Answers.

Thank you, Coach Carlsen. For "Meet the Panthers," I'm Joe Student.

Evaluation Sheet: Interview Project

INTERVIEWER ______________________________

Microphone technique	(20)	________
Quality of questions	(20)	________
Camera presence (eye contact, posture, etc.)	(20)	________
Format/script	(15)	________
Subtotal—Interviewer	(75)	________

VIDEOGRAPHER ______________________________

Proper shot	(20)	________
Steady shot	(20)	________
15 seconds before and after	(20)	________
Background/location	(15)	________
Subtotal—videographer	(75)	________
General Impression	(75)	________

COMMENTS:

Interviewer ________ + ________ = ________
individual team total

Videographer ________ + ________ = ________
individual team total

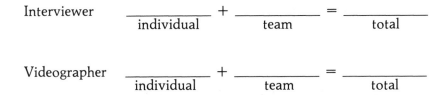

Lesson 3 Postproduction Basics

Objectives

After successfully completing this lesson, you will be able to:

- *use an audio mixer.*
- *recognize and select appropriate audio sources and microphones.*
- *write quality scripts for video production.*
- *select an electronic character generator for the production situation.*
- *compose graphics for television production.*

Vocabulary

Audio mixer. An electronic device that allows selection, combination, and amplification of various audio inputs.

Automatic gain control (AGC). In audio, a feature that automatically adjusts the audio level to the correct setting.

Cart. An audio playback cartridge. A cart is an endless loop of tape wrapped around a hub that provides continuous playback.

Cart machine. A machine that plays and records carts.

Character generator. An electronic device that creates typed letters and displays them on a video screen for use and recording.

Cue. Has two meanings: 1) to set an audio source to the desired point, as in "cue a tape" and 2) a feature on many audio mixers that allows for cuing of an audio source without sending that source out through the master output.

Equalization. The process of adjusting the relative strengths of the audio frequencies. Equalization usually includes separate controls for high, midrange, and low tones.

Fader. A slide used to control the input level of an audio source.

Feedback. The loud squealing sound emitted from a speaker when a microphone "hears itself."

Font. A type style used in character generation.

Postproduction. Video or audio work for the television program that takes place after the original recording.

Potentiometer. A dial that controls input level on an audio mixer.

Trim potentiometer. A dial that fine-tunes and calibrates the input fader or potentiometer.

Voice talent. Has two meanings: 1) the narration performance and 2) the narration performer. Example: 1) "Our audio-dub consists of music and voice talent" and 2) "The voice talent needs to speak into the microphone."

Volume unit (VU) meter. An analog or LED instrument that measures input- and output-level intensity.

ENG is great for simple interviews and news reports. But sometimes television programs require more audio and video than can be possibly or practically created at the site of the original recording. Video or audio work for the television program after the original recording is called postproduction. Postproduction often includes editing, electronic special effects, and digitization. But for our purposes in beginning television production, postproduction consists of audio-dubbing music and script and adding graphics.

Audio Postproduction Equipment

An audio mixer is a device that allows the operator to select, combine, and amplify different audio sources. In its simplest form, an audio mixer could be a switch that selects an audio source. Complex audio mixers are found in recording studios, where dozens of voices and instruments can be combined onto a single tape. Most audio mixers used in television production fall somewhere in between, and it is to that level that this lesson is geared.

Generally, all audio that goes into the videotape recorder during the audio-dubbing process comes through the audio mixer (figure 1.12). Therefore, all microphones and recorded sound sources should be connected to the mixer. For a simple audio dub with narration and music, only a microphone and tape/compact disc (CD) player would need to be connected to the mixer's inputs. For a more complex audio dub, with three narrators, music, sound effects, and voice from another videotaped interview, the technician would probably connect three microphones, an audiotape cassette player, a CD player, and a videotape player to the mixer. Therefore, when selecting a mixer, the technician should consider the most complex project to be completed on the equipment.

Fig. 1.12. Audio mixer.

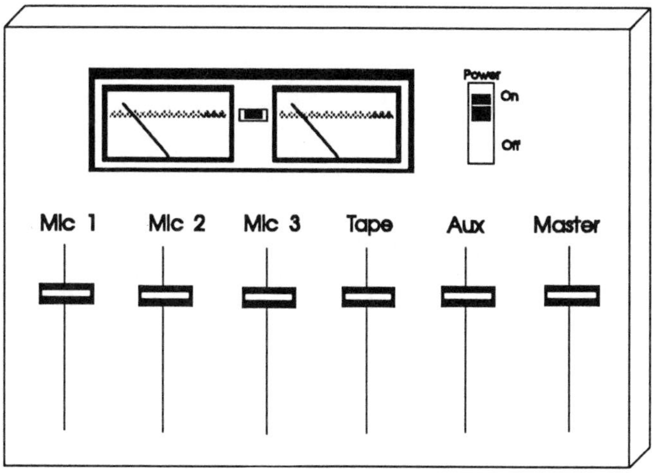

The microphones and audio sources mentioned above are connected to the inputs of the mixer. The inputs for the microphones are generally labeled "MIC" or "M1, M2," etc. Simple mixers accommodate up to three microphones; more complex mixers may accommodate 16 different microphones. Whether the mixer can handle 1 or 100 microphones, it is important to remember that each narrator or voice talent participating in the audio-dub process should have his or her own microphone. For that reason, it is a good idea to have an audio mixer with a few more microphone inputs than you typically need.

A unidirectional (cardioid) microphone is usually best for an audio dub. The cardioid mic allows for single-source recording, and can eliminate recording of most quiet to moderate background noise. An omnidirectional microphone can be used, as long as all voice talent not currently speaking are quiet.

While microphones for voice talent are used to convey specific information, the general tone of the video program can be greatly influenced by the recorded music and sound effects integrated into the audio-dub process through the mixer. Most audio mixers have inputs for audiocassette tape players, CD players, videotape players (audio tracks only), and other, less-frequently used sources. Once again, plan for the most saturated use of your equipment, and then add one or two inputs for those unexpected situations to determine the number of audio inputs needed on your console.

Audiocassette tapes offer an inexpensive, professional source of recorded music for television programs. The audiocassette input on the mixer is usually labeled "tape" or "tape in." The owner's manual can help if the simple connection does not produce the desired result. Music is the source generally associated with audiocassette. But a large library of sound effects can be purchased or recorded on audiocassette, and personal interviews or field recordings where only audio is desired can be recorded on audiocassette and integrated into the audio-dub process through the mixer.

CD players revolutionized audio playback for video programs. The sound is crisper than its cassette cousin. But the boon for the CD player in video applications has been the instantaneous location of a single track on the CD. When the on-camera or voice talent makes a mistake, re-cuing the music on compact disc is usually as simple as pushing a button. And because each track on a CD is time-indexed for each second, an audio technician can re-cue to the middle of a song with ease.

CDs have also made recorded sound effects easier to access and use. Locating a sound effect on a phonograph record can be tedious. Often, a single 33⅓ phonograph record contains 50 sound effects, forcing even the best audio technicians to stick a penlight in their mouth and a magnifying glass in their hand while trying to find the right track. Because the process must be repeated each time the director needs the effect, the result is often scratched records and frustrated students. One hundred sound effects can be recorded on a single CD, and they can be accessed simply by entering the correct number on the CD player. Because most CD players have auto-repeat functions, the sound effect can be repeated throughout the audio dub with ease. For example, let's say you're audio-dubbing a documentary about the circus, and you would like to combine circus sounds with your narration on the audio dub. You locate the appropriate track "circus sounds" on the sound effects CD. However, the desired effect lasts only a minute and your video program is three minutes. You can program the CD player to repeat the "circus sounds" continuously so that the sound effect is seamless throughout the audio dub.

Unfortunately, we are still a few years away from recordable compact discs on the consumer/school level. However, the technology is being developed by several companies. Although it may be a few years before the technology is affordable to schools, rest assured that in the future, compact discs will be considered equal to audiocassettes in terms of recording. The CD player is usually connected to the mixer through the "aux" (auxiliary) jack. A CD player can be connected through a "tape in" or "phono" (phonograph) jack, however, the audio technician should expect to keep the level lower than expected because the CD player generally has a higher output signal level than an audiocassette player or a phonograph. With CD players coming down in price to the level of audiocassette decks, most schools are adding them to their basic audio systems.

Very few phonograph records are being pressed today. The phonograph record continued to thrive in spite of the popularity of the audiocassette format, but the compact disc rendered it obsolete. Except for special dance records used in discoteques and dance clubs, the phonograph is destined to go the way of the 8-track tape—a technology that was useful and popular but has been replaced by a more dependable and portable medium. Schools still buy and use turntables (record players) although the practice will probably die out altogether within the next few years as records accumulate scratches and become warped and worn. Still, many television production instructors own a cache of "classic" (i.e., pre-1990) records that students might find amusing to run over ending credits on the school news show. Most audio mixers have inputs for phonographs, and some mixers distinguish between ceramic phonograph systems and magnetic systems. Connection in the wrong input usually produces unusable audio, so if your turntable is ceramic and your mixer will only accept magnetic turntables, you'll need to buy a preamplifier for the turntable to make it compatible with the mixer.

Other audio sources are used infrequently in television. Sound from a videotape program can be used for an audio dub. For example, let's say your school is beginning a recycling program. You have a videotape interview of the principal explaining the specifics of the new program. You also have a videotape that shows students collecting aluminum around the school, placing it in the recycling bins, and loading it into a truck for delivery to the recycling center. The audio portion of the first videotape (principal interview) can be used as your narration for the audio dub of your second tape (aluminum collection). Simply run a cable from the audio "out" jack of a VCR containing the principal interview tape into the "tape in" or "aux" jack of your audio mixer. Also, connect a video monitor to the first VCR (principal interview) so that you can establish some sort of visual cue as to when to un-pause the first tape. Then, at the appropriate time, un-pause the first VCR and let the principal interview serve as your "voice talent."

Cart machines are also used infrequently in video productions. Cart machines work like 8-track tape players and are similar in appearance (figure 1.13). Carts are tapes wound as an endless loop around a hub in the middle. Therefore, because the tape has no beginning or end, the tape plays forever without stopping. Carts are used for theme music or introductions that are likely to be repeated on a regular basis. Radio stations record most of their commercials on carts. A special inaudible "beep" can be recorded on the cart at the beginning of the song or commercial. This "sync tone" stops the tape right before the song is about to start again. For example, let's say that your school news show uses 45 seconds of the same song as an opening every day. If you have a cart machine, you can record that song onto a 60-second cart. The recording process usually automatically records that "sync tone" right before the song starts. Every day, your 45-second song plays on the cart and then the cart continues to run silently for another 15 seconds (remember, you used a 60-second cart). Right before the song starts again, the cart stops, ready for the next time you push the "play" button on the cart machine.

Fig. 1.13. Cart machine.

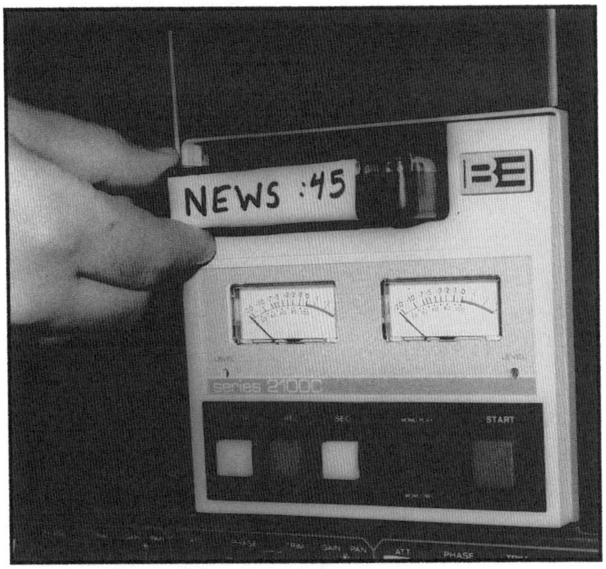

You can see why carts are so popular at radio stations. Most radio stations play about 50 or 60 different commercials each day, and the carts eliminate endless cuing of tapes while allowing local production. In the TV studio, the cart has been replaced by—you guessed it—the CD. Just like the videotape player, the cart machine can usually be connected to the "tape in" or "aux" inputs of your mixer.

The Audio Mixer: A Closer Look

As you can see, the audio mixer is important for connecting and combining several audio sources, and no studio could work without one. However, an audio mixer is more than just a series of connections. Mixers generally have a series of controls that display the intensity of the sound and shape the sound to the needs of the producer.

The level, or intensity, of the sound being input into the mixer is controlled by a potentiometer ("pot") or a fader (figure 1.14). A pot is a dial that controls the sound level. A knob on a car stereo that increases the volume is a pot. Pots are used as level controls on older mixers. Pots are still used in the

Fig. 1.14. Potentiometer.

"sound-shaping" part of the mixer, so they can't be discounted. But the major drawback to using pots for level controls lies in their difficulty of operation. A two-handed audio technician can reasonably adjust only two input pots. Enter the fader (or slider) bar (figure 1.15). Most modern mixers use fader bars to control each input's volume intensity. A fader bar is a sliding version of the potentiometer, with the lower end (bottom) indicating zero input and the upper end (top) indicating maximum input. The correct position is usually somewhere in between. Fader bars are just as accurate as pots, and many faders can be moved at once by adept audio technicians. Almost all mixers manufactured today use fader bars to control audio input intensity.

Fig. 1.15. Fader bar.

But how does the audio technician know how far to move the pots or faders? Certainly the mixer has an upper limit, after which the signal becomes distorted. The audio technician's useful tool is called a VU, or volume unit, meter. A VU meter shows the audio technician the level, or intensity, of the sound entering the audio mixer (figure 1.16). A VU meter is usually labeled -20 to +3. The zero represents 100 percent of the mixer's capability. For convenience, the VU meter is also labeled "0% to 100%," usually along the bottom of the meter. The audio technician should keep the VU meter level below the 0 level (100 percent). If the meter gives a higher reading, the audio will become distorted.

Fig. 1.16. Volume unit (VU) meter settings.

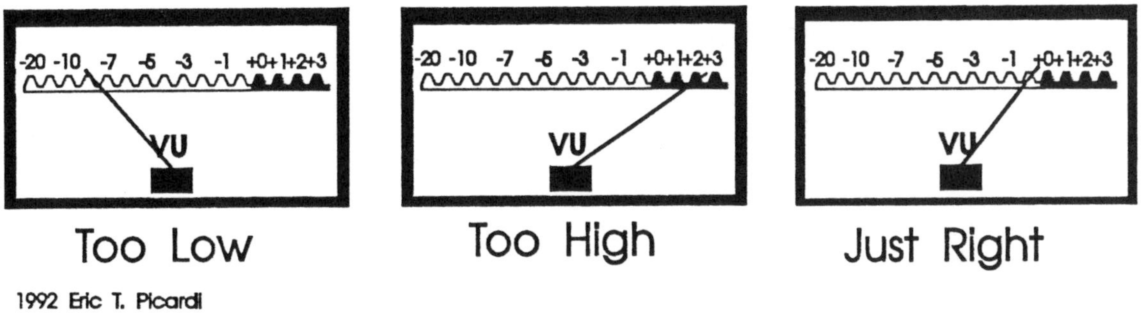

If the VU meter does not approach the 100 percent mark at least every once in a while, the input is set too low, and the sound will be thin and weak, not rich and full. Most VU meters print the area over 100 percent in red ink, and the lower, acceptable area in black. Therefore, a good rule is "the level should approach the red, but not go into it."

The classic VU meter is a needle moving across a graduated background, like a speedometer on a car. But just as cars have turned to LED technology, VU meters can also use LED. LED stands for light-emitting diode. A LED is simply an electronic diode that produces light when a current is passed through it. The audio technician with a LED VU meter simply observes the area that is lit, in comparison to the printed graduate on the side. For ease of use, the lights under 100 percent are usually green, and the lights at and above 100 percent are red. Therefore, the technician simply avoids a continuous stream of red lights. (A color-blind audio technician generally experiences difficulty with a LED VU meter.) Which is better, a dial (analog) VU meter or a LED VU meter? It really depends on the preference of the audio technician. Professional recording studios are often equipped with analog VU meters, but LED is making its effect felt. Because of the constant display of the dial, the analog meter is considered more professional and reliable. After all, a single LED burnout could cause the technician to overadjust the audio, resulting in distortion.

Adjusting a VU meter for a single source is really quite simple. As the music plays or the announcer speaks, the technician simply adjusts the fader or pot to the correct level ("approaching the red, but not going into it"). But what if the audio dub calls for narration and music? Can each source (microphone and tape player) be adjusted independently before the audio dub? No. Volume units are additive—they combine within the mixer. Therefore, a separate pot or fader is usually located on the right side of the mixer and labeled "master." The master output controls the intensity of the final mix produced by the audio mixer. Let's return to our simple example above. A student wants to audio dub using voice narration on microphone 1 and music on a CD player plugged into the "aux" jack on the mixer. The audio technician, wearing headphones plugged into the headphone jack of the audio mixer, plays the CD and asks the narrator to begin reading the script. The technician adjusts the two faders "mic 1" and "aux") so that the mix sounds good—the voice is the dominant part and the music provides a nice background. But the VU meters are still very low. The technician slides the master fader bar up until the VU meter approaches the red, but doesn't go into it. The master control, then, controls the intensity of the final signal being sent from the mixer.

Some audio mixers have automatic gain control or AGC. As its name indicates, AGC automatically adjusts the level on the VU meters for optimum performance. This feature is also available on many higher-quality VCRs. AGC sounds like a dream come true for audio technicians, no more worrying about the correct level. However, AGC is not without its problems. An audio mixer is useful, but it's not smart. Mixers cannot distinguish a soft piano solo from a heavy-metal anthem. All audio is automatically adjusted to the highest level. So while AGC can prevent amateurish catastrophes, it cannot interpret the subtlety required for advanced video projects.

Sometimes, especially with high-powered CD players or loud narrators, the fader bar cannot be placed low enough. With the fader bar at the very bottom, no sound passes through. But the slightest upward movement causes input overload. Conversely, a narrator with a quiet voice might not be able to move the VU meter satisfactorily. For this reason, most high-quality mixers are equipped with trim potentiometers, or "trim pots" for each audio input (figure 1.17). In the cases listed above, the audio technician could adjust the trim pot so that each audio input could be adequately adjusted within the physical range of the fader bar. Think of the trim pot as a calibration of the fader bar.

Fig. 1.17. Trim potentiometers.

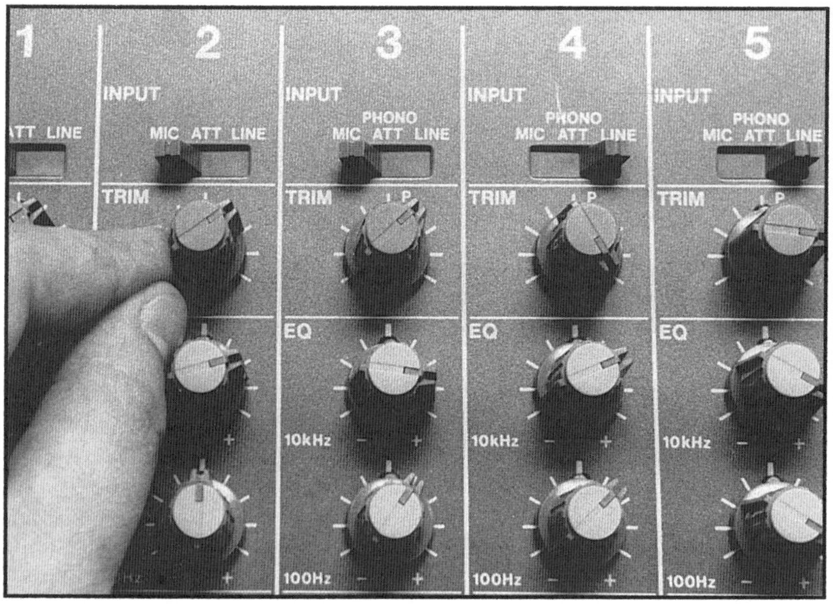

"Cue" is another function found on some audio mixers. Cue allows the audio technician to hear a source before selecting it. For this reason, each audio input has its own cue button. Here's an example. During a 10-minute talk show, an audio technician would like to use two songs from the same audiocassette: song number 1 for the opening theme and song number 2 for the ending credits. In this situation, the audio technician has limited choices: He could hook up a second cassette deck next door, and cue up the tape out of earshot of the talk show hosts and guests, or he could use the counter on the audiocassette player, which is only marginally accurate. Our audio technician could easily use the cue button on his mixer. The cue button above the audiocassette fader is pressed, and the fader itself is left down, so that the sound of the next song being cued does not become part of the master audio output. But as the cue button is pressed, the sound of the audiocassette player comes through the headphone jack of the mixer. Once the closing song is properly cued, the audio technician presses the cue button back to its original position, and the headphones return to the master output. The cue button is quite useful for cuing music during a video production.

Some of the more elaborate mixers have built-in equalization, or EQ. EQ is a complex version of the treble/bass selection on most consumer stereo systems. EQ on a mixer is usually controlled by a series of pots directly above the fader of the input to be equalized. There are usually three EQ pots: one for treble (high notes), one for midrange, and one for bass. By manipulating these EQ pots, the audio technician can shape the sound being sent through the mixer. Narrators can be given rich bass sounds. The sound of a hand-held AM radio can be simulated by turning the treble and midrange pots all the way up and turning the bass EQ pot all the way down. Creative technicians can find many uses for EQ. A word of advice about EQ: Beware of decreasing the EQ pots below midpoint. Once the sound is taken out, it cannot be put back in. For that reason, EQ should be used carefully in video projects to be played back many times in different situations.

Audio Mixer/VCR Connections

The audio mixer must be properly connected to the VCR used for recording/audio dubbing. This is really quite simple. Main outputs, usually labeled "main out" or "master out" are located on the back of the mixer. If your mixer is stereo, there will be two jacks. A shielded cable can be used to connect those outputs to the audio input ("audio in") of the VCR. Once again, if the VCR is stereo, there should be two input jacks. For mono (single-audio channel) VCRs, only one audio input jack will be present. In that case, you have two options. One is to change the mixer from stereo to mono, if that option is given to you. This is usually accomplished with the flip of a switch located near the master output fader. A second option is to purchase a Y-connector at your local electronics supply company. The two output cables from your mixer should be plugged into the Y-connector, and the single output is then connected to the "audio-in" jack on the mono VCR. The first option is obviously simpler, but the mono/stereo switch might not be provided on your mixer. Figure 1.18 illustrates a proper audio/video connection.

Fig. 1.18. Audio/video connection.

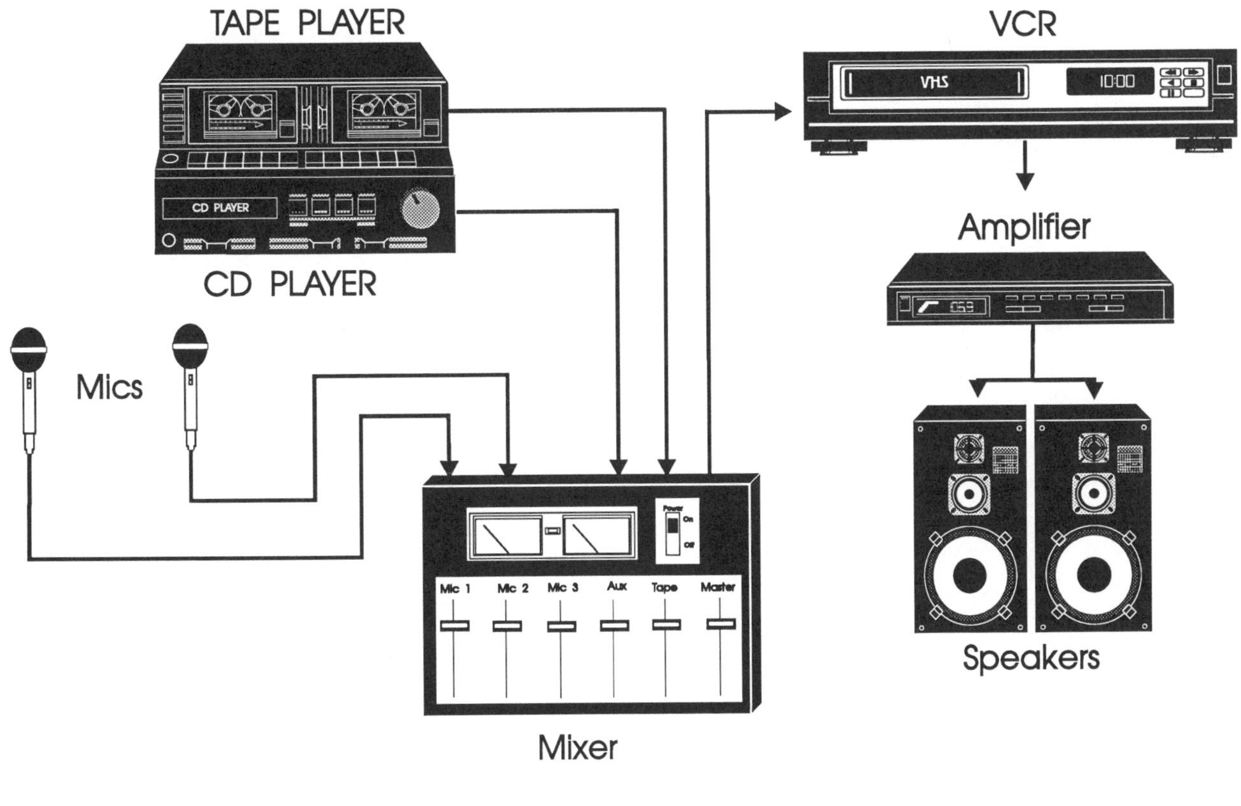

Many of the top VCRs have their own audio input level faders/pots and their own VU meters. The VCR is simply allowing another adjustment for audio input. Adjust the faders/pots on the VCR using the VU meters just as you would the master level on the audio mixer. Make sure to check your VCR to see if it has its own input level. Failure to adjust this level can result in poor-quality audio recording.

After the "audio out" of the mixer is connected to the "audio in" of the VCR and all levels are properly set, quality recording should take place. But what if an audience would like to hear the audio being recorded? The obvious answer is to connect a television to the "RF OUT" ("OUT to TV") on the VCR used for recording. The audio and video are then available to the audience. If a larger audience would like to hear the audio, then the VCR can be connected to an audio amplifier. Most electronic dealers carry simple audio amplifiers at a moderate price. A connection is made from the "audio out" of the VCR to the "tape in" of the amplifier. Once this connection is made and a set of speakers is connected to the amplifier, a roomful of students can hear the audio dub in progress. Notice that this is the first time in the audio process that an amplifier and speakers have been used. Remember the correct configuration: audio sources into the mixer; mixer into the VCR for recording; VCR into the amplifier for loudness control; amplifier into the speakers for large audience output. Of course, the recording of audio can take place without the amplifier and speakers. Because they are connected to the "audio out" of the VCR, they are simply monitoring the audio signal being recorded onto the videotape.

As long as we are referring to audio output, we need to mention audio feedback. Audio feedback is the loud whine/squeal sound that comes from a speaker when a microphone "hears itself." If the audio output of the VCR is to be amplified and played over stereo speakers during a narrated audio dub, the microphone must be placed so that it cannot "hear itself" coming from the speakers. For this application, a cardioid microphone and careful speaker placement are essential. Remember, the feedback will be recorded on the tape just as it is heard during the audio recording.

Audio recording for video production and postproduction requires careful connection of the audio sources and outputs, and attention to the details of correct audio mixer use. With practice and concentration, the audio system can be mastered and the audio will become an essential element in the overall video production.

Successful Scriptwriting

As professionals can testify, successful scriptwriting is a craft to be studied and developed over time (figure 1.19). However, if you follow these general rules, you can avoid common problems of beginning video projects.

The first sentence tells the story. The listener should be able to get a grasp of the material by listening to your first sentence.

Incorrect: "The student council had a meeting yesterday."

Correct: "The student council has decided the theme for this year's homecoming dance."

Keep it short. Simple narration and news items should take only 15-20 seconds.

Incorrect: "The student council has decided the theme for this year's homecoming. The theme was selected by 41 members of the council. Three members voted against...."

Correct: "The student council has decided the theme for this year's homecoming. The theme is...."

Fig. 1.19. A student scriptwriting session.

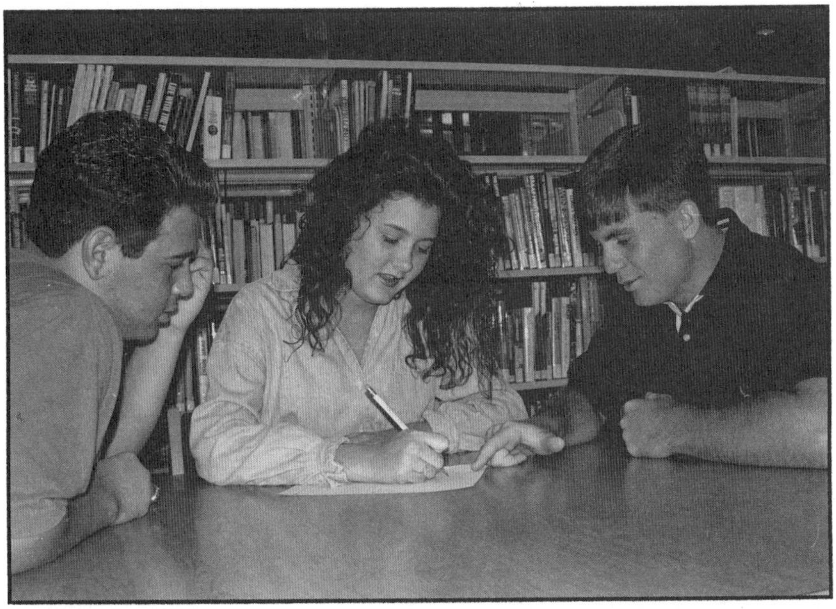

Use active voice; use action verbs.

Incorrect: "The game was won by our baseball team."

Correct: "The baseball team won the game."

Use short words and short sentences.

Incorrect: "The baseball team won the game yesterday, after scoring three runs in the first inning and three more runs in the penultimate inning, anticipating a perennial trip to the district-level tournament, which begins next week.

Correct: "The baseball team won another big game yesterday. The Panthers scored three runs in the first inning and three more in the sixth. The team begins its quest for another district title in next week's tournament.

Don't headline. Every sentence needs a complete, agreeing subject and verb.

Incorrect: "Baseball team crushes Central High."

Correct: "The baseball team crushed Central High yesterday, 6-0."

Use a "people" angle. People like to hear about themselves and other people.

Incorrect: "Three Panthers had two hits each, and another player hit a home run."

Correct: "Scott Mulhan, Tim Bates, and Brian Barber each had two hits. Bobby Hanousek smacked a home run over the left-field wall."

Develop a conversational style. Be "friendly" without sounding frivolous.

Incorrect: "All students who wish to run for the office of student body president should register in room 710 with Mr. Dunlap and prepare to fill out a lengthy application."

Correct: "Have you ever thought about running for student body president? Well, if that sounds exciting, stop by room 710. Mr. Dunlap has the applications.

Give qualifications of names. Don't expect the viewers to know someone just because you do.

Incorrect: "Bill Corrente and John Nadler voted in favor of increased funding to schools."

Correct: "State legislators Bill Corrente and John Nadler voted in favor of increased funding to schools."

Read the story aloud. If the script doesn't make sense to you, it won't make sense to your audience.

Incorrect: "Principal Joann Williams stressed that all grades will be based on class achievement, not the overall achievement of the classwork given to the student in the elective required."

Correct: "Principal Joann Williams stressed that all grades will be based on class achievement, not personal preference of the teacher."

Confirm all facts. If a story sounds too good or bad to be true, it probably is. For example, the following announcement should be confirmed: "Principal Joann Williams announces there will be no school tomorrow!"

Electronic Character Generation

Electronic character generation is used in almost every type of video production. Documentaries, commercials, and even home movies now include titles, credits, and internal graphics describing the task or content. A few years ago, electronic graphics were solely in the domain of professional television production. But recent developments in electronic and computer technology have made character generation possible for most school video production departments. Three types of character generation are found in schools: camera-based graphics, consumer-oriented graphics, and professional graphics.

Camera-based graphics can be created with video cameras and camcorders that have built-in character generators (figure 1.20). These often take the form of a small keyboard installed in the side of the camera. The videographer can simply type the appropriate graphic onto the screen, push a separate button to temporarily erase the graphic, then press the same button again when he or she is ready for the graphic. Some less "friendly" camera-based character generators involve only three or four buttons. The letters are displayed one at a time, "A...B...C..." etc., much like a digital watch. This isn't so bad for titles like "A Bad Cabbage" or "A Cab Ace." But selecting the title "A Buzzing Yellow Zebra" could take all day. Still other cameras/camcorders offer a separate character generator about the size of a hand-held calculator that installs into a specific port on the camera.

Using these camera-based character generators usually involves rolling videotape and recording the graphic, using the viewfinder as a monitor. Most systems record graphics over video footage being recorded simultaneously, as well as graphics over a solid background color. Some offer a choice of character colors, while others offer only black and white. Of course, all of this is rather difficult on a monochrome camera viewfinder. Many school-based video programs use camera-based graphics. However, most schools should consider purchasing a consumer or professional generator after its next fund-raiser or budget allocation.

Fig. 1.20. Built-in character generator.

Consumer-oriented character generators offer a middle step for schools that have graduated from camera-based graphics but do not have the finances or need for a professional system. This equipment takes two forms: stand-alone generators and computer programs.

Several companies produce stand-alone consumer-oriented character generators designed to be integrated into home VCRs and camcorders. These generators usually offer a minimum number of type styles, or fonts. Most are able to scroll (bottom to top) and generate a multitude of colors. Because electronic character generators are really small computers with a single program, many schools decide to forego the purchase of a character generator and instead purchase computer software to run on computers that they already own. These programs range from very simple to quite complex, and their features vary as well. While many of these computer-based generators offer near-broadcast quality, they require the exclusive use of a personal computer. If the school has a very limited number of computers designated for student and faculty use, it may be difficult to dedicate a computer to full-time character generation, and the integration of the computer into the video system may be complicated and time-consuming. Exercise caution before purchasing a relatively inexpensive software program to substitute for even the most elementary stand-alone character generator.

Professional character generators (figure 1.21) offer all of the features of consumer-oriented generators and rock-solid characters that will endure miles of video cable and several generations of duplication. Professional generator prices start at about $1,000 for the most basic models. Many professional character generators offer memory functions, ranging from 10-15 pages stored in the hardware of the generator using a ni-cad battery to internal floppy and hard-disk drives that can store an infinite number of pages and sequences. Ask about all of the possible uses for the equipment and get a demonstration before purchasing.

Character Composition

Successful character generation, like scriptwriting, is a craft and an art. The best graphics grab the audience's attention and convey information verbally in a brief time span. If you follow these simple rules, your graphics will communicate effectively to your audience.

- Be aware of character size as it relates to the viewing situation. If you are preparing graphics for broadcast television, you can use smaller sizes than if you are producing a program to be seen in a classroom from a distance of about 20 feet. The graphics for the latter need to be quite large.

Fig. 1.21. Professional character generator.

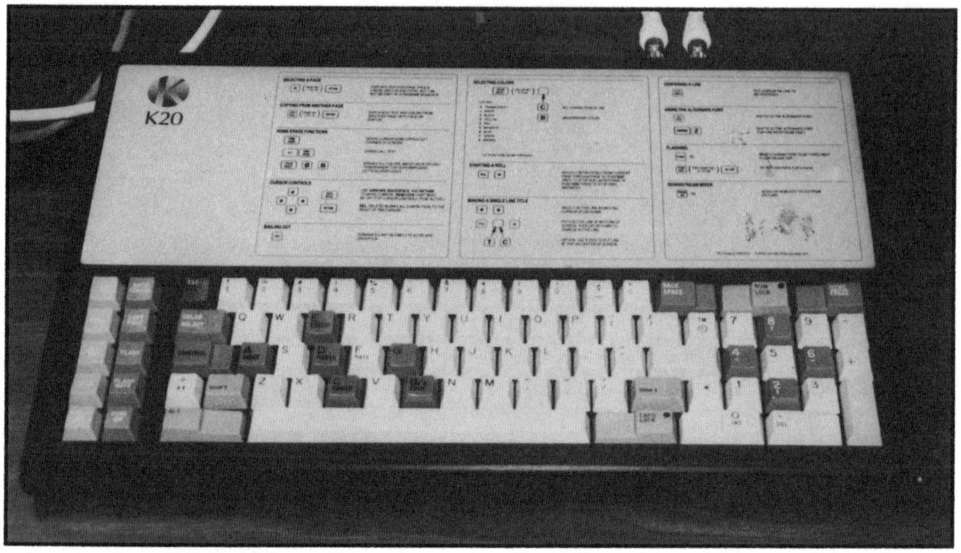

- Use a variety of fonts. If your generator is capable of producing various type sizes, learn to access them and use them in your programs. Your audience will respond favorably to two fonts on a screen (figure 1.22).

Fig. 1.22. Fonts available from a stand-alone character generator.

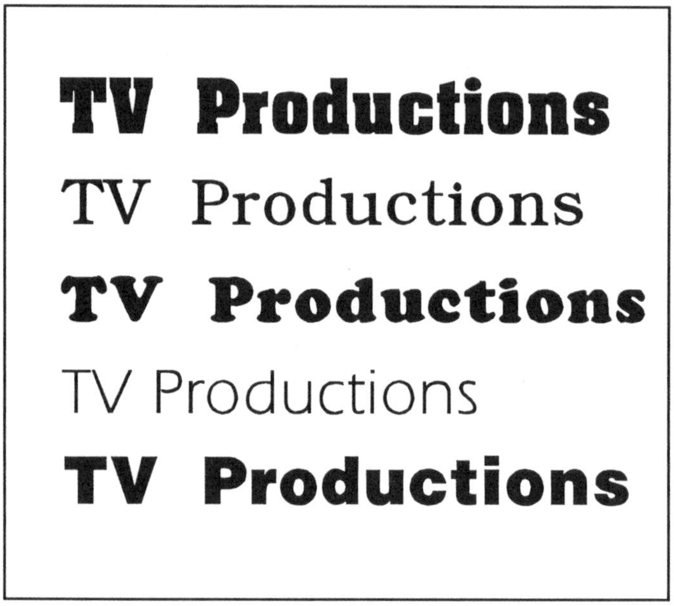

- Use contrasting colors. Go for a high contrast, and avoid pastels that may dissipate when broadcast or duplicated.

- When using a transparent background, be aware of the contrast between the characters and the video footage. White characters may look great on a black background, but when superimposed over a yellow blouse, the white characters are lost.

- Don't overcrowd a page (figure 1.23). Three pages of graphics with two lines each will communicate more effectively than one page with six lines. After two or three lines, your audience will give up. (How many people have actually read the FBI warning on the front of rented video movies?)

Fig. 1.23. Examples of incorrect and correct character composition.

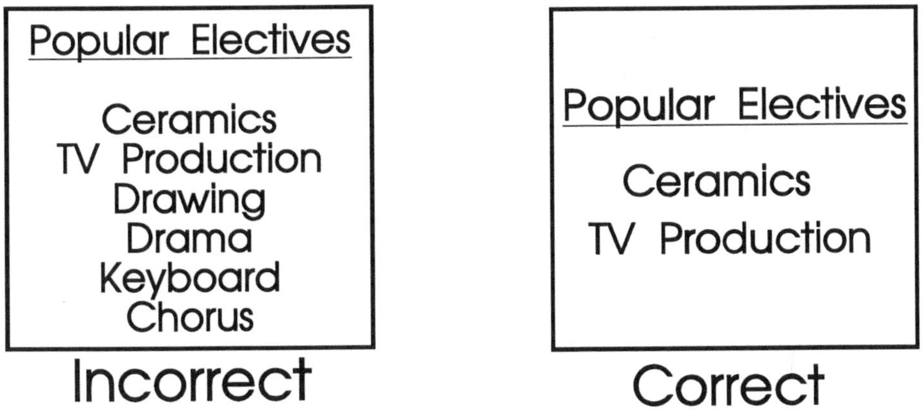

- Keep it simple. Your audience is prepared to watch a program, not read a book. Use characters to accent your video, not replace it.

The use of audio equipment, script, and character generation can certainly add to a video program. Used wisely, these aspects of basic postproduction form the building blocks for the complex video programs that most students want to create and most audiences want to see.

Review Questions: Lesson 3

1. All audio that goes into the videotape recorder should be processed by an [audio mixer, or audio console].
2. A [unidirectional, or cardioid] microphone is usually best for an audio dub.
3. The audiocassette input on the audio mixer is usually labeled [tape or tape in].
4. The compact disc input on the audio mixer is usually labeled [auxiliary, or aux].
5. The level of the sound being input into the mixer is controlled by a [potentiometer] or a [fader bar].
6. A [VU meter] shows the audio technician the level of the sound entering the audio mixer.
7. If the audio input is correctly adjusted, the VU meter should [approach] the red, but not [go into it].
8. The audio input can be calibrated by adjusting the [trim pot].
9. When a microphone "hears itself," the result is called [feedback].
10. Using action verbs in scripts is called [active voice].
11. Every sentence in a script needs a [subject] and a [verb].
12. In character generation, an attractive screen should contain a variety of [fonts], or type styles.
13. A good rule for character generation is: "Keep It [Simple]."

Activities: Lesson 3

1. Record a few commercials from radio or television and analyze them: Who is the desired audience? What are the strong points and weak points? Does the commercial effectively sell the product or service?

2. Visit a local television or radio station and ask to see their audio mixer.

3. While visiting the television station, ask to see the character generator. How does it compare to the character generator that you use in school?

4. Obtain a news script from a radio or television station. How does it compare to the newspaper article of the same news story?

5. Ask your teacher to describe the famous Lake Michigan commercial, as cited in the "Notes to the Teacher," page I-1-116. Create a similar commercial.

Student Project Plan: Audio Commercial

DESCRIPTION OF COMPLETED PROJECT

The completed project will be a 30- to 45-second commercial about a product or service. The audio portion will consist of an announcer reading a script, and appropriate background music. The video will consist of generated graphics, including the announcer's name, class period, the date, the name of the audio technician, and the name of the client (product or service company).

METHOD

1. Each student will write a script for a 30- to 45-second *audio-only* commercial.
2. Each student will select appropriate background music.
3. Students will practice reading their scripts.
4. On the assigned day, the student will type his or her graphics into the character generator, cue up the music, and prepare to read the script.
5. A volunteer will work as the audio technician.
6. The student will record the commercial on his or her videotape.

EQUIPMENT

audio mixer

character generator

microphone

music source (tape/CD player, etc.)

VCR

EVALUATION

The project will be worth 100 points:

script	(25)
graphics	(25)
voice performance	(30)
music selection	(20)

Evaluation Sheet: Audio Commercial

NAME ____

Script	(25)	________
Graphics	(25)	________
Voice performance	(30)	________
Music selection	(20)	________
Total	(100)	________
Letter grade		A B C D Re-do

COMMENTS:

Lesson 4 Complex ENG Assignments

Objectives

After successfully completing this lesson, you will be able to:

- *name, recognize, and create the various shots commonly composed in video production.*
- *understand the concepts of headroom, noseroom, and leadroom.*
- *understand the correct use of automatic gain control, automatic iris, white balance, and other camera features.*
- *storyboard the video, audio, and time of a simple video program.*

Vocabulary

Automatic gain control. A camera feature that, when selected, automatically boosts the video signal to an optimal level.

Automatic iris. A camera feature that, when selected, automatically adjusts the lens aperture according to the brightest level of the video picture.

Bust shot. Video composition that includes the bust area, the head, and a small but comfortable space above the head.

Close-up. Video composition that includes the area of the shoulders up to a small distance above the top of the head.

Extreme close-up. Video composition that includes all or a portion of the face only.

Fade button. A camera operation control that, when used, makes the next press of the trigger a fade to or from a background color, as opposed to a simple tape start or stop.

Headroom. The concept of shot composition that dictates a small but comfortable area above the top of the head of the person in the shot.

Leadroom. The concept of shot composition that dictates an area in front of a moving object. The camera "leads," rather than centers or follows the activity of the person in the shot.

Long shot. Video composition that includes a full body shot of the person in the shot, as well as a moderate area above and below the subject.

Medium shot. Video composition that includes the person in the shot down to the waist or knee area including a small but comfortable area above the head.

Noseroom. The concept of video composition that dictates a substantial area in front of a person in full or partial profile. Noseroom lets the person in the shot "look" across the screen.

Over-the-shoulder shot. Video composition that includes the subject of the shot (animal, vegetable, or mineral) and the shoulder and part of the back of someone's head.

Remote VCR start button. A camera operational control button, usually located near the camera thumb-rest, that allows the videographer to roll videotape. The remote VCR start button is commonly known as the trigger.

Standby. A camera operational control that, when implemented, deactivates most of the power functions of the camera.

Storyboarding. The process of planning a video project that includes drawing a simple sketch of the desired shot, planning the accompanying audio, and estimating the duration of each element in the program.

White-balance. The process of adjusting the colors of a video camera that usually includes displaying the color white in front of the camera and pushing a button or series of buttons.

Television has the power to convey information and emotion more than any other medium. That information and emotion is shaped by the electronic news gathering (ENG) videographer. Whether the topic is a political rally, a museum opening, or a natural disaster, the ENG videographer needs to collect the video footage that tells the story. Because the videographer often doesn't get a second chance to get the right shots, knowledge of the video camera and careful planning play an important role in the ENG process. Three important aspects of field shooting—shot selection, camera operational controls, and storyboarding—are featured in this lesson.

Shot Selection

Although an infinite number of shots can be created with a video camera, certain shots have been established as basic camera angles for television production. These shots are standardized throughout the television industry, so it is important to learn the terminology. By mastering these shots, you will learn the "lingo" of videographers all over the world. Study the photographs and the descriptions, and when a director asks you to line up a medium shot, you'll know exactly what he or she is talking about.

Long shot (LS). In a long shot, the subject's (person's) entire body is in the shot (figure 1.24). There is area above the subject's head and below the subject's feet. Combined, the area above the subject and below the subject should be equivalent to the height of the subject; the area above the subject should be twice the size of the area below the subject. Remember, the subject is not always a person. Imagine a long shot of a chair, a house, or a cheeseburger. For this reason, a specific distance from the subject is not specified. A long shot of a cheeseburger might be taken from 2 or 3 feet, while a long shot of a house would be taken from across the street or down the block.

Fig. 1.24. Long shot.

Medium shot (MS). A medium shot is harder to define. When the subject is a person, a medium shot is taken from the knees up with a small but comfortable area above the person (figure 1.25). A medium shot of a "nonperson" subject usually fills about 75 percent of the frame.

Fig. 1.25. Medium shot.

Close-Up (CU). The close-up is one of the staple shots of video and usually involves a shot of a person. The close-up includes the area of the shoulders up to a small distance above the top of the head (figure 1.26). A close-up of a computer disc would fill the screen with the disc.

Fig. 1.26. Close-up.

Extreme close-up (ECU). The extreme close-up takes the close-up shot a bit closer. An extreme close-up of a person fills the screen with the face (figure 1.27). Areas such as the top of the head, the base of the chin, or the ears may be eliminated from the extreme close-up. While the ECU probably wouldn't be used by a television reporter, it can be very effective in dramatic or persuasive programs.

Fig. 1.27. Extreme close-up.

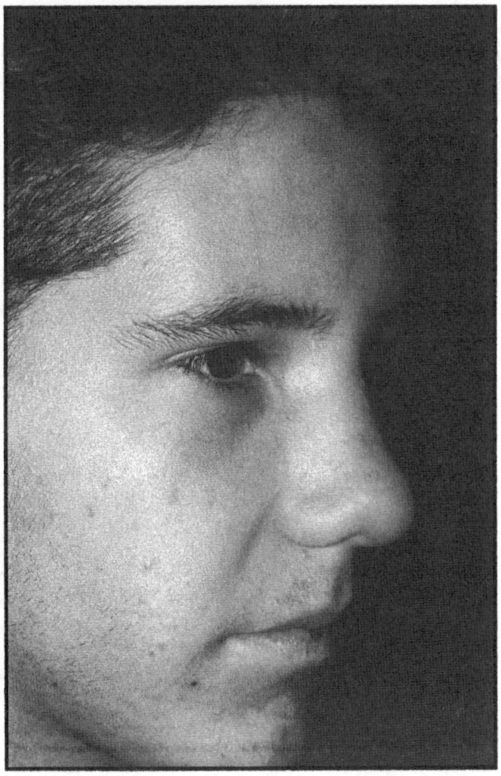

Bust shot (BUST). The bust shot is similar to the medium shot and the close-up. The bust shot includes the bust area while maintaining a comfortable area above the head (figure 1.28). This shot is often used by television reporters because it provides a good picture of the reporter while allowing the viewer to see information behind the reporter or to the side of the reporter.

Fig. 1.28. Bust shot.

Over-the-Shoulder shot. The over-the-shoulder shot, as the name implies, is taken with the camera "looking over a person's shoulder (figure 1.29). This perspective gives the viewer a sense of participation in the shot and offers the viewer a second angle of the content to avoid boredom. An over-the-shoulder shot is generally a bust shot, but with the shoulder and about half of the back of the head of another person visible. An example would be a reporter interviewing a media specialist

Fig. 1.29. Over-the-shoulder shot.

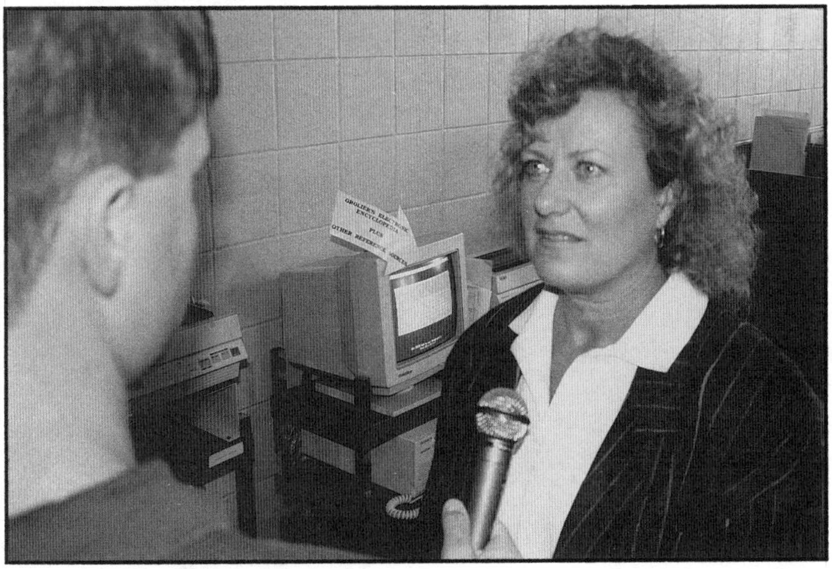

about the new CD-ROM system in the high school, as seen in figure 1.29. The example gives the viewer the perspective of being next to the media specialist as she speaks. In other words, the shot removes the barrier of detachment so often found in television.

Many news reporters are using over-the-shoulder shots for "reaction" shots to insert into lengthy interview sound bites. During an interview with the mayor a reporter asks the question "What can the average person do to help in the recycling effort?" The answer will probably be long, and every word is important. To keep the audience interested, the videographer shoots a few seconds of an over-the-shoulder reaction shot to include in the newscast. The subject in this shot is the reporter, and the shot is taken over the shoulder of the mayor. The reporter nods her head in a response of understanding as the mayor continues to explain the city's recycling effort.

Does the reporter interrupt the mayor during his answer and ask him to continue once the videographer is in place for the over-the-shoulder shot? Or does the station send two videographers to record the interview, one from each perspective? No. The sound bite is recorded exclusively as a bust shot of the mayor. The over-the-shoulder shot is taken after the comment is completed. Sometimes the reporter asks a second question as the videographer records the over-the-shoulder shot. Other times, the reporter simply tells the subject what's happening. Most people who are interviewed on a regular basis know the routine and are glad to help. Of course, during the over-the-shoulder shot, the reporter must not talk (moving lips would not work as an edit) and the subject (in this case, the mayor) must refrain from gestures (such as waving arms) that would seem uncharacteristic for the bust shot. Remember, the mayor's lips are not shown in the over-the-shoulder shot, so the words don't have to be synchronized.

Another use for the over-the-shoulder shot comes when explaining a task for the viewer to learn. Let's say you're making a program for the electronics teacher on how to solder a circuit board. Rather than show two disembodied hands working on the circuit board, you could use a variety of over-the-shoulder shots to give the viewer a size and spatial reference. You can probably think of many other applications for the over-the-shoulder shot in the context of instructional videotape programs.

Headroom. While not a shot in itself, the concept of having the proper amount of headroom is important to television production. Headroom refers to the amount of space above the subject's head in the shot. Unfortunately, this concept is difficult to define. Certainly, a videographer wouldn't want to cut off the top of the head on a close-up or bust shot. Learning to avoid "too much" headroom is a more difficult skill to acquire. The tendency for novice videographers is to center the subject's face in the shot. However, as seen in figure 1.30, this gives the effect of a very short reporter. It seems like the subject is standing on his or her toes, peeking into the shot. Draw an imaginary line about one-third of the way down the shot. The eyes should match that imaginary line (figure 1.31). Once again, setting the appropriate headroom takes practice and instruction from an experienced videographer. After the concept of headroom is mastered, aligning the proper shot will become second nature.

Fig. 1.30. Example of too much headroom.

Fig. 1.31. Example of a proper amount of headroom.

Noseroom/Leadroom. Just as every shot needs a comfortable amount of headroom, every shot in which your subject is walking, running, or just sitting or standing in profile needs a proper amount of noseroom or leadroom. Noseroom is closely related to headroom. When a subject is facing in one direction, during a close-up on a talk show, for example, the shot should not be centered. Instead the camera shot should be about one-third off-center, with the subject given about two-thirds of the screen to look in that direction. This is known as the proper amount of noseroom. Noseroom gives the viewer a stronger sense of direction in close-ups. Let's return to our talk show example. Your class is taping a talk show using two cameras. Camera 1 is a close-up of the host, who is seated on the right. Camera 2 is a close-up of the guest, who is seated on the left. If both camera 1 and camera 2 failed to recognize the noseroom rule, the viewer would have a difficult time distinguishing the placement of the host and the guest on the set. By applying the principal of noseroom, and shooting in a crossing pattern (the camera on the left shooting the close-up on the right and the camera on the right shooting the close-up on the left), the viewers can understand the positioning of the participants and feel that they are in the same room as the guest. Using the proper amount of noseroom gives the subject's eyes space to "see" within the shot and avoids talking lips colliding against the edge of the screen.

When the subject of your video is moving, the principle of noseroom is converted to the term "leadroom." Just as the videographer should leave about a third of the screen empty in front of a stationary subject, he or she should also give the walking or running subject about half of the shot to walk/run toward (figure 1.32). Examples of this rule include football players running down the field, students crossing the stage to receive awards, and surfers chopping through the waves. The scenes described above can be exciting and interesting if shot with the proper amount of leadroom. If we center our football player in the shot as he carries the ball down the field, we have no way of anticipating the bone-jarring tackle he receives from his opponent. With a proper amount of leadroom, the viewer can see the tackle before it happens, adding dramatic effect to the shot. The awards assembly shot is much more exciting if the camera leads, not follows, the student toward her award for being chosen valedictorian. And the thrill of watching the surfing video comes not from seeing the surfer/surfboard centered on the screen, but from seeing the surfer led into the next wave by the expert videographer.

Leadroom and noseroom, just like headroom, are techniques to be practiced and studied. Beginning shots can be analyzed by the student and instructor to learn proper alignment. After mastering the concepts of headroom, noseroom, and leadroom, your shots will be more exciting, involving, and easier for the viewer to understand.

Camera Operational Controls

Whether you're using a new three-chip professional camera or a slightly used camcorder, your camera probably has a few features that you need to know about. The features discussed in the following paragraphs are found on most cameras/camcorders currently on the market. Learning to correctly use these features will add quality to your video programs.

Fig. 1.32. Example of proper amount of leadroom.

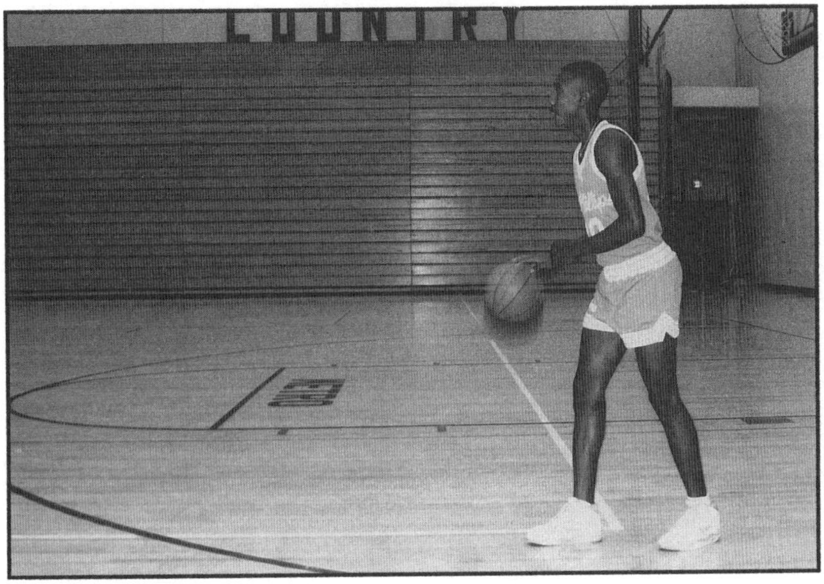

Probably the most important adjustment on your camera is the *white balance.* The white balance adjusts the color response of your camera's imaging device based on the lighting, or "color temperature," of the environment for your shot. A video signal is made of the three primary colors of light—red, blue, and green. These are additive light colors, and different from paint-mixing and still color photography. When all three of the additive colors—red, blue, and green—are present in equal strengths, the result is white light. Therefore, when you white-balance a camera, you are showing the imaging device what the picture should look like when all three colors are being processed at full strength. A simple analogy involves tuning an automobile engine. The mechanic must test the engine at full throttle to assess the car's performance. When you white-balance a camera, you show the camera what video "full-throttle" looks like. The camera then makes electronic adjustments to correspond all colors with the white-balance reading.

Generally, white-balancing a camera involves showing the camera something white—an index card, a white shirt, a white wall—and pushing a button or a series of buttons. The process takes only about five seconds, but the results are critical. Fluorescent lights cast a blue tint onto a shot, changing beautiful blonde hair into a lovely shade of green, and incandescent light gives the entire scene a reddish tinge. Outdoor reflected light can also ruin a shot if the camera is not white-balanced. A person standing in front of a green wall will catch some reflected light from the wall with the result being a greenish complexion. White-balancing on a sheet of typing paper held by the talent can cure the problem.

If at all possible, select a manual white balance over the camera's automatic white-balance settings. Most cameras feature automatic white balancing. Some are equipped with "indoor" or "outdoor" selections. Others offer the choices of "fluorescent" or "incandescent." As you've probably surmised, these settings offer very general choices programmed by a technician many miles away. Also, these settings have a way of deteriorating over time. Tube cameras are more susceptible to deterioration in color than CCD cameras, but CCD cameras have also been known to lose a clear automatic white balance.

Always white-balance your camera immediately before each shot. White-balancing in the classroom will not help the color in the cafeteria. Remember, white-balancing applies to the lighting of the particular environment for the shot. Shots that are not white-balanced should not be used in video production. The distraction of blue faces and green hair far outweighs the content of any scene.

Another common camera feature is *automatic gain control*, or AGC. Lesson 3 indicated that AGC is an audio function that automatically adjusts the sound to an optimum level. On a camera, automatic gain control adjusts the video signal for optimum output in low-light situations. In a general sense, a video AGC is a "power booster" for the video signal. It takes a weak video signal and amplifies it before the VCR records it. As you learned earlier, a camera converts light into a video signal. When the illumination for your videotaping is low, the resulting video signal will be weak. Automatic gain control amplifies that weak signal. Because AGC is an automatic function, the signal will not be amplified unless it is weak. If you turn your AGC button on (or "up"), your camera will amplify weak signals, while leaving strong signals untouched.

There is a disadvantage of using automatic gain control. The amplified weak signal is often "snowy," the slang term for video noise. The weak signal is generally not filtered before it is amplified. In other words, the "noisy" weak signal becomes an even "noisier" strong signal. Sometimes the resulting loss in picture quality outweighs the brightness gained by using AGC.

Most cameras are equipped with *automatic iris controls* (*auto iris*). The iris is the mechanism within the lens of the camera that controls how much light is let into the camera through the lens. The iris controls the small hole, called the aperture, through which light passes. On a bright, sunny day, the automatic iris contracts to make the aperture very small. Indoors, or at night, the automatic iris opens the aperture to allow the lens to gather all of the available light.

Unlike AGC, auto iris really doesn't have any significant disadvantages. Most cameras use auto iris on a continuing basis. However, all videographers should be aware of the theory behind auto iris: Auto iris is determined by the brightest part of your shot. This can pose a problem. Here's an example: An ENG crew (reporter and videographer) is assigned a news story about the dedication of a new band shell at the city's largest park. For her lead-in, the reporter arrives at noon and stands in the shade of the band shell stage as the videographer shoots toward the now-empty seats. The camera's auto iris keys on the bright noon-time sky, not the reporter's shaded face. The result: A perfect background of the seats and a silhouette of the reporter. Unlike the human eye, the camera cannot adjust to such drastic changes in light. The camera's maximum ratio is about 30:1, meaning the brightest point can only be 30 times brighter than the darkest point. Obviously, our example fails this test. The videographer now has three choices.

- Switch from auto iris to manual iris. Opening the aperture with the iris brightens the reporter's face. Unfortunately, the entire scene becomes lighter, and the background becomes an unintelligible sea of white.
- Use a light to illuminate the reporter. The bright light in broad daylight may draw some inquisitive stares from onlookers, but the result will be a balanced shot that stays within the contrast ratio.
- Change locations.

Choice 2—using the portable light—is the winner here, but because some schools don't have access to this equipment, the other choices may have to suffice. Remember, like the other features in this section, auto iris is a tool of the videographer. If the tool is not needed, it should not be used.

Many cameras have a *standby* setting. Standby eliminates power to most parts of the camera, while maintaining warm-up and white-balance capabilities. The main benefit of standby is power savings. Let's say your ENG assignment is to videotape the President disembarking Air Force One upon arrival in your city. Like any good videographer, you arrive early and position your tripod for good composition. But the President has some last-minute details to attend to, and your battery is running down. Turning the camera "off" would lose the white balance. And most cameras take at least a few seconds to warm up to their optimum performance level. Your solution: Use standby to save your battery power. As the door of the jet opens, take the camera off standby. The white balance has been saved, and no warm-up time is required. Roll tape.

Because ENG camera operators have to be ready at a moment's notice, most cameras are equipped with a *remote VCR start button*, called a *trigger* in production lingo (figure 1.33). The camera trigger is usually located near the thumb rest of the video camera. By using this trigger, the videographer can start and stop (or pause and un-pause) the videotape recorder. This convenient feature is frequently used by videographers.

Fig. 1.33. Trigger.

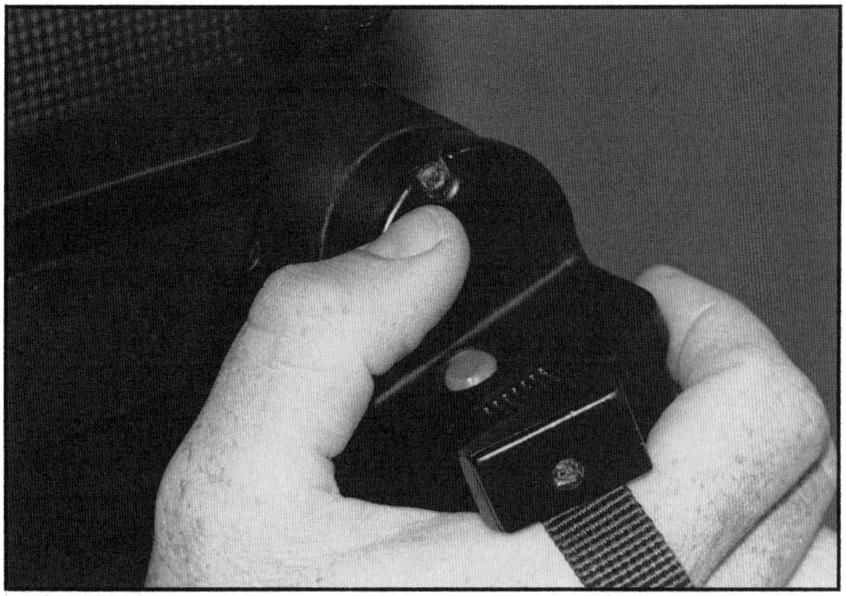

A variation of the trigger is the *fade button*. The fade button allows the videographer to fade out of a shot, rather than have the shot end abruptly. Some cameras fade to black; others to white. Some give a choice.

Another variation of the trigger is the *record review* button. Record review, like the trigger, allows the videographer to control the videotape recorded from the camera. In record review, the VCR switches to "play," searches back about three seconds, plays the last two seconds of video recorded on the tape through the camera viewfinder, and then returns the camera to "record." In other words, record review allows the videographer to see the last few seconds of video made. Perhaps you noticed a time discrepancy in the explanation above; the VCR rewinds three seconds but plays only two. This is your insurance policy to prevent blank tape—a glitch—on your recorded video program. So each time you use record review, you lose about a second of video program. It is possible, then, to cut off an important part of your program by using record review to watch the shot over and over again, and then record another scene on the tape.

Two videotape recorder functions deserve mentioning, as their improper use can sabotage a video production. The VCR *tracking* control aligns the video signal on the tape and should always be adjusted to midpoint when recording. *Tape speed* should always be set at the fastest speed on VHS/S-VHS videotape recorders and camcorders. The fastest speed is known as SP, for "standard play." Other speeds include a speed twice as slow (EP or LP) and one three times as slow (SLP). As you have probably guessed, a faster tape speed gives a better-quality video picture, and most higher-quality videocassette decks can only play on the fastest speed. The only proper use for a slower speed is if an event that you are recording lasts longer than expected and you have to switch speeds midway through the program. In the 1970s, VHS videotape was very expensive—$15-$20 per tape. Because it was strictly for home use (*V*ideo *H*ome *S*ystem) it made sense to record 6 hours instead of 2 hours onto a videocassette. Now, with VHS as a viable format for schools and other closed-circuit applications, and the price of excellent-quality videotape in the $5 price range, the quality given from recording at the fastest speed far outweighs any tape cost. To unnecessarily record on a slower speed is foolish and detrimental to the video production.

Storyboarding

Storyboarding is the process of planning a video production by drawing a simple sketch of the desired video shot, writing the audio portion (or description of the audio), and listing an approximate time for the sequence. Storyboarding is a very important part of the production process. By sketching each individual shot in a format such as that shown in figure 1.34, the production team can create the video project on paper before making costly and time-consuming mistakes on camera. Most video producers can relate stories of the times they thought storyboarding really wasn't necessary for a simple shoot, only to realize during the editing process that a crucial shot had been forgotten.

Storyboard creation is a skill that improves with practice and experience. If you follow these simple pieces of advice, your early storyboarding attempts will be successful.

1. Keep it simple. Even if you're an aspiring artist, stick to simple drawings. Remember, storyboards serve to remind the producers of the composition of the shots. Minor details aren't important.

2. Draw the actual shot. Beginning storyboarders often leave too much headroom in storyboards. Imagine watching the video program on your television, and draw the shot you wish to create (figure 1.35, page I-1-56). If you want a close-up, draw a close-up. Sometimes it helps to close your eyes for a few seconds to visualize the shot before drawing.

3. Consider point of view. Let's say you are planning to videotape a dialogue from a play for your English teacher. You could record the entire scene as a two-shot medium shot, but it would be much more interesting to record some lines from the audience's point of view, some from the first character's point of view, and still others from the second character's point of view. Storyboarding the different points of view can make the final program more interesting to watch.

4. Use the margins for notes. List whether the shot is a long shot, a medium shot, etc. This gives the videographer more information with which to work and can compensate for less talented storyboard artists.

5. Use arrows to indicate panning and camera movement. Remember, the storyboards are your notes. Make notes under the sketches or in the margins. If your opening shot requires the narrator to walk into a medium shot from out of camera range, draw the narrator in the medium shot and draw an arrow pointing from off-camera to the back of the narrator. In the margins, write "talent walks into frame, medium shot." The same technique can be used for pans and zooms.

6. Make a rough estimate of the length of the shot and list that time on the storyboard. If you are editing, make sure to roll the tape at least five seconds before action starts and leave it rolling for about five or ten more seconds after the action concludes. If you are not editing, remember that most videotape recorders require one or two seconds to begin recording on the tape after the trigger is pushed. If your talent begins to speak the moment the trigger is pushed, the first few words will not be recorded.

(Text continues on page I-1-56.)

Fig. 1.34. Storyboard.

Program ______________________ Page ____ of ____

Producers ______________________

VISUAL | TIME | AUDIO

Fig. 1.35. Storyboard.

close-up

working on ceramics

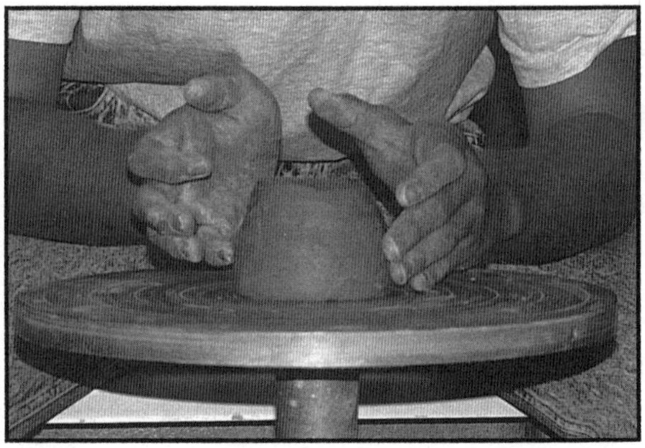

Actual Shot

7. Don't forget to storyboard the audio. If your script is already written, list the first few words of the script for each shot. If your script has not been written, make a note of the content to be covered in the audio. Also, note in the audio section whether the sound is "live" sound (to be recorded at the same time as the video) or a "voice-over," to be audio-dubbed at a later time.

   Music is also selected during the storyboarding process. Good background music is integrated into the program, not just added to pass time between narration segments. If you haven't selected the exact piece of music, list the type of music, for example, "light and breezy," "tough/action music," or "scary music."

Students will invariably ask, "Do I have to storyboard *every* shot?" The answer is an emphatic YES! A local high school video team storyboarded 21 shots for a 1-minute action sequence in which a coward confronted the neighborhood bully. Without such careful planning, such a complex sequence could not have been completed.

Careful storyboarding, knowledge of the different camera angles used in video, and knowledge of the special features of your video camera can make your videos more informative and entertaining.

Review Questions: Lesson 4

1. What is the difference between noseroom and leadroom? [noseroom—subject is stationary; leadroom—subject is moving]

2. Why is it important to white-balance a camera? [White-balancing a camera shows the camera what "white" looks like under the lighting situation. A camera adjusts all of the other colors based on this "white."]

3. What are the three primary colors of light used in television production? [red, blue, green]

4. How does fluorescent light affect the color processed by a video camera? [Fluorescent light gives the picture a blue tint.]

5. What are two problems with using automatic white balance? [1. Automatic white balance represents very general settings; 2. Factory white-balance settings deteriorate over time.]

6. Where and when should white balancing take place? [White balancing should take place at the location of the shoot immediately before the tape is recorded.]

7. Under what conditions should automatic gain control be used? [Automatic gain control should be used in low-light situations.]

8. What is the main disadvantage of using AGC? [AGC amplifies the weak signal, often producing video noise.]

(Review questions continue on page I-1-58.)

9. List three ways to shoot a scene that surpasses the 30:1 contrast ratio. [1. Manually adjust the iris to brighten the subject. 2. Provide more light to the darker areas. 3. Change the location of the shot.]

10. What is the main benefit of the "standby" control? [By shutting down most of the camera functions, standby saves battery power.]

11. What function does the "trigger" perform? [The trigger serves as a remote control start/stop for the VCR.]

12. List the main problem with abuse of a "record review" function. [Abuse of the record review function can lead to erasure of the final seconds of tape because of the "back-up" tape feature.]

13. Which speed should be used for S-VHS and VHS recording? [The fastest speed available, which is SP.]

14. Why is storyboarding important? [Storyboarding allows the production team to create the video project on paper before making costly and time-consuming mistakes on camera.]

15. List the seven rules of storyboarding. [1. Keep it simple; 2. Draw the actual shot; 3. Consider point of view; 4. Use the margins for notes; 5. Use arrows to indicate panning and camera movement; 6. List times on the storyboard; 7. Storyboard the audio.]

Activities: Lesson 4

1. Locate the following buttons on a video camera/deck or camcorder that you use at school: automatic gain control, automatic iris control, white balance, standby, trigger, fade, tape speed, tracking.

2. List the other features available on the camera you used above.

3. Videotape examples of close-ups using the proper amount of headroom, too much headroom, and too little headroom. Do the same with noseroom. View the samples in class and evaluate your performance.

4. Obtain three slide mounts and three slide projectors from your school media specialist. Mount a red gel in one slide mount, a blue gel in the second, and a green gel in the third. Using the three slide projectors, project each slide onto the same screen. What do you expect will happen? What really happens? Which principle of video production does this illustrate? (Important note: Make sure to use professional-quality gel, which looks like tinted transparency material but can actually withstand the heat produced by the slide projector. Using regular tinted plastic will cause damage to the projector. Because you only need a few square inches of each gel, your local vendor may donate a sample.)

5. Connect your camera/camcorder to a television or monitor. Using your manual white-balance control, white-balance your camera on a *red* piece of paper. Try blue and green also. What are the results? How do extremely bright colors differ from dull colors?

6. Connect your camera/camcorder to a television or monitor. Darken your classroom so that your camera has the minimum illumination for processing the video signal. Analyze the picture quality. In what ways does the quality suffer? Then, switch to automatic gain control. How does that affect the shot?

7. Create a simple storyboard of at least three different shots for the following three videotaping opportunities:

   a high school football game

   a dance recital

   an automobile dealership commercial

Student Project Plan: Documentary

DESCRIPTION OF COMPLETED PROJECT

The finished project will be a 3-minute documentary on some facet of life at school. It *may* include an interview. The documentary must contain various camera shots and must contain voice and music audio dub. Titles will be at the beginning, featuring the name of the program and the name of the producers. The last shot will fade to black.

METHOD

1. Students will choose a partner.
2. The team agrees on a topic.
3. The team creates a set of storyboards for the project. Pre-planning is important. There will be no editing.
4. Students use the character generator to compose a title.
5. Students then shoot the documentary in order.
6. Students audio-dub the documentary with voice and music.

EQUIPMENT

audio mixer

camera/deck or camcorder

character generator

microphone

music source

tripod (optional)

VCR

EVALUATION

The project will be worth 200 points:

concept and storyboard	(40)
titles	(40)
camera work	(40)
audio dub	(40)
overall production	(40)

Evaluation Sheet: Documentary

TEAM MEMBERS ____________________

Concept and Storyboard

Project idea	(10)	________
Storyboard video	(10)	________
Storyboard audio	(10)	________
Completion of idea	(10)	________

Audio Dub

Script	(10)	________
Music choice	(10)	________
Mixing levels	(10)	________
Voice talent	(10)	________

Titles

Choice of title	(10)	________
Spelling	(10)	________
Layout	(10)	________
Choice of colors	(10)	________

Camera Work

Shot selection	(10)	________
Steadiness	(10)	________
White balance	(10)	________
Shot variety	(10)	________

Overall Production

Is the viewer more informed on the topic area?	(20)	________
Is the project free from serious production problems?	(10)	________
Is the treatment of the topic fresh, creative, and thought-provoking?	(10)	________

COMMENTS:

Total Points/Percentage ________ / ________%

Letter grade A B C D Re-do

Lesson 5 Single-Camera Studio Production

Objectives

After successfully completing this lesson, you will be able to:

- *identify and describe the connectors used in video production.*
- *explain the function and use of adapters in video production.*
- *explain the difference between shielded and unshielded cable and understand the proper application for each type.*
- *arrange ENG equipment into a ministudio.*
- *understand concepts of basic set design for a small studio news show.*
- *understand and apply the basic structure of small studio lighting.*

Vocabulary

1/4-inch phone. A type of plug or jack used in audio connections.

1/8-inch mini. A type of plug or jack used in audio connections.

Adapter. A small connector that allows conversion from one type of jack or plug to another type.

Backlight. A light used in television production positioned behind the talent and designed to eliminate the shadow caused by the key light.

BNC. A popular twist-lock connector used in video production.

F connector. A jack/plug used to connect VCRs to television sets. Also called an RF connector.

Fill light. A third light used in small studio video production. It is designed to fill shadow areas caused by the use of a key light.

Jack. A receptacle for an audio or video connection.

Key light. The main source of artificial illumination in a video production. The key light is usually facing the on-air talent.

Line-out monitor. The video or audio/video monitor that displays the final signal produced by the audio/video system.

Phono. A type of connector used in audio and video production. Also called an RCA connector.

Plug. The part of the connector that is inserted into the jack.

Shielded cable. An insulated cable used in audio and video production.

Unshielded cable. A cable with little or no insulation used as a stereo speaker cable and headphone cable.

XLR. An audio connector usually used with low-impedance, professional systems.

Schools across the nation are using simple television studios within their schools to create shows that entertain and inform their student body, faculty, and administration. Some schools produce daily news shows that replace the standard morning announcements. Other schools choose a weekly or semimonthly schedule in which documentary and feature programs replace timely news items. Whatever the time frame, the news shows provide a source of information as well as a creative and educational outlet for the students involved.

While some schools have studios that cost half a million dollars and more, a news show can be produced with a minimum amount of equipment. In this lesson, we look at the connections needed to assemble your ENG equipment into a small studio and how to design and light your studio for your program needs.

Audio and video equipment can be configured so that it can work together in more complex programs. As you can imagine, the equipment is connected with a series of wires. Fortunately, the connections do not involve removing the external housing of the equipment and installing new wires. Most items of equipment used in audio and video production have various inputs and outputs used to make these connections.

A receptacle for a wire is called a *jack*. The connector that is inserted into the jack is called a *plug*. There are many different jacks and plugs used in audio/video production. While the industry has no formal standard jack/plug type, some are emerging as prominent connection points on audio/video equipment. Still, it is important to learn the proper name and use of each jack/plug that may be encountered in video production. Because smaller school-based programs often use a hodgepodge of ENG and secondhand equipment, students will likely use many of the different jacks/plugs available.

Connectors Used in Audio

Most audio jacks/plugs are designed for simple connection and disconnection. The main jacks/plugs found in audio production are 1/4-inch phone, 1/8-inch mini, phono (RCA), and XLR.

As can be seen in figure 1.36, the *1/4-inch phone* plug is characterized by a broad metal shaft with an indentation near the end that connects to a plain jack. The 1/4-inch phone plug gets its name from its diameter and its early use by switchboard operators. Now the 1/4-inch phone plug is used for microphone and headphone connections.

The *1/8-inch mini* plug is identical to the 1/4-inch phone plug, except it is about half the size (figure 1.37). The 1/8-inch mini plug was created to accommodate the personal, pocket-sized electronics market. The 1/8-inch mini plug still hasn't made a big dent in studio audio equipment, although its use is increasing in lavaliere microphones and smaller headphone sets.

Music sources are usually connected to an audio mixer via *phono* plugs, commonly referred to as *RCA* plugs, after the company that created and popularized the plug-in home stereo systems. As shown in figure 1.38, the phono plug is a metal shaft that is surrounded by metal flanges that serve to secure the connection. The phone jack is a plain receptacle that is raised from the equipment surface. Phone plugs are popular because of the stereo sound demands of most modern audio equipment. Phone plugs are usually found in pairs: one for the right audio channel and another for the left.

(Text continues on page I-1-65.)

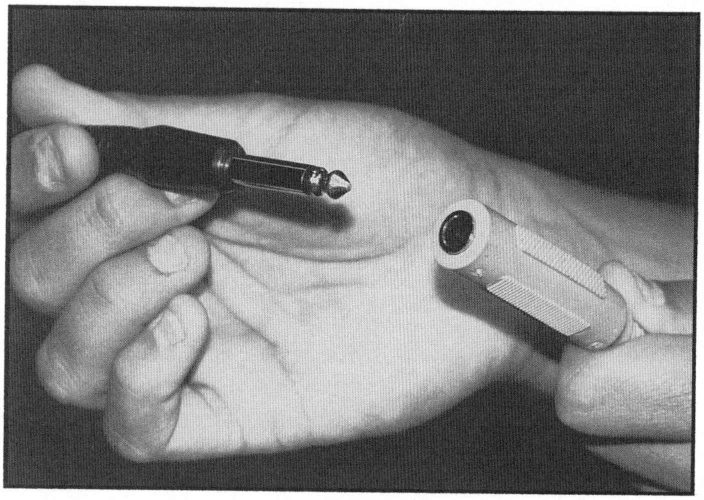

Fig. 1.36. 1/4-inch phone plug.

Fig. 1.37. 1/8-inch mini plug.

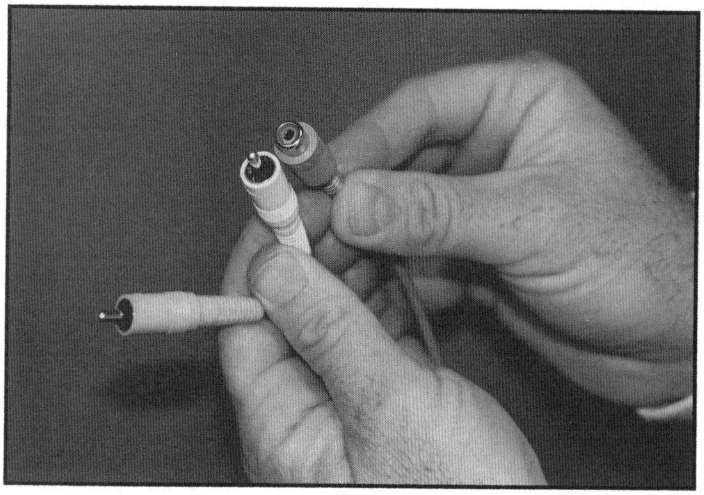

Fig. 1.38. Phono, or RCA, plugs.

They are often colored red and white to avoid confusion when true stereo sound is a goal of the program. (Unfortunately, most school-based television sets are mono, so any channel separation achieved in the studio is often lost on your audience.) Because of the nature of the connection, phono jacks and plugs should be checked on a regular basis for security and firmness. When the audio is not working properly in your system, a loose phono plug is the best place to begin trouble-shooting.

Professional audio systems often use the *XLR* plug/jack system. The XLR plug has three separate plugs encased within a cone-shaped cover (figure 1.39). The XLR jack is simply a unit containing three separate coordinating jacks. XLR plugs/jacks are frequently found in professional TV studios and audio mixers. XLR jacks/plugs are usually used in low-impedance microphone systems using long cable lengths. Often, audio mixers that have XLR jacks also offer the 1/4-inch jack option.

Fig. 1.39. XLR plugs.

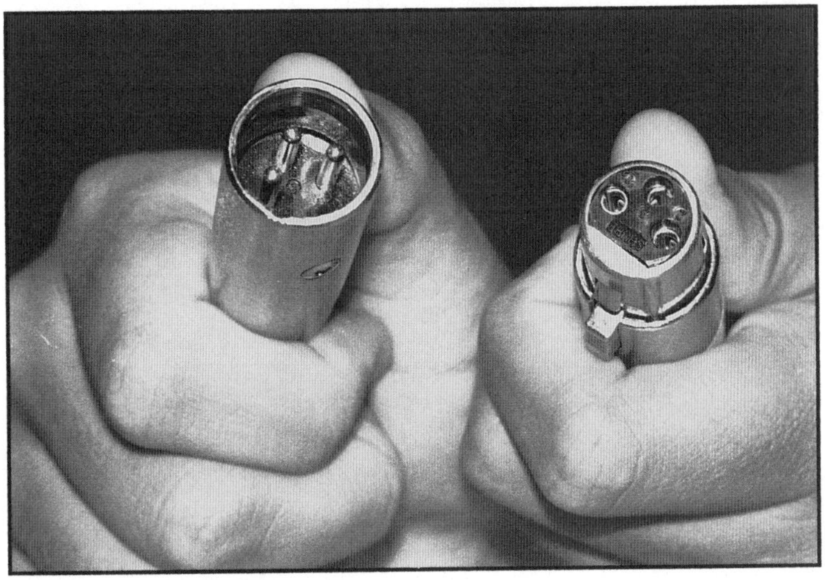

Connectors Used in Video

Video components must be properly connected to work together in the video production. Unlike audio connectors, connectors used in video offer a more permanent installation. The connectors most often associated with video are RF (or F connector) and BNC.

By far, the most common connector used in video is the *BNC* jack/plug (figure 1.40). The BNC is unique in its twist-lock connection. The BNC plug consists of a small post surrounded by a locking assembly that aligns with the jack and twists into place. This locking mechanism guarantees that the cable will not be disturbed by simple jarring or shaking. The connector is large enough to be strong and easily manipulated and small enough to be space-efficient. In an area once crowded with options, the BNC has emerged as the industry standard.

The *RF*, or *F connector* is used to connect VCRs to television sets (figure 1.41). The RF connector is usually considered a permanent installation because it requires several turns of the screw-on post.

RCA/phono connectors are also used in consumer-grade video.

Fig. 1.40. BNC jack/plug.

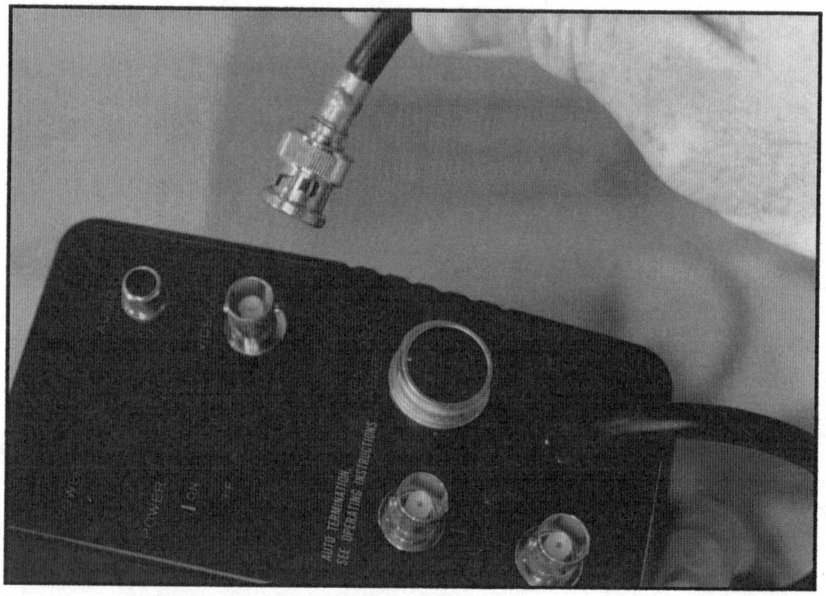

Fig. 1.41. RF, or F, connector.

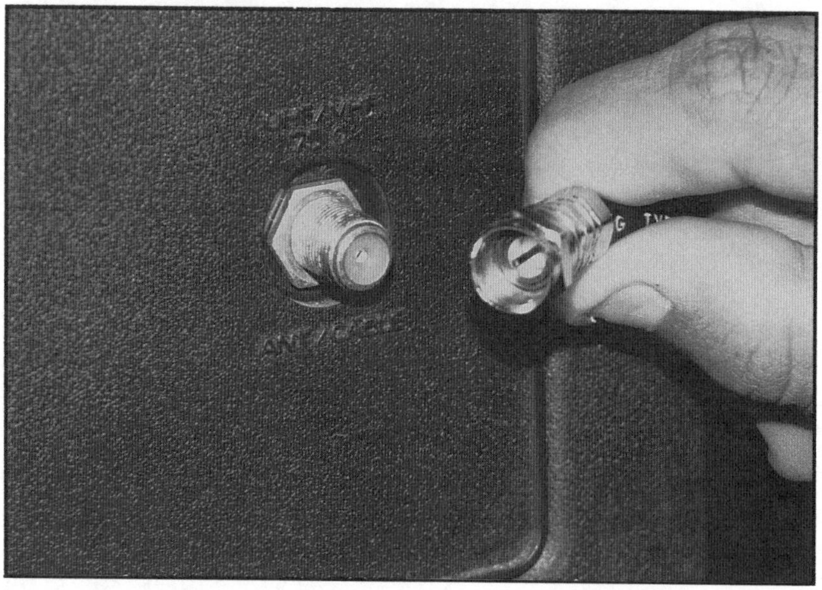

Adapters

Most electronic stores stock a wide variety of adapters that can convert one type of plug or jack to another. For example, an adapter can be used to convert the 1/8-inch mini plug that is on the end of your lavaliere microphone to the 1/4-inch phone plug that your audio mixer accepts. In many cases, like the one mentioned above, using an adapter is the only option other than cutting the original plug and installing a new one. Sometimes the adapter can also cut costs. Schools wired for closed-circuit television frequently have cable with RF plugs on each end left over from the wall-tap to television connections. These cords can be fitted with adapters that convert them to BNC or RCA for use in the television studio. Many schools also maintain a small supply of adapters for use in unexpected circumstances. A tackle box can be used to keep the adapters in order. Older equipment can also be rendered useful, thanks to adapters. One school recently obtained two high-quality monochrome monitors for a very reasonable price but found the connectors to be quite foreign. A visit to the electronics store garnered two adapters that made the monitors fully functional in the television studio. Many years ago, as video technology was emerging, each company that manufactured video equipment used its own connection system, thus you may encounter some obscure connectors. Once again, a trip to your local electronics dealer will probably solve any problems that you encounter.

Shielded and Unshielded Cable

Cable that has been insulated (wrapped) in rubber, foam, or both is called shielded cable. Shielded cable should be used in all audio and video connections. The extra insulation maintains signal strength and keeps out interference from such sources as televisions, computers, and fluorescent lights. Unshielded cable, which is generally just copper wire wrapped in plastic, can be used for connecting speakers or headphones to a system—in other words, audio outputs not to be used again by the system. For example, let's say that your microphone cable is not long enough for a needed application. When you visit the electronics store, you find two cables that are similar in appearance and seem to fulfill your need: shielded microphone extension cable and headphone extension cable. The headphone extension cable is less expensive, but it will not serve as a microphone extension cable. Many manufacturers use gray cable to indicate shielded cable and other colors to indicate unshielded cable, but this is far from being an industrywide practice. The correct information can be obtained from the package label, small writing on the cable, or a query of the salesperson. In order to maintain the integrity of your production and the health of your pocketbook, the correct information should be obtained before buying the cable.

Preparation for System Configuration

Now that you know all about audio and video connectors, you are ready to configure your system into a working studio. Our objective is to produce a single-camera news show with music and voice. Depending on the amount of equipment that you have, you may want to add or delete components.

One concept remains constant in all video connections: the concept of inputs and outputs. Each item of equipment, audio or video, serves to process the signal created by sources—microphones, cameras, and music sources. The input takes in the signal, and the output sends it to the next input. If this concept is cloudy to you, it will become clearer as we continue.

Audio System Connections

Audio inputs for a small studio consist of microphones and music (music intro and conclusion). If you plan to include an ENG segment that has been prerecorded (e.g., an interview with the principal, a story about the first dance of the school year) you will need audio from a VCR (figure 1.42).

Your anchorperson, or talent, can use a lavaliere microphone or a hand-held microphone on a desktop stand. This microphone should be connected to the audio mixer. If you have more than one anchorperson, each should have his or her own microphone. Sharing or passing around microphones can be noisy and lead to loss of sound quality.

If you plan to use music as your show begins and concludes, you need to connect your music source (cassette/CD player) to the audio mixer, too. If you have chosen to use an ENG segment in your news show, you need to connect the segment's audio to the audio mixer as well. (Playing an ENG segment requires a separate VCR.) Run a shielded cable (or pair for stereo) from the "audio-out" of

Fig. 1.42. Audio connections.

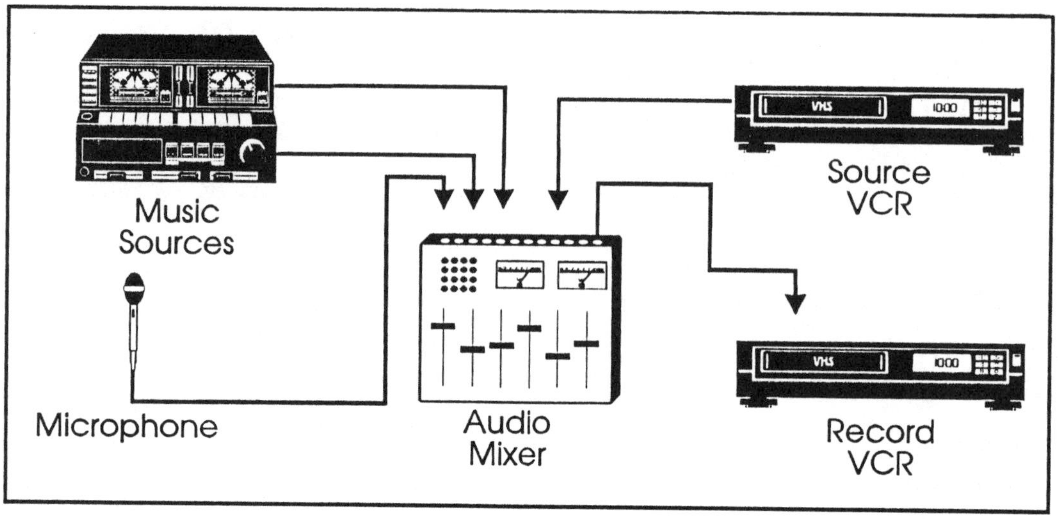

your "play" VCR to an input of your audio mixer. Treat this input as you would a music source, such as an audiotape or CD. Use a pair of headphones so that your audio technician can hear the microphone(s), ENG sound and music, and obtain a proper audio mix.

The audio mixer should have a "main output" set of jacks on the back. Run a shielded cable—or a pair of shielded cables if you are using a stereo-mixing console and VCR—to the audio input jack(s) of your recording VCR. For all practical purposes, your audio connections are complete. If you want other class members to hear the show over stereo speakers as it is being videotaped, you will need a small amplifier and one or two speakers. Run a shielded cable from the audio output of the recording VCR to the tape input of the audio amplifier. Then connect a speaker to the regular speaker output of the audio amplifier.

Video System Connections

The video portion of our small studio setup consists of a camera or camcorder, a switcher, a character generator, a source VCR for playing segments, and a record VCR for recording the final program (figure 1.43). A simpler configuration is available for schools that don't have a switcher and/or character generator, and will be explained on page I-1-69.

A video switcher is similar in function to an audio mixer. A video switcher selects and combines video sources. For our ministudio, we need a switcher that has at least two video inputs and a background color. The video camera/camcorder is connected to an input of the video switcher. In either case, no VCR is used at the site of the camera. Video cameras and camcorders have video outputs. On camcorders, this might involve searching through the accessory pack for an adapter. If you plan to run an ENG segment during your news show, you need to run a shielded cable from the "video-out" of the "play/segment" VCR to another input of your switcher. Now you have both video sources—camera and source VCR—connected to your switcher. Depending on the type of switcher you have, you may be able to make dissolves, wipes, cuts, etc. Your switcher will also probably offer the option of a monitor so that you can preview a video source before selecting it.

Your next connection adds graphics, such as the name of the anchorperson and ending credits. A shielded cable should connect the "video-out" of the switcher to the "video-in" of the character generator. The output of the character generator is connected to the input of the record VCR. By using the "transparent" background color choice on the character generator, the video signal from the switcher will simply "play through" the character generator as the graphics technician adds the titles,

Fig. 1.43. Video connections.

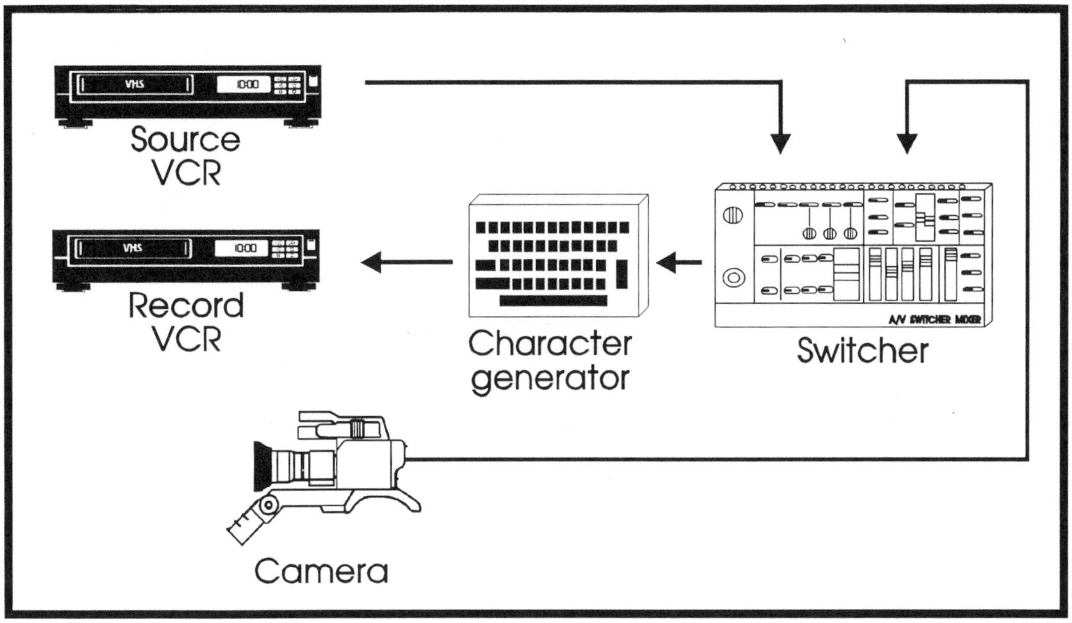

internal graphics, and credits. Most character generators also have "preview out" jacks that can be connected to another monitor to allow the graphics technician to create, select, and preview graphics before they are put on the screen.

Now all audio and video have been connected to the record VCR. Running a shielded cable from the RF out of the record VCR to a television set allows the producer to see and hear the end product. This television is called the line-out monitor.

Let's briefly review the connections explained in the previous paragraphs and also illustrated in figure 1.44. For audio: All sources (microphone/music/source VCR) are connected to the audio mixer. The combined audio signal goes from the audio mixer to the record VCR, where it is recorded simultaneously with the video. For video: Video inputs (camera/source VCR) are connected to a video switcher. The signal is then sent to a character generator for graphics, and then to the record VCR, to be recorded simultaneously with the audio. To see the finished product as it is being recorded, a line-out monitor is connected to the RF out of the record VCR.

But what if we don't have an audio mixer, a switcher, or a character generator? Connect a microphone to your camcorder and go on with the show. If you want to use ENG segments, use the deck-to-deck editing techniques described in lesson 6. For music, use a stereo with a speaker near the anchorperson. Use camera-based graphics. But don't stop production. Make video yearbooks, sell candy, write grants, beg your administration. Spend your well-earned funds on the equipment listed above. But continue to produce your news program.

Basic Set Design

Converting a classroom to a news studio can tax your creativity. Use the following tips to get the job done.

- Keep it simple. A small table with a student or secretary's chair will suffice. Don't distract your viewers with unnecessary items.

- Keep it small. An actual news set can fit in the corner of a classroom. Worry only about what the camera "sees."

Fig. 1.44. Audio and video connections.

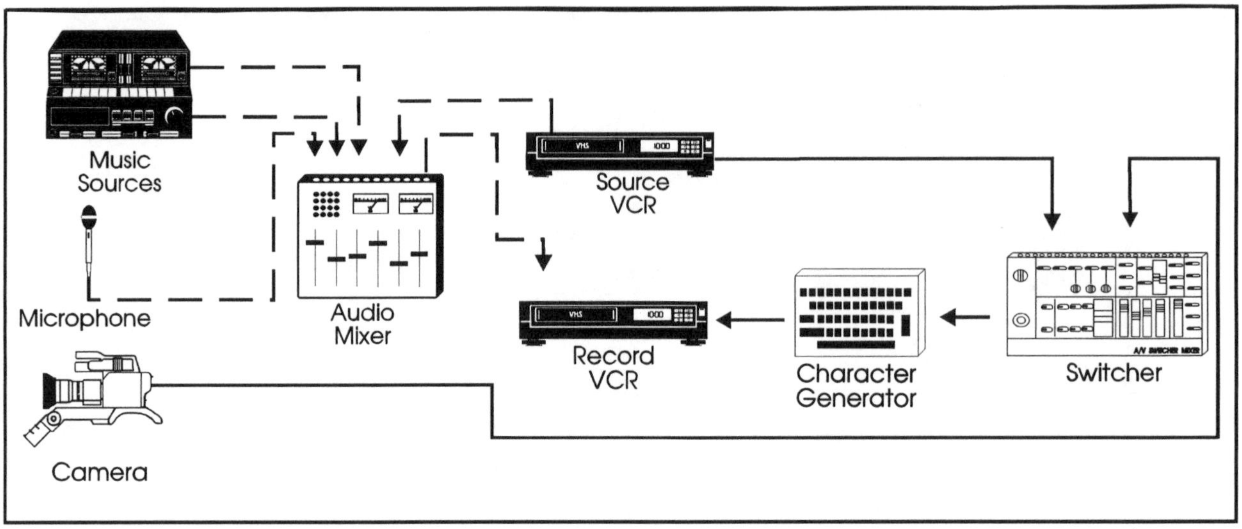

- Seat your anchorperson on a platform. School shop classes might help to construct a wood platform about 4 inches tall. The platform can be 5 to 6 feet long and 4 to 5 feet wide. This platform will allow normal camera operation while eliminating a downward tilt of the camera.

- Use a background. Choose a neutral color like light blue, gray, or tan. Try to use your school colors. Backgrounds can be made of curtains, bulletin board paper, or painted or dyed material. Even ironed bedsheets can be hung on the wall.

- Eliminate empty spots. Fill the screen with your anchorperson and perhaps a simple unobtrusive decoration.

- Constantly think of ways to improve the set. You can probably come up with ideas to improve a basic news set. Use items from around your school to liven up the set.

Simple Studio Lighting

Although your camera or camcorder can operate effectively under classroom lighting, your picture will probably improve with additional lighting. Professional lighting kits are expensive, but many schools have obtained near-professional results using less-than-professional equipment. Perhaps your drama department has an extra light that can be mounted on the wall or on a tripod. Hardware stores sell inexpensive clamp lights, which consist of a regular bulb socket connected to a reflector dish and a clamp. School maintenance departments can help with floodlight fixtures. (A note of warning: All lights mentioned above produce heat. Don't let your creative lighting designs become a fire hazard! Always verify the safety of your connections with the appropriate authorities.)

If you decide to use lighting in your news program, you will probably need at least two lighting instruments: a main key light and a backlight. The key light's job is to illuminate your anchorperson. The backlight is placed behind the anchorperson near ground level and is pointed up and slightly toward the background. This light will help decrease the shadow caused by the key light. If the backlight does not control the shadow, a third fill light may be used from one side pointed at the anchorperson. Work with your lighting until you have produced a safe, aesthetic design.

A classroom can be converted into a small, working studio with a minimal amount of equipment, the knowledge presented in this lesson, and the creativity to work around program limitations. Producing a school news show can be a rewarding experience!

Have fun!

Review Questions: Lesson 5

1. What is the difference between a jack and a plug? [A plug contains the wire to be connected; a jack is a receptacle for that wire.]

2. Several connectors are listed below. To the left of each connector, indicate whether its use is primarily in audio or video.

[audio]	______	1/4-inch phone	[video]	______	BNC
[audio]	______	XLR	[audio]	______	phono
[video]	______	F connector	[audio]	______	1/8-inch mini

3. Which type of connector is usually found in pairs? [Phono]

   Which type of connector is found in professional audio systems? [XLR]

   Which type of connector uses a twist-lock mechanism? [BNC]

   Which type of connector is used to connect VCRs to television sets? [F connector]

4. Video connections are usually [more/less] secure than audio connections. (Circle one.) [more]

5. What is the difference between shielded and unshielded cable? [Shielded cable is insulated, usually using rubber, plastic, or foam. This insulation protects against signal deterioration and interference from outside signals.]

6. Which type of cable should be used in most audio and video applications? [Shielded]

(Review questions continue on page I-1-72.)

7. How can a person determine if a cable is shielded or unshielded before purchase? [You must read the packaging or consult the sales staff.]

8. Why is a line-out monitor important to small studio productions? [The line-out monitor allows the team to see the product being recorded on tape.]

9. List the six tips given for small studio set design. [1. Keep it simple; 2. Keep it small; 3. Seat your anchorperson on a platform; 4. Use a background; 5. Eliminate empty spots; 6. Think of ways to improve the set.]

10. How can a small studio be illuminated with nonprofessional lights? [The following methods can be used: an extra light from the theater mounted on the wall or on a tripod; reflector clamp lights; floodlight fixtures.]

11. What is the top consideration for lighting? [Safety]

Activities: Lesson 5

1. Inspect all of your audio and video equipment. Make a list of all of the connectors used. Are they all found in this lesson? Identify any connectors that are new to you.

2. Identify the connectors used in your home VCR, small electronics, video games, etc. Are they the same as the connectors used in audio and video?

3. Find the names of connectors used in computer equipment.

4. Research the meanings behind the abbreviations BNC, RF, RCA, and XLR.

5. Using a small scale from the science department, weigh equal lengths of shielded and unshielded cable. How do they compare?

6. Visit a local electronics shop. Ask to see all of the connectors and adapters. Bring a catalog back to the class.

7. Make a checklist of all of the equipment mentioned in this lesson. Which items does your school have? Which ones should it consider purchasing?

8. Brainstorm a list of 10 stories that would be interesting for a news show at your school.

9. Make a simple sketch of a news show set design. Make sure to list all of the materials needed. Be realistic.

Student Project Plan: News Brief

DESCRIPTION OF COMPLETED PROJECT

The completed project will be a self-contained news program lasting about three minutes. The project will include opening and ending credits with music, a story read on camera by the anchorperson, a videotape story narrated by the anchorperson, and a complete news segment on videotape. The anchor will introduce all segments.

METHOD

1. Students will choose groups based on jobs and interests.
2. Job descriptions appear on the student handout (see page I-1-75).
3. Titles and assignments are completed.
4. Project is completed using small studio equipment.

EQUIPMENT

audio mixer

camera/camcorder

character generator

lighting (optional)

line-out monitor

microphone

monitors

music sources

switcher

tripod

two VCRs

EVALUATION

The project will be worth 200 points. The group will be given a grade of 100 possible points for professional appearance of the production, coordination, and quality of content. Each group member will also be given a possible 100-point grade based on his or her individual work.

News Brief Handout

FORMAT

Time	Program	Video Source	Audio Source
		fade from black	
:05	opening	graphics	music
:20	story #1	camera/graphics	anchor
:30	story #2	source VCR	anchor
1:00	story #3	source VCR	VCR
:10	goodbye	camera	anchor
:20	credits	graphics	music

PERSONNEL

Each student is assigned specific tasks to complete before (preproduction) and during (production) the actual program.

Student #1 Preproduction: assignment editor, anchor script, lead-ins.
Production: studio anchor

Student #2 Preproduction: learn switching skills
Production: switcher, VCR operator

Student #3 Preproduction: ENG reporter (story #3)
Production: audio technician

Student #4 Preproduction: ENG videographer
Production: videographer/camera setup

Student #5 Preproduction: character generator design, ENG assistant
Production: character generator

Evaluation Sheet: News Brief

SHOW TITLE ____________________

PERIOD ____________________

	Individual Grade	+	Group Grade	=	Total Grade
Student -1 ____________	______		______		______

Comments:

Student -2 ____________	______	______	______

Comments:

Student -3 ____________	______	______	______

Comments:

Student -4 ____________	______	______	______

Comments:

Student -5 ____________	______	______	______

Comments:

Group's comments:

Lesson 6 Instructional Techniques for Video

Objectives

After successfully completing this lesson, you will be able to:

- *select an appropriate topic for an instructional video program.*
- *plan, shoot, edit, and audio-dub an instructional video program.*
- *connect and use a deck-to-deck editing system.*

Vocabulary

Black tape. A videotape onto which a solid black screen and no audio has been recorded. A segment of black tape is used at the beginning and at the end of video programs.

Continuity. The practice of detail orientation that makes sure that the video program is consistent from edit to edit.

Control track. The part of the recorded videotape that stabilizes the video.

Deck-to-deck editing. The process of combining and rearranging videotape segments by connecting two VCRs and duplicating the program in the desired sequence.

Establishing shot. In traditional video production, the first segment of a video program that gives the viewer information about the setting. For example, a video program set in a high school would begin with an establishing long shot of the high school exterior.

Jump cut. The effect produced when similar video segments with significant differences are juxtaposed in the editing process. For example, the first shot contains a woman sitting on a park bench. In the very next shot, the woman is standing. She has "jumped."

Live sound. The audio recorded, using an external microphone or the camera's internal microphone, simultaneously with the video on the videotape. Live sound can be "talent" (someone speaking, singing, or playing a musical instrument) or "ambient" (a naturally existing environmental sound, such as birds singing or waves crashing at the ocean).

Raw footage. The video and audio recorded on the videotape during the shoot. The raw footage is edited to make the video program.

Schools, companies, and organizations around the world are using video to instruct people on a wide variety of subjects. Video is an effective medium for communicating the objectives designed by instructors of many tasks. Since the early days of video technology, class and study sessions have been recorded for people to view at other times and places. Those early efforts usually involved setting a camera on a tripod in the back of a classroom and conducting the class session as normal. Or the entire class was brought into the television studio to accommodate the space and lighting needed by early television cameras. But with the advent of video editing, graphics, and ENG equipment, instructional video took a different form. Instructional programs establish the video viewer as the primary audience of the program, not just as a distant observer.

Today, video is a valuable tool for many institutions. Companies regularly produce instructional video programs to train workers on established procedures, announce new procedures, and conduct informative "video meetings." Schools produce video programs to facilitate distance learning and give special tutoring to students having difficulty with certain topics. Through video technology, people can be trained firsthand by experts otherwise not available. The addition of music and professional narration makes the program even more effective.

Topics for Instructional Videos

Some topics lend themselves naturally to instructional video programs. Video's strongest feature is its ability to convey motion to the viewer. Topics that deal with important behaviors, such as "How to Load a Computer Program" or "How to Make a Fast-Food Sandwich," would make good instructional videos. However, video's strength can also work as a weakness. Topics that require exact, tedious tasks don't translate very well on video, unless still-video technology is used. A video on "How to Connect a Fuse Box" could lead to disaster and might be better suited for a slide show, book, or person-to-person session.

An instructional video must also fit the level of the viewer. A simple rule to follow is to make a "you can" video, not an "I can" video. Instructional video producers should carefully evaluate the current level of expertise of their viewing audience before selecting a topic. For example, a 5-minute video program on "How to Choreograph a Ballet" probably wouldn't work; a 10-minute program on three of the basic ballet positions would be more effective. Remember, tell your audience "you can," not "I can."

For reasons alluded to above, concrete, objective tasks work better as video topics than abstract, subjective topics. "How to Be a Friend" might sound like a great idea for a video program, but the topic is really too personal to communicate real content. "How to Plan a Surprise Party" would capture the same spirit and teach a real skill.

Make sure your instructional programs have real instructions, not just tips. While helpful hints are important, they shouldn't be the entire content of the video.

A topic for an instructional video should be narrow in scope to allow completion of a single skill while achieving some sense of closure. In other words, the viewer should learn to perform a single, complete task. (A single video program on the techniques for video production would be too long and thus ineffective.) After learning more than a few new skills, most viewers suffer from "information overload," that feeling that you have at the end of a class when it seems like your brain just can't hold anymore! Instructional video programs on topics like television production, cooking, or auto repair are usually broken into appropriate subject areas and presented as a series of programs lasting a few minutes each. These programs can be selected for appropriateness and reviewed by the learner as the need arises.

Remember: Not all topics are suitable for instructional video programs. Topics that show simple, concrete skills that the learner can master after one or two viewings work best in the medium of television.

The Structure of Instructional Video Programs

Like a good novel or short story, an instructional video program should have a beginning, a middle, and an end.

Many options exist for the beginning of instructional video programs. Let's choose a topic and work through many possible introductions. Imagine that you have been contacted by a local sandwich shop to produce a 10-minute video program on the preparation of its new roast beef sandwich. You could begin with a graphic "How to Prepare a Roast Beef Sandwich" on the screen. This reading activity would surely get your audience involved in the task. Perhaps an announcer could dub those words on the tape as the graphic appears. This "traditional" approach works well in formal topics, or when the client wants a serious treatment of the subject matter. But maybe your client recognizes that most of his sandwich shop workers are high school and college students. They might respond better to a humorous opening. You could produce a brief scenario involving what would happen if the sandwich was prepared incorrectly, with the roast beef sliding off the bread and the condiments dripping on the floor. The flip side of this comical introduction could show the correctly made sandwich being enjoyed by a customer. Showing the desired end product is a good way to begin an instructional program.

An even more serious approach than the "traditional" opening would be the exposure of the problem that resulted in this program being produced. A program could begin with magazine articles and statistics about food poisoning resulting from poorly prepared food. Whatever the approach, it is easy to see that the beginning of the instructional video program performs two important tasks: 1) It tells the viewer what task(s) will be learned and 2) it sets the tone for the program to follow.

The "middle" of an instructional video program contains most of the information that the producer wishes to communicate. The body of the video program contains all of the audio and video that are essential to learning the desired task. Narration and graphics are used to reinforce the content. As you complete this lesson, you will see how the body is shaped into effective video communication.

The end, or conclusion of an instructional video program, like the beginning, can take many forms. A review of the pertinent points of the procedure makes a great conclusion. Try to summarize the entire program in your concluding sentences. Show the finished product and the rewards for a job well done. A return to the introduction gives the viewer a sense of closure and completion. Remember, the conclusion makes a lasting impression on the viewer and sets the tone for the execution of the task. While "How to Kick a Soccer Ball" might end with people playing their favorite sport, "How to Jump-Start Your Car" should end on a more serious note.

To borrow an old adage from public speaking: Tell them what you're going to tell them, tell them, and then tell them what you told them!

Planning an Instructional Video Program

Like any other video program, an instructional video program takes careful planning. Unlike other forms of presentation, the instructional video has a specific behavior to teach and reinforce. The instructional video planning session must strive for completeness as well as presentation.

The first step in most instructional videos involves diagnosing or identifying the problem. One fine student-produced instructional video is called "How to Add Oil to Your Car." You might think that this student production group's first instruction was "open the oil bottle" or "take off the oil cap." But this perceptive group went back to the beginning. They told the viewer how he or she would know that the car needed oil. The students videotaped someone routinely checking the oil level under the hood and even showed the illuminated "oil" light on the dashboard. (Actually, the "oil" light was a mock-up using red plastic and a penlight flashlight.)

Another important step to include in an instructional video program is the gathering of the appropriate materials. Along with showing an oil funnel and a towel to wipe up any spills, the student group also videotaped a student reading the car owner's manual to determine the correct type of oil for the car. Naturally, the task is not completed until all of the tools used are cleaned and prepared for the next use. Oily rags can start a fire, and the improper storage of unused oil can be messy and dangerous. The philosophy behind instructional video is that it is always the "maid's day off," so show the viewers how to complete the task. Don't leave them hanging!

Earlier, we mentioned the need to assess the level of the learner. When planning your instructional video, be aware of what the viewer does or does not already know about the topic. If in doubt, assume that your viewer knows little or nothing about your topic. It is better to have a few informed viewers bored during a minute of background information than to have most of your viewers confused by a program that assumes information not known or tasks not yet mastered. (Just why *do* cars need oil, anyway?) Remember, if in doubt, write it out!

Storyboarding is the next step. Lesson 4 fully explained the concept of storyboarding. As you can imagine, storyboarding is very important in the creation of instructional video programs. The omission of a single shot can make your video program incomplete, confusing, and ineffective. Besides making sure that every shot is completed, there are some general rules for storyboarding an instructional video program.

1. *Display your task from many different angles* (figure 1.45). Try to think of all of the camera angles you can possibly use for your project. Remember, each different camera angle might add new information to your program. A long shot is good for establishing the scene.

Fig. 1.45. Experimenting with a different camera angle.

Close-ups mixed with medium shots can give the viewer a sense of participation. Overhead shots can give the viewer an unobstructed view. Creativity is a big plus in instructional video. One student decided to make an instructional video program on "How to Bag Groceries." His objective was to show the viewer how to effectively use the space in the grocery bag while making sure not to crush the more fragile items. After videotaping several shots from various camera angles, he carefully cut the bottom out of the grocery bag. Then he put a piece of plexiglass between two tables and placed the bottomless bag on the plexiglass. Then, by positioning the camera on a tripod *underneath* the plexiglass, he created the unique "in-the-bag" camera angle that helped the viewer understand the exact positioning of each item in the grocery bag.

While the "different angles" approach leads to a more educational and watchable production, it does present one problem: the jump cut. A jump cut describes the situation in which a person or object "jumps" across the screen when a segment is edited. Let's go back to our example of adding oil to a car engine. Your first shot is your talent on camera sitting in the driver's seat of the car giving a 15-second intro to the program (figure 1.46). Your second shot shows your talent outside the car lifting the hood (figure 1.47). How did your talent magically jump from the inside to the outside of your car? This is a jump cut, and should be avoided. There are many solutions to this problem. Most are simple, but they need to be planned and storyboarded. You could end the first shot with the talent exiting the car and

Fig. 1.46. Introducing the video program.

Fig. 1.47. A jump cut.

walking off camera. Then the talent could walk into the second shot. Or, you could storyboard a graphic and edit it in between the first and second shots. This, in the mind of the viewer, would give the talent "time" to exit the car and walk around to the front. Carefully critique your storyboards and look for possible jump cuts. Even on television, viewers expect the world to make sense.

The concept of continuity also comes into play here. If a container of motor oil is opened in one shot, it cannot appear closed in the next shot. Even if videotaped on different days, your talent should be wearing the same clothing. And don't shift from day to evening scenes unless that time shift is important to your topic. Even though your shooting may take place in several locations over a period of a few days, your audience will feel more comfortable thinking that everything is happening as they are watching the program. Don't detract from your program by adding confusing jump cuts or continuity discrepancies. Consider assigning a detail-minded member of your group the task of keeping continuity on track and avoiding jump cuts in the raw footage.

2. *Make sure to show the appropriate detail that the viewer needs.* If the task involved requires manipulation of small items or the reading of print, you need to storyboard several macro-position shots to let your viewer get close to the action. Two students recently created an instructional video program on "How to Build Model Cars." They used many macro shots to let the viewer see the assembly of the small parts. Another popular project (because TV production class is often taught in the media center) is "How to Locate a Book in the Media Center." Whether using a traditional or electronic card cataloging system, the videographer needs to use the macro position to show the location of the information in the card catalog.

   Showing the right details doesn't just mean using the macro lens of your camera or camcorder. Make sure to storyboard *all* of the concepts that you plan to mention in your script.

3. *Storyboard a "tips" section, if it applies to the topic.* Earlier we stated that an instructional video program should be more than just a series of tips. However, helpful hints are an important part of any program. Whether you offer this advice throughout the program, or at the end, make sure to let your personal experiences in the topic area work for the viewer. If you brainstorm, you can probably think of five or six helpful pieces of advice. Remember, the viewer may not have *any* experience with the task at hand.

4. *Storyboard the graphics.* Graphics are helpful tools for the instructional video producer. Plan for these graphics by determining the abilities of your character generator (number of lines, number of spaces per line, colors, etc.) and writing the graphics in a storyboard box just as you would storyboard any other shot. If you're following the project plan after this lesson, you will *not* be able to superimpose graphics over a camera shot. That's a more advanced skill. For now, plan to use letters on a solid background. Actually, this is a good technique for instructional videos. The switch from the camera shot to a solid background lets the viewer know that important information is about to be revealed. It also gives the viewer a sense of transition, allowing him or her to "shift gears" in the middle of the program.

5. Decide whether you will use live sound or do a total audio dub after the task is edited. There are advantages to each approach, and a combination of both can work well also. Live sound can work for an on-camera introduction and/or conclusion, and audio dub is best for the body of the program. The decision must be made in the storyboarding process, as it will affect your camera angle selection.

Shooting the Instructional Video Program

After all this planning, actually shooting the raw footage may seem anticlimactic. Don't be fooled. Good camera work is the essence of an instructional video. And the best editing can't save terrible raw footage. The following tips should help.

1. Use a tripod. A shaky camera can distract the viewer from the ever-important content. And with close-ups and macro shots, the camera exaggerates even slight motions.

2. Avoid zooms and pans. These camera movements are distracting to the viewer trying to concentrate on learning a task. Establish your camera angle, then roll tape and perform the step of your task (figure 1.48). Move the camera, then roll tape again. Remember, you're not just performing the task in front of a camera. You're making a program that will teach a skill.

Fig. 1.48. Establishing a camera angle.

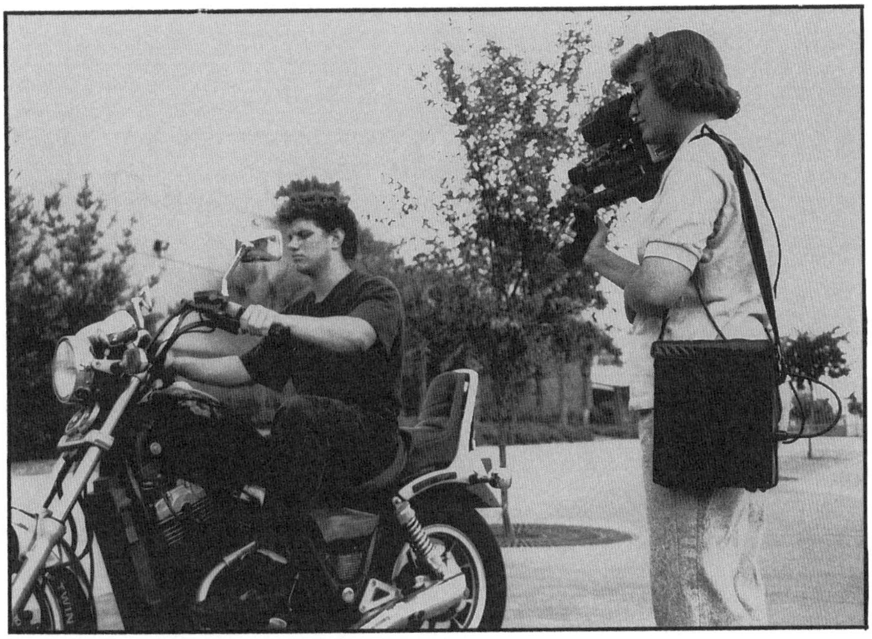

3. Plan for several cycles of your task. If your task is "How to Make a Salad," you should bring duplicates of all of the ingredients so that your preparations can be videotaped from several angles. Once a tomato is sliced, it can't be put back together!

4. Use your storyboards during the shoot. Don't rely on memory to supply the shots.

5. Shoot to edit. If your class is following this text in order, this is the first project that you will be editing. Let the camera run a full *5 or 10 seconds* before you perform the task. Whether you're using the deck-to-deck editing system explained later, or a professional editing suite, you need that time to properly edit your shots. Also let the camera run a few seconds after the task is completed. Don't conserve videotape! Shoot the best, and edit the rest.

Editing the Instructional Video Program

After all of your raw footage is shot and all of the graphics produced, you are ready to edit your program. If your school has a professional editing suite already in place, you probably won't have to worry about proper connections. But editing can be performed using two VCRs or even camcorders.

Videotape cannot be edited like film. If you have worked in film, from home Super 8mm to professional 35mm or 70mm, you know that film is edited by cutting, splicing, and taping or gluing the scenes together physically. In video, this is not possible. Cutting and pasting videotape has disastrous results. Film is actually a series of transparent pictures that is projected very quickly upon the screen. Videotape is magnetic, recording the signal onto the tape using electrical charges. One of the "tracks," or recording sections of a videotape is the control track (figure 1.49). Cutting the videotape will destroy the control track and ruin the project. Also, because videotape comes in direct contact with the VCR heads as it plays, a dab of film glue or splicing tape could ruin a VCR. To edit a videotape, you need two VCRs—one to play and another to record.

Fig. 1.49. Tracks on a videotape.

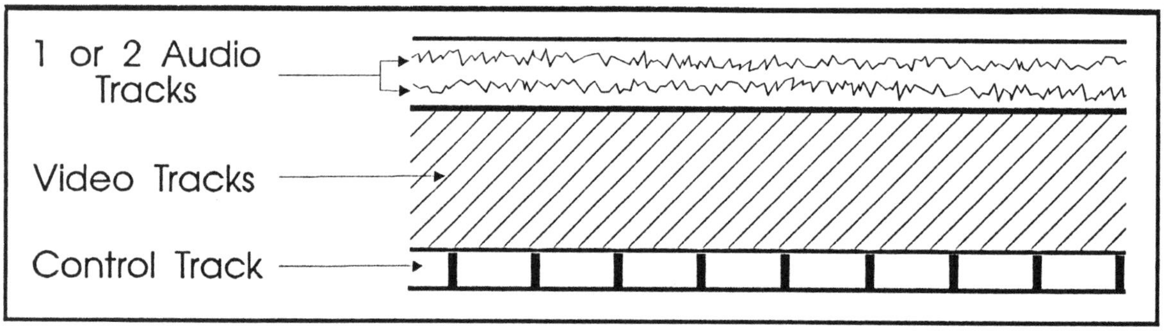

Because many schools don't have full editing suites, let's look at the proper connections to set up your own editing facility. Two simple rules apply.

Rule #1: Use four-head VCRs and camcorders when possible. This allows clear still-frame tape cuing and smoother edits.

Rule #2: Use only shielded cable in connecting these machines. This will give much cleaner tape-to-tape transfer.

To connect a simple deck-to-deck editing system, you need two video decks (or VCRs or camcorders), two televisions or monitors, and four or five lengths of shielded cable with connectors to fit your equipment. This connection is actually quite simple, and we'll break it into two parts: 1) connecting the VCRs to each other, and 2) connecting the VCRs to monitors or televisions.

Connecting the VCRs to each other. Set your VCRs on a table either side by side or, if ventilation is available, on top of one another. The left VCR, or top VCR will be your source (play) VCR and the right VCR or bottom VCR will be your record VCR (figure 1.50). This setup is standard in the industry and will avoid confusion if you have the opportunity to edit at another facility.

Next, locate the "video out" and "video in" jacks of your VCRs. Run a length of shielded cable from the "video out" jack of your source VCR to the "video in" jack of your record VCR. Your video connection is now complete.

Fig. 1.50. Deck-to-deck editing system connections.

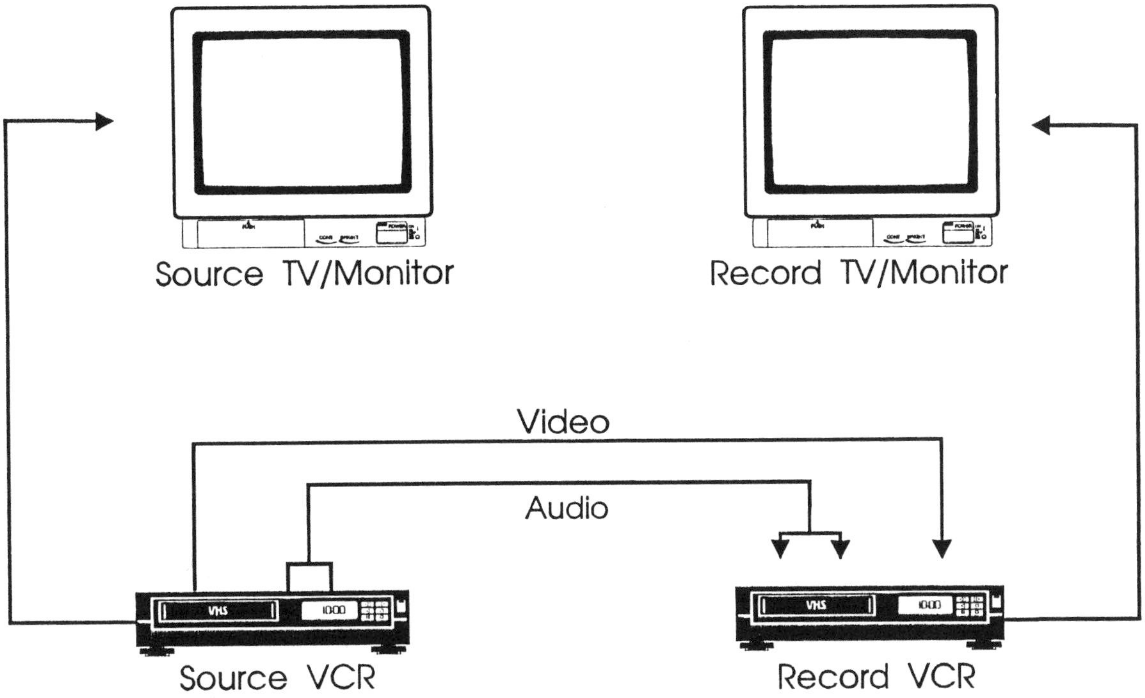

Now, locate the "audio in" and "audio out" jacks on the back of the VCRs. Run a length of shielded cable from the "audio out" jack of your source VCR to the "audio in" jack of your record VCR. If you are using stereo VCRs, there will be two sets of audio jacks, color-coded for left and right channels. Your audio connection is now complete.

Connecting the VCRs to monitors or televisions. Now, the only connection left to make is that between the monitors or televisions and the VCRs so that you can see the video being played/recorded on the VCRs (figure 1.51). First, determine if you have monitors or televisions. There are two major

Fig. 1.51. VCR-to-monitor connection.

differences: 1) Monitors have inputs for audio and video signals very similar to the jacks on the back of VCRs, while televisions have only the RF connector for composite audio/video signal; and 2) televisions have tuners (channel selectors) and monitors do not. Some people can argue for the advantages/disadvantages of monitors and televisions. Right now, it is really not that important. Monitors are connected to a "video out" of each VCR. This may pose a problem for your source VCR if you have only one "video out." If you are using televisions, connect them to the "RF out" of each VCR. (This will output video as well as audio—an advantage to using televisions.) How can you tell if your system is connected properly? A tape played in the source VCR should play through on both monitors/televisions.

The deck-to-deck editing process. The system that you have just created is called a deck-to-deck editing system, because you are editing from one VCR to another without the aid of an editing control unit. If you do have an editing control unit, the connection is the same, with the connection of the control unit to the VCRs. This lesson teaches the technique of deck-to-deck editing without an editing control unit.

Remember the concept of editing videotape: Videotape cannot be cut and spliced together like film. In order to combine and rearrange scenes, you must make a duplicate of the tape, copying the scenes in the correct order.

First, load the tape onto which you want to edit into the record VCR (right or bottom). This tape should be blank, or at least have a few minutes of blank tape left on it. Remember: You cannot edit a scene *before* another scene. This will destroy the control track.

It is nice to have a few seconds of black or neutral screen before your program begins. Blank videotape is not black and silent, but snow and "white noise." Our first edit then, will be this "black." Do you have a "black" tape? You should. A black tape is a videotape onto which a black screen has been recorded with no sound. To create a black tape, record a videotape in a camera or camcorder with the lens cap on, the iris closed, or the camera pointed at a piece of black material hanging on the wall. To eliminate the sound, attach an adapter, but no microphone, to the "mic" jack of your camcorder. If you have a character generator, you can record a black screen. A black tape is usually kept at the editing station for this purpose. Pull out the erase tab so that no one can record on the black tape.

Load the black tape into the source (left or top) VCR. Now each VCR has a videotape loaded. By using the record VCR controls, find the place that you want to begin creating your new program. Put the record VCR on "record" and "pause." Now, push "play" on the source VCR to begin playing the black tape. Push "pause" on the record VCR to start the recording tape rolling. Both televisions/monitors should display the black video. After you have recorded 15 or 20 seconds of the black tape, pause the record VCR, then stop the play VCR. Eject the black tape from the play VCR, while leaving the record VCR on record/pause. Now, find the first scene of your instructional video (use your storyboards!) and load that tape into the source VCR. When you find the proper starting point, put the source VCR on "play/pause." Your record VCR should still be on "record/pause." (*Note:* Most VCRs will hold a tape on pause for only a few minutes. Until you master the deck-to-deck editing technique, your record VCR may automatically stop while you are cuing your next scene. You *must* re-cue the record tape if it turns off automatically. Pushing record/play again is not enough. Even an inch of blank tape can ruin 10 seconds of edited project.) Now both VCRs are on their respective play or record and on pause. Un-pause both VCRs to get the tapes rolling. But which VCR is rolled first? The source or play VCR must be un-paused *slightly* before the record VCR. This will ensure the recording of rolling tape. If the record VCR rolls before the play VCR, you will be recording a second of still frame. This technique may be desirable, but at this point it is an error. After the segment that you wish to edit is complete, pause the record VCR, then the play VCR. Once again, this will ensure that you do not record a paused image. Now you have completed your first edit! Load/cue your next scene and get to work. When your program is complete, run more black, so that your viewer will not be exposed to the flash and loud noise of blank tape after the program is finished.

What happens if you allow more of your source video to be recorded than you intended? You need to re-cue your record tape so that the unintended segment will be recorded over on your next edit.

Let's review the procedure for a deck-to-deck edit:

1. Place the source tape in the play VCR and the tape onto which you will be recording into the record VCR.
2. Cue each tape.
3. Put the source tape on play/pause and the record tape on record/pause.
4. Un-pause the source VCR, and then un-pause the record VCR.
5. Allow the segment to be recorded.
6. Pause the record VCR, then pause or stop the source VCR.
7. Leave the record VCR on record/pause. Find your next scene on the source VCR.
8. Repeat the process for each subsequent scene.

Following are some deck-to-deck editing tips:

- Log each source tape that you use. Write down each shot and its approximate length.
- If possible, use a separate tape for graphics and each scene that you record. This will eliminate much of your rewinding and fast-forwarding. For example, if "How to Add Oil to Your Car" has scenes shot in the parking lot, scenes shot in the auto parts store, and graphics, it would be easier to use three separate tapes.
- Become adept at using your VCR's "search" functions. They will help you quickly locate shots.
- Be patient. It takes a few edits to master the technique. Before long you will be editing like a pro!

Here are some content suggestions:

- Beware of jump cuts. If a jump cut is inevitable, use a graphic to make the transition.
- Some VCRs have slow-motion and still-frame (clear, clean pause) capabilities. These can be used effectively, but are prone to abuse. Ask yourself, "Do I need to slow this down for viewers to understand?" If the answer is "yes," use your slow motion. Two students recently used slow motion quite effectively in a video entitled "How to Stepdance." Close-ups of dancing feet were slowed to show the viewer each subtle movement.
- Remember to intermingle shots of various angles and distances to maintain viewer interest. The first shot of each new scene is called an establishing shot, and makes the viewer aware of the location. In "How to Add Oil to Your Car," the students used an exterior shot of the auto parts store to begin the "shopping" section.
- Consider a "built-in pause" section in your instructional video if the tape is designed to be played while the viewer performs the task. For example, a viewer might watch "How to Knit" while holding yarn and knitting needles. One of the first techniques explained would be casting on—the process of weaving the yarn onto a knitting needle. After this process is shown and explained, you might want to add a 30-second shot of the completed cast-on while you narrate, "This is what your knitting needle should look like. If it doesn't look this way, rewind the tape and view this section again." After the completed cast-on is on the screen for about

30 seconds, continue the process of knitting with your next shot. A graphics screen can be substituted for the extended shot.

- Remember to make the video flow smoothly. Experiment with timing. A shot shown for too long bores the viewer, while the quick shot confuses.

Audio-Dubbing Your Instructional Video Program

After you have edited your instructional video program, you need to complete the audio portion. The audio can either make or break an instructional video. The two parts of the audio discussed here are script and the audio-dub process.

The script. A good script can explain the task at hand and reinforce the video. A poor script can overwhelm and confuse. Follow this advice.

Guide the viewer through the program using the script. The narrator should convey a friendly and helpful tone. Write in second-person, active voice to draw the viewer into the project. For example, "Oil is now added to the driver's car" becomes "Now, slowly pour the oil into your car." Avoid "Here you see ..." phrasings. Make the viewer the active participant.

Use the script to explain any activities that are not clear within the video. Practice reading the script to achieve an appropriate balance. Too much script is overwhelming, and too little script leaves the viewer with a feeling of abandonment. Don't add useless or trivial information. Stay focused. Remember, the task may be entirely new to the viewer. Finally, write the script in the appropriate style. As discussed above, some topics require a formal treatment while others can take a more casual tone.

The audio-dub process. After the program is planned, shot, edited, and scripted, many students "see the light at the end of the tunnel" and subsequently do a sloppy job of audio-dubbing. But if you have properly shot and edited your video, your viewer will expect a professional audio track to match.

Practice reading your script aloud. Don't mumble your way through it. Like it or not, your audience will judge your professionalism based on your script delivery. And you can't truly practice script reading silently. Say the script aloud many times. Write your script on notecards. The microphone will pick up rustling papers. Numbering the notecards will help keep them in order. Choose an appropriate voice style. If the topic is serious, speak in a serious tone. Use a casual tone for lighter topics.

Music is important and should be chosen with the topic of the video in mind. A fast, rock-and-roll tune might work for "How to Skateboard" but would probably be out of place in "How to Arrange Flowers."

Instrumental music usually works best, but vocals are not out of the question. Check soundtracks and jazz collections for good instrumentals, and avoid songs with strong vocals that will usually overwhelm the narrator. Also beware of lyrics that have absolutely nothing to do with the topic. The Beach Boys' "Sail on Sailor" would be great for a videotape titled "How to Prepare for a Day of Sailing" but would be out of place in "How to Scramble Eggs." Don't forget to pay careful attention to the mixing levels. While the song may be really great, it is *never* more important than the script.

Did you use "live" on-camera sound during your instructional video? *Do not* audio-dub over that sound. It will be erased. *Before you begin* your audio dub, play your tape through and note the counter number when your live sound begins. Stop the audio-dubbing VCR when that number approaches. Then, resume your audio dub at the next section. Audio-dubbing erases the existing audio track. And once it's gone, it's gone!

Instructional video production is fun and rewarding. As each member of your class creates a different project, you will learn new skills and probably be impressed at just how much your friends know! Instructional video production is also a useful job skill for those interested in video as a career.

Review Questions: Lesson 6

1. How do modern instructional video programs differ from classroom programs created in the early days of television? [Modern instructional programs establish the video viewer as the primary audience of the program, not just a distant observer.]
2. What type of topics work best in instructional video programs? [Concrete, objective tasks that deal with important behaviors work best in instructional video programs.]
3. What type of topics do not work very well in instructional video programs? [Topics that require exact, tedious tasks; topics that are abstract or subjective.]
4. What does it mean to say that an instructional video program should be "narrow in scope"? [The viewer should learn to perform a single, complete task.]
5. What two things are done by the introduction of an instructional video program? [The introduction tells the viewer what task(s) will be learned and sets the tone for the program to follow.]
6. What is the first step in planning an instructional video program? [Diagnosing or identifying the problem.]

(Review questions continue on page I-1-90.)

7. If you don't know the learning level of your viewer, what assumption should you make? [Assume that your viewer knows little or nothing about your topic.]
8. How can jump cuts be avoided? [1. Use careful storyboarding; 2. Show talent walking out of a shot; 3. Use a graphic.]
9. What is the best way to avoid continuity problems? [Assign a detail-minded member of your group the task.]
10. Why can't videotape be edited with the cut-and-paste method? [This would destroy the control track of the videotape.]
11. In deck-to-deck editing systems [four-head] VCRs and [shielded] cable should be used.
12. When arranging VCRs in the deck-to-deck configuration, which VCR should be on the left or on the top? [Source]

    Which one should be on the right or bottom? [Record]
13. When should a "built-in pause" be used in instructional video programs? [A built-in pause should be used if the tape is designed to be played while the viewer performs the task.]

Activities: Lesson 6

1. Visit your local video rental store or public library. Make a list of 10 instructional videotapes available.

2. Using the *TV Guide* or another TV listing, make a list of the instructional video programs available on television.

3. Ask your school media specialist what topics are covered by the school's collection of instructional videotapes.

4. Using a magazine about video programs, find the most popular instructional video program. How much does it cost?

5. Visit a local business and ask if they use videotape to train their employees. (Tip: fast-food restaurants use video to train employees.) Ask to see one of these programs.

6. Ask one of your teachers about tasks that they would like to have made into instructional video programs.

7. Watch an instructional videotape program. Does the program use the same techniques discussed in this lesson?

8. After you have become a skilled editor, create a short program packed full of jump cuts and continuity problems. Show it to your friends and ask them to make a list of all the problems they see.

9. Watch the movie *Plan 9 from Outer Space*, commonly known as the worst movie of all time because of its continuity problems. Make a list of the production problems. (And be prepared to make a long list!)

Student Project Plan: Instructional Video Program

DESCRIPTION OF COMPLETED PROJECT

The completed project will be a 3- to 5-minute videotape program instructing the audience on a certain task. The project must include at least five different camera angles, music, titles, end credits, and internal graphics.

METHOD

1. Students will choose a task and list the steps needed to accomplish the task.
2. Students will storyboard the project.
3. Students will generate graphics and record them. At least three pages of graphics must be used: a title, an end credit ("Produced by ... "), and at least one page of graphics to be used within the program to help the viewer learn the task.
4. Students will shoot the raw footage.
5. Students will edit the raw footage, making the program.
6. Students will audio-dub the program by adding narration and music where needed.

EQUIPMENT

audio mixer

camera and deck or camcorder

character generator

microphone

music sources

tripod

two TVs/monitors

two VCRs

EVALUATION

The project will be worth 200 points. Each team member will receive the same score.

instructional value	(50)
graphics	(25)
audio	(25)
editing	(25)
camera work	(25)
script	(25)
storyboards	(25)

Evaluation Sheet: Instructional Video Program

STUDENTS ______________________________

Period ______________________________

Total Points __________ %

Letter grade A B C D Re-do

Instructional value (50 points)

Appropriate task	(10)	________			
Step-by-step process	(10)	________			
Appropriate rate	(10)	________			
Did we learn?	(20)	________			
			Total	(50)	________

Graphics (25 points)

Title screen	(5)	________			
Internal graphics	(10)	________			
Credits	(5)	________			
Color contrast	(5)	________			
			Total	(25)	________

Audio (25 points)

Mixing levels	(10)	________			
Narration performance	(5)	________			
Music selection	(5)	________			
Overall polish	(5)	________			
			Total	(25)	________

(Evaluation Sheet continues on page I-1-94.)

Editing (25 points)					
Technical quality	(10)	________			
Program length	(10)	________			
Pace	(5)	________			
			Total	(25)	________
Camera work (25 points)					
Shot selection	(10)	________			
Five angles	(5)	________			
Focus	(5)	________			
Appropriate detail	(5)	________			
			Total	(25)	________
Script (25 points)					
Appropriate amount	(10)	________			
Good explanation	(10)	________			
Appropriate style	(5)	________			
			Total	(25)	________
Storyboards (25 points)					
Completion	(15)	________			
Visual	(5)	________			
Audio	(5)	________			
			Total	(25)	________

Lesson 7 Multicamera Small Studio Production

Objectives

After successfully completing this lesson, you will be able to:

- *connect the equipment needed for a talk show.*
- *understand and execute basic camera movements using a tripod.*
- *select an appropriate guest for a talk show.*
- *formulate good questions for a talk show.*
- *write a good introduction and conclusion for a talk show.*
- *design a simple talk show set.*
- *successfully complete a talk show assignment.*

Vocabulary

Cut. A video transition in which one video source instantly and completely replaces another video source.

Dissolve. A video transition in which one video source fades out as another video source fades in.

Dolly. A camera movement in which the camera is rolled on a tripod dolly or studio pedestal toward the subject ("dolly in") or away from the subject ("dolly out").

Electronic field production (EFP). Complex video production outside the television production studio. EFP is more elaborate and involves more equipment than ENG.

Fade. A video transition in which one video source is gradually replaced on the screen by a background color. A fade is a dissolve to a background color.

Follow-up. A question in an interview based on the answer to a previously answered question.

Pan. A side-to-side camera movement as the camera base remains stationary.

Tilt. A vertical camera movement as the camera base remains stationary.

Tripod dolly. A tripod mounted on a dolly base ("spreader").

Truck. A lateral movement of the camera achieved by moving the tripod dolly or studio pedestal to the left ("truck left") or to the right ("truck right").

Wipe. A video transition in which one video source is replaced by another video source with a definite line of transition.

Many of the longest-running and most successful programs on television are talk shows. Whether the topic is political, social, or purely entertaining, talk shows continue to gain popularity in many time slots throughout the nation. We know our favorite talk show hosts by their first names—Phil, Oprah, Arsenio, Jay, Geraldo, Sally Jesse.

Talk shows are usually relatively inexpensive to produce because they don't require lengthy scripts or exotic settings. Although talk shows may not require a great deal of technical preproduction, they do provide an opportunity for spontaneous, "as-it-happens" television production work. At the outset of the program, no one involved knows exactly what will happen. Prepared and professional television production personnel can make the talk show happen, capturing that controversial comment or getting a reaction shot that really tells the story.

While most professional talk shows are produced in elaborate television studios, schools can produce talk shows in their studios or by configuring ENG equipment. While many schools have television production studios, many do not. The next few paragraphs describe assembling your equipment into a working, talk show studio.

Equipment Connections

The equipment connection for a talk show is very similar to the connection for the "News Brief" student project plan described in lesson 5. The only addition is a second (and possibly third) camera and a microphone for each participant. Figure 1.52 illustrates such a connection, with the necessary additions, to help in this process. Remember, alternate connections can be made, depending on the availability of equipment. If you aren't ready to turn back to lesson 5 right now, the process is as follows. For video, connect both camera outputs to the inputs of the switcher. The video output of the switcher is daisy-chained through the character generator and the signal is sent to the record VCR. For audio, all audio inputs (mics and music) are connected to the audio mixer. That audio signal is sent to the record VCR. Audio and video monitors are used where appropriate.

Fig. 1.52. Talk show equipment connections.

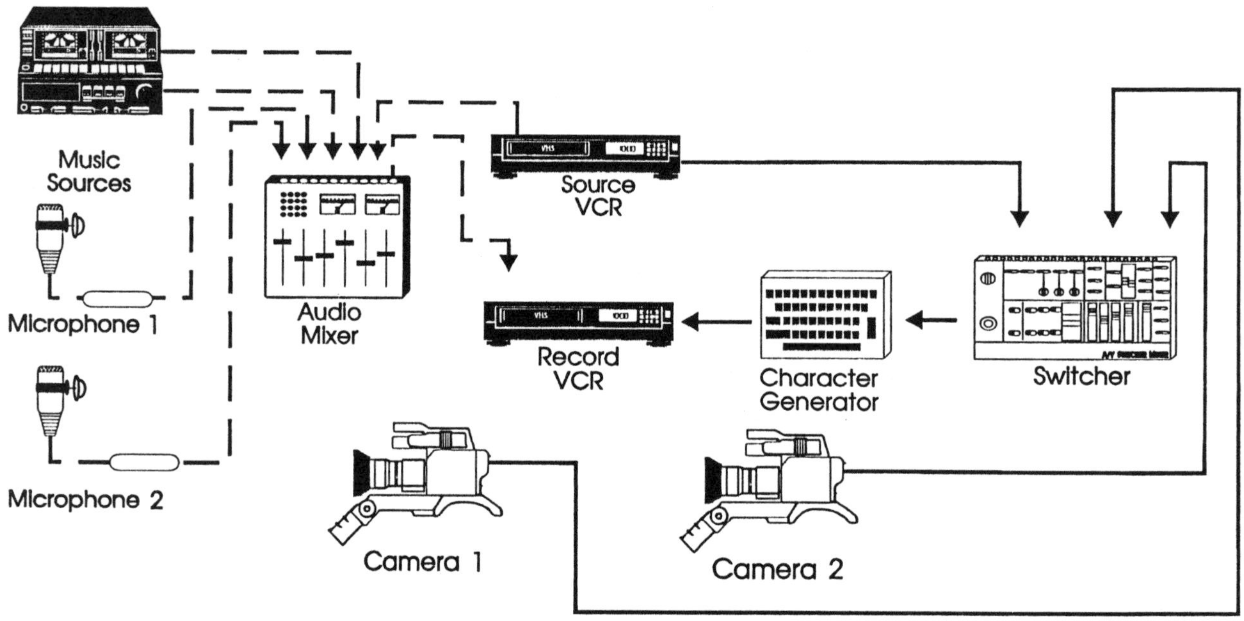

Obviously, if you have a television production studio in your school, you will use this for your talk show. However, the configured ENG system can be great for producing remote talk shows. This type of video work—assembling studio or ENG components for production in the field, is called EFP, or electronic field production. EFP differs from ENG in the complexity of the equipment taken into the field. A reporter conducting a brief interview, recorded by a single camera operator, is ENG. A video production team using two cameras, a switcher, a character generator, and an audio mixer to record an academic awards assembly is EFP.

Tripods

Tripods help the videographer achieve a steady shot during program production. The tripod provides a firm base and tireless service not otherwise possible. Even the strongest, most experienced videographers cannot be expected to hold a steady shot for more than a minute or two.

Tripods also facilitate smooth camera movement. The four camera movements most often associated with tripods are pans, tilts, dollies, and trucks. *Panning* a camera means moving the camera from side to side on the tripod. During a pan, the tripod remains stationary. The camera pans atop the tripod. Pans are useful when following the action, showing the expanse of a shot, or making minor adjustments in the picture composition. But pans should not be used to "look" for a good shot. All pans used in a video program should have a purpose.

A *tilt* is similar to a pan, except that in a tilt, the camera motion is vertical, not horizontal, atop the tripod. Like pans, tilts should be used to emphasize the height of the subject, or to make a minor adjustment in the composition.

Many tripods can be fitted with wheels or casters to allow the tripod to roll smoothly across the floor. This wheel or caster assembly is called a dolly, and the tripod becomes a tripod dolly when a dolly is attached. Dollies are also known as "spreaders" because many have the ability to adjust, or "spread," to meet the tripod's base. Moving the tripod dolly toward the talent or away from the talent is called *dollying.* A lateral (side-to-side) motion of the tripod dolly is called a *truck.* Videographers can be instructed to "dolly forward," "dolly back," "truck left," or "truck right."

Many tripods and tripod dollies used in television production have a special means for attaching the camera to the tripod. The quick-release assembly is quite common. Screwing the camera into a tripod can be a time-consuming, knuckle-bruising experience. These quick-release methods save time and effort. The tripod includes a special plate or post assembly that screws into the bottom of the camera (figure 1.53). That plate or post can be quickly and conveniently attached to the tripod (figure 1.54). Most video production tripods now incorporate such a device.

If possible, select a tripod that doesn't have too many loose parts. In school television production, students often work against the 50-minute class period. Small parts that are easily detached from the tripod can quickly become lost. If you have the opportunity, select a tripod that doesn't easily disassemble itself!

Preproduction Activities

As mentioned earlier, talk shows are often unpredictable and spontaneous. While some things are out of the production team's control, careful attention to preproduction details can help the team be ready for those unexpected moments.

Unless your talk show topic requires a specific guest, carefully select the person who will appear on your show. Choose someone who is interested in the topic, usually answers questions in complete sentences, and uses proper grammar and words that your audience can understand. Perhaps most important, choose someone who really wants to help with the program. Many students in the past have begged popular teachers and students to appear on a talk show, only to have the guest cancel at the last minute or provide lackluster conversation.

(Text continues on page I-1-99.)

Fig. 1.53. Plate assembly for tripod.

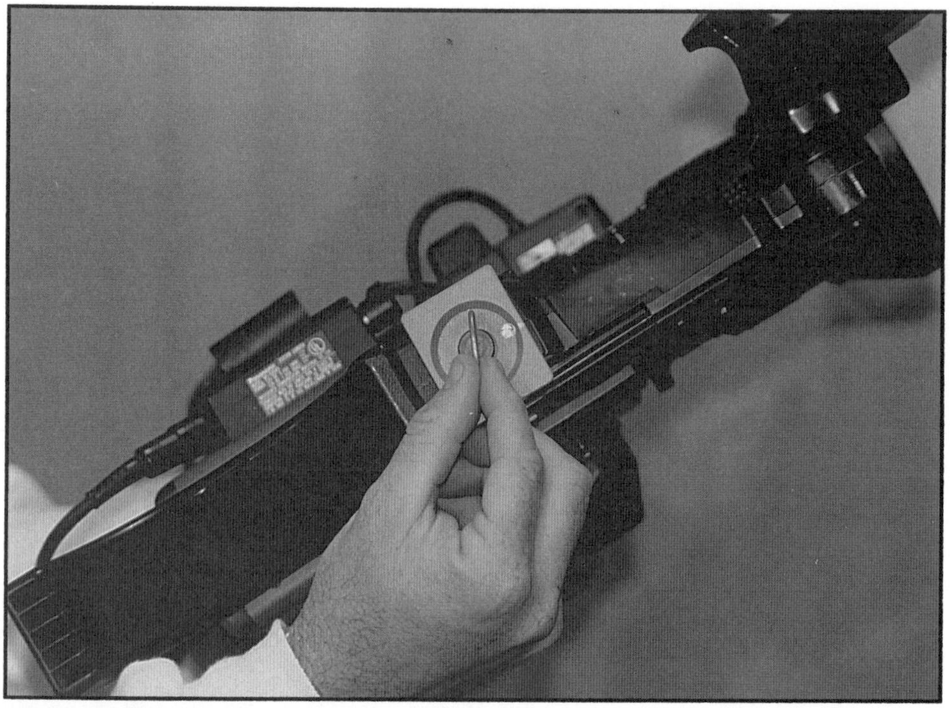

Fig. 1.54. Attaching plate assembly to tripod.

Application of the above criteria means that production teams will usually, but not always, choose adults as talk-show guests. (Some student guests can handle a 15-minute conversation *and* the distraction of the television crew and equipment.) Don't forget about community members who can help with this project. Doctors, police officers, paramedics, crisis counselors, and airline pilots are among the most memorable guests. One group even coordinated a visit by the local Guardian Angels.

It is wise to remember that most people have an interesting story to tell. One group surprised many classmates by introducing one of the school cafeteria workers as a guest. Instead of a conversation about school food preparation, the audience was treated to a conversation about the worker's religious missionary experience in Africa. Another group interviewed a school custodial worker about his experiences in the Pacific during World War II. A good host looks beneath the surface to find the best topic for discussion.

Obviously, it is important to determine the main topic of discussion for your interview and stay with that topic until it has been covered exhaustively. One group interviewed the head football coach, who is also a driver education instructor at the school. The first question was "What can we expect from the football team this year?" The second question was "What is the most important thing a student can learn in driver's ed?" You can probably imagine the mental whiplash experienced by both the guest and the audience. Within the course of a 15-minute talk show, the program can reasonably cover two, or maybe even three, topic areas. But those topics should not be intermingled within the program.

Once the host determines the topic area, he or she should formulate a list of questions to ask during the program. Generally, there are two types of questions: open-ended questions and closed-ended questions. Closed-ended questions can be answered with one or two words. "What is your favorite class in school?" is a closed-ended question. Your guest could answer in one word. Another closed-ended question is "Do you like your job?" By using only closed-ended questions, the interviewer could easily ask question #100 5 minutes into the program! In order to remedy this, some talk show hosts tack on "Why?" to the closed-ended question. Although this might extend the answer, asking "Why?" after each response will probably put the guest on the defensive and result in a cross-examination style of interview.

The solution to the closed-ended question is not to ask "Why?" but to use the open-ended question instead. The open-ended question inherently requires explanation and elaboration. "How can a person become an airline pilot?" is an example of an open-ended question. Instead of asking "Do you like your job?" ask "When did you receive the most satisfaction from your job?"

Usually, the open-ended question will lead to a follow-up question. A follow-up question is a question that is based on the answer to a previous question. For example, the question "How can a person become an airline pilot?" can lead to the follow-up question "How important was your military service to obtaining your pilot's license?" An alert talk show host will listen to the answers and ask questions that the audience would want to ask if they could. In other words, they *talk* with the guest. One talk show host asked a doctor what influenced her to enter the medical profession. The guest replied that she was inspired by the poor medical conditions in her homeland. Without missing a beat, the talk show host turned a routine interview on careers in medicine into a 20-minute dialogue on medical conditions in third-world countries.

Great questions and inquisitive follow-ups will mean nothing if the viewer is not paying attention to the program. A carefully crafted introduction will capture the audience's attention and draw them into the program. An all-too-common opening sounds like this: "Hi, we're here today with Ms. Nancy Lugo, who is a counselor at the crisis center." On the surface, that sounds OK. But it really does nothing to bring the viewer into the program; the viewer should feel that he or she has a personal stake in the program. Let's try another introduction: "Have you ever felt depressed? Did you ever think that there was no one to turn to? Well, there's always someone to listen. Someone who cares is just a phone call away. Nancy Lugo is one of those people who will listen to you, and she's our guest today."

A successful talk show needs a strong conclusion that will summarize and further personalize the interview. "Well, that's all the time we have today ..." is commonly used, and doesn't end the show on a positive note. The conclusion should be mentally prepared by the host throughout the program. The host can even jot down a word or two on a small notepad while the camera is on a close-up of the guest. Our interview with the crisis counselor might conclude: "If you ever need to talk to someone, you can call Nancy Lugo and her friends at The Crisis Hotline at 555-1234. Remember, no problem is too large or too small. Thank you very much for joining us today, Ms. Lugo. For Campus Outlook, I'm Adam Whiteside." A good interview deserves a good conclusion!

All interviews need a place to happen. A good talk show set can add tremendously to your program, and it really isn't as hard to create as it sounds (figure 1.55). The first thing to remember in set creation is that you really only need to worry about what the camera sees. A simple, two-person talk show set is really quite small—about 10 feet wide, 6 or 7 feet high, and 5 or 6 feet deep. As long as the camera remains within these boundaries, your set design need not extend beyond this minimal area.

Fig. 1.55. Talk show set.

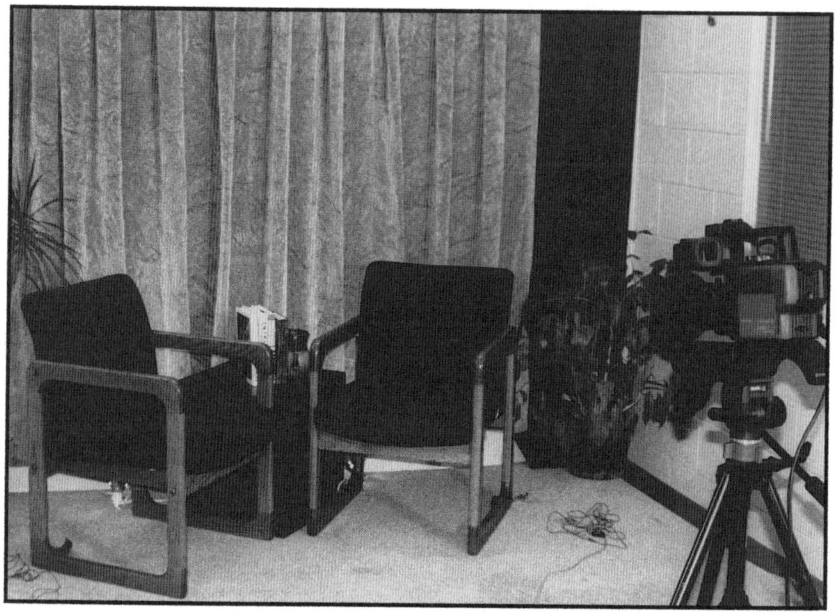

Office or reception-area chairs work well for a talk show. Remember to place the chairs close together to avoid too much empty space on the set. A background can be fashioned from a curtain, a set of miniblinds, or even bulletin board paper. Try to avoid the extremes of black and white when selecting your background.

Your set can be "dressed" to give it the "living room" approach. Potted plants give the set color and warmth. Hardbound books on a small end table and natural artifacts, such as rocks, seashells, and potted plants, can also dress the set. A bookcase filled with books and knickknacks works well. Use your imagination to create a simple, yet effective set.

Lighting the set can be achieved in many different ways. For many newer video cameras, the natural classroom lighting, combined with light coming through doors and windows, can create enough illumination. Simple clip lights, available at most hardware stores for a few dollars, can illuminate the dark parts of the set and provide backlight. Small professional light kits, usually containing two or three lights on stands, are available for a few hundred dollars. Such purchases represent a wise investment for schools producing talk shows on a regular basis. Remember to white-balance your cameras *after* your artificial lights have been turned on. Different types of light can drastically change the color response of your cameras.

Some other important preproduction notes: Carefully consider the host's wardrobe for the show. Scruffy jeans or shorts generally look sloppy on camera, especially in light of the complexity of this assignment. Men should consider wearing a tie, and ladies a dress or skirt/blouse ensemble. Remember to dress on the level of your guest; an off-campus guest may be wearing a business suit. Also, encourage your guest to wear his or her uniform if it will add to the atmosphere of your program.

Paramedics, police officers, and firefighters are just a few of the uniformed professionals who will make your viewers sit up and watch.

Storyboard the basic shots that you want in your interview program. This simple task will probably take only a few minutes, but will dispel any confusion about the "look" of your show. Will your talk show feature medium shots and bust shots, or two-shots and close-ups? Carefully consider the types of shots you want to use in your program.

Fig. 1.56. Crossing pattern.

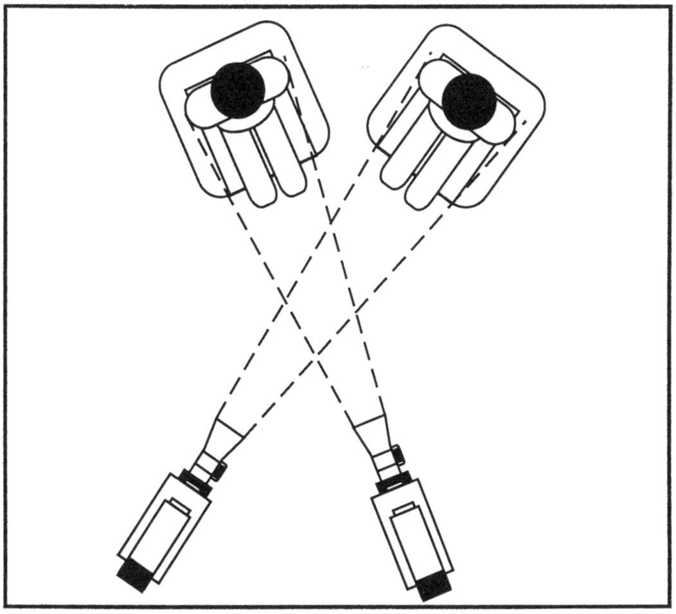

Plan to shoot the program with two cameras in a "crossing pattern," as shown in Figure 1.56. In other words, the camera on the left should get the close-up of the person on the right, and the camera on the right should get the close-up of the person on the left. This approach will achieve the 45-degree profile desired for a talk show. A left camera/left guest approach gives a full profile, and is often disorienting to the viewer.

Plan which channels on your audio mixer you will be using for your talk show. For a simple program, you will need two "mic" channels and one music source channel. Determine the audio mixing levels *before* the show begins.

Probably the most important aspect of preproduction is working as a team. Unfortunately, this aspect is almost indefinable. But there are some tips to follow. Make sure to listen to all members of the group when making decisions, and be willing to compromise with all members of your group. Everyone in your group will have something to offer. Remember: In a good working group, the final product is more than the sum of the parts. Make sure that you are contributing to further the goal of the group—to make a great talk show program.

Production Activities

Many schools have access to a character generator. Generated titles can make your program appear more professional. Plan to use a title for your talk show. Use the last line of your character generator page to create "name tags" for the talk show host and guest(s). Superimpose these graphics over the first few close-ups of your host and guest(s). Display the graphics long enough for the viewer to read them—very slowly. Use the graphics again near the middle and end of the program. Create a separate page for credits, and display that page after the talk show is complete.

Once your guest and host are seated on the set, establish the shots storyboarded in your planning sessions. Make sure to allow the correct amount of noseroom in your close-ups. Practice directing the camera operators and switcher. Common director commands are "Ready to cut to camera 1. Go 1." "Dissolve to camera 2. Go 2." The team should become accustomed to giving and taking directions without bruising every ego.

Some sort of communication system is needed between the director, the switcher, and the videographers. The audio technician and the graphics generator also need to be in communication with the director. The two most common types of communication systems are wired and wireless intercom systems. Wireless intercom systems use radio frequencies that broadcast between the units (figure 1.57).

Fig. 1.57. Wireless intercom system.

The range and quality vary by manufacturer. When using wireless intercom systems, check the frequency of the system against the frequency of a wireless microphone system you may be using. The wireless microphone system receiving station will receive any signals broadcast on that frequency, including the signals generated by the wireless intercom. Wireless intercom systems can be used when using intercom cable is impractical (across a gymnasium floor) or impossible (communicating across a lake or river). Wired intercom systems are usually more expensive and durable. Most professional cameras and switchers have built-in wired intercom systems already in place.

During production the switcher can perform transitions between shots. The most basic transition, a *cut*, is simply replacing the first shot with the second shot. A cut usually involves pushing the desired button on the same *bus* or row of buttons. A *dissolve* slowly replaces the first shot with the second. As the first shot fades out, the second shot fades in. A third type of transition is a *wipe.* A wipe replaces the second shot with the first shot with a definite line. This wipe could go from top to bottom, side to side, corner to corner, etc. Many modern production switchers have 50 or more different wipe patterns. The final type of transition, used at the beginning and end of the program, is a *fade.* A fade is a dissolve that changes from the first shot to a background color. That color is often black. But many switchers allow fading to an infinite number of background colors.

You may choose the option of rolling videotape from a separate VCR into your talk show. For example, during an interview with the football coach, the talk show production crew may want to include videotape of a scoring drive and have the coach describe what's happening on the field. The source VCR should be connected to the switcher just as the cameras are connected. Then at the appropriate time, the tape in the source VCR can be played as the switcher selects the appropriate source. Rolling footage can make the talk show more entertaining and informative.

Before the show begins, plan a signal to let the host know how much time is left in the program. On shows requiring exact times, a darkroom timer can be used. If the program has no maximum time limit, a signal can be devised to inform the host when the minimum time for the program has been reached. Make sure that the guest knows the signal, too. Waving a red handkerchief may seem like a good way to tell the host when she has reached the 15-minute mark. But it may confuse, confound, or even panic the unsuspecting guest. What would you think if you were the guest on a talk show and a camera operator began waving a bandanna?

More sophisticated shows may want to add the audience participation aspect. This should be attempted only after the team becomes quite experienced at talk show production. Consider the studio audience as extra guests on your show. You need to be concerned with lighting, camera angles, and the appearance of your studio audience members. If you plan to have an audience participation portion of the talk show, you need to plan camera angles and microphone access. While this approach can have impressive results, proper execution requires meticulous planning, experience, and professionalism.

Producing a talk show is a fun, entertaining way to display your television production expertise (figure 1.58). With correct equipment connection, preproduction teamwork, careful planning, and thoughtful production, the talk show can be a valuable experience in television production class.

Fig. 1.58. A television talk show.

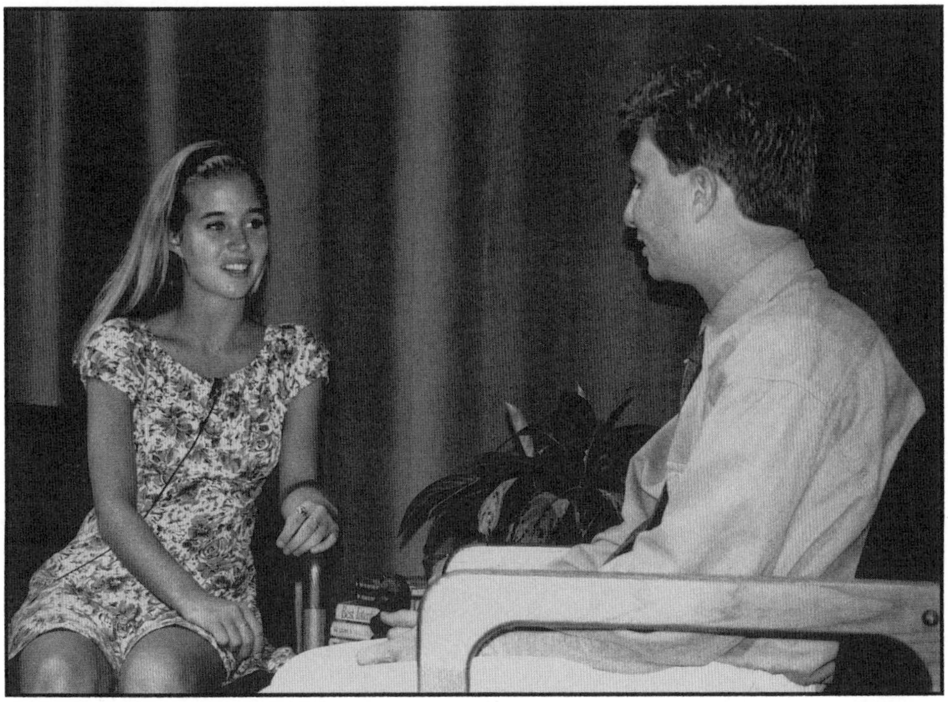

Review Questions: Lesson 7

1. What is EFP? [complex video production outside the television production studio]
2. What is the difference between ENG and EFP? Give an example of each. [EFP is more elaborate and involves more equipment than ENG. An example of EFP would be a production team using two cameras, a portable video switcher, an audio mixer, and a portable character generator to produce a news show from a remote location. An example of ENG would be a reporter and videographer shooting a 1-minute segment about the science fair.]
3. What are the four basic tripod dolly movements? [pan, tilt, dolly, truck]
4. List the criteria that should be applied in the guest selection process. [someone who is interested in the topic you would like to discuss; a person who answers questions in complete sentences; uses proper grammar and words your audience can understand; someone who really wants to help with the program]
5. What are the three types of questions used in interviews? [closed-ended; open-ended; follow-up]
6. Convert the following questions into open-ended questions.

   "Do you like your job?" [What things do you like about your job?]

   "How many years have you lived here?" [What was the most interesting thing that's happened since you've been in town?]

   "How many years did you study to become a lawyer?" [What was the hardest part about studying to become a lawyer?]

   "Do you think people should vote in every election?" [What are some of the most important duties of a citizen?]
7. What is a follow-up question? [A follow-up is a question based on the answer to a previous question.]

8. What items can be used to decorate a set? [potted plants, hard-bound books, rocks, seashells, a bookcase, knickknacks]
9. What wardrobe guidelines should be used by talk show hosts? [men—dress shirt, dress slacks, tie; women—dress or skirt and blouse ensemble]
10. What does it mean to shoot in a "crossing pattern"? [The camera on the left frames the subject on the right; the camera on the right frames the subject on the left.]
11. List the three ways graphics are used in a talk show. [title screen, super-imposed "name tags," ending credits]
12. What are the two types of intercom systems used in talk shows? [wired, wireless]
13. What is the difference between a dissolve and a fade? [dissolve—video of one camera is replaced by video of another camera; fade—camera video is replaced by a background color]
14. What new considerations are presented when the talk show includes audience participation? [The studio audience should be considered extra guests on your show. You need to be concerned with lighting, camera angles, and appearance of your audience. For audience participation, you need to plan camera angles and microphone access.]

Activities: Lesson 7

1. Write introductions for the following topics:
   - school board member—requirements for graduation
   - student body president—prom plans
   - firefighter—career inquiry

2. Write conclusions for the following topics:
   - race car driver—most exciting moments
   - school principal—scheduling classes for next year
   - foreign exchange student—adjusting to life in the United States

3. Watch your favorite talk show and complete the following activities:
   - Storyboard four different camera angles used in the program.
   - Analyze the introduction and conclusion used by the host.
   - List three questions used by the talk show host.
   - List follow-up questions used by the host.

4. Survey the students and faculty at your school. Ask them to name their favorite talk show. Report the findings to the class.

5. Find out which talk show is the highest-rated talk show in your area and in the nation.

6. Find out which talk shows have won Emmy awards in recent years.

7. Many talk shows, especially the ones that air in the mornings and afternoons, are syndicated. Find out what this means.

8. Call a local television station and ask how much it spends on syndicated talk shows. Also ask how much it costs to buy a 30-second commercial during that talk show.

Student Project Plan: Talk Show

DESCRIPTION OF COMPLETED PROJECT

The completed project will be a 10- to 15-minute talk show. The program will be totally self-contained. The show will include opening music and graphics, two people on camera (the interviewer and guest) conducting an interview session, internal graphics featuring the names of the host and the guest, end credits, and music. The program will use two cameras and a switcher. No postproduction will be used.

METHOD

1. Each student will select a job that best suits his or her educational goal: videographer, graphics, audio technician, switcher, host, production coordinator.
2. Students will be assigned to teams based on that interest.
3. Students will then plan the video project. Emphasis will be placed on selecting a guest who will give the program a professional demeanor.
4. Each group will have at least one class session to practice production skills as a team.
5. Each team will have one class session to videotape the program.

EQUIPMENT

audio mixer

character generator

lavaliere microphones

monitors

music sources

switcher

tripods

two cameras

VCR

EVALUATION

Each student in the group will receive an individual grade and a group grade. Each grade is 100 points, for a total of 200 points.

Evaluation Sheet: Talk Show

SHOW TITLE ______________________________

PRODUCTION DATE ______________________________

	Individual Grade	+	Group Grade	=	Total Grade
Host ______________	______		______		______
Comments:					
Production Coordinator ______________	______		______		______
Comments:					
Switcher ______________	______		______		______
Comments:					
Audio ______________	______		______		______
Comments:					
Graphics ______________	______		______		______
Comments:					
Camera 1 ______________	______		______		______
Comments:					
Camera 2 ______________	______		______		______
Comments:					

Instructor's Comments:

Notes to the Teacher

Lesson 1: Macro-Lens Project

EQUIPMENT SETUP

1. The camera or camcorder should be mounted on a tripod. The camera lens should be at about the student's chest level when mounted (figure 1.59). A video camera needs to be connected to a video deck. (The camcorder is self-contained.)

Fig. 1.59. Proper positioning of camera lens at chest level.

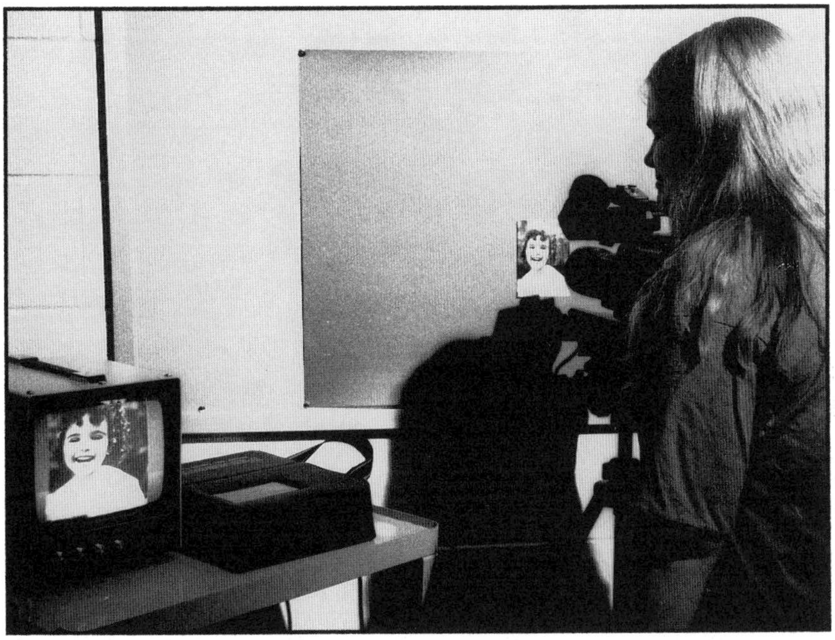

2. The output of the video deck or camcorder should be connected to a television set or video monitor. This will enable the student to get a clear view of the project being recorded (figure 1.60). If a television is used, then the signal should be taken from the "RF out" jack of the video deck or camcorder. If no such jack exists, an RF modulator must be used between the video source and the television. Most camcorder accessory packs include a simple RF modulator. Connection to a monitor does not require the high-powered RF signal. A connection should be made from the "video out" jack of the video deck or camcorder to the "video in" jack of the monitor. The monitor should be placed on a media cart or table in easy view of the student composing the macro-lens shot.

3. The video camera/camcorder on the tripod should be facing the wall, with the lens about 1 foot from the wall. Tape a piece of cloth (felt, corduroy, etc.) on the wall in front of the lens to accommodate very small or odd-sized items (for the overhang!).

Fig. 1.60. Macro-lens project equipment connection.

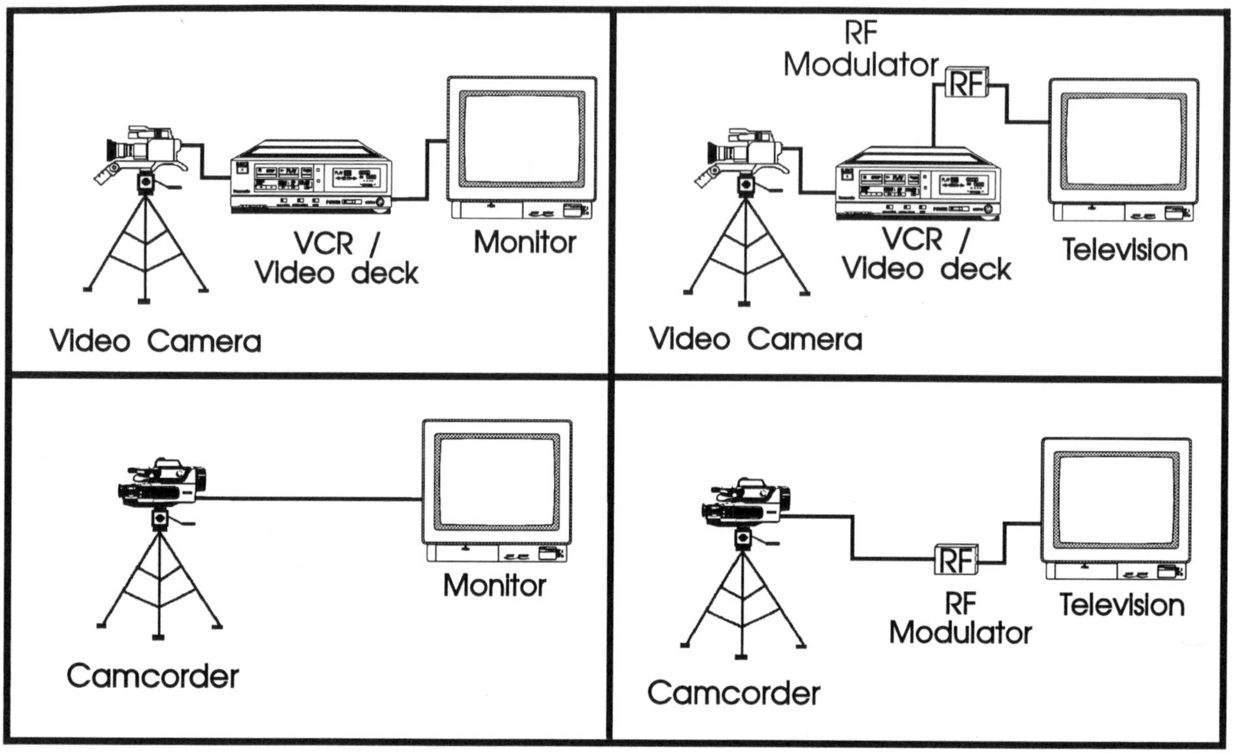

TITLE CARDS

4. Students can make title cards using 3-by-5-inch note cards and felt-tip pens. Since the width-to-height ratio (aspect ratio) for TV production is 3 inches by 4 inches, not 3 inches by 5 inches, an inch will have to be trimmed from the card so that it will properly fit on the video screen. This makes a 3-inch-by-4-inch card. Encourage students to bring items from home to decorate their title cards. Students often bring in stickers, gold stars, and other items to give their title cards a glitzier touch.

5. Because this is the first project, most students will be using new videotape. Do not record on the first 20 seconds of the tape. Chances are, the clear leader lasts that long, and, of course, you cannot record on the leader! Record black on the first minute of the program. Black can be recorded by recording with the lens cap on or by simply recording the material on the wall in front of the lens. Remember, unrecorded tape is "snow" and "white noise." Neither is desirable immediately before a program begins. After the project is complete, have the students record 30 more seconds of black in order to eliminate the disturbing flash that will otherwise appear at the end of the program.

6. As stated in the project plan, students should fade in on the title card and fade out on the last shot. The fade is a function of the camera, so the manual should be consulted. Fading in and out of every shot should be avoided, as it reminds one of a dream sequence from a bad soap opera.

7. Masking tape works well for sticking the photographs onto the material. It is not too sticky and it is easy to remove.

8. Use the camera remote record button ("trigger") to pause the video deck/camcorder between pictures. Your transitions should be relatively clean. Remember, this is a first project. The finer points will come later.

9. Depending on the amount of equipment at your disposal, you may want to set up several taping stations around the room.

10. Students may use an assistant to help them with the masking tape. Make sure the assistant doesn't become a director.

AUDIO DUB

11. Follow your owner's manual for correct audio-dub procedure. Many modern camcorders are able to audio-dub.

12. Because most popular tunes are longer than this 2-minute project, require students to fade out the music as the last picture fades.

13. Some of your more ambitious students will want to combine many songs on their one project. Experience tells us to stick with one song for this project. Keep it simple.

TOPICS

14. You may determine the subject matter for the projects, or leave it up to the students. An autobiography is great fun and a good icebreaker for the start of the year. The students can try to guess whose project they are watching as the creator "ages" before their eyes. Other topics could be hobbies, sports, trading cards, family photos, and calendar photos. Many students can get extra credit for other classes by making science or history-oriented projects.

GRADING

15. A grading sheet is enclosed (see page I-1-10). You may want to change it based on your own areas of emphasis.

16. Schedule a class period to watch and grade the projects. Everyone always claps for every project. Have fun!

Lesson 2: Interview Project

EQUIPMENT SETUP

1. Each team will need the following items of equipment:

   a. camera/video deck or camcorder
   b. microphone (preferably a dynamic cardioid hand-held model)
   c. headset or earphones
   d. videotape

   If your class has more than one setup, you may want to put each one on a different media cart. This arrangement helps to keep the items inventoried from class to class.

BEFORE SHOOTING

2. In each group of two students, one will be the videographer and one will be the interviewer (figure 1.61). It is best to have the students choose their jobs before they choose their partners.

Fig. 1.61. Shooting an interview.

One method is to ask the class to line up against the wall—either the interviewer wall or the videographer wall. Then, like seventh graders at the first school dance, they can choose someone from across the room with whom to work. This might mean that best friends don't get to work together. But because best friends usually have a few ideas in common, chances are they'd argue about who got to operate the camera and who got to be the interviewer.

3. Each group should then decide who they would like to interview. Experience says that adults are preferable interviewing subjects. They are usually not nervous about being interviewed by students, and they generally speak in complete sentences. Students, on the other hand, tend to get very nervous while being interviewed and often grunt their answers. Also, we generally don't like to pull students out of class.

4. When the students decide who they would like to interview for this project, they should write a brief letter to the person requesting permission and scheduling input. You may want to make a form letter for the students to copy. The students can either hand deliver the letters or have them placed in the teachers' mailboxes. Replies can either be verbal or in writing.

FORMATS

5. Because this is the first real out-of-class assignment, a format for both the camera shot and the script is recommended. A two-shot waist shot is a good all-purpose interview shot, but a two-shot bust shot may also be used. Another suggestion: Have the videographer hold the same shot for the entire 1-minute interview. Zooms get very tedious. A sample script is included on page I-1-24. The script serves two functions: First, it relieves the students of the burden of having to write their own script, and second, it familiarizes students with formats, which are used at most television stations.

PRACTICE

6. Students can practice their interviews by interviewing classmates or their parents. This practice helps the students become more comfortable once the tape is rolling.

VIDEOTAPING THE PROJECT

7. Make sure to test all of the equipment before leaving the classroom.

8. Give each team 30 minutes to complete the project. A team should be able to make 1 minute of tape in 30 minutes.

9. The videographer should roll the tape at least 15 seconds before the interview starts and leave it rolling for at least 15 seconds after the interview is completed. Once the trigger on the camera is pushed, it takes the videotape recorder about 3 or 4 seconds to start recording tape. Allowing the tape to roll before and after the interview compensates for this lost time. This is a good habit to start because this time will be required when the students begin editing on later projects.

10. The camera operator should make sure to white-balance the camera at the site of the interview. Since white balancing sets the color under the lighting conditions, white-balancing in the classroom before leaving to interview would be a waste of time. The camera operator should also check the tracking control for proper adjustment.

11. Some of the interviewers will be quite excited about this project, but their excitement may make their guest nervous. The interviewer should remain calm so that the guest will be relaxed.

AFTER SHOOTING

12. Upon completion of the projects, the students should write a brief thank-you note to their guests.

13. As always, watch the interviews as a class and offer constructive criticism. Have fun!

Lesson 3: Audio Commercial

EQUIPMENT CONNECTIONS

1. For this project, your character generator should be connected to the "video in" jack of your VCR, and your audio mixer should be connected to the "audio in" jack(s) of the VCR (figure 1.62). When your VCR is on "record," the graphics and audio should record on the tape.

   If you use your camera/camcorder as a character generator, you need a different approach. You can connect the "video out" of the camera/camcorder to the "video in" of the recording VCR.

   If you don't have a stand-alone character generator *or* camera-based graphics, you can simply make the normal camera/VCR connection and create the graphics by hand (figure 1.63), as you did on the macro-lens project described in lesson 1.

Fig. 1.62. Audio project connections.

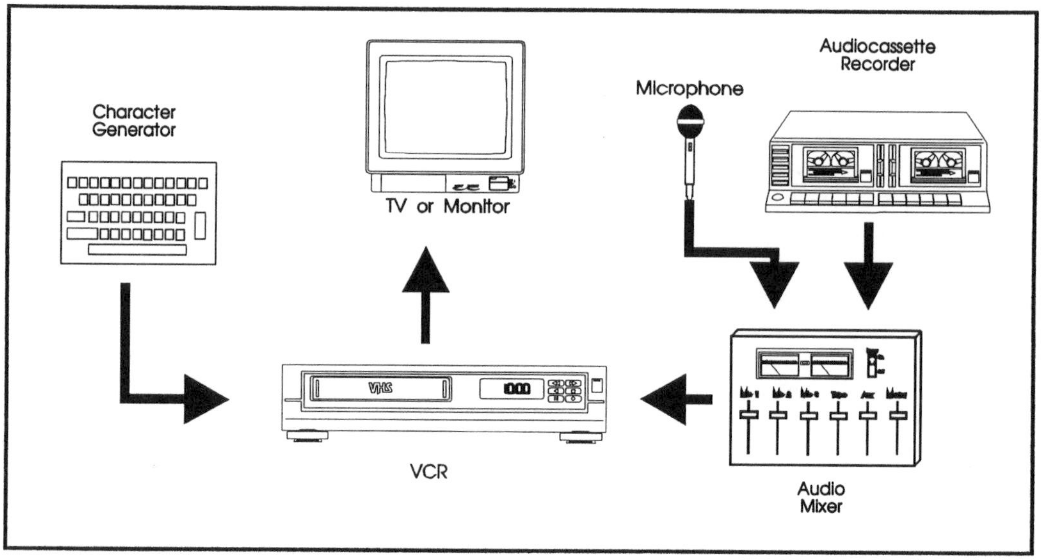

Fig. 1.63. Hand-created graphics.

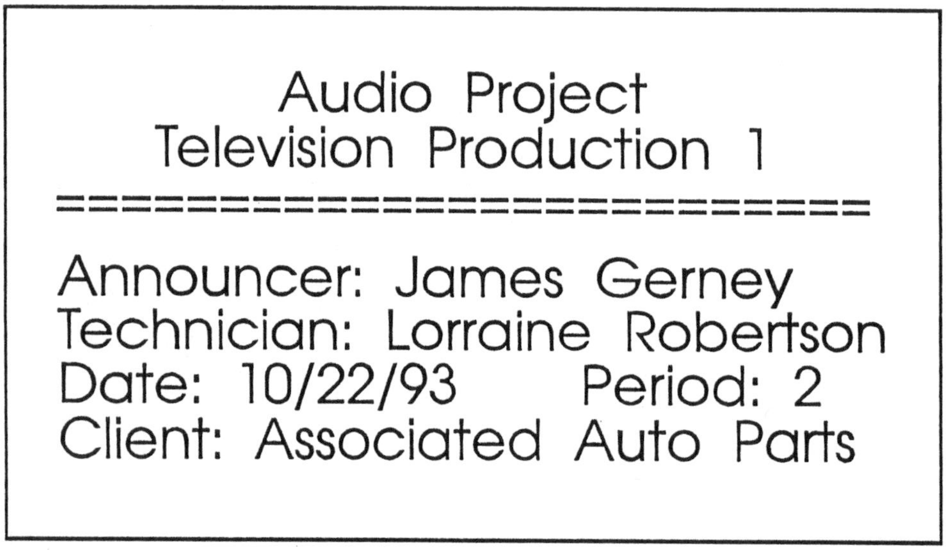

THE AUDIO MIXER

2. A mixer with three microphone inputs might be just fine for your school news show, but if your principal asks you to videotape a discussion group with five experts on the panel, you are left to ask your guests to pass around microphones (and probably record the "crunching" sound of a microphone being passed around). The impedance of the audio mixer should also be verified before selection. (See part I, lesson 2 for a complete discussion of impedance.) Some mixers can handle both low- and high-impedance situations, but most accept only one. Therefore, a careful inventory of the microphones that you already have should be a factor in your mixer choice. The purchase of new microphones to use with a new mixer is a luxury for most schools, and the money could probably be spent more wisely on the other needs of the program. As mentioned previously, the less-expensive high impedance system is adequate for most school-based video production.

CHARACTER GENERATORS

3. Aside from cost, considerations for purchase of mid-range character generators include individual character quality, system integration, and features. Request a sample tape or demonstration of a generator before purchase. Remember, many boot-up (first) screens are the result of complex programming and do not display the true capability of the character generator. Character quality ranges from 9-pin dot-matrix to near-professional structure. If your school is wired for closed-circuit television, make sure to run a program of graphics through the closed-circuit system and monitor the program from various rooms of the school. Many characters that look good on the initial screen break apart, shake, or "vibrate" when sent through thousands of feet of cable.

   A second consideration is the integration capability of the generator. Many of the less-expensive generators are just that, character generators. They can produce screens of color graphics to be recorded onto tape. But the better models have a series of "video in," "video out," and "preview" jacks that allow integration into the video system. Ideally, the character generator should include "transparent" among its choices for background color, allowing the characters to be written over moving video. Without that "transparent" choice, the technician is forced to choose between live footage and graphics with solid background. The preview channel allows the technician to see the graphic before it is added to the program. This preview output is connected to a separate color monitor for the technician to use during the program. The preview channel allows the technician to generate new graphics during the program. The main output of the character generator is connected to the main video input of the VCR for recording. This simple process—camera to switcher, switcher to character generator, character generator to VCR—is known as "daisy-chaining" the system and is necessary for connection of a system with a limited number of inputs and outputs. All character generators designed for use in a production setting should have this capability.

   A third consideration for purchase of a stand-alone character generator involves the features offered by the equipment. Features often include the number of type styles (fonts), the number of pages in memory, and the number of colors. These features are important to the smooth operation of the generator. Once again, brainstorm with administrators, colleagues, and students regarding the maximum use of the character generator. It is better to buy more than less.

SCRIPT WRITING

4. It is preferable for students to write about "real" products and services over fictional ones. Students who dwell on creating a cute or avant-garde topic probably aren't focusing on the true objective of the project. If a student insists on creating a fictional client, insist that it be equivalent to one typically advertised on television or radio. Topics such as "nuclear waste disposal service" and "antihomework spray" don't pass this test.

5. Students should stick to one concept for their commercial, avoiding commercials that try to describe every aspect of the product or service. For example, if a student is creating a commercial on a house-painting service, he or she should focus on the company's record of service, the quality of the paint, or a special sale, but not all three concepts. Thirty seconds is not very long, and in this exercise, it is better to present complete information about one concept than vague information about three or four.

6. Remind the students to remember the "client aspect" of advertising. Radio and television commercials are *very* expensive, and the client usually expects a big bang for the buck. Focusing on the client is one way to encourage your students to create professional-quality scripts.

7. Remember: This project is *audio only*! The students can be creative with sound, knowing that they aren't responsible for the video. We can recall a student entering the classroom one day in a three-piece suit. His explanation? His commercial was about a men's clothing store, and his first line was "I bet you're wondering how much I paid for this suit." He understood that the commercial was audio only. He just hadn't thought it through! One of the most famous radio commercials of all time starts with a helicopter sound effect and an "airborne" reporter describing the draining of Lake Michigan (with full sound effects). The dry lake bed is then filled with ice cream and covered with chocolate syrup (the client). At the end, an Air Force bomber flies over and drops a huge cherry, with a whistle and splunk! The narrator and technician effectively convince the listener that Lake Michigan is now a giant ice cream sundae, painting a picture in the mind's eye.

8. If your students are having trouble with ideas for the script, record an hour's worth of radio and play the commercials for the students.

9. Newspaper advertisements can provide specifics such as price, product description, and store location. Plan to have a few copies of the newspaper on hand for the scriptwriting session.

10. How do you get to Carnegie Hall? Practice, practice, practice. That rule applies to this project. Students should practice aloud. Ideas: Have students write or type their scripts on note cards for easy reading; have students double-space their scripts; have students write in red ink the words they want to emphasize when reading.

BACKGROUND MUSIC

11. Background music should remain in the background. Unless a concert or a CD is being advertised, strong vocals should be discouraged in the student commercials.

12. Your public library or school media specialist should be a good source for modern instrumental music. Ask the AV librarian or the school media specialist for help.

13. Don't be afraid to have your students use sound effects. A wide variety of sound effects are now available on compact disc and are priced very reasonably. Your public library or school media center may already have a collection ready for circulation.

RECORDING THE COMMERCIALS

14. The concept of cross-training—teaching employees to perform a variety of tasks necessary for the completion of the project—applies here. All students should serve as a technician for a classmate. A "technician grade" can be added to the grading sheet at your discretion. One way to ensure that all students gain such experience is to have the student work as the audio technician immediately before or after the completion of his or her own commercial.

15. Schedule students in advance for their recording times. A student probably needs 5 to 7 minutes to record his or her commercial. Some students who claim they are not ready are really just too nervous to perform. Unfortunately, this phenomenon can continue through beginning production classes. Deal with these students as you see fit, but encourage them to complete the project on schedule.

16. Make a sample tape for the class. Showing the correct procedure can help many students understand the process, and a good leader never asks the class to do something he or she wouldn't do.

Lesson 4: Documentary

PLANNING THE PROJECT

1. A documentary is a work of nonfiction television. Avoid dramatized situations. Most beginning TV students have a movie in mind but, at this point, they probably don't have the video skills to pull it off. (Movie dreams can be tackled after students have gotten a few projects under the belt.) Remember: The objective at this point is to encourage proper planning, shooting, and audio-dubbing techniques.

2. Students should choose a simple topic that will not lead to frustration. Early video experiences should be positive.

3. Students should plan a variety of shots and should be allowed to visit locations to storyboard the project.

4. Many students will want to interview faculty members and classmates even though interviews are not required for this project. Because no editing is used on this project, any interviews the students wish to do must be done correctly the first time.

5. Be aware of bickering among partners over topic selection. At this point in the instruction, the topic is not as important as the demonstrated competency. Remind the students that many projects will follow and that many good ideas will be used throughout the year.

6. Because no editing is used, storyboarding is crucial!

GRAPHICS

7. In more complex projects, graphics are added after the raw footage is shot. But at this level, the title page must be recorded before the raw footage. The program should start with about 20 seconds of a blank screen, followed by the title screen for about 10 seconds, and then another 20 seconds of the blank screen. When it is time to shoot the project, play the tape through the title screen and stop after the title screen goes off. Then record the project. The 20 seconds of blank screen that you initially record over gives the VCR a strong control track to start the program.

SHOOTING

8. Each team should have about an hour to shoot the project. Most 3-minute projects can be created in an hour. Students who are high achievers or are prone to self-criticism may need encouragement here. The "perfect" program has yet to be created. Your positive comments can go a long way toward the development of your students.

9. Remind the students to fade on the last shot.

10. Documentaries without interviews can be dubbed straight from start to finish. The audio-dubbing process must be stopped when an interview appears. It is not enough to simply turn down the audio mixer. The videotape recorder must be stopped and re-cued to the end of the interview.

11. Encourage students to practice reading their scripts before doing the actual audio dub.

12. As always, schedule a class period to view and evaluate all projects. Establish a reasonable deadline; don't delay the entire class for one or two procrastinating stragglers. Everyone claps for every project. Remember to expect some mistakes because no editing was allowed.

13. If your personal video experience is limited, make a project yourself before grading your students' work. This will give you a perspective of the task at hand.

POSTPRODUCTION

14. As an instructor, it will be up to you to inspire your students to work creatively with the limited resources of their learning and your school's equipment, while maintaining the excitement and integrity of their video production. Many great television programs have been created with simple postproduction techniques. In fact, the entire golden age of television, when television programs were broadcast live, can be considered television without postproduction. The challenge, just like the challenge presented to the producers of "I Love Lucy" and "Your Show of Shows," is to use the existing postproduction techniques to augment an already great idea and script.

    Remember, it is difficult to "save" bad raw footage with good postproduction. No matter how adept your students become at postproduction, they still need to exert considerable energy into planning and executing a good video shoot. While some students naturally enjoy the gimmicks and gizmos of postproduction, the emphasis must remain on planning and camera work, the bread and butter of school-based video production.

COPYRIGHT LAW

15. A word about copyright: Most of you have probably been made aware of copyright law by district or school-level media personnel. If not, you need to ask. Schools are liable for all copyright infringements, and large corporations have sued schools and won. Instructors are among those who are financially and criminally liable for violations. Through interpretation of current copyright law, schools or, more specifically, students, get a break. Under the current law, a student can use copyrighted music while 1) displaying a competency, 2) in a class, and 3) for a grade. For example, it is fine for your students to use a current song for audio dubbing as long as they meet all three of the criteria above. However, they do *not* have the right to run copies of that tape, sell the tape(s), or both. The explanation is brief at best. All TV production instructors should contact their building and district-level media centers for the latest updates and interpretations of current copyright law.

Lesson 5: News Brief

BEFORE THE PROJECT IS ASSIGNED

1. Depending on the equipment that you have, this project may have to be adapted slightly or drastically. The section of the lesson that discusses audio and video connectors is geared toward those schools possessing a moderate level of equipment—schools that have acquired portable equipment, but not a studio. If you work with only camcorders, you will probably have to work around the tasks of audio mixing and character generation. If you have an equipped studio, you can implement the format presented in the project plan while using your studio equipment.

2. Depending on the requirements of your switcher, you may encounter synchronization problems when using the source VCR. The problems are manifested in a shaky, discolored, unstable picture. Two solutions are available. One is to purchase a time base corrector that will convert the unstable VCR signal into a rock-solid video signal. Unfortunately, this is a very expensive option. For this project, the second option makes more sense. Instead of connecting the source VCR to an input of your switcher, connect the source VCR as a link between your character generator and your record VCR, as shown in figure 1.64. Now, your video configuration is: camera into switcher, switcher into character generator, character generator into source VCR, source VCR into record VCR. The video signal of the camera/graphics will play through the source VCR until you push "play" on the source VCR. At that point, the tape in the source VCR will override the incoming camera/graphic signal. A side effect may be a slight jump in the picture when you stop the source VCR to return to the camera video. Without the expensive time base corrector, this problem is unavoidable. However, it does not detract significantly from the finished project or the educational experience of producing a news show.

Fig. 1.64. Alternative video connections.

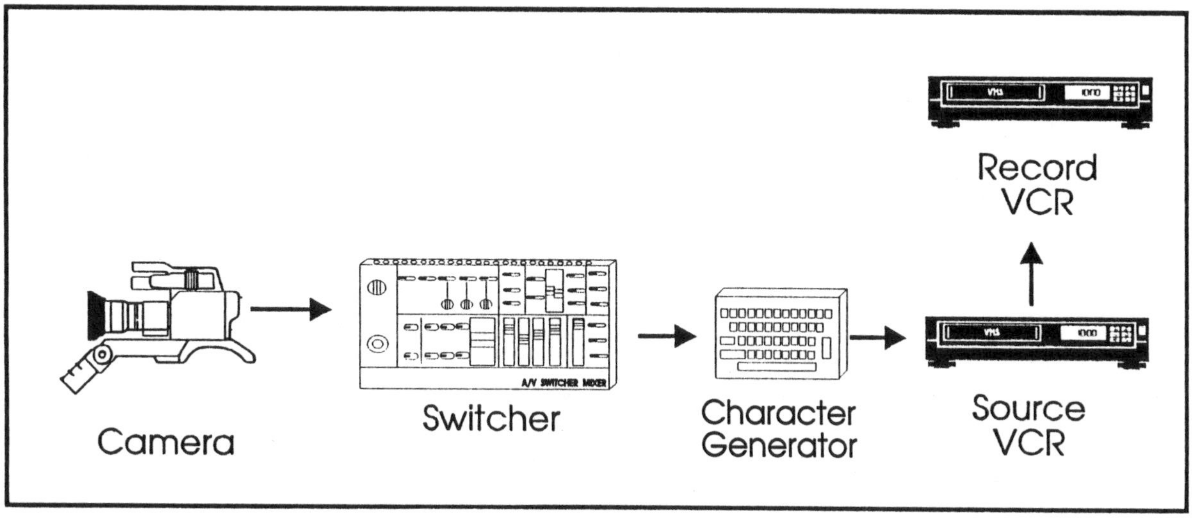

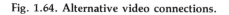

3. There are many ways of choosing students to work together. Probably the least effective for this project is allowing students to form their own groups. Chances are, all of the anchors will form one group, all of the camera operators will form another, etc., and bickering over positions will result. One successful method involves having students select the job they want to perform (#1, #2, etc.) and making a list by calling the roll. Students in overselected jobs may have to name a second choice. Then the instructor meets with all of the #1s and a "draft"-style selection process is conducted. This process retains the educational integrity of the project while allowing the students a moderate amount of control over team membership.

PROGRAM PREPRODUCTION

4. Set a time frame for completion of all ENG assignments. Four to 5 days is usually sufficient.

5. Once again, actual, real-world news stories are preferable to fictional accounts. Fictional auto thefts or gang fights really don't help your ENG reporter learn anything about reporting.

6. Each team should be able to complete their 30-second (video only) segment and their 1-minute ENG report in one class period.

7. While the ENG teams work, present 30-minute workshops on the switcher and character generator for all students not working on reports.

DURING THE PRODUCTION

8. Once a team has recorded its ENG footage, the anchor has written the script, and the switcher and graphics technician are competent in their jobs, production of the actual news brief can begin.

9. The production should be accomplished in one class period. Plan for a half-speed walk-through, a full-speed run-through, and the actual recording of the program. You, the instructor, should serve as the director. Students at this point are still learning about television production and are probably not ready to take full responsibility for such a program.

10. This project is designed to be a no-edit show. If a mistake is made, re-cue and reset, and begin again. This is how real-world news shows are done (except for the mistake part).

GRADING

11. Remember to grade on preproduction *and* production work.

12. If time permits, show all news briefs to all classes. Ask students to compare approaches to stories. A discussion could follow about how real news stations can approach a story from different perspectives.

13. Refrain from grading the projects immediately after their completion. Let them "ripen" a little, especially if the production was frantic. Remember, this is the students' first show. Don't let anxiety during production translate into poor grades.

14. As always, everyone watches all projects and applauds in appreciation of a job well done!

FROM PROJECT TO SCHOOL NEWS SHOW

15. While this project is designed to be a class exercise, it may be adapted as a regular school news format for those schools wired for closed-circuit television. A thorough presentation of school news shows appears in part II, chapter 2. Get a few shows under your belt, then show your students' best work to the school administration.

PURCHASING EQUIPMENT

16. A word to instructors about equipment purchases: As your television production program receives funding through budget allocations, grants, or fund-raising, be very judicious about your purchases. Evaluate your current level of equipment and the *real* needs of your program. Most of us are impressed by flashy graphics and digital video technology, but these purchases should be considered as secondary to the acquisition of basic audio and video components. Many schools considering the purchase of a "cutting edge" special effects generator don't even have a basic audio mixer or a lavaliere microphone. Special effects may get students and administrators excited about your program, but this "all smoke and no fire" approach usually leads to disappointment and apathy. Make sure that your studio is firmly grounded in basic video equipment before adding the "icing" of special equipment.

The equipment listed below is basic to television production, and is really quite inexpensive. At the time of this writing, a simple, five-input (three microphone and two music source) audio mixer could be purchased at a leading electronics chain store for about $125. Good microphones could be purchased from the same source for less than $50 each, and at least one company offered a user-friendly character generator for less than $1,000. Assuming that your school already owns a camera/camcorder and a VCR, the "ministudio" conversion can be made for less than $1,500, or about one-third the price that many underequipped and underfunded programs are spending on flash-in-the-pan technology.

Lesson 6: Instructional Video Program

PLANNING THE PROJECT

1. Students can work in groups of two or three. There really isn't enough work for more than three students.
2. Make sure that all students are involved in the program production. Do not allow any students to serve strictly as talent. On-camera talent can work in other areas of the production as well.
3. Retain the right to approve topics. Be very careful that the students choose topics that will serve them well and be aware of potentially dangerous topics. You will *not* be stifling creativity by emphasizing safety.
4. Make a schedule for shooting the instructional programs. Shooting can begin on the third day of the project, leaving ½ day for project introduction and 1½ days for storyboarding.
5. Carefully review the storyboards of each group before they shoot.

PRODUCTION

6. Each team should be able to complete shooting raw footage in one class period. Students who finish *too* quickly probably haven't shot enough raw footage.
7. While some groups are shooting, others can record graphics. Unlike the documentary project, which was not edited, this project does *not* have to be shot in order.

POSTPRODUCTION

8. Set deadlines for project completion. You may want to establish a deadline for each group, depending on how long that group has had to work with the equipment. For example, a group could follow this schedule:

   Monday—shoot raw footage
   Tuesday—evaluate footage
   Wednesday—create graphics
   Thursday—edit
   Friday—audio-dub

   Because you may not have enough equipment to let all groups shoot on the first day, the groups that shoot on later dates should have later deadlines.

9. Make sure that all groups stay on task. Many of the steps listed above can be completed without all of the group members present. If the project is storyboarded properly, much of the post-production work can be accomplished by one or two group members.

VIEWING AND GRADING

10. As always, schedule a day or two in class for project viewing and grading. Everyone claps for every project.

11. The grade sheet provided for this project is quite elaborate. Because this is the first major project of the course, any deficiencies in training should be corrected at this point. The projects get more difficult, and tasks not mastered at this point will present continuing problems throughout the course of study.

Lesson 7: Interview Program

GROUP ASSIGNMENTS

1. After you have explained the project to the class, ask each student in the class to name his or her job preference for the interview program. Remember, you'll need a camera operator for *each* camera! Surprisingly, the preferences will be reasonably distributed among the various jobs. If too many students express the same preference, ask them to name a second choice.

   You may want to eliminate the job of "production coordinator." An aggressive, organized production coordinator can take care of many group details. However, some unmotivated students will request this job as a way to avoid a specific task. Evaluate your class and decide for yourself.

2. Gather your hosts (in a corner of the room to avoid the bruised egos of other students) and hold a "draft" to complete each team. The host who picks first for the first job will pick last for the next job, etc.

PREPRODUCTION

3. After the groups have been formed, allow them to meet for a few minutes with no specific tasks. This "get-acquainted" time is a natural function of groups.

4. Next, the groups should begin the task of selecting a guest. Review the criteria in the text of this lesson. The host should have the final say in guest selection.

5. Make sure to get administrative clearance for off-campus guests. A paramedic or firefighter on campus can panic the assistant principal!

6. Depending on the skill retention or experience of your students, you may need to hold "switcher school," "audio school," etc., to review equipment operations.

PRODUCTION

7. Keep the projects simple. Allowing the firefighter to demonstrate the proper technique for extinguishing a grease fire might make exciting video, but it will also require a larger set, different camera angles and a *very* dangerous situation for the school. (Do you *really* want to set off your school's smoke detectors?)

8. Become active in the production. Offer leadership of experience. Become the director of the production, if necessary.

GRADING THE PROJECTS

9. Carry a clipboard, and write comments as the show is being produced. Grade the students as the show happens.

10. Upon completion of the projects, ask each group to select their favorite 5-minute segment from their programs. Show all of these segments to the class and encourage constructive criticism.

2 CURRICULUM INTEGRATION

Videotaping School Events and Activities

Objectives

After successfully completing this unit, you will be able to:

- *identify the equipment needed to videotape various types of school events and activities.*
- *successfully videotape a school event or activity.*

Television production students are often asked to assist teachers and other students in videotaping and producing videotapes for various school events and activities. These requests range from simply videotaping a classroom guest speaker or student classroom presentation to a multicamera event in the school auditorium. School plays, fashion shows, talent shows, athletic contests, and school award presentations are routinely videotaped and later shown to classes and school organizations. Television students properly trained in videotaping these events can be a valuable resource to the entire school, as well as the television production program.

Learning to professionally videotape these events and functions, along with the necessary skills and concepts needed to correctly hook up the equipment, can lead to career opportunities in the community. Hotels, motels, and convention sites provide these resources for guests and community groups and are willing to hire personnel trained in the audiovisual support services. Local production companies are also eager to hire well-trained and experienced videographers.

This chapter will provide you with the information and concepts required for successfully videotaping many school events and activities. Although the equipment models and facilities vary from school to school, the techniques remain the same.

Classroom Applications

Guest Speakers

A visit by a guest speaker, a common and enriching experience, allows teachers to utilize the talents and knowledge of citizens in the community to provide students with up-to-date information in their field of study. Videotaping your guest speaker has several advantages:

1. It allows flexible scheduling for your speaker. Guests can choose the time that is best suited to their needs, rather than having to meet the teacher's request for a certain period or time.

2. Speakers can be scheduled for small classroom situations rather than large auditorium settings.

3. It allows you the opportunity to "revisit" a speaker with your class for discussion and comments. Students who were absent can also take the tape home to view when they return.

4. Teachers can share their tapes and take advantage of each other's contacts in the community.

Generally, most guest speakers can be videotaped with a single-camera system. The equipment should include:

- video camera/deck system, or camcorder
- microphone and mic extension cable
- AC power adapter
- extension cord/gaffer's tape
- tripod
- headphones
- videotape

Most problems can be easily eliminated by following some simple guidelines.

- *Always use a tripod.* A steady camera is a must, and no one can hold a camera still during the length of time a speaker is presenting information to the class. Set your camera/tripod a comfortable distance from the speaker; close enough for a good shot but not so close that you will distract him or her during the presentation. Be aware of backlight and glare from classroom windows and lights. If there is to be interaction between guests and students, be sure you can pan to capture all areas of the class. Check with the speaker before the presentation to find out if there are visual aids that should be included in the videotaping.

- *Make sure you have an uninterrupted power source.* Batteries will often "die" at the most inopportune times. Use an alternating current (AC) power adapter for your power source. Use gaffer's tape or masking tape to tape down your extension cord in areas where people will be walking to prevent accidents and loss of power during taping.

- *Ensure that you have good sound.* Always use an external microphone. Don't rely on the internal camera microphone. A lavaliere mic can be attached to the speaker's clothes, or you may decide to use a shotgun microphone to capture a question-and-answer period with the class. Dynamic microphones placed on a floor or desk stand can also be used. Use headphones to monitor your sound as you are recording. (See part I, lesson 2, for a full explanation of microphones.)

- *Don't forget to label your videotape.* Include the speaker's name and title, topic, and teacher's name and date. When the videotaping is completed, you can add the length of the presentation.

Experiment and practice videotaping "speakers" in your television classroom. Review the tape with your teacher and classmates, identify areas that need improvement, and note outstanding sections. After a few sessions of taping, you will be developing your skills as professionals as well as building a valuable resource for your school.

Lab / Science Experiments

A picture is worth a thousand words, and in 30 pictures per second (frames) a video can describe quite a bit in a short amount of time. A science experiment or lab can be difficult to describe, but easily shown on tape. Even procedures used in the lab (safety, setups, cleanups, emergency procedures, etc.) can be videotaped and shown periodically throughout the year. With the use of some simple editing, audio-dubbing, and additional graphics, these labs can be "saved" and used as needed.

Depending upon the type of situation you are videotaping (teacher demonstration, group work, experiments), some equipment considerations should include:

- camera setup
- microphones and mic cables
- tripod
- power source
- extension cords
- lights (if needed)
- videotape

The placement of cameras and possible use of a switcher depend upon the program you are taping. A teacher demonstration, for example, would be best videotaped using two cameras and a switcher. One camera would be set for a medium shot and another for close-ups of the activity being demonstrated. A lavaliere mic on the teacher would be sufficient for recording sound.

If a lab or experiment by a group of students is being taped by a single camera, the camera operator will need to move around and record from several angles. Some shots need to be close-ups, even macro shots, and others can be filmed at a medium distance from the students. For sound recording, a shotgun mic can capture all of the group's discussion, or a Pressure Zone Microphone© (PZM) placed on the table can be used. In this situation, there would be a need for editing to make a good copy for later use in the classroom.

In some cases, the use of simple lighting would assist in videotaping experiments and procedures. For close-ups and macro shots, the areas need to be well lit for videotaping. Classroom lighting is often not enough to adequately videotape these types of experiments.

Work closely with the science department at your school to identify what types of activities are scheduled that would be best to videotape and use for classroom instruction. Coordinate your activities to provide a situation that benefits both the science department and the television production program. You'll be able to develop your skills as a videographer and provide a teaching resource for your school.

Athletic Events

Taping athletic events is rewarding to the videographer, the athlete, the coach, and the school. Careers in sports videography abound, and quite a few colleges will give full scholarships to "team managers," who are solely responsible for videotaping games and practices. In viewing the videotapes, the athlete can benefit by analyzing his or her performance, and the coaching staff can see how well their game strategy worked. Many athletic coaches review every game for strategy and to record game statistics. Sports highlights can be edited and audio-dubbed for viewing at the annual sports banquet. Television students gain valuable experience taping the games, and it makes great public relations material for the school. These highlights can be shown at awards banquets and booster club meetings and can be included in video yearbooks.

Sports activities that lend themselves best to videotaping include gymnastics, football, basketball, wrestling, diving, track, and cheerleading. These can easily be taped on a single-camera system. Baseball, volleyball, and softball are more difficult to tape with one camera due to the nature of the action of the game. Highlight tape is easily shot, but continuous play is more difficult.

One of the best ways to learn sports videotaping is to preview some games already taped and note specifics, like camera position, camera start/stop time, and game versus highlight taping. The following list of suggestions can assist you in videotaping athletic events at your school.

1. *Camera start/stop time.* Most camcorders/VCRs will "roll back" slightly each time the camera "record" button is pushed to stop recording. If the camera operator pushes the trigger at the end of each play, as the VCR rolls back, the last few seconds of each play will be erased. To avoid this, allow 3 to 5 seconds after the completion of a play, or event, before depressing the "record/pause" button. To avoid color bars from appearing in your sports highlights, start recording action 5-9 seconds before the start of each play.

2. *Camera positioning.* This will vary with each sport, but allow yourself to experiment and find the best angle to record the action, both on the field and in the stands. Some of your best footage will come from the reaction of fans, coaches, and players on the sidelines! Camera positioning varies with the purpose of the taping. Coaches will prefer wider-angle shots to view the position of all players on the field, whereas highlight taping looks best from close-ups and tighter shots that depict the intensity of the game.

3. *Scoreboard/Clock.* Most coaches prefer that the scoreboard be taped following time-outs and at the end of each period of play. In football, it is generally suggested that the videographer tape the scoreboard after each score. Gymnasts and wrestlers like to have their points taped after each event. Basketball, because of the nature of the game, has a lot of scoring. Usually shots of the scoreboard are reserved for time-outs and the end of each period.

4. *Game versus highlight taping.* When you are videotaping a game for a coach to analyze or to obtain player statistics, a wide-angle view is recommended. Try to keep all of the players within the field of view. Keep the camera rolling at all times, stopping only during time-outs or breaks between periods of play. Avoid extreme close-ups, and follow the action on the field of play. Fan reactions, cheerleaders, and other sideline actions are *not* important in this type of videotaping. Follow the suggestions in this chapter for scoreboard and clock shots.

   Highlight videotaping for your school news show, video yearbook, or class reports varies tremendously from complete game videotaping. Some of your best footage will include fan reactions, player "celebrations," and the sights and sounds that accompany the sport. Close-ups and "aesthetic" shots will enhance your videos, as well as some game footage. Your task here is to make the viewer relive these moments and feel the excitement and emotion of the players, fans, and the sport itself.

5. *Reviewing games.* Review parts of each game with the coach or your teacher. Accept suggestions and note areas where taping could be improved. The more games you tape, the more you will improve.

Dramatic Performances

School plays, musicals, faculty follies, dance recitals, talent shows, and many other school performances are fun to watch but difficult to videotape well with a single-camera system. The problems one often faces include too much or too little light on stage, too large a scene to tape without a lot of panning and zooming, the camera in the way of the audience or the audience in the way of the camera, and of course, the question of "Can I have a copy?" from the participants. Here are some suggestions that can improve your taping skills in this area.

1. *Lighting.* Stage lighting often washes out the faces of the performers. Try using a manual iris setting and avoid the "auto" functions of your camera. Open or close the iris manually as the lighting conditions dictate during the course of the performance. Bring a monitor with you the first few times so you can see how your video looks in color. Viewfinders can be deceiving, especially in low light or extreme lighting conditions. White-balance your camera in the lighting conditions within which you will be taping.

2. *Scene size.* Some scenes are just going to be too large to capture on videotape without standing so far back that everyone will be unrecognizable in the video. Don't worry about videotaping all of the performers all of the time. Follow the action as best you can, staying with the main characters most of the time. *Do not* use a lot of pans and zooms! Occasionally a *slow* zoom and pan of a group will be fine, but do not overuse this technique.

3. *Audience.* Reserve a small area (figure 2.1) to isolate yourself from the audience. Make sure all camera and "mic" cables are securely taped to the floor with masking/gaffer's tape. Place your microphone(s) in an area where they can record stage sound but will not pick up conversations, loud comments and laughs, or thunderous applause from the audience. Sometimes it is necessary to "tape off" a small area for microphones as well as cameras.

Single-Camera Setups

Place your camera about 9-12 rows back from the stage area. Set up to the left or right of stage center. This location will enable you to obtain close-ups or to cover almost all of the stage action from a wide-angle shot (figure 2.1).

Always use a tripod. Utilize AC power, and bring some extension cords and gaffer's tape.

Sound quality can be improved by placing a shotgun microphone (or two) near the front of the stage on a floor stand and connecting this to your camcorder/VCR. This eliminates the "echo chamber" effect when relying on your internal camera microphone. Use headphones to monitor your sound. If at all possible, record the audio directly from the soundboard into your recording VCR.

Avoid a lot of zooms and pans. Follow the action smoothly and maintain a "good shot" as much as possible.

Follow all copyright laws concerning duplication and sale of videotapes.

Fig. 2.1. Single-camera positions.

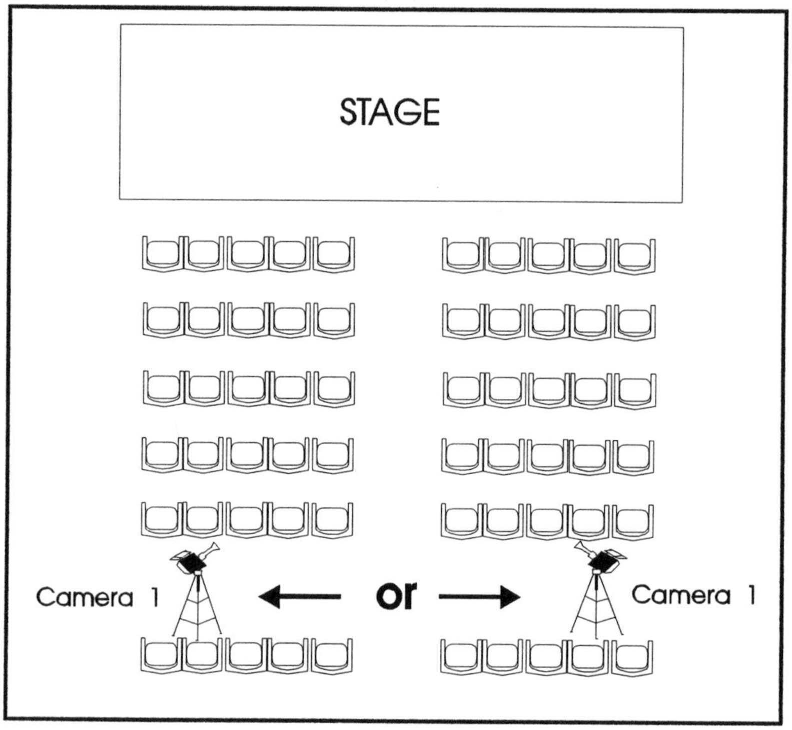

Multiple-Camera/Switcher Systems

Place one camera 7-10 rows back from the stage for close-ups, and place the other camera far enough back to cover the entire stage scene (figure 2.2).

Sound quality can be balanced and improved by placing one or two shotgun microphones several rows from the stage and using a small audio mixer to balance and mix the sound. Some switchers come equipped with this function.

Avoid a lot of zooms and pans by one camera. Use slow dissolves and cuts to switch camera angles.

Communication between the technical director and the camera operators is important. You can use a wireless or wired headset system. Generally, a wired system will have fewer problems in the long run.

Make sure all cables are taped securely to the floor in any areas the audience and performers are walking over.

Follow all copyright laws concerning duplication and sale of videotapes.

Miscellaneous Video Production

Within your school are numerous possibilities for creative videos familiarizing students with programs, course offerings, school services, guidance functions and services, as well as many of the school's policies and procedures on a variety of topics. School orientation videos for new students

Fig. 2.2. Multicamera positions.

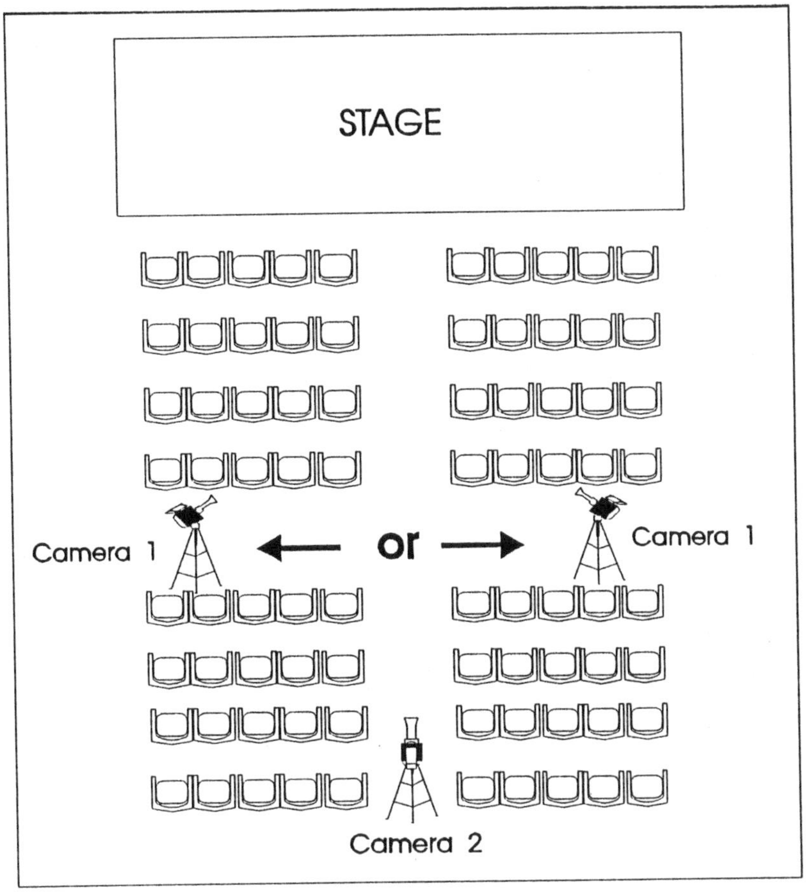

registering at the school, media center orientation videos for classes about to embark on that "research paper" voyage to the library, or teacher education videos demonstrating the latest classroom management practices or discipline strategies are just a few of the topics that may be suggested to you by your principal or teacher during the course of the school year. As you are contemplating production of these projects, here are some guidelines you might find helpful:

1. Have those personnel most familiar with the topic write, or assist in writing, the script. It's hard to research and write about programs and procedures that are unfamiliar to you.

2. Keep the video short and to the point. Only use the essential information. It's an informational video, not an Oscar award-winning movie.

3. Always direct your video to appeal to the viewing audience. A video produced for students should appeal to their likes and interests. Music and dialogue should reflect their norms. Likewise, videos aimed at faculty, staff, or parent groups should also be geared to their interests.

4. Allow plenty of time for planning, storyboarding, and scriptwriting, as well as videotaping and postproduction.

5. Work as a team to complete the job as quickly and effectively as possible. Share ideas and use the talents of all involved. Avoid criticism and encourage everyone to work with a positive attitude.

6. Review your project periodically with your teacher. Revise and review your storyboards as needed. Preview your footage as soon as possible to make sure you have videotaped what you need before you begin postproduction.

7. Always make a backup copy of a tape as soon as possible. Pull out the record tabs on all of your recorded tapes.

Producing school-related videos can be an enriching and rewarding experience for all involved. Establishing guidelines and policies, working closely with your peers as a team, setting appropriate timelines and frameworks, and coordinating production and use of these videos can facilitate and enhance these projects for all involved!

Activities: Chapter 2

1. You have been selected to videotape a Vietnam War veteran speaking to an American history class at your school.

   a. List the equipment you will need to tape this speaker.

   b. What information do you need prior to taping?

   c. Describe some postproduction techniques you might utilize to enhance this video for future use.

2. Plan a visit to observe a science class or laboratory. Discuss possible ideas for videotaping some labs or experiments with the teacher.

   a. What were some tentative ideas suggested?

   b. List the equipment you will need for taping.

   c. What problems do you anticipate might occur, and how will you overcome them?

3. Videotape an athletic event at your school. Shoot 10 minutes of "game" footage, and 5 minutes of "highlight" footage. Preview this footage in class. Identify and compare the differences in style and picture composition, as well as the utilization for the coach and "news show" highlights. Write down your ideas and opinions. Compare them with those of your classmates.

Equipment Checklist

PROJECT ______________________________ DATE______________

LOCATION ______________________________

- ________ video camera(s)/camcorder
- ________ VCR
- ________ videotape
- ________ AC adapter
- ________ battery(ies)
- ________ tripod(s)
- ________ microphone(s)
  - ________ lavaliere
  - ________ hand-held
  - ________ shotgun
  - ________ other
- ________ lighting instruments ______________________
- ________ monitor
- ________ switcher
- ________ audio mixer
- ________ audiocassette deck
- ________ CD player
- ________ turntable

Client Consultation Worksheet

CLIENT: ______________________________ Phone # (   )____________

PRODUCER: ____________________________ Phone # (   )____________

Working title:

Target audience:

Suggested program length:

Desired outcomes/objectives:

1.

2.

3.

4.

Resources of client:

1.

2.

3.

Cost of production not to exceed $__________.

Notes:

Notes to the Teacher

Videotaping Scientific Experiments

1. Videotaping scientific experiments has many advantages. Groups can watch each others' tapes and note significant differences in results and procedures. A student who is absent will be able to make up these labs much easier. The teacher may also view the labs to see how effectively they teach the concepts and skills being presented.

2. A PZM mic works well with groups.

3. Once you have begun videotaping, you and your students will develop guidelines that best suit your situation. Include members of the science department in planning and reviewing your videotapes.

Videography for Athletic Events

4. One of the best ways to "train" students in sports videotaping is to preview some games previously taped and point out specifics, like camera start/stop time, camera positioning, and game versus highlight videotaping. For instance, a game taped for a coach to review and record statistics would be taped differently than a tape being made for highlight film. The coach will want the game taped in its entirety, play for play, with no action or game time deleted for camera cuts and repositioning. Scoreboard shots and game time are also recorded after scores (football) and at the end of periods. A wide-angle shot should be used to enable the coach to view the position and play of all the athletes on the field or court. Highlight film will include some of the overall action and scoring but should also include close-ups of the players and coaches, cheerleaders, and crowd shots. Only portions of the game will be videotaped. These are similar to what you would see on a typical daily news broadcast.

5. It is good practice to accompany your crew the first several times they are taping a particular sport. Hook up a small monitor to each camera setup so you can comment on camera angles, subject framing, and pan speed. You'll be surprised at how well your students progress from game to game. Review parts of each tape with the students and point out areas of improvement or items that need to be changed during the next videotaping. You can even have the coaches write comments about the taping and pass these along to the students.

Miscellaneous Video Production

6. Avoid at all costs those projects that carry the "I need it in a hurry" label. They are usually poorly done and reflect the lack of planning needed to produce a good informative video.

7. Work closely with your students to make video production an enjoyable experience for all involved. Allow students to make production decisions involving script, camera shots, and post-production techniques. This hands-on experience will teach them lessons that classroom lectures and presentations cannot possibly illustrate.

8. Test-market your project on several individuals or small groups before school-wide broadcasting or distribution. Obtain feedback from these groups and revise your video if needed. Sometimes when you are involved in a project, you can overlook some small details that can affect the message or effectiveness of the project.

Tutorial Libraries

9. In any given subject area there are skills and objectives critical to understanding the major concepts of that discipline. Having a set of videotapes that contain teaching lessons, practice exercises, and review skills would be invaluable to teachers and students. These tapes could be located in the media center for student checkout. Students would then view them at home and return them the next day. Several copies of each skill could be duplicated if needed.

   For example, a math teacher could present a lecture on simplifying algebraic equations. Students would watch the teacher solve several problems and then be presented a problem to solve. They would stop the tape, solve the example, and then continue watching the tape to see if the answer was correct. The possibilities for this type of program are endless. Foreign languages, history lessons, science skills, and many other disciplines could all be cataloged and placed in the media center or within the departments and classrooms themselves.

10. With the advent of "corporate video," more and more employees are being instructed in company procedures and technical skills with the use of video. The taping of these tutorial libraries can be as much of an education for the television students as the students who will be viewing the tapes. With some simple editing, use of graphics, maps and macro shots, perhaps even some music for background or mood setting (history lessons!), these tapes can be a valuable resource and an excellent training session for all involved.

Videotapes for Substitute Teachers

11. Every teacher knows how difficult it is to adequately prepare class instruction for a substitute teacher. Even with advance notice, which isn't always possible, the substitute generally is used to maintain the status quo of the classroom. But what if a lesson is prepared in advance on videotape! Sure, students might enjoy watching that copy of *Star Wars* for the fifth time, but they might actually learn something through the use of these "substitute tapes."

    The ideal tapes would be designed to present information (a review or introduction to new material), and also give instructions for text, workbook, or even handout information. The substitute would play the tape for the class, maintain class focus, and then pass out accompanying handouts or text material. Talk about taking the stress out of calling in sick! Each teacher might tape one to three lessons, duplicate any needed material, and place them in the office in labeled manila folders. Once the substitute arrives, all he or she needs to do is request a VCR from the media center and pass out the information in the envelope.

12. Other ideas would include:

    a. A videotape designed for all substitute teachers to view containing school policies on attendance, lunch procedures, passes out of class, and other school and classroom procedures. These tapes could be viewed by all substitute teachers used at the school.

    b. A "teacher emergency tape" containing three consecutive lessons and material designed by the teacher to be used in cases where the teacher may be absent for an extended amount of time.

Public Service Announcements and Community Projects

13. As your television production program grows and develops into a strong communication facility, community and civic groups will undoubtedly seek to use this invaluable resource for production purposes of their own. These requests will range from simply asking you to broadcast pre-produced tapes to writing/directing/producing videos about a wide range of community resources and programs. Usually these requests are initiated by a telephone call or letter stating "We thought this would make an excellent student project...."! In reality, the reasons most of these requests are made are:

    a. There are no funds available to do the project.

    b. Equipment is not available to produce the project.

    c. The group believes that everything has to be done on video.

    d. The group would like to provide free advertising to your students.

    e. There is a legitimate concern for student welfare and interests but no experience in video production.

    f. The group is pursuing an excellent idea that will provide a vehicle for enriching experiences in production for your students, as well as a viable communication tool for the school or community.

    Needless to say, only those projects/ideas that meet criteria 5 and 6 should be considered. All others can be easily dismissed with a simple "Thank you, but we cannot...." It is a good idea to have a policies and procedures manual for your studio to cover these types of requests. If you are considering the request, always ask for a letter explaining exactly what the group is requesting the school to produce or provide for them. Present this letter to your principal and obtain his or her approval before you begin the project.

14. Some other considerations to keep in mind before undertaking the project include:

    a. Time, personnel, and equipment constraints. Do you have enough time to plan, tape, and produce this video? Will there be adequate numbers of students available to perform the necessary jobs during scheduled production times? Do you have the right equipment needed to complete the assignment?

    b. Teacher-student expertise: Do you and your students possess the necessary knowledge and skills needed to complete the job to everyone's satisfaction?

    c. Intrinsic value of the project. Is it worthwhile to devote the resources needed to complete the project?

15. Even though most projects involve your students, it is you, the teacher, who must oversee all phases of production. Most students lack the necessary maturity and sophistication that these types of projects require even though they may possess the necessary video skills! These projects must be produced along with all of your other classroom duties, so be careful not to undertake an overwhelming amount of extracurricular work.

16. Once a project is completed and the group is satisfied with the results, request a letter from the group to your principal thanking him or her for the time and effort you and your class put into the project. It is also a good idea to make a copy or two of the project to keep in your class and to give to the principal to view. If you feel the community or civic group involved could afford to make a donation to your program, such a request could be sent along with the final project. Most groups are glad to be able to help, especially if they think they will need to call on you in the future for further assistance.

    Working with community and civic groups can provide meaningful video production experiences for you and your students, as well as fostering a positive image of your program and school in the community. These videos can be a valuable tool in providing information for the school or community members and, at the same time, develop the skills and abilities of television production students.

Special Note on Curriculum Integration

17. A well-developed and coordinated television production program is truly an asset to the school and community. By providing video production as a resource, the television production program can integrate numerous areas of the curriculum, as well as school policies and procedures, within the framework of the educational system. Using the talents and skills of teachers, students, parents, and community resources, an innovative television production program can provide a communication link in the school and community, as well as train and develop video production skills for the students.

    Curriculum integration means working with, not doing for other programs and services offered in the school. A carefully planned project using the skills of you and your students, in conjunction with the content skills of other faculty members, can provide a useful and informative video project for all involved. Avoid those situations, however, where someone offers you the idea and you are left with all the work. These situations usually result in lackluster projects and ill feelings for those involved.

    Curriculum integration offers the best opportunities to apply the television skills and concepts developed in the classroom to the real-world challenges of the educational system. It can be a rewarding learning experience, providing an exceptional resource for instruction.

Part II
STUDENT EDITION, BOOK II

1 INTERMEDIATE TELEVISION PRODUCTION

Lesson 1 Reviewing Basic Television Production Skills

Objectives

After successfully completing this lesson, you will be able to:

- *explain various equipment checks to be completed prior to ENG videotaping.*
- *white-balance a camera.*
- *manually focus a camera.*
- *record videotape to be used in postproduction.*
- *identify and describe several camera angles.*
- *list and describe some postproduction techniques.*

Vocabulary

Camera remote. An electronic adjustment on a video deck that allows the functions of the video deck (e.g., play, record, search, rewind) to be controlled by the video camera.

Gain. Adjusts the video signal for optimum output in low light situations.

Iris. Adjustable lens opening, which controls the amount of light entering the camera body.

Tape speed. Adjusts the amount of time recording on a videotape.

SP—Standard Play (2 hours per T120 tape)
LP—Long Play (4 hours per T120 tape)
EP—Extended Play (6 hours per T120 tape)

Tracking. An electronic adjustment on a video deck that adjusts the way the video heads trace the videotape during recording and playback.

White balance. Adjusts the color response of the camera's imaging device based on the lighting environment of the shot.

In earlier lessons, you learned about basic equipment setup, camera techniques, production skills, and project planning. This lesson is designed to review those basic concepts and also to expand those skills into developing and producing more complex projects. The emphasis of intermediate television production is to combine the basic skills of camera operation and reporting techniques with the introduction of advanced postproduction methods. The end result contains the elements required for planning, writing, and producing advanced projects designed to develop your communication and journalism abilities. Following are step-by-step instructions for setting up equipment.

Camera/Video Deck Systems

Connect the camera to the video deck using the pin connector. Check the following functions on the video deck:

- Tracking. Adjust to record at the optimal position.
- Recording speed. Set the video deck to record at SP speed.
- Battery power. Insert the battery and turn on the power to the deck. Check the battery power on the power indicator. Do not use the battery if it is less than 50 percent charged.

Load your videotape in the video deck. Make sure your tape has a record tab in place. Once your video deck has been checked, turn on power to your video camera. Complete the following camera checks before leaving class for videotaping:

1. Check to make sure camera power is on by looking for an image in the viewfinder. Some cameras may have a "standby" position that may have to be switched to "on" before an image will appear.
2. Check the camera lens for smudges and fingerprints. Use a lens cleaning paper to clean the lens.
3. Check to be sure the camera is switched to the "record" position (not the "play" position), which allows control of the video deck functions through the camera.
4. Adjust the iris and gain positions to "normal."
5. Insert the headphones into the camera and check the camera's internal microphone sound. If you are also planning to use an external microphone, plug it into the microphone jack and check the sound level.

After completing these equipment checks, turn off all power to the video deck and camera.

Camcorder Units

When using a camcorder unit for videotaping, conduct the following equipment checks before leaving the classroom for videotaping:

1. Adjust the tracking to the optimal position.
2. Set the recording speed to SP.
3. Adjust the iris and gain positions to "normal."

4. Insert the battery and check the power level in the viewfinder. Some units have a "display" button that will display the battery power level indicator in the viewfinder. Do not use a battery that is less than 50 percent charged.

5. Inset the videotape. Check to make sure the tape has a record tab in place. Set the camera to the "record" position.

6. Plug in the headset and check the camera sound. If an external microphone is to be used, plug it in the external mic jack and check the sound levels.

Once your equipment checks have been completed, turn off the power to the unit.

Performing these equipment checks before leaving the classroom to videotape eliminates a lot of the problems and mistakes that often occur during videotaping ENG projects and reports. Confidence in the ability to videotape events and activities comes from knowing the equipment is operating effectively. Once engaged in the "heat of battle," excitement and confusion can overcome the best of crews and create problems. Some of these mistakes may be avoided by routinely performing equipment checks as part of the instructional program. Use an equipment checklist (see page I-2-10) before leaving for ENG videotaping. After a while, these checks will become second nature and may be performed quickly and efficiently.

Once the production crew arrives at the taping site, the video camera can be adjusted to the unique environmental conditions existing in that area. The videographer should do the following:

1. White-balance the camera in the lighting conditions in which you will be taping. To manually white-balance a camera, follow this procedure:

    a. Switch to manual white balance.

    b. Hold a white index card approximately 10 to 12 inches in front of the lens.

    c. Press the white balance "set" button.

    d. Hold until the word *white* ceases to flash in the viewfinder.

2. In extremely low or bright light, adjust the gain and iris controls to optimum positions.

3. Switch the camera to manual focus. To manually focus a camera, follow these steps:

    a. Zoom all the way in to the object you are taping.

    b. Turn the focus ring until the object is in focus.

    c. Zoom out to the appropriate framing for your shot.

If either the videographer or subject moves and changes distances, the above procedure will need to be repeated. Manual focusing eliminates the blurring effect that occurs as the autofocus mechanism adjusts the focus when the camera or subject moves. Once you have developed your skills and abilities with the video camera, adding creative camera shots, such as selective focus shots, macro shots, and unique angles, can enhance your final video projects.

Camera Start/Stop Time

Always start recording tape at least 10 seconds before the beginning of your required shot, stand-up, or interview. This is called "getting up to speed" and will eliminate the color bars that appear on the first few seconds of footage as a video camera begins taping from the record/pause mode. This is especially important when taping on a new videotape, or at the beginning of a videocassette, because an editing system will need 3 to 7 seconds to roll back before it can make an edit. Information recorded in the first 3 to 5 seconds will be unavailable for editing purposes. Continue recording 7 to 10 seconds after completing the shot so that the roll back feature of the video deck or camcorder will not cut off the end of the shot as you begin taping your next shot.

Allow the camera to run between takes of a reporter's stand-up or interview. If the reporter makes a mistake, keep the camera recording as he or she resumes the stand-up or interview. If a series of shots is required in a given area, allow the camera to run as you frame, focus, and record each shot. Videotape is very inexpensive, so don't feel like you are wasting tape. If you need a 5-second shot of a student reading a book, record at least a 20- to 30-second shot. Then when you begin editing, you can select the best 5 seconds for your project. If there is going to be an extremely long pause between shots, say 1 or 2 minutes, switch the camera to standby to conserve battery power.

Camera Angles

The best projects usually contain creative and well-framed camera shots. Although a storyboard is helpful for planning your video project, you can't always indicate all possible shots before arriving at your taping destination. For example, your storyboard might indicate a need for a shot of an instructor teaching a class. It is up to the director and videographer to obtain the "best possible shot" for use in the project. In any given situation, there are three possible shots:

1. The obvious shot
2. Another angle shot
3. The unique angle shot

Let's continue our example of the instructor teaching. The *obvious shot* would be to place your camera in the back or side of the classroom facing the instructor. *Another angle shot* could include an over-the-shoulder shot of the instructor to give the viewer a feel for what it's like standing in front of a class of students. The *unique angle shot* could include a camera shot from the point of view of a student sitting at his or her desk listening to the teacher's presentation. To obtain this camera angle, the videographer could sit in the desk and videotape from this position. By using all three of these camera angles in your final project, you can convey the atmosphere and experiences of that classroom to your viewer, which is the ultimate purpose of your project.

The successful videographer needs to capture the scenes as they appear to those involved in the action. Creative camera shots, along with the use of "live sound," enables the viewer to perceive the event as it actually happens.

Postproduction Suggestions

Postproduction is generally the most exciting, and usually the most expensive, part of video production. Although students do not usually have to incur the cost of renting a postproduction facility, their editing time in class is limited by class size and the availability of editing equipment. Reducing the amount of time needed for post-production can save time and resources for your program. The following suggestions for completing video projects can assist in reducing the amount of time needed for postproduction:

1. Use several videotapes for taping raw footage. Tape 1 can be used to tape reporter lead-ins and summaries. Tape 2 can include all of the student and teacher interviews. Tape 3 can be used for all required shots/scenes included on the storyboard. Additional footage can be taped on Tape 4. This technique eliminates a lot of the time spent rewinding and fast-forwarding tapes for the shots needed when editing the final project.

2. Preview footage as soon as possible after videotaping. If additional footage is needed, or there are problems with lighting or sound, it's a lot easier to return that day, or a day or two later, than it is to try and get the shot you need in the middle of postproduction.

3. Label and log the tapes while previewing footage. Know where each tape is located. Rubber-band the tapes to keep them together.

4. Record sound bites, audio-dub music, and titles/graphics before beginning editing. Place all recorded sound on one tape. It is easier to locate each sound bite if it is recorded over a title/graphic identifying the sound.

5. Revise and rewrite the storyboards to include additional footage shot during production before editing.

Many of the ideas and suggestions presented in this lesson will develop into routine skills for completing video projects. Production personnel will systematically develop their skills in camera operation, on-camera experience, and postproduction. For students, the learning process includes organization, routine practice and performance, and many hands-on experiences with equipment. Mistakes and problems always occur when details are overlooked. Spend a few minutes reviewing equipment checks, organizing and logging tapes, discussing camera shots and angles, and developing good videographic skills. These basic concepts will develop into the components needed to consistently produce quality projects in appropriate timeframes.

Review Questions: Lesson 1

1. Why is it important to white-balance your camera before videotaping? [White balancing adjusts the color response of the camera's imaging device according to the lighting conditions of the shot. Videotape colors will not be correct if the camera is not properly white-balanced.]

2. What are the four steps necessary to white-balance your video camera? [1. Switch camera to manual white-balance setting. 2. Hold a white card/paper approximately 10-12 inches in front of the lens. 3. Press the white-balance set button. 4. Hold until the word *white* ceases to flash in the viewfinder.]

3. List some equipment checks that need to be completed for each piece of equipment:
   a. Video deck (list at least 3 items in any order) [tracking set to nominal position; recording speed set at SP speed; check battery power levels]
   b. Video camera (list at least 3 items in any order) [camera is receiving power; check lens for smudges/fingerprints; camera set to record position; iris/gain in normal position; internal microphone sound levels]
   c. Camcorder (list at least 3 items in any order) [tracking is set to nominal position; set recording speed to SP speed; adjust iris and gain to normal positions; check battery power level; check camera microphone for sound levels]

4. Describe a taping situation in which you would use the following camera angles: obvious angle, another angle, and the unique angle. Briefly describe each shot, according to a specific situation.

   Situation: [Student answers will vary for each angle.]

5. Describe three timesaving ideas when videotaping for postproduction. [Use several tapes for recording raw footage. Preview footage as soon as possible after videotaping. Label and log all videotapes.]

6. Fill in the blanks on the following tape log:

Show #	Description	Counter #	Length
1	Black	0:00-0:10	[:10]
2	Assorted School Shots	0:30-2:28	[1:58]
3	Project: From the Teacher's Desk	[Times will vary]	2:52
4	Graphics	5:41-6:02	[:21]
5	News Show	[Times will vary]	3:40

Activities: Lesson 1

1. Place several camera setups around the classroom. Deliberately sabotage each setup by adjusting some of the camera or video deck controls, or both (open iris all the way, set to play mode, adjust tracking, change recording speed). Solve each problem by performing an equipment check.

2. Videotape some scenes around your school with the camera white-balanced and some without white-balancing your camera. Play back the footage in class. Discuss each scene in terms of lighting conditions, color balance, and color hue.

3. Videotape scenes around the campus using the obvious angle, another angle, and unique angle. Play back and discuss the scenes in class. Identify camera angles and compare picture composition and framing.

Lesson 2 Planning and Producing Video Projects

Objectives

After successfully completing this lesson, you will be able to:

- *identify the steps in planning a video project.*
- *complete a project proposal.*
- *complete a storyboard.*
- *write a script.*
- *identify and perform an assemble edit.*
- *identify and perform a video insert edit.*

Vocabulary

Address. A specific location on a videotape as specified by a time code.

Assemble mode. The process of editing videotaped footage with its control track, video track, and audio track in consecutive order.

Audio track. The sound portion of a videotape.

Complexity. The use of editing to intensify the screen action.

Continuity. Preserving the visual coherence and perceived reality of an event.

Control track. The portion of the videotape that records synchronization information essential for editing.

Cutaway shot. Video used to intercut between two shots in order to avoid jump cuts and continuity problems.

Frame. The smallest picture unit on a videotape, 1/30 of a second.

Insert mode. The insertion of video shots or audio information onto an existing recording. Must have a previously recorded control track.

Jogging. The frame-by-frame advancement of a videotape.

Postproduction. Video editing, sound mixing, and the addition of titles and graphics to produce a completed project.

Pulse count. The most common type of address code system used to find exact locations on a videotape. It counts control track pulses and translates them into frames, seconds, minutes, and hours.

Record VCR. The videotape recorder that receives and edits various program segments.

SMPTE time code. An electronic signal recorded on the cue track or audio track of a videotape that provides an address code in frames, seconds, minutes, and hours. Appears on screen.

Sound bite. A videotaped segment in which the video track and audio track must remain in sync.

Source VCR. The videotape recorder that provides the raw footage to be edited in the record VCR.

Storyboard. A paper visualization of a video project that contains video sketches, time allotted for each shot, and the audio information for the project.

Sync roll. A vertical rolling of a video picture caused by a bad edit or loss of synchronization.

Creative and informative video projects don't just happen. They are a result of careful planning and production expertise. The steps for producing video projects begin with the idea and end with the final review of the completed project. All of the steps in the production process are important for producing high-quality video projects. Taking shortcuts in planning, scripting, storyboarding, and production leads to inadequacies in the final project. Each step needs to be completed before moving to the next phase of production. The following basic production steps will assist you in producing video projects:

1. Project orientation. Present and discuss the project information and format.

2. Brainstorming. List and discuss topics and ideas.

3. Identification of project topic. Narrow down ideas to a single topic that is attainable within time, money, and resource constraints.

4. Topic research. Search for available background information on the topic.

5. Storyboard. Assemble storyboard, complete with visual, audio, and time information. Complete script and camera shots.

6. Videotape footage. Record necessary footage needed for project completion.

7. Preview footage. Review footage to ensure that all required information has been recorded. Check for lighting and sound problems. Log and label all tapes. If additional footage is needed, record at this time.

8. Revise storyboards. If needed, revise storyboards to include additional footage that could be included in the final project.

9. Postproduction. Edit video and add additional audio tracks and graphics/titles.

10. Review final project. Critically view the final project in terms of complexity, continuity, and overall appeal. Correct any problems that appear during playback, such as sync rolls, extra frames, or audio glitches.

11. Turn in project for grading.

As you can see, the production process includes not only production activities, but review and critical viewing activities as well. By following these steps and taking the time to critically review and analyze your work, you can produce high-quality video projects that are creative and informative.

Project Planning

After assigning and discussing the overall project concept and format, you should form groups and begin to select topics. Groups can be as small as one or two students, but should not be larger than the required amount of personnel needed to complete all of the jobs necessary to finish the project.

One of the best ways to identify and select your topic is by "brainstorming." This technique involves forming a group and listing topics for possible projects. During this phase, all topics are listed as they are mentioned, with no discussion concerning feasibility or usefulness. Once all of the topic ideas have been listed, the group discusses each topic idea, dismissing those that seem unattainable or unusable. One by one the remaining topics are discussed until the group narrows the topic down to the best choice. Some of the criteria used for topic selection should include:

1. Availability. Topics selected need to be within your ability to obtain adequate video footage and information about those involved in the activity.

2. Feasibility. Equipment, time, and technical expertise must be available to complete the requirements for this project.

3. Compatibility. The project topic must meet the requirements and needs of your school program.

After the group has narrowed their list to one topic, they should submit that topic to the instructor for approval. Groups can meet individually with the instructor to discuss the proposal, explore ideas, and listen to suggestions. Once approved, the project proposal form (figure 1.1) can be used for record keeping and monitoring of group topics.

Storyboarding

Once your topic has been selected, you can begin the storyboarding phase of production. The storyboard will be a "map" for the production crew to follow in producing the project. The visual, audio, and time elements of the storyboard will provide a framework for the production team. A well-planned storyboard reduces production problems, decreases production time, and assists in editing and postproduction.

Scriptwriting is a key element in completing your storyboards. Information and ideas must be condensed into a written script before you can include the video shots in your storyboard. Include all of the important aspects about the topic, but don't overwhelm your viewer with script. Keep the intended audience in mind while you are writing your script. A viewing audience of teenagers is quite different from a PTA audience. Background music and dialogue should be geared toward the norms of the viewing audience. Professional broadcast journalists like to use the *Rule of Three's* in writing their scripts: three sentences of stand-up or lead-in; three sentences of live sound, interviews, or comments; and then three sentences of narration dubbed over footage. This format not only prevents the viewer

Fig. 1.1. Video project proposal form.

VIDEO PROJECT PROPOSAL

Title of Project ______________________________

Brief Description of Video ______________________________

____

____

Production Staff for Project

Names	Jobs
______________	______________
______________	______________
______________	______________
______________	______________
______________	______________

Starting Date of Project ______________________

Estimated Time of Completion ______________________

Approved ______________________

- -

VIDEO PROJECT PROPOSAL

Title of Project ______________________________

Brief Description of Video ______________________________

____

____

Production Staff for Project

Names	Jobs
______________	______________
______________	______________
______________	______________
______________	______________
______________	______________

Starting Date of Project ______________________

Estimated Time of Completion ______________________

Approved ______________________

from being inundated with script, but it increases the complexity of the project along with viewer attention and interest.

Use interviews and comments from the participants involved in the activity. List the questions you are going to ask the participants on the storyboard; obviously you won't be able to write their comments until after you've completed your videotaping. Comments, interviews, and live sound bites convey the energy and atmosphere of the event to your viewers.

Obtaining information about your topic is essential for writing interesting and accurate script. Some of the ways you can obtain this information include:

1. Observing the activity. If possible, visit and observe the activity about which you will be writing. Spend 20 to 30 minutes observing the activity and jotting down notes concerning script and possible camera shots.

2. Preinterviewing. Talk with individuals involved with the project. Discuss ideas and obtain information. (This can be done over the phone.)

3. Researching. Many topics require background information and reliable statistical information. A visit to your school media center or public library can be tremendously helpful.

Obtain as much information as possible about your topic, but really concentrate on the who, what, when, where, why, and how of each activity.

When you begin the video component of your storyboard, remember this basic principle: *Best Video First!* The first few seconds of your project are critical in obtaining viewer interest. Use your creative shots, most interesting live sound bites, or an intriguing opening to draw the viewer's attention. For example, let's say your video topic is "Driver's Education Classes" at your school. Rather than opening your video with a reporter doing a lead-in, you could use a close-up of a hand turning an ignition key in an automobile as the engine roars to life! The viewer is now "behind the wheel" and actively involved in the project. Don't begin every project with a stand-up! Sometimes the sights and sounds of an event create a unique and interesting opening by themselves. Remember: If it's a boring project on paper, it will probably be boring to viewers when they watch it!

Sound is another important aspect of your video project and needs to be included in your storyboard. The excitement and energy of the moment can be captured on tape with sound. For example, the "Football Game" video would not be complete without the cheers of the fans, the sound of the "hits," and the band's fight song. All too often students tend to dub over with their style of music and the viewer loses the sense of hearing the event as well as seeing it on television. Professional broadcast journalists use the actual sound of an event and dub their voice on only one channel. Sound bites are just as important as video shots when producing a video project that conveys the feelings and emotions of any activity.

Storyboards are a guide to producing a video, but they are not etched in stone. Directors, reporters, and videographers need to take advantage of every opportunity to videotape significant footage as it becomes available. If you see a great shot, take it! You can always revise your storyboard after you preview your footage. Look for the best shot, seek out the faces and emotions of the participants, and capture the event with the excitement and energy that exists all around you. That's where the story is, and that's what you'll need to produce the best video!

Editing Video Projects

Editing occurs during the postproduction phase of your television project, after the completion of videotaping and previewing of footage. Some of the reasons editing is routinely used include:

1. Raw footage assembly and rearrangement. Editing is done primarily to combine various shots into a meaningful sequence of events. Reporter lead-ins and summaries, topic activities and events, along with interviews and comments may be shot out of sequence and recorded on separate videotapes, then later edited in order on a master tape for broadcast or duplication.

2. Mistake correction. By editing the videographer can use the best camera shots, reporter comments, and sound/lighting conditions. The editor can select the best take and avoid or cover up unusable footage.

3. Time reduction. Events and activities that last for hours can be edited to a few minutes or seconds of highlights. Using selected camera shots, edited comments, audio sound bites, and some narration, an edited project can convey the atmosphere and excitement of an entire event.

4. Show production. Through the use of editing, an entire show or program can be produced from numerous segments and recorded video footage. Especially in a film-style production, where each scene is recorded by a single camera with numerous takes, editing enables the videographer to select the best take and edit it in sequence to produce a completed video. Titles, graphics, sound effects, narration, and music can all be added in postproduction during the editing process. News shows, documentation, and television magazine shows can be recorded in small segments and then edited together to produce the final program.

Address Code Systems

An address is a specific location on a videotape as specified by a time code. An address code system enables the editor to identify and locate a specific shot on a videotape quickly and accurately. This system is also used when setting each "in-" and "out-" cue during the editing process. The most common form of address code system is the *Pulse Count System.* This system simply counts the pulses on a videotape's control track and translates them into frames, seconds, minutes, and hours. The biggest advantage of the pulse count system is that no special code must be recorded onto the videotape, because the control track is automatically recorded as part of any videotaping. Recording any video footage, even black with a lens cap on the camera, records a control track onto your videotape. Although the pulse count system is not 100-percent frame accurate, it is easy and efficient to use. For most student projects and ENG reporting the pulse count system is very reliable.

Figure 1.2 illustrates a typical pulse count system address code.

Fig. 1.2. Typical pulse count system address code.

Hours	Minutes	Seconds	Frames
1	36	50	28

Figure 1.3 illustrates the typical pulse count system address code after the advancement of two frames.

Fig. 1.3. Typical pulse count system address code after the advancement of two frames.

Hours	Minutes	Seconds	Frames
1	36	51	00

As you can see from the above chart, the additional two frames created another second of video in the seconds cell.

Another address code system used in video production, the *Society of Motion Picture and Television Engineers (SMPTE) Time Code System,* is an electronically produced signal recorded on an address track or additional audio track of a videotape (figure 1.4). This code provides a specific address for each electronic frame, identifying each frame in terms of frames, seconds, minutes, and hours. Some VCRs have a built-in time code generator. However, the SMPTE Time Code can be added to a program during the postproduction process. The SMPTE system is extremely accurate, and is therefore used in most professional videotape and film productions.

Editing Modes

The two types of editing modes are (1) assemble mode and (2) insert mode. Most editing systems contain both modes and allow the editor to select and switch modes as needed.

Fig. 1.4. Society of Motion Picture and Television Engineers (SMPTE) Time Code System.

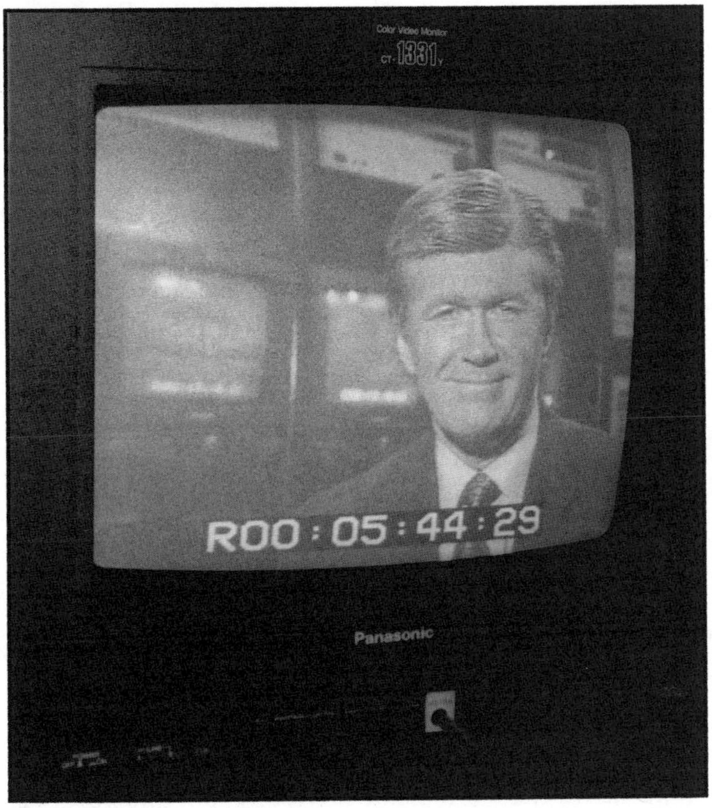

When editing in the assemble mode, each edit transfers the video, audio, and control track from one shot to another. Because the control track from each shot is edited to the control track of the previous shot, the edits must be done in consecutive order (figure 1.5). For example, Shot 1 is edited, then Shot 2, followed by Shot 3, and so forth. Once the shots have been edited, you cannot change or replace a shot in the sequence in the assemble mode. This will cause a break in the control track and leave a huge glitch at the end of the edit. In the assemble mode, the record VCR sometimes will not exactly match the control tracks. When editing in this mode, it is advisable to jog the VCR frame by frame and examine each edit point for sync rolls or glitches. These will appear as a vertical "rolling" of the video picture or a video distortion at the top of the video frame.

Fig. 1.5. Assemble edit mode.

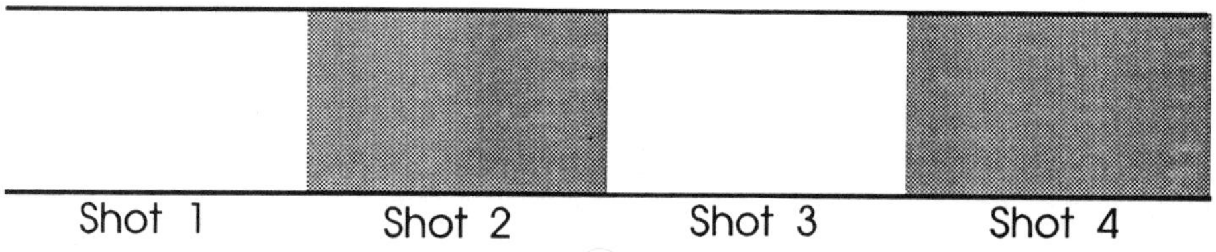

When editing in the insert mode, a control track must first be recorded because each shot will not transfer its control track when edited. The control track must be at least as long as the completed video project is expected to be upon completion. *Never* underestimate; instead, allow several extra minutes for security. A control track can be established by:

1. Placing a lens cap on a camera and recording black on your videotape. You can also manually close the iris and record black. Remember to unplug or bypass your camera microphone or you will have background sound on your control track.

2. Recording black on your tape in a VCR, using a switcher or character generator to create a black screen. If no signal is input into your VCR, a control track will not be recorded.

3. Assembling editing black from a previously recorded videotape onto your videotape. Most edit stations and production studios have tapes of black specifically made for this.

The insert edit mode enables the editor to selectively edit the video, audio, or any combination of the two for any camera shot. For example, if we were to edit a shot of a drummer in the band using the insert edit mode, we would be able to edit in any one of the following ways:

- the video of the drummer and no audio
- the video of the drummer and channel 1 audio
- the video of the drummer and channel 2 audio
- the video of the drummer and channels 1 and 2 audio
- the audio from channel 1 (no video)
- the audio from channel 2 (no video)
- the audio from channels 1 and 2 (no video)

In terms of the production process, the insert mode has many more postproduction applications. Via split-line editing, audio and video channels can be used and reserved as needed. Sound effects, audio narration and music dubs, and video inserts can all be used and edited with accuracy in the insert edit mode.

Another advantage of the insert mode is the ability to edit shots in random order, or to go back and change a shot after the editing is completed. Because you are not editing a control track, you can rearrange or substitute shots without causing a glitch on your videotape.

Video inserting is also used to enable the viewer to see as well as hear what a reporter or interviewee is discussing. For example, let's look at how a video insert could be used during an interview project (figure 1.6).

Fig. 1.6. Insert edit mode.

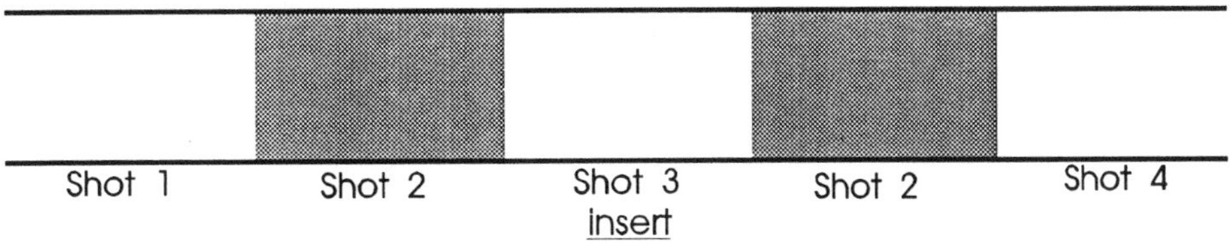

In this example we are interviewing a drama teacher about a school presentation of the play *Grease.* Shot 1 is a stand-up of a reporter in front of the stage as the actors are rehearsing the play. Shot 2 is a "talking head" of the drama instructor describing the play, its actors, and exciting scenes. During the instructor's comments, a video insert (Shot 3) of a scene from the play is inserted over the instructor's voice. The viewer will continue to hear the audio of the instructor, but will now be watching the play. The audio remains intact during this insert because you have selected to edit only a video insert. If you wanted to see and hear the play as well as the comments of the instructor, you could edit video and audio channel 1 (or 2). If you adjust the audio input on channel 1 on the record VCR, you can balance both the sound of the instructor and the sound from the play! The viewer will then hear the teacher, as well as see and hear the play. The overall effect will enhance viewer interest as well as convey the information about the performers.

As you become more and more experienced with your editing system, you can take advantage of the opportunities available when editing in the insert mode.

Editing Systems

Editing systems vary in their sophistication and complexity, depending upon the manufacturer, model number, and the amount of peripheral equipment connected to the editing system (figure 1.7).

Fig. 1.7. Editing system.

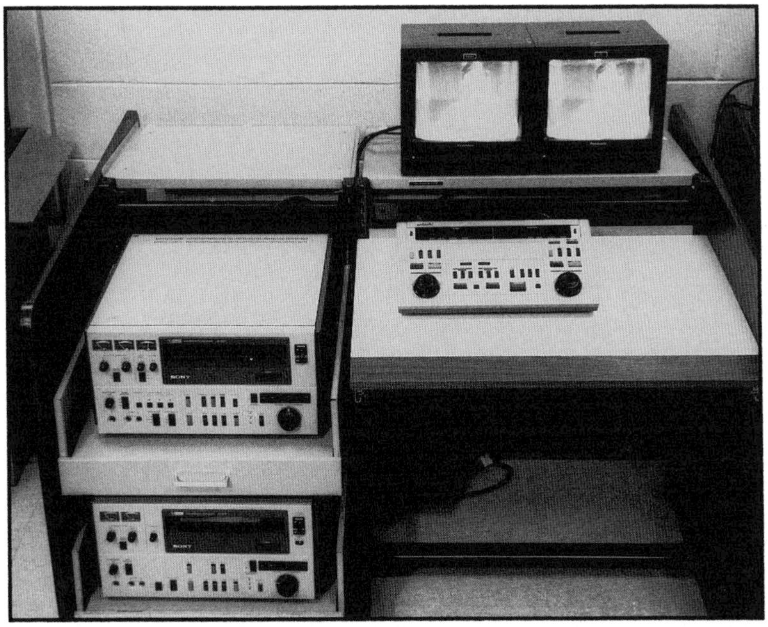

Most editing systems contain the following pieces of equipment:

- Source VCR. Supplies the raw footage to be edited in the record VCR.
- Record VCR. Receives and edits various program segments.
- Source monitor. Displays video footage from the source VCR.
- Record (program) monitor. Displays footage as it is edited and played back in the record VCR.
- Edit remote controller. Controls the operation of the source and record VCRs, as well as programming edit cues. Also called an ECU (editing control unit).

Additional equipment may be added to a basic editing system to create special effects, add titles/graphics, or monitor sound more effectively (audio components).

Editing Techniques

1. Make sure all tapes are appropriately labeled.
2. Locate the record VCR. Place the tape that the footage will be edited onto into this VCR.
3. Edit a control track onto your master tape. Remember: You cannot edit on a blank tape! Even using the assemble edit mode, your first piece of video must have a control track to be edited onto your master tape. Before beginning editing, record a 20- to 30-second black leader onto the master tape. If you are going to use the insert edit mode, record enough black to edit the entire finished video.
4. Identify the source VCR. This is where the tape containing the raw footage is loaded.
5. Before editing, check the following functions on the record VCR to make sure they are set appropriately:

    a. Audio levels—adjust input to desired level.

    b. Tracking—set to optimal position.

    c. Dolby—On/Off?

    d. Counter—reset to 0:00:00.

6. Select the edit mode (assemble, insert) to be used to begin editing the video project.
7. Review your storyboards! These can assist in the editing process by providing a guide to follow.
8. Cue the source VCR to the first "in-" cue (where the first edit is to begin). Jog the record VCR to the first edit point. Set the "in-" cues for the source and record VCRs. Next, jog the source VCR to the "out-" cue (where the first segment will end) and set the "out-" cue. The edit can be previewed by pressing the "preview" function on the edit remote control. This enables you to see how the edit will look before the edit is actually performed. Watch the record monitor carefully to view the previewed edit. Once the preview has been completed, the VCRs will return to their original positions. All "in-" and "out-" cues will remain set. If the edit appears satisfactory, press the "edit" function on the remote controller and the edit you previewed will be completed.

9. Continue this process until the video project has been completed. It is not necessary to preview all the edits, but those where timing and intricate video/sound editing are critical should always be previewed.

Reviewing the Edited Material

Once the project has been completely edited, it is essential to critically review the project in its entirety. Rewind the record VCR to the beginning of the project and play it uninterrupted. Carefully screen the project for deficiencies in the following areas:

1. Sync rolls and glitches. These can occur at the edit points of each edited sequence. A slight vertical picture "roll" or video picture distortion at the top of the video frames will appear if there is a problem. These flaws can be corrected by using video/audio inserts over the sync rolls. If a control track has been broken (due to incorrectly using the assemble edit mode to insert a video or audio segment), a huge glitch will appear at the end of the edit. Unfortunately there is no way to repair this, and the project will have to be reedited from that point to the end of the project.

2. Complexity. The completed video may lack the intensity it needs to keep viewer interest and attention. (It's boring!) This could be the result of long, uninteresting camera shots, too many talking heads, an overabundance of script, or simply a lack of creativity in approaching the topic. Revitalize the video, if possible, by using shorter and more creative camera shots, adding some video inserts to your talking heads, and blending in some live sound to re-create the excitement of the event. Or look for another way to introduce or summarize your topic.

3. Continuity. Problems with continuity—the visual coherence of the overall video project—can occur as jump cuts, a series of unreal events that could not happen that way in real life, wardrobe and makeup inconsistencies, or simply a matter of timing. Jump cuts occur when two nearly identical scenes are edited together and the characters in the scene appear to jump from one position to another. For example, a teacher is writing on an overhead in one scene; immediately following is a scene in which he is standing by the overhead asking a question of the class. As the viewer watches the edited scenes, the teacher will appear to jump instantly from one position to another. This is commonly referred to as a jump cut edit. To avoid this, a cutaway shot must be edited between the two scenes of the teacher. A proper cutaway shot for this scene could include:

   a. A student taking notes.

   b. A macro shot of the teacher's hand writing on the transparency.

   c. A shot of the overhead screen displayed in class.

   By editing one of these shots in between the teacher shots, a jump cut edit can be avoided.

   Continuity problems can also result when projects are videotaped over a series of days or weeks. Reporters and actors need to be consistent with clothing, hairstyles, makeup, and even their demeanor and intensity of emotions. This is especially true when taping "film-style." Each scene must appear as if it were recorded at the same time.

   Timing the edits so that an action continues from one shot to another also helps to preserve the continuity of the project. Preview edits so that actions occur naturally and avoid pauses as characters enter/leave camera angles.

   Sound is another critical factor in maintaining continuity. Background, or ambient, sound creates an environment in which an event takes place. Avoid editing scenes in which the background sound abruptly changes (music, voices, environmental sounds) or ceases unrealistically. Never try to match a person's voice and lips by editing first the video and then adding the sound. This routinely produces the "B-grade monster flick" style of sound track where the lips are rarely synchronized with the sound!

4. Sound. Maintaining consistent sound levels throughout the video project, especially when a variety of sound sources (camera mics, external mics, audio dubs) are used can be a problem. By carefully examining and adjusting the audio input levels each time an edit is made, discrepancies in sound volume can be avoided. Establish the base sound level by monitoring your live sound, such as reporter lead-ins, interviews, and live sound bites. Adjust the input levels on the record VCR so that each edit's sound matches the previous sound levels. When adding an audio dub, adjust the sound input to match the edited sound already existing on your videotape. Carefully examining and balancing sound levels is just as critical as previewing the video edits.

5. Ethics. Is the video an unbiased and accurate presentation of the facts and a realistic portrayal of the event or activity? Avoid editing only those shots and comments that present one side of an issue. Never create or stage a scene simply to produce an exciting video. There is enough excitement, energy, and drama in any event to produce an interesting video project. It is the production team's responsibility to capture the emotion of an event, not to simulate it through actors and set-up situations. Viewers, classmates, teachers, parents, and administrators expect truthful, responsible, and accurate reporting. Trust is important in video production, just as it is in life in general. Use good judgment at all times.

Editing is one of the most enjoyable phases of production. Creating an interesting and informative video project from a collection of raw footage is an exhilarating and enriching experience. Watching a completed project after many painstaking hours of production can certainly be rewarding and satisfying. The editor, much like an artist, takes a blank videotape and creates a video with his or her own unique style and character. Developing editing skills and techniques is a continuous, lifelong process. Critically watch other videos, movies, and television programs to pick up new techniques and ideas. Work with a variety of people to expose yourself to new ideas and concepts. Explore, experiment, and extend your editing skills to develop videos that are informative, accurate, and interesting.

Review Questions: Lesson 2

1. Match the following terms to the descriptions in a through j below:

Continuity	Storyboard	Complexity
Jogging	Control track	Address
Frame	Sync roll	Audio track
SMPTE code	Pulse count	Cutaway shot

a. Used to intercut between two camera shots to avoid a jump cut edit. [Cutaway shot]

b. The smallest picture unit on videotape, 1/30th of a second. [Frame]

c. The two most common forms of address code systems. [SMPTE code] [Pulse count]

d. A frame-by-frame advancement of a videotape. [Jogging]

e. The portion of the videotape that contains the synchronization information essential for editing. [Control track]

f. A vertical rolling of a picture caused by a bad edit or a loss of synchronization. [Sync roll]

g. A specific location in a television recording as specified by a time code. [Address]

h. The portion of the videotape containing sound information. [Audio track]

i. The visual coherence or perceived "reality" of a project. [Continuity]

j. Intensifying the screen action through editing. [Complexity]

(Review questions continue on page II-1-22.)

2. Place the following production steps in sequence.

Videotape footage	[6]
Project orientation	[1]
Topic research	[4]
Preview footage	[7]
Identify topic	[3]
Brainstorming	[2]
Review project	[10]
Revise storyboard	[8]
Postproduction	[9]
Storyboard	[5]

3. Describe three ways you can obtain information about a topic.
   a. Observing the activity—[Visit and observe the activity about which you will be writing.]
   b. Interviews—[Talk with individuals involved in the activity. Take notes about important details.]
   c. Research—[Obtain background information and statistics from reliable sources.]
4. Identify the following statements as indicative of either assemble editing or insert editing.
   a. Segments must be edited in consecutive order. [Assemble editing]
   b. Transfers its own control track. [Assemble editing]
   c. Must have a previously recorded control track. [Insert editing]
   d. Transfers video and audio with each edit. [Assemble editing]
   e. Allows you to select to edit the video track, audio track, or a combination of the two. [Insert editing]
   f. Shots can be edited in random sequence. [Insert editing]
   g. Used to edit video shots over a preexisting audio track. [Insert editing]

5. Complete the following address code:

Hours	Minutes	Seconds	Frames
1	32	46	27

Advance: 2 minutes, 23 seconds, 8 frames

Hours	Minutes	Seconds	Frames
[1]	[35]	[10]	5

6. Describe three problems associated with complexity. Answers should include:
   a. [Long uninteresting camera shots]
   b. [Too many "talking heads" or interviews]
   c. [Overabundance of script]
   d. [Lack of creativity in approaching the topic]
7. Describe three problems associated with continuity.
   a. [Jump cuts in editing phase]
   b. [Series of unreal events]
   c. [Wardrobe and makeup inconsistencies]
   Also: [Timing between shots/scenes]

Activities: Lesson 2

1. Bring one of your favorite video movies to class. Watch 1 minute of a portion of the tape and count the number of edits you observe during that scene. How does this affect the complexity of the scene?

2. The rule "Best Video First" is a standard in the industry to create viewer interest in a journalist's report. List an interesting camera shot or creative opening for each of the following topics:
   a. A baseball game—
   b. An orchestra class—
   c. A ceramics class—
   d. A track meet—
   e. Student elections—
   f. Driver's education class—
   g. Lunchroom report—

3. Sound is just as important as video in conveying the atmosphere and excitement of an event. Record scenes around the school with the lens cap on the camera. Play these back in class and let classmates guess what activities are taking place.

4. Record a local television news report about a community topic. Replay it in class and discuss the following topics:
   a. How is the topic introduced?
   b. How is "live" sound used in the project?
   c. How does the reporter "format" the report? Does he or she use the "Rule of Three's"?
   d. What is the most interesting camera shot during the video? Where does it occur in the report?
   e. How is the report summarized?

5. Deliberately "break" the control track of a video segment by assemble editing another piece of video in the middle of it. Answer the following:
   a. Describe the glitch.
   b. Where does the glitch occur during the edit?
   c. What happens to the segment of video immediately following the glitch?
   d. Replay the segment and observe the counter numbers as the video rolls through the glitch. What did you observe?

Student Project Plan: From the Teacher's Desk

DESCRIPTION OF COMPLETED PROJECT

A 1- to 2½-minute video describing a program or class offered at school. The project will be worth 100 points.

FORMAT

Each project must contain the following:

1. An establishing shot (stand-up or narrated over footage).
2. Classroom footage with voice-over (music or live sound background).
3. Interviews with or comments from students or instructors, or both.
4. A closing (narrated over footage or stand-up).

PRODUCTION TEAM

Director/Writer ______________________________

Reporter/Narrator ______________________________

Camera/Editor ______________________________

METHOD OF PRODUCTION

1. Pick a topic, choose a team, and designate jobs.
2. Introduce the team to the instructor, research the topic, and set up observation times.
3. Observe a class or classes. Note suggested shots and questions.
4. Complete the script and storyboard.
5. Set up videotaping dates and times. Record the footage.
6. Preview and evaluate the footage according to one of the following:
    a. Satisfactory. Log the tapes and revise the storyboard, as needed.
    b. Unsatisfactory. Reshoot the video.
7. Edit the tape and complete postproduction tasks.
8. Review the final project, revise as needed, and turn it in for grading.

EVALUATION

Content	25 points
Camera work	25 points
Audio	25 points
Editing	25 points

Evaluation Sheet: From the Teacher's Desk

PRODUCTION TEAM

Director/Writer ______________________________

Reporter/Narrator ______________________________

Camera/Editor ______________________________

TOPIC

Class/Program ______________________________

Instructor ______________________________

EVALUATION

1. Content: Adequate and accurate information about the class, defined skills and class outcomes, syntax, and vocabulary.

   ___________ out of 25 points

2. Camera work: Camera shots are white-balanced. Shots are focused and show a use of quality camera angles.

   ___________ out of 25 points

3. Audio: Audio levels are consistent and balanced. Music is used appropriately and enunciation is clear.

   ___________ out of 25 points

4. Editing: Editing is precise (no sync rolls, glitches) and includes the following: a 20-second black leader and tag, complexity, and continuity.

   ___________ out of 25 points

Total points ___________

Teacher's comments:

Lesson 3 Audio Techniques for Television Production

Objectives

After successfully completing this lesson, you will be able to:

- *use audio insert editing to produce sound tracks for video projects.*
- *edit sound effects in video projects.*
- *complete a tape log.*
- *perform split-line editing.*
- *edit music sound tracks on video projects.*

Vocabulary

Audio insert. Use of an editing system to insert audio onto a prerecorded control track.

Audio dub. Adding additional sound to a prerecorded videotape.

Distortion. An unnatural deterioration of sound.

Potentiometer. Sometimes referred to as a "pot." Also, a dial that controls the sound level.

Sound bite. Videotaped segments in which the sound and video must remain intact, such as an interview or reporter stand-up.

Split-line editing. Editing the video or audio tracks independently using the insert editing mode.

Volume unit meter. An analog or LED instrument that measures input and output sound level intensity.

The use and control of audio in television production is just as critical to the development of the overall project as the video component. Viewers not only see a video, but they also listen to obtain information and concepts. Sound tracks are used to reinforce the visual images, disseminate information, and convey the atmosphere or mood of a particular scene. The reporter's stand-ups and narratives, participant comments and interviews, and background sound communicate the information and emotions of an activity to the viewer. Even silent movies weren't really silent, but used a musical score to create an "atmosphere" for the screen action. Effectively using and controlling the audio portions of a video project can enhance the effectiveness of the video and increase viewer attention and understanding.

The ability to produce consistently balanced sound tracks is essential in producing videos. It is very distracting to the viewer to have the sound volume increase and decrease throughout the video, even to the point where the volume must be turned up or down on the monitor. The following techniques will assist you in controlling the volume of edited video segments, as well as developing audio sound tracks for your video projects.

Identifying the Sound Volume: VU Meters

Unless the sound inputs are adjusted and controlled during videotaping by using an audio mixer (most projects aren't), the sound levels for recorded segments will vary from scene to scene. This is especially true when recording a variety of sound sources, such as reporter narratives, sound bites, participant interviews and comments, and reporter stand-ups. More than likely each of these sound elements will vary in intensity (volume). This is even more likely if different microphones are used to record each segment (e.g., lavaliere, shotgun, and camera internal microphone).

The first step in balancing the sound levels is to identify the volume level of each recorded segment on the videotape. This can be done while previewing the raw footage prior to editing. As each segment is added to the tape log (see page II-1-37), write down the volume level of the recorded sound, obtained by carefully watching the VU meter on the VCR (figure 1.8). The meter readings can be written down as a percentage (0-100%) or as a volume unit (-7-0) measured in decibels. This will identify which sound recordings need to be "trimmed" up or down during editing. A typical tape log is shown in figure 1.9.

Fig. 1.8. VU meter settings.

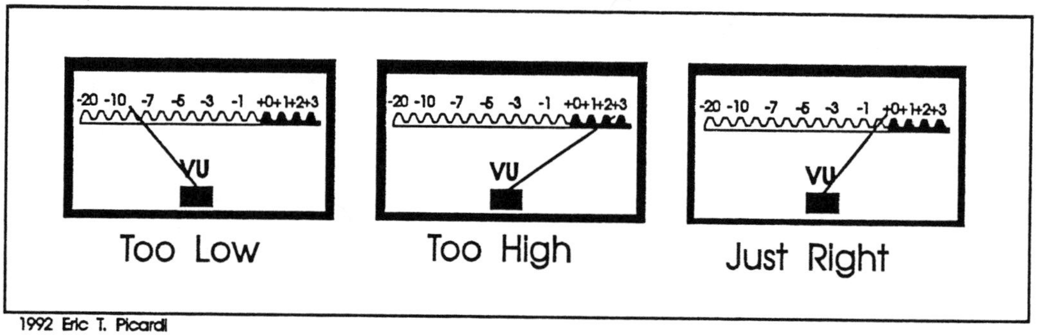

1992 Eric T. Picardi

Fig. 1.9. Typical tape log.

Video/Audio	Tape Counter #	Length
1. Reporter lead-ins (80%) VU	0:00 - 2:10	2:10
2. Shots of electronics class SOT (60%) VU	2:10 - 4:35	2:25
3. Interview—teacher (60%) VU	4:35 - 7:10	2:35
4. Reporter narration (80%) VU	7:10 - 10:20	3:10
5. Interview—student (80%) VU	10:20 - 11:40	1:20

From the above tape log, it is obvious that most of the sound is recorded at the 80% sound level. When editing the final project, the sound portion of the tape recorded at 60% levels should be increased, or "trimmed" up as it is edited onto the master tape.

Controlling the Sound Volume

Adjusting the volume of recorded videotape can be accomplished during the editing phase of postproduction. The level, or intensity, of the sound inputs can be adjusted using the potentiometer ("pot") on the record VCR as each edit is performed. Generally, there is a pot for each audio channel. An adjustment to these pots can be used to increase or decrease the sound as it is edited from the source VCR to the record VCR. The ability to "boost" sound is limited though, and cannot be used to create sound that is not there due to a videotaping problem. The pot can be used to completely eliminate sound from one or two channels during the editing process simply by turning the input level to 0%. The process of controlling sound input during editing is relatively simple:

1. Load the tapes in the appropriate VCRs. Set the "in-" and "out-" cues for the first edit.
2. Adjust the audio-input pots on the record VCR (increase/decrease recorded sound).
3. Preview the edit and note the sound level on the record VCR's VU meter.
    a. If sound levels are correctly adjusted, perform the edit.
    b. If sound levels need further correction, readjust the input pots and continue to preview and adjust until correct.
4. Continue this routine for each edit.

This process can effectively produce a consistent sound recording for every video project. Minor adjustments to sound levels made during the editing process can eliminate sound volume problems that occur during playback.

Controlling Sound Characteristics

Just as every person has a unique timbre or voice characteristic, so does each style of microphone and audio mixer. Sound recorded with a lavaliere microphone during an ENG report will be distinctly different than sound recorded using a unidirectional microphone in the postproduction studio. For some video projects, maintaining a consistent sound quality or ambience is essential in preserving the continuity of the video project. Movies, for example, need to maintain consistent sound characteristics to ensure the reality of the scene for the viewer. Sound effects, voice-overs, and even dialogue must remain consistent in tone and volume throughout the entire movie. Otherwise, the viewer will be able to differentiate between what is real and what has been contrived in the studio. The same can be said for ENG reports and "live at the scene" projects. All too often the audio-dubbed portion of the videotape is distinctly different in tone, volume, or intensity from the rest of the project. Some of the ways to eliminate these sound differences include:

1. Microphones. Use the same microphone throughout the project. If a lavaliere mic is used for reporter stand-ups, use that same mic to record participant comments.
2. Narration. Rather than doing the reporter narration in the studio during postproduction, record it "live" at the scene. Simply bring a copy of the script/storyboard to the scene and record it on camera using the microphone already available. Now the reporter's narration,

when edited into the final project, will have the same tone or character as the rest of the project.

3. Background sound. Try to use as much of the real sound as possible when producing the video project. Recorded "live sound" can add authenticity and realism to the completed video by conveying more of the atmosphere surrounding the activity to the viewer. For example, a project featuring the school chorus should include a few songs or musical selections in the audio portion of the tape. A school basketball project would not be complete without the cheers of the crowd, the squeak of shoes on the gym floor, or even the swish of the net on a three-point shot. Adding the naturally occurring sound of an activity heightens the experience for the viewer.

Synchronizing Audio and Video

Getting the audio track to exactly match or synchronize with the video track can be accomplished by editing the sound track rather than dubbing the sound. An edited sound track can be as precise as 1/30th of a second! Editing the audio and video tracks independently is commonly referred to as *split-line editing.* Since split-line editing uses the insert mode, a control track should be recorded prior to editing the video and audio tracks.

The following example illustrates how insert editing can be used to synchronize the audio and video components: The narration states that "Ceramics students are eagerly preparing for next week's art festival. Students are busy molding clay, shaping pots and bowls on the potter's wheel, glazing and baking their creations in the kiln, and finally preparing them for display."

The editor's task is to position each video shot so that it exactly coincides with the audio narration. The viewers see the shot as they hear the descriptive audio. The following steps will illustrate how this task can be accomplished using split-line editing:

1. Record a control track on the master tape long enough to edit the entire project. Allow at least 1 minute of additional time.

2. Audio track. Switch the edit system to the insert mode. Select to edit audio channels 1 and 2. Leave video input off. Place the tape containing the recorded audio track (script) in the source VCR and the master tape in the record VCR. Set the "in-" and "out-" cues for the source VCR (at the start and end of the narration), and set the "in-" cue on the record VCR approximately 15 seconds into the prerecorded control track. Preview the edit and note the sound levels on the record VCR's VU meters. Adjust if needed, then perform the edit.

3. Video track. Switch the edit system so that the audio channels are "off" and the video input is "on." Place the videotape containing the selected camera shots in the source VCR. Now the video edits can be matched with the corresponding audio. By playing the record VCR, the editor can first listen to the audio track and use the sound to set the "in-" and "out-" cues for the video edits. For example:

   Audio—"Ceramics students are eagerly preparing for next week's art festival."

   Video—Shots of students placing pots on shelves, handling clay.

   Audio—"Students are busy molding clay ..."

   Video—Over-the-shoulder shot of hands molding clay.

   Audio—"shaping pots and bowls on the potter's wheel ..."

   Video—Shot of student "throwing" pot on the wheel.

Audio—"glazing and baking their creations in the kiln ..."

Video—Shots of students glazing pots, placing in kiln.

Audio—"and finally preparing them for display."

Video—Students printing display cards, students standing next to and admiring finished pots.

Using split-line editing to create this finished project will enable the viewers to see each shot as they hear the audio information. There are no silent pauses between shots or extended periods of silence, as in the case where the script is audio-dubbed after the editing process is finished. Split-line editing eliminates the "read faster" syndrome where there is too much script for the edited video footage, or the need for background music to fill in the empty spaces where there is not enough script to cover the edited footage. Split-line editing increases visual and audio continuity, as well as presenting concise information to the viewer.

Editing Sound Effects

The ability to blend sound effects with a previously recorded sound track is extremely useful in producing creative and entertaining videos. The ambience of a scene can be enhanced with the use of sound effects. For example, consider a scene in which three characters are sitting around a campfire in the middle of the woods discussing the day's exciting events. To really create the atmosphere of "a night in the deep, dark woods," some sound effects (crickets and frogs chirping, an owl hooting, and the crackling of the fire) are necessary. By adding these sounds in postproduction, viewers can truly feel as if they are watching the scene take place outdoors at night. The authenticity of the scene is enhanced by the audio track. Retaining the original dialogue and adding the sound effects can easily be accomplished by the following process:

1. Record the selected sound effects on videotape. If several sounds need to be heard at the same time, mix them on an audiotape before transferring them to videotape. Note: It can often be difficult to locate sounds and sound effects on a black videotape. Try recording graphics that list the sounds at the same time the sound effect is recorded. That way the editor can see the effect at the same time he hears the effect. Make sure the tape is rolling at least 15 seconds before recording the sound effect to eliminate unwanted color bars or control track problems.

2. Place the tape containing the sound effects in the source VCR. Select the insert edit mode on the editing system. Use one of the audio channels (channel 1 or channel 2) to add the sound effects. Remember: Whatever sound was recorded on this channel will be erased as the sound effect is added! Place the master tape in the record VCR.

3. Set the "in-" and "out-" cues on the record VCR (where the sound effect is to begin and end). Set the "in-" cue on the source VCR at the beginning of the sound effect. Preview the edit, and carefully monitor the placement and volume level of the sound effect. Adjust the audio input pot to increase or decrease sound volume, and the "in-" and "out-" cues for sound placement. Continue to preview the edit until all adjustments have been made, then perform the edit. Replay the scene in its entirety to ensure correct sound placement and volume.

Some videotaped scenes are edited so they fade in or fade out at the conclusion of each scene. In this case, the sound effects should also fade with the video. This can be accomplished by slowly turning the audio input pot on the record VCR while the sound is being edited to fade the sound with the video.

Editing sound effects can also be a lot of fun, and they can be used to create some very entertaining videos! The addition of a few honks, bells, crashes, and whistles can create great blooper videos from school sporting events.

Patience is the key when performing sound effects editing. Timing these edits so they coincide with the video action is essential. Preview each edit to check the placement and volume of the sound effect. A minor time difference in the sound and video portions of the picture will easily be detected by the viewer, and the effect will lose its desired impact.

Music Sound Tracks

Music is frequently used in movies and video presentations to create a mood for a scene. After all, can you imagine a scary, suspense scene in a movie without the "thrill" music to coincide with the scene. Music sound tracks for films have become best-sellers at music stores around the country. Movie viewers can relive the scenes in the movie as they listen to the sound track at home.

Music sound tracks are also used to eliminate some awkward pauses in script and character dialogue. A scene that continues for longer than a few seconds without some type of audio appears boring and uninteresting to the viewer. Music sound tracks are used to carry the action from scene to scene.

Music sound tracks can be edited easily on the master tape using the audio-insert mode of the editing system. Select either audio channel 1 or channel 2 for the musical sound track. The process is identical to that of editing sound effects, except that the music sound track is generally longer in length and may last an entire scene or video presentation. Some suggestions include:

1. Record the sound track on a videotape using graphics to identify the music title and length.

2. Adjust the audio-input pot on the record VCR so that the music volume does not overpower the dialogue or naturally occurring sound on the remaining audio channel. Preview the edits and monitor the sound carefully (using headphones) so that sound placement and volume are correct before performing each edit.

3. If the scene fades in and out, so should the music sound track.

4. Review each scene carefully before going on to edit the next scene.

The use of music sound tracks and the ability to edit them into scenes will enhance the impact of the video on the viewer. Be sure the music selections establish the right mood for each scene and assist the actors in conveying this feeling to the viewer.

Editing sound tracks, sound effects, and reporter narration creates a precise and accurate process for creating sound tracks in television production. Sounds can be accurately positioned (within 1/30th of a second) and edited, rather than audio-dubbed. Using the editing system for audio postproduction enables the production team to accurately position the sound to coincide with the video, control the volume level of the edited sound, and carefully monitor the sound as it is being edited.

Review Questions: Lesson 3

1. How is a VU meter used during editing? [The VU meter indicates relative sound volume. By observing the position of the VU meter during editing, the editor can make minor adjustments to sound levels during the editing process.]
2. List one technique for preserving sound continuity for each of the following:
   a. Microphones— [Use the same microphone throughout the project.]
   b. Reporter narration— [Record narration live at the scene using ENG camera and microphone.]
   c. Background sounds— [Use background sounds recorded at the scene to add authenticity and realism to the project.]
3. What is split-line editing? [Split-line editing is editing the sound and video portions of the tape independently.]
4. How can you use split-line editing to synchronize sound and video? [First edit the sound or narration track, then video-insert the images to match the script.]

(Review questions continue on page II-1-34.)

5. List some possible sound effects for each of these scenes:
    a. Fishing on a lake— [Responses will vary for each scene.]
    b. Stock car races—
    c. Neighborhood playground—
    d. Football game—
6. List three reasons for adding a music sound track to a movie scene.

    Student answers should include:

    [1. Creates a mood.

    2. Eliminates awkward pauses in script and character dialogue.

    3. Enhances the effect of the movie on the viewer.]

Activities: Lesson 3

1. Videotape three scenes around the campus without recording sound. Use the editing system to add a music sound track to each scene.

2. Videotape a classmate clapping hands without recording the sound. Record the sound of hands clapping using a cassette recorder. Try to edit the sound of hands clapping on the original footage.

3. Bring one of your favorite video movies to class that uses music to enhance a scene. Play it in class and discuss the following:

   a. Did the dialogue continue with the addition of the music?

   b. What feelings did the producer try to elicit with the music?

   c. Do you think the music was effectively used at this time?

Student Project Plan: Students' Choice

DESCRIPTION OF COMPLETED PROJECT

The student(s) will choose and develop their own topic for a video project. The project is worth 100 points.

METHOD OF PRODUCTION

1. Choose a topic for a video project. Submit the topic to your instructor for approval.
2. Form a production team (if needed).
3. Complete the storyboards for the project.
4. Sign up for videotaping dates.
5. Videotape required footage. Preview footage and complete tape logs (see figure 1.10).
6. Sign up for editing dates. Edit and complete postproduction. Review finished project.
7. Turn in completed project and evaluation sheet.

EVALUATION

Content	25 points
Audio	25 points
Camera	25 points
Editing	25 points

Fig. 1.10. Tape log.

Show #	LOG SHEET Description	Counter #	Length
1			
2			
3			
4			
5			
6			
7			
8			
9			
10			
11			
12			
13			
14			
15			
16			
17			
18			

Video Project Evaluation Sheet: Students' Choice

PROJECT TITLE ______________________________

Length (Time) ____________

Purpose of project ______________________________

____

Production Staff

Names	Jobs
____________	____________
____________	____________
____________	____________

EVALUATION

1. Content: Information about topic is adequate, accurate, and detailed.

   (25) ____________

2. Audio: Features natural sound, adequate audio levels for music/narration, smooth transitions, and appropriate music for audio dub.

   (25) ____________

3. Camera: Video has good quality of shots, uses continuity and complexity, contains smooth pans, and steady shots that are focused and white-balanced.

   (25) ____________

4. Editing: Video contains clean edit points, good use of inserts, effective length of shots, black leader and tag, and is of a good overall length.

   (25) ____________

Total points ____________

Teacher's comments on overall project:

Student Project Plan: Music Video

DESCRIPTION OF COMPLETED PROJECT

The students will use video insert editing to produce a music video. The project is worth 100 points.

METHOD OF PRODUCTION

1. Record a control track on the master tape approximately 4 minutes in length.
2. Submit the selected topic and music for approval.
3. Complete storyboards.
4. Videotape footage (if needed).
5. Audio-insert or audio-dub a 1- to 2-minute music selection on the recorded control track. (Start the music selection at least 15 seconds into the control track, and fade the music out at the appropriate time.)
6. Video-insert images correlating to the beat and/or the message of the music.
7. Edit graphics on the end of the music video. Graphics *must* include:
   a. Name of performing artist(s).
   b. Title of song.
   c. Production team members/jobs.

   Graphics should fade out simultaneously with music.
8. Be sure to leave at least a 15-second leader and end tag of black.
9. Review completed project. Turn it in with the evaluation sheet for grading.

EVALUATION

Content	25 points
Graphics	25 points
Editing	25 points
Camera work	25 points

Evaluation Sheet: Music Video

PRODUCTION STAFF

Names	Jobs
____________________	____________________
____________________	____________________
____________________	____________________

Song title ____________________

Performing artist ____________________

GRADING

1. Content: Video depicts mood/message and/or beat of the music.

   (25) ______________

2. Graphics: Video includes name of artist, song title, production team members, names are spelled correctly; contrast and aspect ratio are good.

   (25) ______________

3. Editing: Contains complexity; avoid sync rolls, glitches, extra frames, and black frames. Edit to the beat and/or message.

   (25) ______________

4. Camera: Shots are white-balanced, focused, and stable; good picture composition.

   (25) ______________

Total points ______________

Teacher's comments:

Lesson 4 Electronic Graphics for Television Production

Objectives

After successfully completing this lesson, you will be able to:

- *identify the purpose of television graphics.*
- *identify elements of readability for television graphics.*
- *list functions found on character generators.*
- *compose graphics for television production.*

Vocabulary

Aspect ratio. Refers to the proportions of the television screen, for example, three units high, four units wide.

Character generator (CG). An electronic device that creates typed letters and displays them on a video screen for use and recording.

Crawl. The horizontal (left/right) movement of graphics across the video screen.

Digital store system. An electronic device that can use a single frame of video stored in digital form on a disk.

Keying. Electronically "cutting" letters into a background image.

Roll. A vertical movement of graphics (up/down) on a video screen.

Electronically produced television graphics are used in almost every type of television program today: network shows, commercials, news shows, religious programming, documentaries, and music videos, to name a few. They appear on every channel, every station, and are used for a variety of reasons.

Why are graphics used so frequently in television programming? Research has shown that viewers will assimilate information to a much greater degree by reading or seeing the information as well as hearing the information. Let's look at an example using a sports reporter on a local news show. The reporter could simply just announce the scores from last night's baseball action on camera at the anchor desk. Most viewers would not be able to follow or remember the scores presented in this fashion. The report would also appear uninteresting to the viewing audience. However, this same information could be presented using a page or two of graphics with the names of the teams and scores displayed as the reporter announces them. The viewers are more likely to maintain interest and remember the information they see in this latter format. By reading and listening to the information, viewer interest and comprehension can be increased.

Television graphics are used for the following reasons:

1. To provide specific information. Graphics are used to highlight essential information about topics and events. Specific dates, times, prices, a person's name and title, and other important information are just some of the examples used for graphics.

2. To get viewer attention. A graphic can often be used to increase and hold viewer attention (as in the sports scores example). Sometimes this information is in the form of an "incredible sale price of just $$$" and flashes boldly across the screen.

3. To identify products. Some graphics are used to identify specific forms of programming, products, or companies. Logos, for example, are routinely used to identify channel programming. Ask any teenager to identify the logo for MTV!

Designing Television Graphics

The main idea in producing television graphics is to present the information in a readable manner to the viewing audience (figure 1.11). Several key factors determine the readability of television graphics, among them time, quantity of information, contrast, and style.

Fig. 1.11. Designing television graphics.

Viewers need adequate *time* to read the graphics. Don't rush the graphics portion of the video project, especially if the graphics contain essential information necessary for viewer comprehension. Ending credit time can often be reduced, as this information is not as critical to the viewer. A good rule of thumb when producing graphics is to actually read them at a reduced pace so that most viewers' reading rates are accommodated.

Keep in mind the *quantity of information* you are presenting. Be careful not to overload the viewer with too much information on the screen at one time. If there are several important facts or ideas that need to be presented, use several graphic pages or screens to display the information rather than trying to squeeze it all in one page. The following examples illustrate how to effectively reduce the information presented on each graphics page.

Fig. 1.12. Example of an overcrowded graphic screen.

Orlando High School Presents ...

The Fifth Annual
"Battle of the Bands"

5 Live Bands in 1 Exciting Show!!!

Friday March 19, 1993
7:30 - 10:30 P.M.

Admission $5 at the door

It is obvious from figure 1.12 that there is too much information for the viewer to assimilate in a reasonable amount of time. This problem can be solved by separating and presenting the information in a series of graphics (figure 1.13). Readability will be enhanced along with the overall project presentation.

Fig. 1.13. Example of a series of graphic screens.

Orlando High School Presents ...

The Fifth Annual
"Battle of the Bands"

5 Live Bands
in
1 Exciting Show!!!

Friday
March 19, 1993
7:30 - 10:30 P.M.

Admission $5 at the door

By using several graphics pages, each presenting just a few facts, the information is much more readable to the viewers. The complexity of the project will also be increased because there will be several page changes rather than one long period of time with one page of graphics. Increasing the complexity also increases viewer interest.

Contrast refers to the difference between the lightest and darkest portions of the screen. In terms of graphics, increasing the contrast between the letters and the background screen makes them more readable. Select graphic colors that stand out from the background color or image on the screen. The best color combinations include:

> A high-energy foreground (bright) with a low-energy background (dark), for example, white letters on a black screen.
>
> A low-energy foreground (dark) with a high-energy background (light), for example, black letters on a white screen.

This is also true when keying letters over a video background. If the reporter is wearing a dark blue blouse, keying letters in black would make them difficult for viewers to read. In this case, the background color (dark blue) would suggest a light foreground color for the letters (white or another light color). If the reporter's blouse was white, then the letters should be keyed in a dark color.

The *style* of the graphics should reflect the overall mood of the message. For example, the bright, flashy graphics used to promote a "Battle of the Bands" contest may not be appropriate to use during a documentary on child-related diseases or a similar serious subject. Some sophistication is necessary when designing graphics for television production. The viewers' needs and emotions must be taken into consideration.

By carefully using these elements, graphic operators and artists can design graphics that are readable, interesting, and increase viewer comprehension.

Producing Television Graphics

In most television studios today, the CG has become an essential piece of equipment (figure 1.14). A wide variety of models provide an opportunity to select a CG that is appropriate for each particular school's use and program budget. With the advent of the electronics age, CGs are available with numerous functions at moderate prices. The following functions can be found on many of the CGs used in school television production studios today.

1. Letter styles (fonts). Many CGs provide a selection of letter styles that can be used for producing graphics. Lower-priced models may offer a selection of one or two letter styles, while higher-priced models may allow a selection of as many as 10 fonts, including the use of some symbols/pictures.

2. Letter sizes. Depending upon the make and model of the CG, a choice of several letter sizes may be available.

3. Letter/background color. The ability to select letter/background colors is essential in producing quality, readable graphics. Contrasting the graphics with the video image is especially important when keying the graphics over a video image. The greater the selection of colors, the more opportunities there are for creativity and design.

4. Border/shadow edging. Placing a border around graphics enhances them and creates a distinct contrast when they are keyed over video footage. Shadowing the graphics creates a distinct 3-D image in the letters.

Fig. 1.14. Character generator.

5. Pages. The ability to type and store several pages of graphics is extremely helpful, especially in producing school news shows or complicated programs requiring the use of multiple pages and styles of graphics. These pages can usually be manually changed during the course of a program, or in more advanced models, can be programmed to change (see "Sequencing" below).

6. Sequencing. Some advanced models of CGs allow the graphics operator to program the CG to automatically change pages according to predetermined time and page numbers. This function eliminates the time differences that can occur when manually sequencing pages of graphics. For example, the ending credits of a school news show may consist of four to five pages, which are keyed over video footage at the conclusion of each day's show. The graphics operator could program the CG to automatically change each page after displaying the page for 5 seconds. Each page would then appear for the same exact length of time throughout the end of the show, rather than one page appearing for 3 seconds and another one for 7 seconds.

7. Roll (scroll). Some CGs have the ability to "roll" pages of graphics in a vertical movement up and down the screen, much like credits at the end of most movies. Advanced models can identify start and stop cues, which allow the graphics operator to roll selected pages from those available on the CG. Lower-priced models generally begin the roll on page 1 and continue sequentially through the pages until they complete the last page or are manually stopped.

8. Crawl. Graphics that move horizontally across the screen are often used for "urgent" messages or continuous broadcasting of graphics information. Some examples include weather bulletins that appear during network programming, stock market quotations during the daily broadcast of CNN's "Headline News," or the "news flash" of an important event that occurs during network programs.

9. Storage/Retrieval (disc-operated systems). Several recent advanced CGs have the ability to store and retrieve information using a disk-drive system, much like a typical computer system (figure 1.15). Graphics can be typed and stored for later use. Being able to store and retrieve large quantities of graphics, like those used for a daily news show, can eliminate a lot of time necessary in preparing for each day's events.

Fig. 1.15. Character generator with storage and retrieval capabilities.

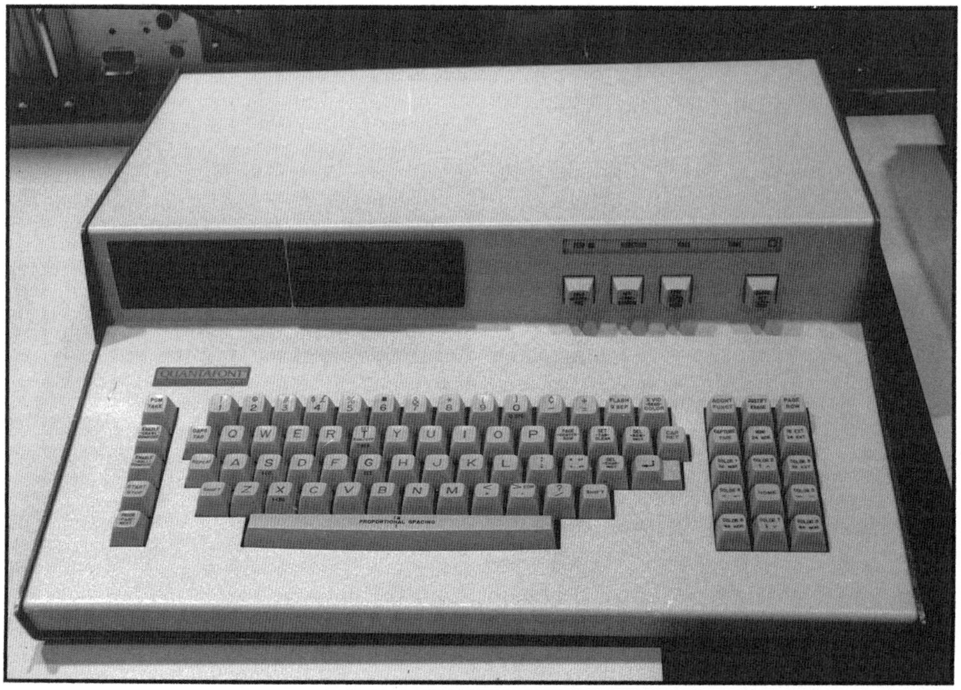

These are just some of the more common features found on character generators being used in today's television production programs. Depending upon budget and purchasing constraints, the character generator used in a program may contain one or all of these functions. The ability to use these functions will come with obtaining and reading the CG operator's manual, practicing keyboard and typing skills, and correctly programming the functions on the CG system. Classes like typing, word processing, and some computer experience can also improve your skills with the character generator.

In television production, careers for graphic operators and artists are appearing in most community production facilities. It's no longer only the message that counts, it's how the message is delivered and received by the viewer. Color, balance, style, and creativity have become even more necessary in today's competitive television industry.

Review Questions: Lesson 4

1. An electronic device that produces typed letters and displays them on a video screen for use and recording in television production is called a [character generator].
2. A horizontal movement of graphics across the screen is a [crawl].
3. [Contrast] refers to the difference between the lightest and darkest portions of the video screen.
4. [Keying] is the term used for placing graphics (e.g., a reporter's name) over background video.
5. A [roll] is the vertical movement of graphics up or down the screen.
6. List and describe three reasons graphics are used in television production.
   a. [Provides specific information.]
   b. [Increases viewer attention.]
   c. [Helps to identify products (logos).]

(Review questions continue on page II-1-48.)

7. Briefly describe how each of the following items can affect the readability of graphics.
   a. Time— [There must be adequate time on screen for viewers to read and comprehend the graphics.]
   b. Quantity of information— [Do not overload the viewer with too much information on each screen of graphics.]
   c. Contrast— [Select graphic colors that stand out from backgrounds.]
   d. Style— [The style of the graphics should reflect the overall mood of the message.]

8. Give an explicit example of how each of the following graphic styles is used in television programming.
   a. Roll— [Student answers will vary for each item.]
   b. Crawl—
   c. Sequenced graphic pages—
   d. Keyed-over video footage—

Activities: Lesson 4

1. Create a poster from graphic logos, symbols, or pictures cut out of newspapers and magazines.

2. Design a logo for your school's news show or your television production program. This activity could even be developed into a contest on your school news program!

3. Videotape examples of the following forms of graphics from a variety of television programs.
    a. Roll
    b. Crawl
    c. Sequenced pages
    d. Keyed-over footage
    e. Logo or station identification

4. Visit a local television production facility's graphics department. What type of equipment do they use? Who works in the department? What do they produce and where can it be seen?

Student Project Plan: Composing Graphics

DESCRIPTION OF COMPLETED PROJECT

The students will use a CG to produce television graphics. The project will be worth 100 points.

METHOD OF PRODUCTION

Produce the following graphics using a CG. Each page should be recorded on your videotape for 15 seconds. Fade in and fade out of each page.

Graphic #1

TELEVISION PRODUCTION

Graphics Project
By
[Student's Name]

Graphic #2

Directed By:
[Student's Name]

Produced By:
[Student's Name]

Graphic #3 Key the following title over *your* video image.

[Your Name]

Television Production

[School's Name]

Graphic #4 Compose the following graphics using a "roll."

Orlando High School

Visual and Performing Arts

Drama

Speech

Drawing

Ceramics

Jewelry

Painting

Media Production

Television Production

EVALUATION

Each page is worth 25 points.

Evaluation Sheet: Composing Graphics

NAME ____

Turn in your videotape and assignment sheet for grading. Make sure your tape is cued to the first page of graphics.

1. Each page of graphics is worth 25 points.

2. Each misspelled word results in a deduction of 3 points.

3. Each incorrect punctuation or capitalization results in a deduction of 3 points.

4. Any instances of insufficient style, contrast, incorrect format, or time discrepancies result in a deduction of 3 points.

page 1 (25) ______________ page 3 (25) ______________

page 2 (25) ______________ page 4 (25) ______________

Total points ______________

Teacher's comments:

Lesson 5 Switchers and Special Effects Generators

Objectives

After successfully completing this lesson, you will be able to:

- *identify switcher components.*
- *identify switcher functions.*
- *perform switcher operations.*
- *identify effects produced by special effects generators.*

Vocabulary

Bank. A pair of buses.

Bus. A row of buttons located on a switcher that select video inputs.

Chroma key. A special effect that uses color for keying graphics or video.

Cut. An instantaneous switch from one video source to another.

Dissolve. A gradual transition from one video picture to another during which the video images overlap.

Fade. A video effect produced by dissolving an image to a black (or another color) screen.

Fader bars. Levers located on a switcher that activate buses and can be used to perform switcher operations and effects.

Joystick. A switcher control that is used to position an effect on the video screen.

Key level. An adjustment on the switcher that enables graphics and other keyed effects to appear clear and sharp without breakup or distortion of picture quality.

Line-out. A switcher bus that directs the video source to recording deck or broadcast unit.

Mixing. Combining various video images using a switcher.

Mosaic. A digital effect that breaks the picture image into equal-sized squares or tiles.

Posterization. Sometimes referred to as "paint." A digital effect that creates a "watercolor" posterlike image from a video picture.

Preview bus. A switcher bus that enables the previewing of camera angles, videotaped segments, graphics, or switcher effects prior to being accessed to the line-out.

Program bus. A switcher bus that directs video sources to the line-out.

Strobe. A special effect that produces programmed intervals between video frames during playback. Sometimes referred to as "stop-action."

Super. The simultaneous display of two overlapping video images. Short for "superimposition."

Technical director (TD). The person who operates the switcher.

Wipe. An effect produced when one video image seems to push another image off the screen in a predetermined pattern.

Wipe key. Keying done using a wipe pattern.

Switchers enable the production crew to select and use multiple video sources at the same time to tape and record an event or program. These sources can be combined to produce a variety of transitions and special effects, as well as changes in camera angles during production. The number of video sources that can be used by a switcher varies with the model and complexity of the switcher used in production. Switchers that contain several (three or more) video inputs allow more flexibility and complexity in designing camera and video configurations and producing programs and shows.

All switchers are designed to perform several basic functions, including:

- Selection of appropriate video sources from a variety of inputs.
- Performance of video transitions from one video source to another.
- Creation of special effects.

Using a switcher during the taping of a program or show (switching) enables the producer to use several cameras and camera angles without the need for editing. Not only does this reduce the time of production, but it can also reduce costs associated with real-world postproduction. Many switchers also offer a variety of special effects that can be used while simultaneously recording the program.

Switcher Functions

Although switchers vary in their design and features, most switcher functions are comparable. Each video input (camera, CG, VCR) is delegated to a button located on one of the switcher buses. Pressing that button accesses that particular video input. Some switchers contain several rows of buttons, called buses. In this case, a fader bar is used to select which particular bus is activated. When two or more buses are used together to produce an effect, they are called a bank. By moving the fader bar up or down, the selected bank(s) are activated. Fader bars labeled "mix" perform the mixing functions of the switcher: dissolves, fades, and supers. Fader bars labeled "wipe" generally are used to produce the effects on a switcher: wipes, keys, and split-screens. Some switchers use a set of buttons labeled "wipe" and "mix" and one fader bar to achieve the same results. In this case, pressing the "mix" button and moving the fader bar from bus A to bus B will produce a fade, dissolve, or super. Pressing the "wipe" button and moving the fader bar from bus A to bus B will produce a wipe, key, or a split-screen effect. Control and operation of the fader bars are discussed in the "Switcher Operation" section of this chapter below.

Most switchers contain a preview bus. This bus routes the video signal to the preview monitor (rather than the line-out) and allows the technical director to see or preview a video source or effect before it is accessed to the program bus. This is especially helpful in ascertaining whether the forthcoming video segment is properly cued and ready, if the graphics are correctly typed and prepared, or to preview a special effect. The preview bus is totally independent from the program buses and will not be seen by the viewer or directed to the recording system. The preview bus is used by the producer and the technical director throughout the production phase, so the placement of the preview monitor should be in a position that is accessible to both. For example, during the taping of a news show a videotaped segment showing football practice needs to be "rolled in" immediately following the sports reporter's introduction. By pressing the VCR "input" button on the preview bus and looking in the preview monitor, the technical director can see the video cued and ready for playback. Meanwhile, the program bus continues to input the anchor desk and reporters to the line-out. The preview bus needs to be accessed and carefully scrutinized during production to maintain program continuity.

Many switchers contain an effects bank. When activated, these effects can be incorporated with the video sources to produce special effects. Several effects can be used simultaneously to produce a variety of effects for programming purposes.

Switcher Operation

Certain standard switcher operations can be performed on most switchers available in television production programs. A *cut* is an instantaneous switch from one video source to another. Cuts are used for a rapid change in camera angles, much like in a talk show. A cut is achieved by simply pressing another video source button on the same bus, or row, that is currently activated (figure 1.16).

Fig. 1.16. Switcher operation for a cut.

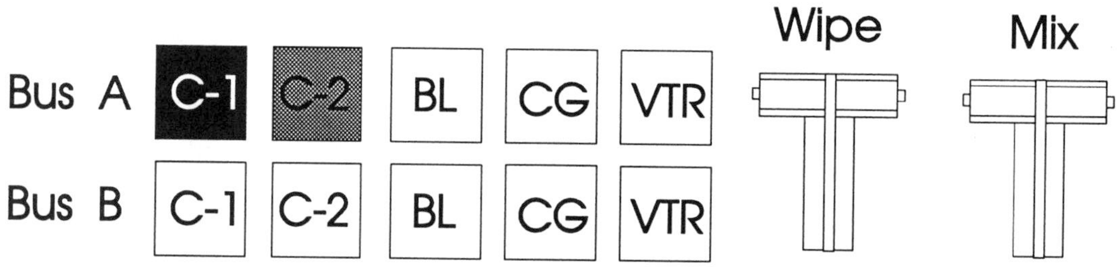

For example, camera 1 is activated in bus A. To cut to camera 2, the technical director (TD) will press the camera 2 button in bus A. The program monitor will now show camera 2 instead of camera 1. The fader bar is not used to produce a cut.

A *dissolve* is a transition from one video source to another, with image overlap at some point. To perform a dissolve, a video source is activated on bus A and the second source to be dissolved into should be selected in bus B. The fader bar (mix function) should be moved from bus A to bus B. The slower the bar is moved, the slower the dissolve. Some switchers contain an adjustable automatic speed control for completing dissolves, fades, and wipes (figure 1.17).

For example, camera 1 is activated in bus A. Press the camera 2 button in bus B. Now move the fader bar (mix function) down from bus A to activate bus B. The dissolve is now complete.

A *super* is achieved by performing a dissolve, but this time the fader bar is only moved halfway between bus A and bus B. Both buses will be activated at the same time and both pictures will be seen simultaneously. By moving the fader bar slightly up or down, one video image can be favored over another.

Fig. 1.17. Switcher operation for a dissolve.

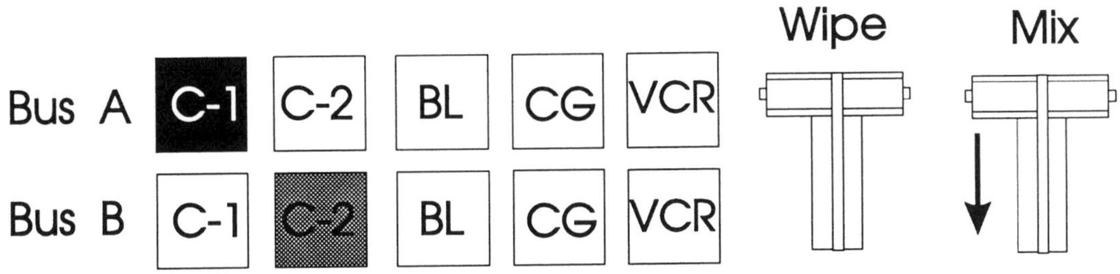

A *fade* is accomplished by simply dissolving a video image, or graphics, to a black (or other color) screen. Most switchers contain a "background color" selection, which can be used for this purpose. If none are available, a blank screen on a CG will also work (figure 1.18).

Fig. 1.18. Switcher operation for a fade.

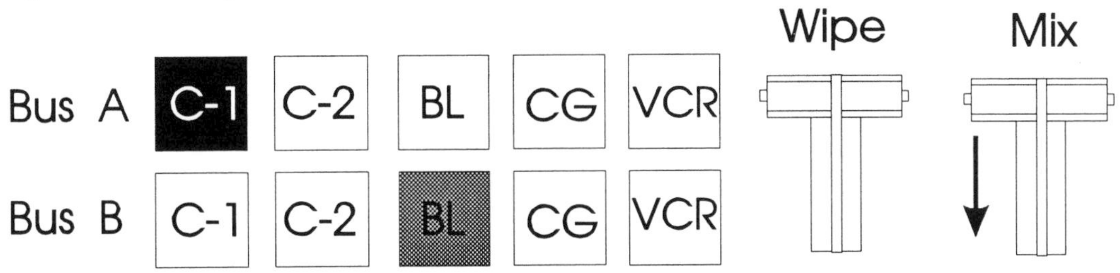

For example, camera 1 in bus A is currently activated. By pressing the button labeled "black" in bus B and moving the fader bar (mix function) to bus B, the video image from camera 1 will now fade to black. To fade in to a picture, simply reverse this process.

Most switchers designate dissolves, fades, and supers as a "mix" function. Look for a separate fader bar labeled "mix" or a button to delegate the mix function to the switcher's fader bar if there is only one bar.

The wipe functions generally include wipes, keys, and some special effects. During a *wipe*, it appears to the viewer that one video picture seems to "push" another picture off the screen. Wipes can be created in a variety of shapes and patterns, depending on the complexity of the switcher being used to produce the wipe. Some of the wipes available on switchers include:

- Soft wipes. Wipes that allow the TD to soften the edge between the two images used in the wipe.

- Border wipes. Wipes featuring a colored border/edge used to distinctly separate the two images. Often the border edge can be adjusted for color and thickness.

- Patterns. Wipes can be produced in an array of patterns. Most switchers offer a selection from which to choose when selecting wipe patterns.

The use of a joystick, much like that of any video game controller, allows the TD to position the wipe to begin at any point on the screen. The joystick can be used to create some effects, such as a spotlight effect (using a circular wipe pattern and positioning it strategically on the screen to spotlight a particular image) or to simulate a key over a reporter's shoulder (using a box wipe to reveal an image from another video source and positioning it over the reporter's shoulder).

For example, to wipe from camera 1 to a video segment, the following steps would be performed.

1. Select the wipe pattern to be used.

2. Select the video source (VCR) and press that button in bus B.

3. Move the fader bar (wipe function) from bus A to bus B (figure 1.19).

Fig. 1.19. Switcher operation for a wipe.

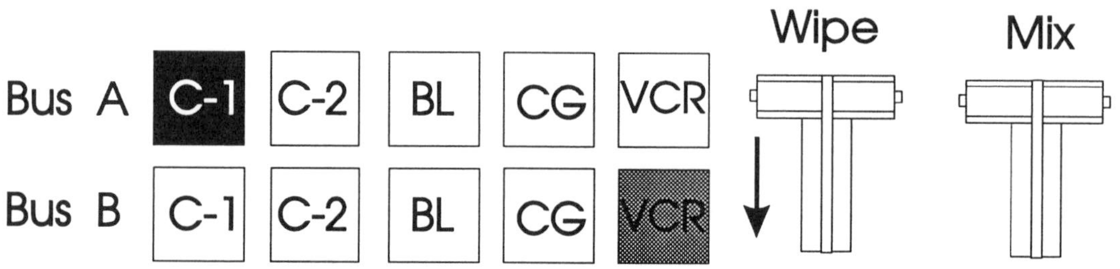

The speed of the wipe can be controlled on some switchers by setting a pot labeled "speed" to the appropriate setting. A *split-screen* image can be achieved by stopping the fader bar halfway between buses while performing a wipe.

Finally, keying refers to the process of electronically cutting out portions of a video picture and filling them in with graphics or other video images. Some of the key effects offered on today's switchers include:

- Wipe key. Allows the keying of graphics/video to be achieved using one of the wipe patterns available on the switcher.

- Matte key. Allows the cutout portions of the video image to be filled in with a selected color generated by the switcher.

- Chroma key. Allows the use of color (hence the word *chroma*) to create the key effect. For example, an actor standing in front of a green curtain (one of the key colors) can be electronically keyed onto another image supplied by the other camera, VCR, or CG. A good example of this effect would be the use of chroma keying to produce a daily weather show. The weather reporter actually stands next to a blank wall painted a key color (blue, green, red) and weather maps are electronically placed on the screen. The reporter actually looks at a television monitor located off camera to see the maps, temperatures, and weather information.

To produce one of the above key effects, the following steps would be performed.

1. Select the appropriate key function (chroma, wipe, matte).

2. Select the video source on bus A and the key source on bus B.

3. Move the fader bar (wipe function) from A to B. When keying, both buses will be activated.

Sometimes the key level will need to be adjusted to prevent picture breakup or deterioration. This can be done by adjusting a pot labeled "key level." Simply turn the pot to adjust the key level (increase/decrease) to establish a correct image.

Digital Video Effects

Some switchers, and a variety of special effects generators, are frequently used to create special video effects. These devices, known as digital video effects (DVEs), can change the normal (analog) video signal into a digital (numerical) signal. By digitizing the video information, the switcher can manipulate the signal, store the signal, and then retrieve the signal on command. Some of the following special effects are routinely used in television production:

- Still frame. The DVE can grab a single frame of video and freeze it, much like a snapshot or photograph.
- Posterization. Sometimes referred to as "paint," the DVE manipulates the brightness and shading of the picture area to create a painted, posterlike image.
- Mosaic. The DVE divides the picture into minute squares, or tiles, to obtain a mosaic tile look.
- Strobe. Sometimes referred to as "stop-action," the video appears to jump from one video frame to another. The amount of time (video frames) between video frames elapsed during playback can be increased or decreased with an adjustment on the switcher.

DVEs and other special effects generators can be added to an existing video system quite easily. Many studios have added DVEs to their editing systems to create special effects during postproduction.

The use and operation of switchers is essential for producing complex shows and programs, reducing editing and postproduction time and costs, as well as creating a program that is useful and interesting to the viewer. The technical director should be very familiar with the switcher functions and their operations. Routine practice and repetition are two of the ways students can develop these abilities.

Review Questions: Lesson 5

1. List the three basic functions of a switcher.
   - [Select appropriate video source from a variety of inputs.]
   - [Perform video transitions from one source to another.]
   - [Create special effects.]
2. Describe the following switcher operations.

   Dissolve— [A transition from one video source to another. At one point the images will overlap.]

   Fade— [Dissolving an image into a black (or other color) screen.]

   Super— [Like a dissolve, but fader bars are only moved halfway between two video sources so that both images are seen simultaneously.]

   Wipe— [One picture appears to push another picture off the screen in a predetermined pattern.]

   Cut— [An instantaneous change from one video source to another.]
3. What is the difference between a program bus and a preview bus? [A program bus directs the video source to the line out for broadcast or recording purposes. A preview bus directs the video source only to the preview monitor(s).]

4. Use the following terms to complete the sentences in a through h:

cut	mixing	key level
bank	program bus	wipe bar
joystick	wipe key	chroma key

a. The [program bus] directs the video source to the line-out.

b. [Mixing] refers to the process of combining various shots via the switcher.

c. A pair of buses is called a [bank].

d. The [key level] enables graphics and keys to appear clear and sharp without deterioration.

e. [Wipe key] is the ability to electronically superimpose graphics over a video picture using a predetermined pattern.

f. A [cut] is an instantaneous switch from one video source to another.

g. The device with which we can position an effect anywhere on screen is called a [joystick].

h. A [chroma key] uses a colored background to produce a special effect.

5. What is a technical director? What are some of the responsibilities of the technical director?

6. Complete each of the following switcher operations by drawing diagonal lines on the selected video inputs and indicating fader bar movement with arrows. The first one (see page II-1-60) has been completed as an example.

(Review questions continue on page II-1-60.)

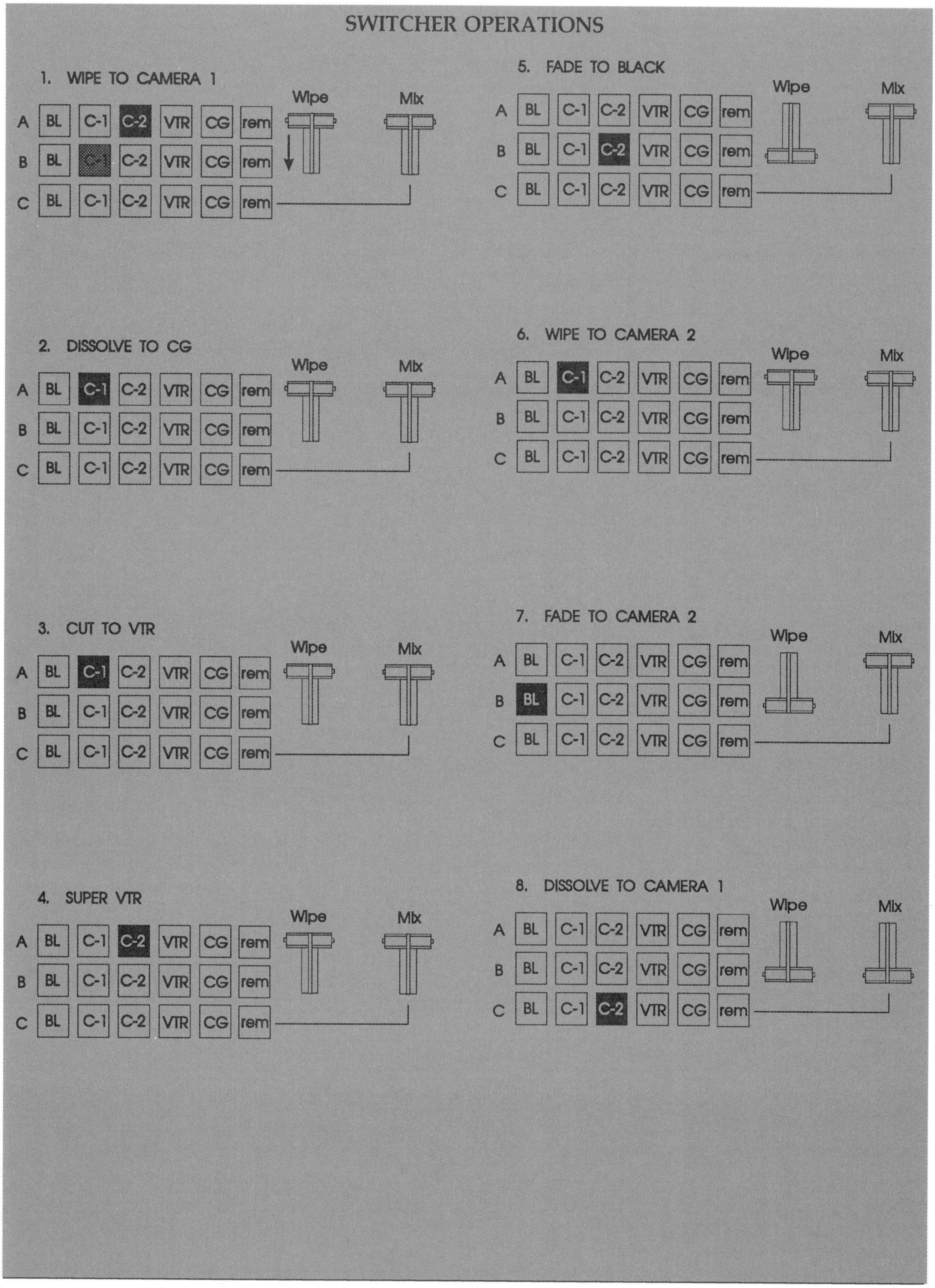
SWITCHER OPERATIONS
1. WIPE TO CAMERA 1
2. DISSOLVE TO CG
3. CUT TO VTR
4. SUPER VTR
5. FADE TO BLACK
6. WIPE TO CAMERA 2
7. FADE TO CAMERA 2
8. DISSOLVE TO CAMERA 1
A
B
C
BL
C-1
C-2
VTR
CG
rem
Wipe
Mix

Activities: Lesson 5

1. Record about 15 minutes of one of your favorite television programs. Identify some switcher operations (e.g., wipes, dissolves, cuts, supers) used in the recorded telecast.

2. Locate a video sales catalog containing switchers and some DVEs. See if you can identify a model available for each of these price ranges. Identify each by manufacturer and model number:

   a. Under $1,000— ____________________ ____________________

   b. $1,000-$2,000— ____________________ ____________________

   c. $2,000-$3,000— ____________________ ____________________

   d. $3,000-$4,000— ____________________ ____________________

   e. More than $3,000— ____________________ ____________________

   [Student descriptions will vary.]

3. Draw a diagram of the switcher used in your television production program. Label each button with its video input (camera 1, camera 2, CG) and identify all of the special effects buttons.

Student Project Plan: The Switcher

DESCRIPTION OF COMPLETED PROJECT

The students will become familiar with the functions and operations of a switcher and digital video effects.

ACTIVITY #1

Method

1. Set the cameras to the following shots:

   Camera 1 - 1 shot
   Camera 2 - 2 shot

2. Record the following switcher operations on your videotape:
   a. Cut from camera 1 to camera 2.
   b. Dissolve from camera 2 to camera 1.
   c. Super camera 1 and camera 2.
   d. Wipe (vertical) from camera 2 to camera 1.
   e. Wipe (horizontal) from camera 1 to camera 2.
   f. Fade from camera 2 to black.

ACTIVITY #2

Method

Record 20 seconds of video using each of the following effects:

a. Posterization (paint)
b. Mosaic
c. Strobe (stop action)
d. Still frame

ACTIVITY #3

Method

1. Form groups of four students.

2. Assign each person in the group one of the following jobs:
   a. Technical director: Operates the switcher.
   b. Producer: Coordinates production crew and monitors recording times.
   c. Camera/graphics operator: Sets up camera shots, types in graphics, and changes pages.
   d. Videotape operator: Cues up videotape and calls out time cues during playback.

3. Set up for the switcher activity.
   a. Set up cameras: camera 1 - 1 shot   camera 2 - 2 shot
   b. Type in graphics:

      Page 1   Switcher Project

      By

      [Names (4)]

      Page 2   [Key Graphics]
   c. Cue up videotapes: Tape 1 (Record project)

      Tape 2 (Roll in footage)
   d. Set key levels.
   e. Reset record VCR counter to 0:00:00.
   f. Load videotape for recording project.

4. Record the following switcher operations. Each step should be recorded for the exact time listed! Record this activity without pausing the record VCR.
   a. Black (:20)
   b. Fade to graphic page 1 (:15)
   c. Cut to camera 2 (:20)
   d. Cut to camera 1 (:10)
   e. Key graphics page 2/camera 1 (:20)
   f. Dissolve to VCR footage, first segment (:30)
   g. Cut to camera 2 (:10)
   h. Dissolve to camera 1 (:15)
   i. Key graphics page 2/camera 1 (:10)
   j. Dissolve to VCR footage, second segment (:30)
   k. Dissolve to graphics page 1 (:10)
   l. Fade to black (:20)

5. Cue up tape and turn it in for grading.

EVALUATION

Activity #1 is worth 30 points, activity #2 is worth 20 points, and activity #3 is worth 84 points.

Evaluation Sheet: Switcher Project

NAME ______________________________

Date______________________

ACTIVITY #1 (30 points)

Each switcher operation is worth 5 points.

1. cut ______________
2. dissolve ______________
3. super ______________
4. wipe (vertical) ______________
5. wipe (horizontal) ______________
6. fade ______________

Total points ______________

Teacher's comments:

ACTIVITY #2 (20 points)

Each digital effect is worth 5 points.

1. posterization ______________
2. mosaic ______________
3. strobe ______________
4. still frame ______________

Total points ______________

Teacher's comments:

ACTIVITY #3 (84 points)

Personnel

Technical Director ______________________________

Producer ______________________________

Camera/graphics operator______________________________

Videotape operator ______________________________

Grading

Each switcher operation is worth 5 points.

Time components are worth 2 points each.

a. Black (:20) ____________
b. Fade to graphic page 1 (:15) ____________
c. Cut to camera 2 (:20) ____________
d. Cut to camera 1 (:10) ____________
e. Key graphics page 2/camera 1 (:20) ____________
f. Dissolve to VCR footage, first segment (:30) ____________
g. Cut to camera 2 (:10) ____________
h. Dissolve to camera 1 (:15) ____________
i. Key graphics page 2/camera 1 (:10) ____________
j. Dissolve to VCR footage, second segment (:30) ____________
k. Dissolve to graphics page 1 (:10) ____________
l. Fade to black (:20) ____________

Teacher's comments:

Lesson 6 Advanced ENG Reporting

Objectives

After successfully completing this lesson, you will be able to:

- *list and describe equipment needed to complete ENG reports.*
- *identify the videographer tasks necessary for producing ENG reports.*
- *identify the reporter tasks necessary for producing ENG reports.*
- *write scripts for ENG reports.*
- *record an ENG report.*
- *produce an ENG report.*

Vocabulary

ENG. Electronic news gathering. Refers to the process of reporting events and activities that occur outside of the television studio.

Lead-in. The first few sentences of script that establish the setting of a news story. Introduces the topic to the viewer.

Sound bite. A videotaped segment in which the audio and video portions of the tape must remain in sync.

Stand-up. Refers to an on-camera shot of a reporter as he or she presents information about the topic.

ENG reporting is the cornerstone of any news show. Recording the events and activities as they happen and presenting that information to the viewer is what news is all about. The reporter and videographer need to record on tape the drama, actions, and emotions that surround the story and convey them to the viewer in an interesting and informative manner. The ENG reporter must quickly ascertain what is important about the activity and how it affects the participants and viewers. Reproducing the excitement and energy of an event on videotape for broadcasting purposes is a skill; it doesn't just happen. Professional reporters spend many hours writing scripts, interviewing people, and editing videotape. The information about an event must be presented accurately and fairly. Both sides of an issue should be reported in an honest and unbiased style. ENG reporting requires both on-camera and behind-the-camera skills.

ENG Equipment

In ENG reporting, there's no going back to the studio for equipment. Reporter and videographer must be prepared for every situation that might present itself during the reporting of an event. To avoid problems, follow this checklist:

1. *Always* check camera and recording equipment before leaving the studio for taping. Turn on the camera and deck and make sure they are operating correctly. Microphones and mic cords should also be checked for sound quality.

2. Bring several power sources. Besides a few extra (charged!) batteries, it is wise to bring an AC power supply and a battery charger.

3. Don't forget the essentials: videotapes, tripod, headphones.

4. What about lighting? If you think you might need it, bring it.

5. Use a durable equipment bag to pack and carry the equipment. Carefully pack and store equipment so it will not be damaged during travel.

6. Before leaving, recheck the bag to make sure nothing has been left behind.

Getting the Story

Once the ENG crew has arrived at the scene, each member has specific tasks to perform (figure 1.20). The *videographer* should quickly set up the camera equipment. Videotape needs to be loaded and checked to make sure everything is operating correctly. Camera functions (iris, focus, white balance) should be adjusted for recording conditions. Start recording the activity as soon as the equipment has been checked and prepared.

Fig. 1.20. ENG crew.

The *reporter* needs to quickly observe and identify what is happening at the scene upon arrival. Find out what activities are planned, who is in charge, and any important information concerning times and locations of events you can relay to the videographer. Write down the information on a small notepad for later use in reporter lead-ins, stand-ups, or narratives. Assist the videographer in selecting shots that can be used in the project.

Let's look at an example of how a typical ENG crew would cover an assignment: A reporter and videographer have been assigned to report on the International Dinner and Dance sponsored by the school's foreign language department. Upon arriving, the reporter should:

1. Locate a foreign language teacher in charge of the event. Ask about details of the event: number of students involved, what the profits from the event will be used for, and what activities are planned for the evening. This information should be written down and used for scripting the reporter's lead-in or stand-up.

2. Talk to several students involved in this project. Find out their names, foreign language classes they are enrolled in, and their opinions about this activity. Ask them about participating in some on-camera interviews later in the evening.

3. Prepare a lead-in for the story.

The videographer should:

1. Immediately set up and check the camera equipment.

2. Record any activities that are going on at the time: students arriving for the dinner dance, banners and hall decorations, dancing, and food preparations.

3. Discuss camera shots and locations with the reporter. Verify shots and locations, as well as times, for stand-ups and interviews.

This example illustrates how each production crew member has to assume individual responsibilities as well as coordinate group efforts. The reporter and videographer work together as a team to quickly record and report events and activities.

Recording the Story

A good videographer will develop an eye for shots and angles that effectively capture the actions and emotions of an event. While the reporter is concerned with telling the story, the videographer must be concerned with recording the story in images and sound. This does not mean that hours of tape need to be recorded for every event and activity. Rather, the videographer should record several minutes of each activity as it occurs. It is also important to note that sometimes the people watching the activity are more interesting than the event itself.

Camera angles and shots should reflect the atmosphere and mood of the event. Facial expressions and emotions of the people involved can be effectively recorded on tape. Close-ups and camera angles that bring the viewer into the scene create interest for the audience.

Sound is also an important element of every story and can be used during postproduction to re-create the mood of an event. If the videographer consistently records only brief moments at a time, starting and stopping the camera after a few seconds, the sound track will be practically unusable for postproduction. Effectively use sound, as well as video, for recording an event. The dinner dance, for example, would contain a multitude of sounds that could be effectively used in postproduction: international songs and dances, students engaged in conversation in various foreign languages, and perhaps some cultural presentations representing different countries. These sounds could be used as a background for reporter narration as well as conveying the sights and sounds of the events to the viewer. The videographer needs to record these sounds on tape without cutting the sound track with frequent camera stops.

Interviews and comments from participants and others involved with the event are important in getting another aspect of the story. The videographer will be called upon quite frequently to record these comments during the course of the activity. Some suggestions for improving videotaping of on-camera comments include:

1. Roll tape! Start recording even as the reporter and interviewee are getting set for the interview. Doing so eliminates color bars and control track problems, as well as providing an opportunity to effectively check microphone sound quality. Continue to roll tape throughout the interviews, even during bloopers and retakes. Let the tape roll at least 30 seconds after the completion of the interview to eliminate any lost footage due to VCR roll back.

2. Always wear headphones when recording interviews and sound bites. If the record deck has VU meters, check input volume level prior to, and during, each segment.

3. Shoot "talking heads." Obtain a nice close-up or bust shot of the individuals making the comments on tape. Avoid using a 2-shot for recording comments and statements. Try to keep the microphone out of the shot whenever possible. Be constantly aware of the background for each shot so it adds to, rather than detracts from, viewer attention.

A good videographer will work with the reporter to develop a style for their reports. Spend some time discussing possible camera shots and unique story angles that can add to the effectiveness of the project, as well as the logistics (time and place) for recording reporter stand-ups, narratives, and interviews.

Telling the Story

It is the reporter's task to tell the story that surrounds each event. The lead-ins and narratives should be informative, accurate, and brief. Present the information in a professional and unbiased manner. Do not editorialize! The purpose of the report is to present all of the information the viewer needs to make his or her own judgment. Remember: Every issue has two sides. Opinions do not belong in news reporting.

The reporter's lead-in is essential for informing the viewing audience about the topic. The first sentence or two should contain enough details so that the viewer can quickly grasp the content of the report.

Incorrect: "The foreign language department has been working hard the last few days."

Correct: "The foreign language department is hard at work preparing for tonight's International Dinner and Dance."

All ENG reports do not have to begin with a shot of the reporter, mic in hand, doing a stand-up. A sentence or two of narrative can also be effective in introducing a story. This can be recorded on camera and simply audio-inserted during postproduction. Recording the narrative at the scene keeps the sound quality consistent throughout the project and effectively uses background ambience to keep the atmosphere of a live report.

Sound bites are another effective way to begin a report. A few seconds of "live" footage/sound can grab the viewer's attention and create interest in the report. In the dinner dance report, the opening shot could include a shot of some "senors and senoritas" dancing to the sounds of a Spanish song.

Almost all ENG reports contain some information that usually is audio-dubbed over video footage. In order to ensure sound continuity throughout the project, record the script on location using an external microphone and the camera recording unit. This maintains a consistent sound quality throughout the audio portion of the edited project and preserves the ambience of the event on tape. Use audio inserts during postproduction for editing the script onto the master tape.

Comments and statements made on-camera are another good way of telling the story. These give the viewer the perspective of the participants involved in the activity. Although the reporter may ask several questions during each interview, the comments should be edited so only brief insightful passages are actually used in the edited project. The videographer will be focusing on the interviewees, so the reporter should not be concerned with his or her on-camera appearance during the interviews. If a person being interviewed does not appear to understand the question, or answers the question in a one- or two-word sentence, the reporter should rephrase the question to elicit a more eloquent response. For example:

Reporter: "Did you help with the decorations?"

Interviewee: "No."

Reporter: "What were some of the things you had to do to prepare for this dinner dance?"

Make sure all of the names and titles of interviewees are written down for use in postproduction graphics.

The closing, or summary, of the report needs to reflect the content of the rest of the project. The closing is a brief statement made on- or off-camera by the reporter. Sometimes it is beneficial to record several summaries and choose the best one during postproduction.

Producing the Story

Editing the parts of the story together is comparable to an artist creating a painting from a blank canvas or a beautiful vase from a lump of wet clay. The raw footage and story parts are edited together to create a unique and interesting news report.

Before starting the editing phase, preview all of the raw footage and complete a tape log. This will assist in quickly locating certain shots and audio information while editing. It is also helpful to develop a working storyboard, or outline, to follow during postproduction. Editing on the fly, without an outline or storyboard, can be extremely difficult and takes longer to complete.

Every report needs to have a beginning, a middle, and an end. Earlier in this chapter (lesson 2, page II-1-11) we referred to the *Rule of Three's* for writing scripts and producing news reports. As you remember, the rule states that the reporter uses three sentences of stand-up or lead-in, then three sentences of comments and interviews, three sentences of narration over footage, and finally, a summary or closing. Following this rule keeps the report interesting by increasing the complexity and pace of the report and reducing the tendency of the reporter to add too much script to it. Using the previous example of the dinner dance, let's examine how this report can be produced and edited using the *Rule of Three's.* Notice how each component uses two to three sentences to tell the story.

1. Lead-in (reporter stand-up): The foreign language department is hard at work preparing for tonight's International Dinner and Dance. Students and teachers are preparing the food, decorating the hall, and planning the schedule for the night's entertainment. (*Note the three activities.*)

2. Comment 1 (student on-camera): The dinner is really delicious because you can sample a lot of food from many different countries!

   Comment 2 (teacher on-camera): Besides raising money for student classroom materials and activities, this event provides an excellent opportunity for students to really experience the culture and foods of other countries.

   Comment 3 (student on-camera): I really like dancing to all of the different kinds of music, and the costumes are quite interesting! (*Note that the comments are limited to three sentences.*)

3. Narration (over video footage): Dining and dancing weren't the only activities to enjoy this evening. Foreign language skits, movies, and even a fashion show were included in tonight's events.

4. Closing (reporter off-camera): The foreign language department would like to thank everyone who helped make this year's dinner and dance a big success.

   (*Reporter on-camera seated at table with a huge plate of food*): As for me, I'm going to enjoy these culinary delights. For WDOC News, I'm [reporter's name]. (*Note the use of three sentences for the closing.*)

In between these portions of the report, sound bites can be used to convey the sights, sounds, and atmosphere of the evening. These are short (7 to 10 seconds) clips that contain video and audio tracks that remain in sync. Some good sound bites to use in this project could include:

- People dancing to an ethnic tune.
- Students performing a skit or modeling costumes in the fashion show.
- Some sights and sounds from the buffet table.
- Students speaking in foreign languages.

Carefully planning the project after viewing the raw footage can eliminate a lot of the "what should we put next" that comes with trying to edit spontaneously. Continuity results when the sequence and presentation of material have been planned and produced.

Postproduction Tips

1. Use the insert mode for editing the project. Simultaneously edit audio and video inserts in sections where the synchronization of lips and actions (stand-ups, comments/interviews, sound bites) must remain intact. Use audio inserts to lay down narration (script) and then edit the video track to match the audio information.

2. Use graphics to identify students, teachers, or guests who appear on-camera commenting about the activity. A simple graphic that contains the individual's name and title is effective:

   Mr. Steven Long
   Teacher

   Patty Smith
   Student

3. Complexity is essential for maintaining viewer interest and attention. Edit camera angles and shots that portray the drama associated with the event. Avoid long camera pans and long shots that leave out detail. A series of 2- to 3-second shots is more interesting and informative than a long 12-second pan.

4. Use as much of the live sound as possible. Inserting a dubbed sound track from a favorite tape or CD usually changes the character and mood of the video.

5. Critically watch the completed project in its entirety. Don't be afraid to make changes to sections of the video that do not meet your expectations.

Producing quality ENG reports enhances the effectiveness of school news shows and television production programs in general. Developing good reporting skills and habits can prepare students for entrance to college/vocational programs, as well as lead to careers in the television industry.

Review Questions: Lesson 6

1. List the equipment needed to complete an ENG report titled "Homecoming Dance." (*List should include the following items.*) [camera, batteries, tripod, microphone, videotape, AC adapter, battery charger, lights, headphones]
2. Identify three tasks that the videographer should complete during an ENG report.
   - [Quickly set up equipment.]
   - [Record a variety of shots from a variety of angles.]
   - [Shoot "talking heads." Obtain close-ups of interviewees making comments on camera.]
3. Identify three tasks that the reporter should complete during an ENG report.
   - [Quickly observe and identify what is happening at the scene. Take notes for lead-in and narration.]
   - [Talk to someone involved in the activity to get information and set up interviews.]
   - [Assist the videographer in identifying camera shots.]

4. Describe the *Rule of Three's* as it applies to ENG reports. [Each component of the report (stand-ups, narrations, comments) should be limited to three sentences.]
5. Describe three elements of recording and editing comments and statements on-camera that can make them more effective in an ENG report.
   - [Shoot "talking heads" or bust shots of individuals making comments on tape.]
   - [Utilize graphics to identify individuals giving comments and statements on-camera.]
   - [Limit comments to two to three sentences of important facts and opinions.]
6. What is a sound bite? How are sound bites used in creating effective ENG reports? [A sound bite is a videotaped segment in which the audio and video portions of the tape must remain in sync. They can be used as background for narration as well as conveying the sights and sounds of the event to the viewer.]

Activities: Lesson 6

1. Record an ENG report from a local news show. Discuss the following aspects:

   a. How did the report begin (sound bite, stand-up, narration)?

   b. Did the report follow the *Rule of Three's*?

   c. Did the reporter use comments and statements from participants?

   d. What sound bites were used in the report?

   e. What graphics were used in the report?

   f. What was the total length (time) of the report?

   g. What made the report interesting to the viewer?

2. Write a two- to three-sentence stand-up for each of the following topics:

   a. A school basketball team plays in the district championship.

   b. An art student receives a national award.

   c. The debate team wins the state championship.

   d. A math teacher is honored as "Teacher of the Year."

   e. Rain causes heavy damage to the student parking lot.

   f. Attendance is a student's responsibility.

3. News reports are also produced for daily radio news shows. Record a radio news ENG report. How does it compare to a television ENG report? What are some differences and similarities?

Student Project Plan: ENG Reporting with On-Camera Comments

DESCRIPTION OF COMPLETED PROJECT

The students will become familiar with the format and structure of a professional ENG report by using on-camera statements/comments.

FORMAT

Each project must contain the following:

1. Story lead-in (stand-up or narrative)

   A two- to three-sentence lead-in describing the topic, situation, or problem involved in the report.

2. Comments/statements (on-camera)

   These are edited comments and statements made on-camera that express the various opinions and ideas of people involved in the topic. Three statements must be included. All sides of the issue need to be expressed in this section. Use of a 1-shot (interviewee) is used in this format.

3. Summary (stand-up or narrative)

   Reporter summarizes the feelings and attitudes expressed in the project, as well as possible consequences/outcomes. Summary ends with "and this has been [reporter's name] reporting for ___________ news."

NOTES

1. Only one stand-up can be used in this report. If the project begins with a stand-up, it must end with a narrative. If a narrative is used to begin the project, a stand-up is used to summarize the report.
2. All comments/statements made on-camera must be taped using a 1-shot of the participant.
3. Total length should not exceed 1½ minutes.

EVALUATION

Content	25 points
Audio	25 points
Editing	25 points
Camera work	25 points

Evaluation Sheet: ENG Reporting with On-Camera Comments

PROJECT STAFF

Reporter/Writer ________________

Camera/Audio ________________

Director/Editor ________________

EVALUATION

1. Content: Appropriate topic, audience appeal, informative, use of appropriate comments/ statements, summary

   ____________ out of 25 points

2. Audio: Levels balance, audio dub clear and concise

   ____________ out of 25 points

3. Editing: Comments edited precisely, degree of continuity and complexity demonstrated, clean edit points, black leader/tab

   ____________ out of 25 points

4. Camera: White-balanced, use of 1-shot for comments, steady camera shots, variety of camera angles, focused shots

   ____________ out of 25 points

Total points ____________

Teacher's comments:

Lesson 7 Directing Talent for Television Production

Objectives

After successfully completing this lesson, you will be able to:

- *identify the director's roles in a production.*
- *distinguish between performers and actors.*
- *identify on-camera techniques for improving talent performances.*
- *identify and perform floor director's cues.*
- *use cues to direct production crews.*

Vocabulary

Actor. A person who portrays someone else in a dramatic role.

Blocking. Planned movement and actions of talent and crew.

Floor director. Directs talent during production, relays director's cues to talent and studio crew, and supervises all floor activities and personnel.

Performer. On-camera talent who portray themselves.

Talent. Refers to anyone performing on camera.

Directing talent and supervising production crews can be an exciting and fulfilling job. The responsibilities of the job can also be very demanding. The director must assume a variety of roles that enable him or her to achieve the goals involved in producing a television program.

The director acts as a *motivator* to encourage talent and crew to give 100 percent of their effort during all phases of production. Everyone has to be reminded to concentrate on the job at hand, whether it is a rehearsal or the tenth take of a scene. Everyone must be treated as an individual, yet be motivated to work as a team to complete the job on time. The director must overcome both technical and ideological difficulties and maintain an atmosphere that will encourage each team member to do his or her best.

The director acts as a *technical advisor* to overcome the technical problems that always seem to appear during television production. A good director knows each crew member's job description and expertise, as well as his or her limitations. Recognizing and solving technical problems can improve a director's standing among crew members and reduce production time and costs.

The director acts as a *supervisor*. He or she is responsible for the actions and activities of everyone involved in the production. Coordinating the efforts of all of these crew members can often be difficult. The director must treat everyone with respect but be firm and fair in making important decisions. A director needs to manage the crew so that everyone's efforts assist in producing the program and make the effort fun and enjoyable.

The director is responsible for coordinating both talent and production crew members. Let's look at how this is accomplished.

Directing Talent

On-camera talent can be broken into two groups: actors and performers. An actor portrays another character and assumes the personality of that role while on-camera. Performers always portray themselves while on-camera. Arsenio Hall, for example, is considered a performer when hosting the "Arsenio Hall Show." He is portraying himself throughout the show. Kim Basinger, an actress, assumes the character's personality she is portraying in a movie or film.

Directing actors and performers for television production is quite different from directing the performances given in front of an audience. In television, the camera is the audience. The on-camera talent needs to be directed to perform to the camera at all times. Often, a director can improve a performance by offering some helpful techniques to the talent. Some of these include:

1. Look directly into the camera lens. Maintaining eye contact with the camera is absolutely crucial in establishing rapport with the television audience. Averting the eyes or looking away from the camera can distract the audience. Especially during close-ups, the talent needs to be reminded to maintain good eye contact.

2. Blocking is extremely important in television production. Camera crews and audio operators are positioned to obtain the best camera angle possible. Rehearsed positions are critical in maintaining program continuity. On-camera talent, as well as production crew members, need to adhere to all predetermined actions and positions.

3. When multiple cameras are being used for videotaping programs, the talent has to be aware of which camera is "hot" at all times (figure 1.21). Carefully read and review shot sheets and camera positions before production begins. Follow all floor cues immediately! Do not jerk your head around if you find you are looking at the wrong camera. This only makes the error more obvious.

4. Performing on-camera is quite different than performing onstage. Actions and expressions are less animated in television, especially in the field of news reporting. Head and hand movements can distract the viewer from the information being reported. The director needs to observe the talent and eliminate distracting actions and mannerisms that appear on camera.

5. Timing is critical in television production. Shows and programs are scheduled with strict adherence to time slots and program length. The production crew members, as well as the on-camera talent, need to be aware of recording times and follow all time cues quickly and accurately.

Relaying the director's cues to the on-camera talent is the responsibility of the floor director. The director and floor director generally communicate instructions and cues via a two-way headset or intercom system (figure 1.22). Each headset is equipped with a small microphone that enables the directors to speak and hear each other's cues and directions.

Many of the floor director's cues are relayed to the talent through nonverbal cues or hand signals, so the cues will not be picked up on an open microphone and recorded on the master tape. Both the floor director and the talent have to be skilled in the use of these cues. The following cues, shown in figure 1.23 (page II-1-80), are routinely used in television production.

Fig. 1.21. "Hot" camera.

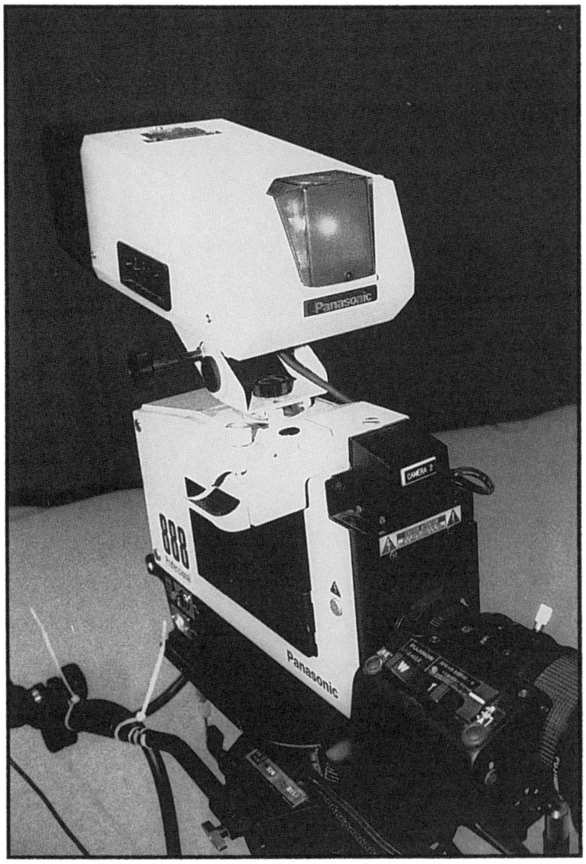

Fig. 1.22. Headset with microphone.

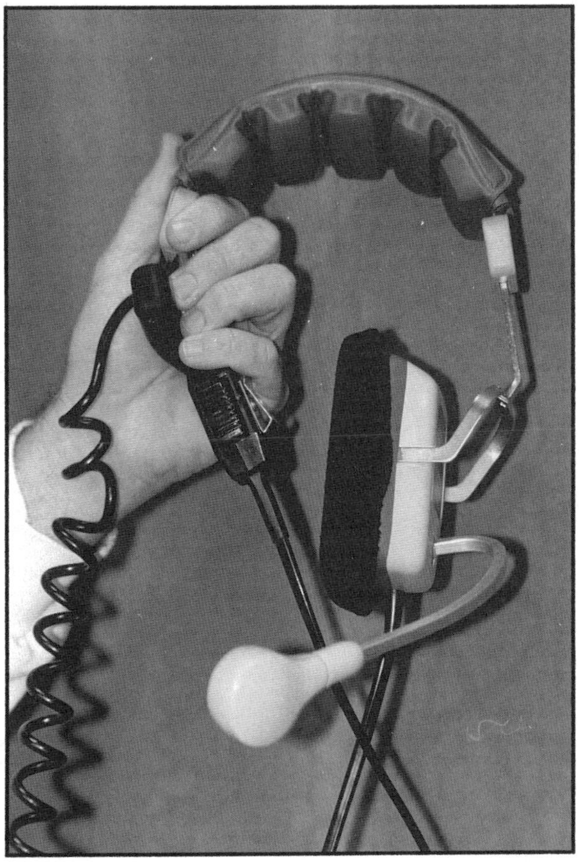

Fig. 1.23. Television production cues.

Cue	Picture	Signal
1. Stand-by (Show is about to start)	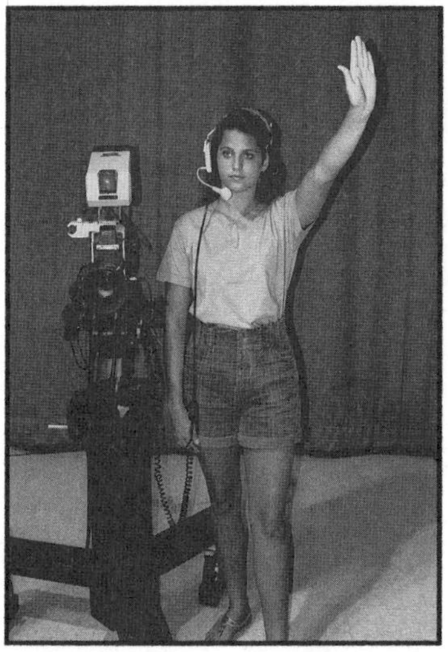	Extend one arm above head with palm facing talent.
2. 1/2 minute (:30) (:30 to go for program start or video segment completion)	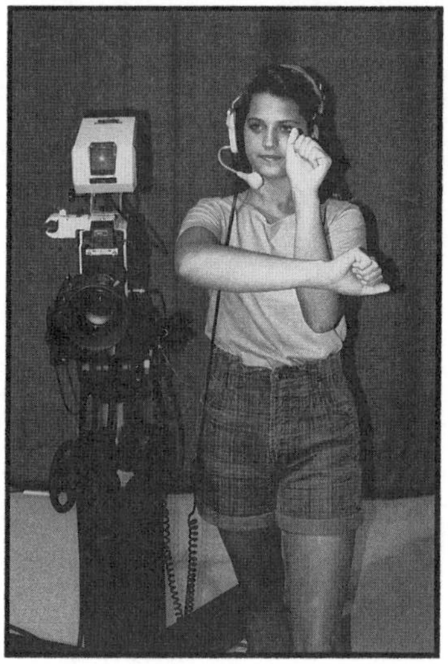	Form a cross with both arms.

Cue	Picture	Signal
3. :15 seconds (15 seconds to go for program start or video segment completion)	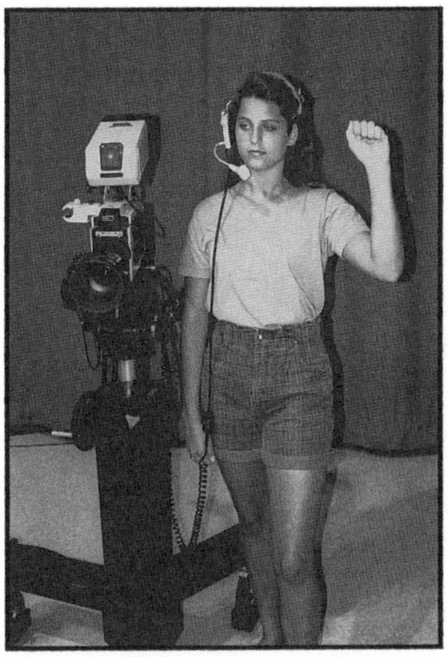	One arm is half-raised with hand clenched into a fist.
4. 5, 4, 3, 2, 1 ... (seconds to go before program start or video segment completion)	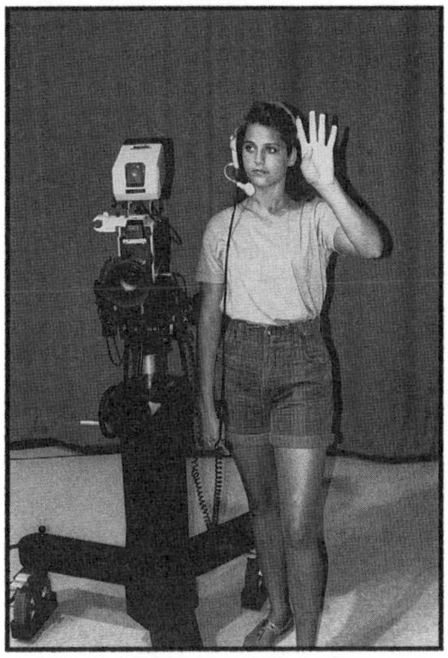	Raise hand and hold up number of appropriate fingers. Lower each as countdown progresses.

Cue	Picture	Signal
5. Cue (Camera is hot)	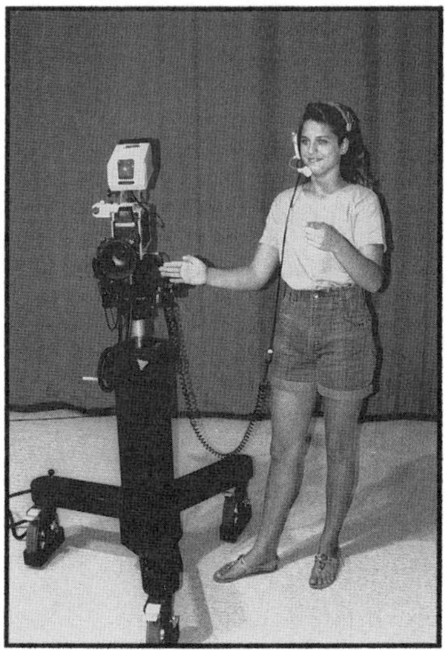	Point to performer and indicate camera.
6. Speed up (Accelerate what talent is doing/saying at the time)	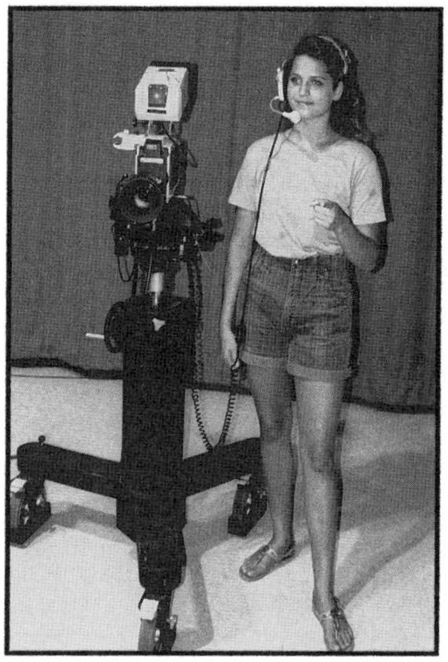	Point index finger and rotate hand clockwise. The more urgent the message, the faster the rotation.

Cue	Picture	Signal
7. Wind up (Finish what talent is doing/saying at the time)	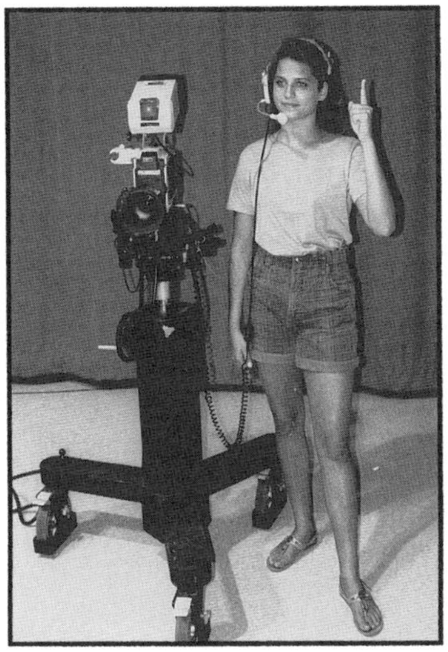	Raise one arm above the head, extend forefinger, and rotate clockwise. The more urgent the message, the faster the rotation.
8. Cut (Stop immediately, cease action)	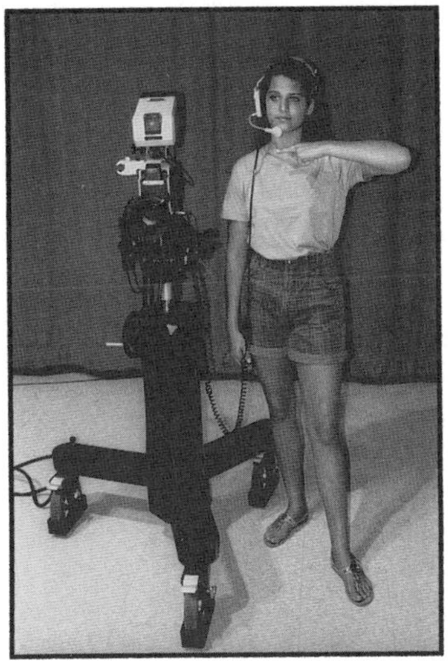	Extend forefinger and move horizontally across the throat.

Cue	Picture	Signal
9. Rolling VCR (Taping is beginning, video segment is coming up)	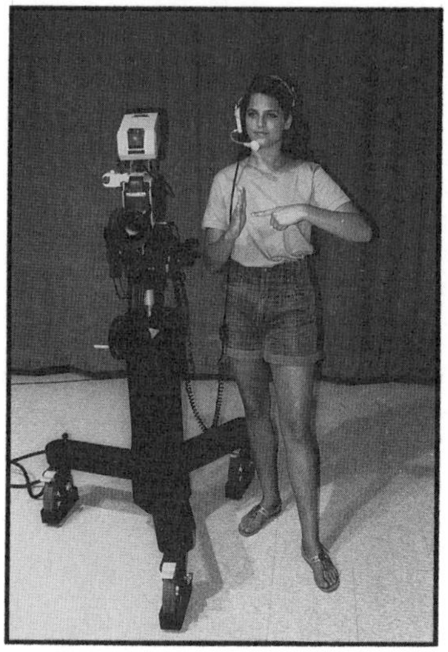	Place palm of one hand in front of extended forefinger of the other hand, which is rotating clockwise.
10. Speak up (Talk louder)	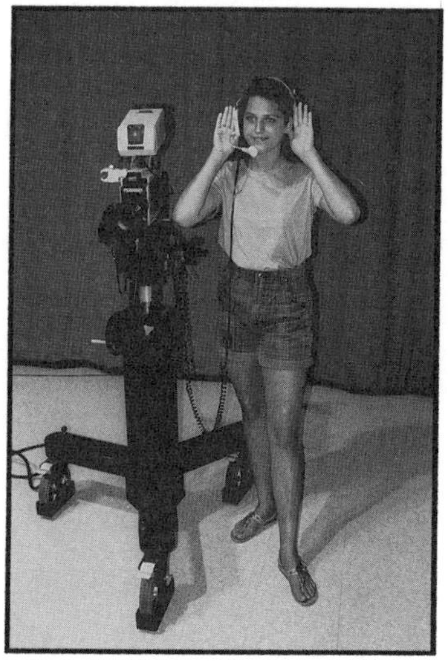	Place both hands cupped behind the ears.

Cue	Picture	Signal
11. Tone down (Speak quieter, become less animated)	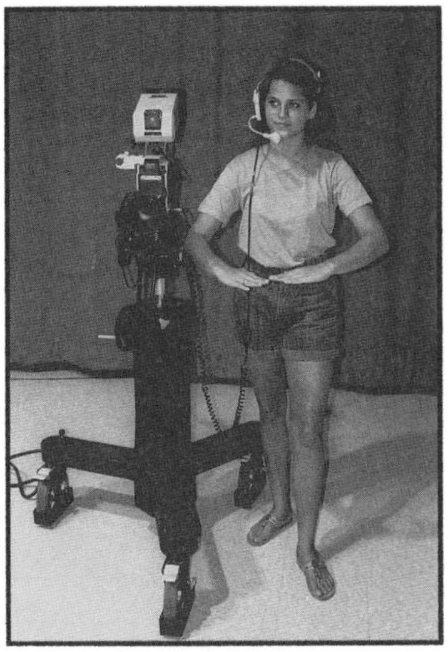	Place hands together, palms facing the floor and move in a pushing down direction.
12. On time (Program is continuing according to schedule)	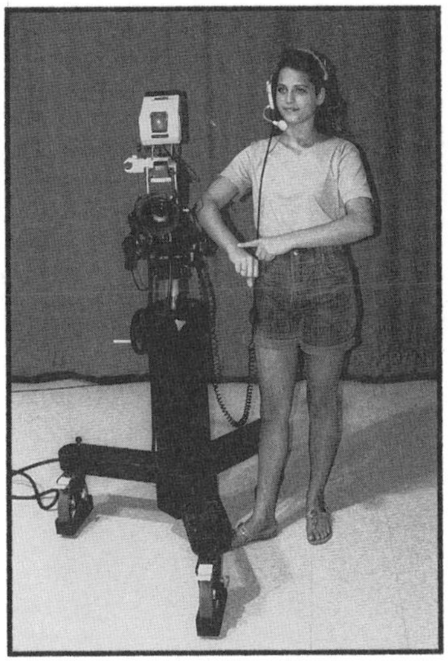	Place forefinger on nose, or on wrist to simulate a watch position.

These cues should be memorized by the floor director and talent. Cues are used during program taping. Each cue is given in a sharp, deliberate manner. Remember, the floor director is directing the talent by cues relayed from the director. Every cue needs to be immediately followed by talent as soon as it is given.

Directing Production Staff

Besides directing the on-camera talent, the director must also coordinate the efforts of the production crew. Each member of the staff has specific responsibilities and tasks to perform. The director is responsible for using the skills and expertise of each member and coordinating those efforts to produce a quality program. Personality traits and egos, as well as personal problems, must be set aside so each member can fully contribute to the production team. The director should quickly recognize and resolve conflicts and problems as soon as they appear. The interaction among crew members should be as professional and cordial as possible.

During the course of production, crew members are usually directed according to position, rather than by personal names and titles. For example:

"Pan left, camera 1."

"Camera 2, ready to pan left."

"Audio, cue intro music in :10."

"Roll tape in 5, 4, 3 ..."

Whenever possible, the director should give each staff member a "ready" signal prior to initiating a task. Some examples include:

"Ready to cut to camera 2 ... cut to 2."

"Ready for ending graphics ... roll graphics."

"Ready to roll opening ... roll opening."

"Ready to key graphics over camera 1 ... key graphics."

Directors often experience stress and frustration at technical and performance mistakes. Correcting mistakes quickly and effectively can be best accomplished by calmly assessing the mistake and identifying the correct procedure to eliminate the error. Never yell, berate, or degrade crew or talent for making mental or technical mistakes. Doing so only causes tension and creates hard feelings among staff members.

When the taping has been completed, the director often meets with the technical crew to discuss problems that may have occurred and identify steps to avoid the same problems in the future. Positive praise is also important during these discussions. Take the time to thank the crew for a job well done.

The director's job can often be difficult and full of stress, but the feeling of accomplishment when taping is complete is very rewarding. Directors need to be self-confident, patient, and professional. Knowledge of equipment and operations is important, as well as social skills in working with production crews, talent, and staff. A good director knows how to plan, coordinate, and complete a television production program.

Review Questions: Lesson 7

1. List and briefly describe the three roles a director must assume in television production. (*Descriptions will vary, but students should identify the following.*)
   - [Motivator ...]
   - [Technical advisor ...]
   - [Supervisor ...]
2. Describe a technique or suggestion for improving on-camera performances in each of these areas:
   a. blocking— [The talent needs to adhere to all predetermined movements and positions.]
   b. camera switching— [Talent must be aware of all camera switches and know which camera is "hot" or recording the shot.]
   c. body/head movement— [Restrict actions and movements. Be less animated than when performing on a stage. Avoid distracting movements and actions.]
   d. timing— [Pay strict attention to time slots and time cues.]

(Review questions continue on page II-1-88.)

3. What is the difference between an actor and a performer? [An actor portrays someone else in a dramatic activity. Performers always portray themselves.]
4. Why are floor cues given by hand signals rather than verbally? [Hand signals are given so that an open mic will not pick up any audible cues.]
5. List three typical duties a floor director would perform.
   - [Relay the director's cues to the on-camera talent.]
   - [Coordinate the efforts of the production crew.]
   - [Quickly recognize and resolve conflicts.]

Activities: Lesson 7

1. Research the life of a well-known director. Write a brief report about his or her life. Include the following information:

   a. Biographical information (place/date of birth, family history)

   b. Education

   c. Professional works

   d. Professional awards/highlights

2. Write a letter to one of your favorite television actors (in care of the television studio address). Explain why you enjoy his or her work and request an autograph or picture. Display these in the classroom, along with any responses you receive.

3. Locate information about floor cues not presented in this chapter. Present this information to the class.

4. Survey two of your other classes to find out their current favorite:

   a. actor

   b. performer

   c. movie

   d. television show

   Compile the results and share them with the class.

Student Project Plan: Floor Director's Cues

NAME ______________________________

Date ____________________

Period ____________________

DESCRIPTION OF COMPLETED PROJECT

The students will become familiar with some commonly used cues in television production by taping the cues on videotape.

FORMAT

1. This project is to be completed in groups of two students. One student will be the director, and the other will assume the role of floor director. After completing the project, the students will switch roles.
2. The floor director will be on camera. The camera should be set so that all hand signals will be recorded (perhaps a waist shot) with enough headroom for overhead hand signals.
3. The director will read out the cues in order and assist in recording the hand signals given by the floor director.
4. Each cue is worth 5 points.
5. After completing the cues, rewind the tape and turn it in along with this form.

Evaluation Sheet: Floor Director's Cues

NAME ____________________

The cues are worth 5 points each. The project is worth 60 points.

1. Stand-by ____________
2. Thirty seconds (:30) ____________
3. Fifteen seconds (:15) ____________
4. 5, 4, 3, 2, 1 ... (countdown) ____________
5. Cue ____________
6. Speed up ____________
7. Wind up ____________
8. Cut ____________
9. Roll VCR ____________
10. Speak up ____________
11. Tone down ____________
12. On time ____________

Total points awarded ____________ out of 60 points

Teacher's comments:

Student Project Plan: Teen Conflicts and Social Issues

DESCRIPTION OF COMPLETED PROJECT

Students will present information about a social issue or conflict that affects teenagers' lives today in a 3½- to 5-minute videotape format. The project is worth 100 points.

FORMAT

Every project should include:

1. a reporter stand-up
2. graphics showing relevant statistical information
3. video footage with voice-over
4. on-camera statements or interviews
5. ending graphics (Ending credits include personnel and job descriptions, special guests/interviews, and acknowledgments.)

METHOD

1. Describe the social issue or conflict.
2. Define the problems associated with this issue.
3. Present research information and statistical data.
4. Present various views/opinions on the topic:
   a. quotes/comments
   b. interviews
   c. statements on-camera
5. Identify possible solutions or outcomes to the topic.

NOTES

1. Begin researching your project immediately.
2. Contact several professionals related to your topic for information and possible on-camera interviews.
3. Additional information and video footage may be available from your local library or school media center.

EVALUATION

Content	25 points
Camera	25 points
Audio	25 points
Editing	25 points

Evaluation Sheet: Teen Conflicts and Social Issues

Names	Job Descriptions
1. ______________________	______________________
2. ______________________	______________________
3. ______________________	______________________
4. ______________________	______________________
5. ______________________	______________________

Content: ______________ (25)

Information provided on topic was complete and accurate. Report contained statistical data on the subject; defined problems; and identified solutions and outcomes.

Camera: ______________ (25)

All shots were framed, focused, and white-balanced. Report featured use of a 1-shot for on-camera statements and comments, and a variety of camera angles and backgrounds.

Audio: ______________ (25)

Audio levels were consistently balanced, audio dubs were clear, and audio transitions were smooth.

Editing: ______________ (25)

Report maintained project complexity and continuity with smooth transitions. Contained 15-second leader and tag of black. No glitches, sync rolls, or extra frames.

Total points ______________

Teacher's comments:

Lesson 8 The Role of the Television Producer

Objectives

After successfully completing this lesson, you will be able to:

- *identify program constraints.*
- *identify personnel needed to produce television programs.*
- *describe production personnel tasks.*
- *plan a television program.*
- *complete a production schedule.*
- *produce a television program.*

Vocabulary

Producer. The person who creates and organizes television programs. In some cases, he or she supervises production personnel.

Slate. A small blackboard that identifies the program/show title, scene and take numbers, date, and time. This information is recorded at the beginning of each videotaped segment.

Producing television programs is an exciting and challenging responsibility, involving a lot of creative and technical expertise, as well as social skills in working with talent and production personnel. Producers have the responsibility of ensuring that television programs meet technical, creative, and budgetary standards. They must coordinate a variety of tasks from program conception to program completion.

Designing the Program

Television programs are produced to fulfill a need or interest of the viewing audience. Such programs can be as simple as those providing nightly entertainment or as complex as those identifying and solving national and community problems. If there is a lack of viewer interest in the topic, chances are the program will not be very successful. Citizens' concern for the environment, for example, can serve as an impetus for creating programs about environmental awareness and community action.

Once a program topic has been selected, the producer must analyze several factors before deciding if the show is feasible. These program constraints include:

1. *Time.* Is there enough time to produce the program before viewer interest or need has diminished? For example, if an election is being held in two weeks, a producer would have to make a judgment as to whether or not there would be enough time to produce a program highlighting each local candidate's qualifications and position on the issues. This type of program would not be feasible to produce if it could not be aired prior to the election.

2. *Budget.* Will the cost of the program exceed the financial constraints of the station or production company? Most programs do not have an unlimited budget, and financial concerns are important in making the decision to produce a television show. The producer must carefully estimate the cost of each program in terms of equipment, talent, production personnel, sets, props, and wardrobe.

3. *Equipment/expertise.* Is the equipment available to produce the program? Are there enough qualified personnel to operate it? A program on scuba diving would be great with an underwater camera available for capturing exciting action footage. A camera could be obtained (rented, leased) but you also need someone to operate it.

Satisfying these constraints can often require some creative planning and expertise on the part of the producer.

Producers also need to identify intended viewing audiences, evaluate their viewing needs and desires, and distribute the program in a way that will best reach the greatest number of viewers. Surveys and polls can be used to estimate viewer concerns and interests. Ratings are often used to determine which type of programming is successful in obtaining viewing audiences. Producers must analyze these data and use them to determine program content as well as program distribution.

Organizing the Program

Once a topic has been selected and approved, the producer must coordinate equipment, facilities, and personnel necessary for producing the project.

The personnel needs of the program should be identified. Individuals should be selected based on expertise, experience, and availability. A list can be created identifying all possible job tasks/positions. Depending upon the format of the program, the number of personnel used for the project will vary. Smaller production companies often use one or two individuals to perform several tasks. Some of the personnel may include:

- *Director:* In charge of directing on-camera talent and production personnel.
- *TD (Technical director):* Operates the switcher.
- *Art director:* Creates and designs sets, displays, scenery, and props.
- *Writer:* Transforms ideas into a written script/storyboard.
- *Audio engineer:* In charge of setting up and operating audio equipment.
- *Graphics:* Types and stores graphics for program, operates character generator during production.
- *Videotape engineer:* Operates VCRs for recording/playback.
- *Videographer:* Operates camera used for recording program.
- *Talent:* Performs and acts on-camera.
- *Floor director:* Relays cues from director to talent.
- *Lighting:* Sets up and operates lighting equipment.
- *Editor:* Edits program material to make final master copy.

After each position has been filled, equipment and supplies must be identified and secured. The lighting director, for example, may request several types of lights, fixtures, gels, and scrims for setting up various lighting conditions. The audio engineer might need several types of microphones, extension cables, and windscreens. Each production crew member should identify necessary equipment and supplies, compile a list, and submit the list to the producer. The producer can locate sources for equipment rental or purchase.

Sets, props, costumes, and accessories can be accumulated and stored so they will be available as needed. Make a list, scene by scene, of all necessary props. Cross each item off the list when it has been obtained. Props for each scene should be stored together, perhaps in large boxes clearly labeled with program title and scene numbers.

Sets need to be built and locations identified as soon as possible. Sets should first be designed on paper and then built to specifications. If several people are working together to construct a set, it is much easier to complete if there is an established guideline to follow.

The producer needs to conduct periodic meetings with cast and crew to determine progress, identify and solve problems, and maintain enthusiasm for the project.

Scheduling the Production

Production schedules are used to coordinate the activities of cast and crew. They include locations, talent and crew information, and dates and times for rehearsals and videotaping. Production schedules are important. They provide crew and talent the opportunity to plan and organize their activities so they will be prepared for each day's events. Last-minute problems ("We don't have the ...!") can be avoided by reviewing upcoming production activities with program personnel. Production schedules should be given to all talent and production personnel.

A production schedule for a television program titled "Today's Schools: Protecting the Environment in Education" might look like that shown in figure 1.24.

This production schedule illustrates the planning and details necessary for completing television projects. The more complicated the production, the greater the need for organization and planning. Post the production schedule in an obvious place, and duplicate the schedule so that all cast and crew members have their own copy.

Recording the Program

Organizing and coordinating the efforts of cast and crew during program taping can be a monumental task. Delegate some of the supervisory roles to the director, technical director, and floor director (figure 1.25). These personnel can direct camera operators, lighting technicians, audio technicians, and on-camera talent. Delegating prevents the producer from being overcome by the endless details involved in recording the program. The producer can assist in coordinating the various groups involved in the production by working closely with these subordinates.

During the actual recording of program material, the producer can assist in directing talent and crew, and offer suggestions for solving problems and concerns that occur during production.

Keeping program segments and tapes organized is crucial when producing complex programs. Each tape needs to be clearly labeled and identified for editing purposes. There are often several takes for each program segment. A log should be kept with each tape identifying the scene and take numbers. A slate can be used to identify each segment as it is being recorded on tape. This is extremely helpful during the editing phase of production.

Fig. 1.24. Sample production schedule.

Show/Scene	Date/Time	Location	Talent/Crew
Opening/Closing	Aug. 21 1:00 P.M. - 3:00 P.M.	Orlando H.S. Front Entrance	John T. - Reporter Crew #1
Scene #1	Aug. 22 2:30 P.M. - 3:30 P.M.	Orlando H.S. Dumpster	John T. - Reporter Mr. Nadel, Jerry
Scene #2	Aug. 23 12:00 P.M. - 12:45 P.M.	Orlando H.S. Cafeteria	Jen W. - Reporter
Scene #3	Aug. 24 1:00 P.M. - 2:00 P.M.	Riverside H.S. Science Lab	Jen W. - Reporter Mrs. Fipps
Scene #4	Aug. 24 3:00 P.M. - 4:00 P.M.	Riverside H.S. Rm. 221	Jen W. - Reporter Environmental Club
Scene #5	Aug. 27 9:00 A.M. - 11:00 A.M.	Orange County School Board Office	Jen W. - Reporter Mr. Church

The producer should review each tape as soon as possible to check video and audio quality, program continuity, as well as overall production quality.

During postproduction, the producer makes decisions about edit points, special effects, and other postproduction techniques that can enhance the quality of the final program. The producer reviews and evaluates the final master copy before the project is considered to be complete. Technical, as well as aesthetic qualities of the tape are evaluated by the producer. If the program meets technical standards, as well as program objectives, the tape is ready for broadcast!

Producing television programs requires a combination of technical skills and social expertise. The television producer has to be prepared to work with people and equipment. The producer must anticipate possible problems and offer solutions. Creativity and originality are traits that all producers must have to design and produce innovative programs for the viewing audience. Television producers truly take ideas and turn them into reality!

Fig. 1.25. A technical director operates the switcher during production.

Review Questions: Lesson 8

1. What is a slate and how is it used in television production? [A slate is a small blackboard that identifies program/show title, scene, take numbers, dates, and times. It is recorded at the beginning of each scene/take to assist in editing and postproduction.]
2. Identify and describe the three constraints when deciding program feasibility.
   - [Time—Is there enough time to produce the program before viewer interest or demand is diminished?]
   - [Budget—Will the cost of the program exceed the financial constraints of the company?]
   - [Equipment/expertise—Is there enough equipment to produce the program? Are there enough qualified personnel to operate it?]
3. Identify the personnel for each job description.
   a. Sets up and operates audio equipment. [Audio engineer]
   b. Types and operates character generator. [Graphics operator]
   c. Operates VCRs for recording/playback. [Videotape engineer]
   d. Operates the switcher. [Technical director]
   e. Cues on-camera talent. Relays director's cues to talent. [Floor director]

f. Coordinates the activities of production personnel. [Director]

g. Transforms ideas and concepts into a written script/storyboard. [Writer]

h. Designs and creates sets. [Art director]

i. Edits program material. [Editor]

j. Sets up and operates lighting equipment. [Lighting engineer]

k. Operates cameras used for recording program. [Camera operator]

l. Performs and acts on-camera. [Talent]

4. What is a production schedule? What program elements are included in a production schedule? [A production schedule is a chart that lists the activities of cast and crew. It's the production schedule that includes show and scene numbers, dates and times of production, locations of each scene, and the talent and crew members needed for each scene.]

5. What are two ways a producer can determine if a program idea is going to meet viewer needs and interests? (*Answers should include the following.*)

- [Polls, surveys, and ratings.]
- [The producer analyzes data to see if the show/program meets the needs and demands of the viewers.]

Activities: Lesson 8

1. Carefully watch the credits for three of your favorite television shows. Write down the producer's name. Compile a list of this information in your class.

2. Research the A. C. Nielsen ratings used in television today. Write a brief paper about the Nielsen ratings.

3. Create a survey to use in two of your other classes to find out what types of programs students currently watch and what types of programming they would like to see on television currently not available.

4. Write a brief report about the life of a television producer. Find out the following information:

   a. Educational background

   b. Professional experience

   c. Professional awards

   d. Current job/program involvement

5. All television programs are categorized by the Federal Communications Commission (FCC) into eight categories. Use your local television guide to identify a program that fits each category:

   (A) Agricultural—

   (E) Entertainment—

   (N) News—

   (PA) Public affairs—

   (R) Religious—

   (I) Instructional—

   (S) Sports—

   (O) Other—

Student Project Plan: Studio Video

DESCRIPTION OF COMPLETED PROJECT

The students will become familiar with the planning, production, and postproduction aspects of studio videotaping; will develop an understanding of the role of a producer in television production; and will develop expertise in the use of studio equipment by producing a 2- to 5-minute video project using studio television equipment. The project will be worth 100 points.

FORMAT

1. Show opening. Must include title of show, video, and audio track. Should not exceed 20 seconds.
2. Show content. Must be videotaped using studio equipment.
   a. Should include at least two camera angles.
   b. Must include one videotaped segment or footage rolled in during program taping.
   c. Topic must be approved by instructor.
3. Graphics. Ending graphics must include personnel and job descriptions. Graphics may be keyed over camera or video footage. Ending credits must contain an audio track.

PERSONNEL

Producer/Director: ______________________________

Assigns jobs. Responsible for program content and completed storyboards. Maintains production schedule and coordinates personnel during program taping.

TD: ______________________________

Operates switcher. Assists in coordinating show taping.

Audio technician: ______________________________

Sets up studio microphones. Operates audio equipment. Obtains necessary music and assists in producing prerecorded segments.

(Student Project Plan continues on page II-1-102.)

Videographer(s): ______________________________

____

Operates cameras during studio taping. Records video material for opening and videotaped segments. Cues talent and relays director's cues.

Graphics operator: ______________________________

Types and stores graphics for program use. Operates CG during production.

Videotape operator(s): ______________________________

____

Operates VCRs for recording and playback. Calls out time cues for prerecorded segments rolled in during production.

Talent: ______________________________

Assists in writing script. Responsible for wardrobe, props, and set design.

NOTES

1. Start production on videotaped segments and show opening as soon as storyboards and script have been completed.
2. Keep it simple. Don't try to do too much too soon.
3. Meet as a team and review storyboards, program content, and production schedules. Duplicate storyboards for each production personnel.
4. Remember, this is a *group* effort. Everyone contributes to the success of the program.

EVALUATION

Show content	25 points
Technical aspects	25 points
Format	25 points
Production aspects	25 points

Evaluation Sheet: Studio Video

Project Title: ______________________________

Description: ______________________________

PERSONNEL

1. Producer/director: ______________________________
2. TD: ______________________________
3. Audio technician: ______________________________
4. Camera operator(s): ______________________________

   ____
5. Graphics operator: ______________________________
6. Videotape operator: ______________________________
7. Talent: ______________________________

   ____

GRADING

Show content: ____________ (25)

Topic and content appropriate for intended audience; informative, thorough presentation of subject matter.

Technical aspects: ____________ (25)

Professionally produced, camera shots effective, switcher operations performed satisfactorily, program contains a high degree of complexity and continuity.

Format: ____________ (25)

Program format consistent with project outline.

Production aspects: ____________ (25)

Topic maintains viewer interest, length is appropriate for subject matter, and editing is consistent with program continuity.

Total points: ____________ out of a possible 100 points

Teacher's comments:

Notes to the Teacher

(There are no notes for lesson 1.)

Lesson 2: From the Teacher's Desk

TOPIC SELECTION

1. Topics or classes that are being taught during the periods you are teaching your television production class are the most accessible and feasible to select as subjects for video projects. Obtain a curriculum schedule from an administrator that lists subjects and classes, instructors, and room numbers by class period. Prepare this information for each of your television classes on a handout or an overhead transparency so that students will be aware of their options when selecting topics. For example, it would be extremely difficult for a third-period television production student to do a project on a fifth-period art class. Some subjects could be covered during lunch, but students need to be advised that they are, in effect, volunteering to shorten or omit some of their lunchtime to obtain the necessary video footage and information.

2. Help students select classes and programs that offer interesting and creative project ideas. Classes such as Driver's Education, Typing, Marketing, Art, Ceramics, Drama, and Music can easily provide interesting video and viewer interest. It's more challenging to create an interesting project with an English class, for example.

GROUP SELECTION

3. Students can form groups based on topic rather than individual preferences. For example, you can ask "Who would like to work on a project about Student Council?" rather than "Who wants to work with Jim?"

4. Allow each team to be only as large as the number of jobs required for completing the project. The project in this lesson can be done in groups of two or three.

5. Make sure everyone is included in a group. If one or two students are having trouble finding a team, form a group of two and assist them in selecting a topic. Discretely enlist the aid of your students in finding a group for a lone classmate.

RESEARCHING THE TOPIC

6. After the groups have narrowed their ideas to one topic or class, allow them to leave class a few minutes early to go and introduce themselves to the instructor of the class on which they will be reporting. At this time they can schedule some dates for classroom observation and videotaping. Remind them to ask the teacher for a copy of the class syllabus.

7. Classroom observation is extremely helpful in planning the storyboards and scripts. Encourage the production team to take a clipboard and paper on which to take notes, jot down camera shots, and list script ideas.

STORYBOARDING THE PROJECT

8. Scriptwriting is critical. Work closely with your groups to develop scripts that are accurate and interesting.

9. Review each storyboard with the team before you allow them to sign up for videotaping. Suggest creative openings, camera shots, and summaries for groups that are having trouble being creative.

SCHEDULING

10. Hopefully you have established a scheduling procedure for videotaping and editing in your class. A large monthly "Planning Calendar" can be laminated and used as a taping/editing schedule board. Use different color overhead transparency pens for observation dates, taping dates, and editing times.

11. Encourage groups to start immediately! Motivate your students and discourage procrastination. Wasting time with too much "planning" and not enough "production" results in projects not getting completed on time. Set a realistic deadline for final completion of the project and consider using a point reduction system for late projects.

12. Set limits on the amount of time students can engage in each production phase (allowing some margin for individual differences and student absences).

    Observation: Limit to one class period.

    Videotaping: Two or three class periods are sufficient for obtaining all required footage.

    Editing: Depending upon the skills of the students, and the complexity of their projects, set a two- to three-day limit for each group.

STORING PROJECTS

13. As each team turns in its project for grading, duplicate the project on a master tape for future broadcast and viewing. Keep a current tape log with this tape so you can quickly locate projects as you need them. This project readily lends itself for use in:

    a. curriculum fairs

    b. school news shows

    c. PTA open houses

    d. video yearbooks

14. Each student should copy the completed project on his or her own tape for future use (e.g., video resumes, portfolios). All student tape logs should be updated after project completion.

Lesson 3: Students' Choice

TOPIC SELECTION

1. This is an opportunity for students to work on a topic or project that they are personally interested in producing. Encourage creativity in the selection of topics, but inform students that the topic must conform to program, school, and community standards. Some of the students will select topics that are not appropriate for a school-based television program. Discuss such considerations with your students and encourage them to select another topic, or approach the topic in another way.

2. Do not let students take days or weeks to select a topic. Set a deadline for topic selection and forming the production group. Sometimes selecting a topic can be difficult, but students need to realize that this is an important part of the television production process.

3. Don't reject a student's choice of topic simply because you do not feel it is important or interesting. Allow students the opportunity to work on something they like.

GROUPS

4. Some topics can be produced by individual students. These might include editing football highlights to music, or doing a documentary on a community/national problem.

5. After one or two days, check to be sure every student is involved in a group or working individually on a project.

6. Don't allow students to form groups that are too large for the number of production jobs needed to complete the project. Students have a tendency to want to work with their friends rather than form groups strictly to perform a job.

PRODUCTION

7. Monitor each group's progress in terms of time, production scheduling, and personnel workload. Remind students that this is a group effort and that everyone must share in the workload.

8. Students often have a topic in mind but are unable to decide how to approach the topic in a video project. Assist them in developing a creative and informative approach to their topic. For example, they may choose to do a video project on "Skateboarding." Their idea is to re-edit a few skate videotapes using their own music and editing style. You could suggest that they also include some of the following skateboarding ideas:

   a. skater's clothes

   b. skateboards—where to buy them, different styles

   c. skateboarder's lingo—what they say and how they say it

   d. careers in skateboarding

   By suggesting ways to expand the topic ideas, you can encourage students to produce more effective videos.

GRADING

9. A grading sheet is included in this lesson.

STORAGE AND VIEWING

10. Edit the completed projects on a master tape for rebroadcast or classroom viewing. Complete a tape log so that projects can be quickly and accurately located.

Lesson 3: Music Video Project

MUSIC SELECTION

1. Discuss with your students the criteria for appropriate music selection. All selected music needs to conform to the standards and rules established by your program, school, and community.

2. Adhere to the time criteria established for the music selection. Many students will want to create a music video for the entire song, but most school-based television production programs have limited equipment. Due to time constraints, students need to produce their video in a few days. Until they actually begin editing, most students do not realize how complicated producing a music video can be.

3. Many students will be requesting to use a certain song that they do not currently possess. Posting a list of requested songs in your classroom can assist students in sharing music selections.

AUDIO TRACK

4. The audio track can be recorded in several ways:

    a. A control track and audio track can be recorded simultaneously by recording black and music at the same time. Remind students to allow the tape to roll at least 15 seconds before and after they add the music.

    b. Record the control track (black) and the music selection on separate tapes. Use the audio insert mode on the editing system to transfer the song onto the master tape.

5. Most songs are longer than the length of the project. Students should fade out the music at the appropriate time.

6. Remind students to carefully monitor the VU meters to keep the music below the distortion point (100% VU).

VIDEO TRACK

7. Before students begin editing their video tracks, have them watch a few music videos. Point out the use of many camera angles, brief shots, and quick edits. This increases the complexity of the video and keeps viewer attention focused on the video. If the students edit long, uninteresting shots in their music videos, the result will be unappealing to viewers.

8. Once the audio track has been recorded, students will begin to video insert images on the master tape. Constantly remind students to always double-check the editing mode before they begin editing to make sure it is on video insert only! If they edit on the assemble mode, the control track will be broken and they will have to start the entire project over again. (This is sure to happen at least once each semester!)

9. Some editing systems do not add a few extra frames and roll back to the "out-" cue in the video insert mode. This can result in some black frames being left between the edits. In this case, students should add a few extra frames (5-10) at the end of each edit and manually roll the master tape back a few frames at the end of each edit. This will eliminate the chance of leaving black frames between the edit points.

10. Some students will want to lip sync parts of their music video. Although this is difficult to do without the use of SMPTE time code, it can be done. Students should play the music selection on an audiocassette player at the same time they are videotaping the lip sync segments. Then, with a lot of patience and preview editing, they can synchronize the video and audio portions of the tapes. Using some special effects while editing (strobe, paints, mosaics) can disguise slight variations in the synchronization. This technique is often used in music videos anyway.

GRAPHICS

11. The project does not require an opening title, but some students may wish to use one. Ending credits should include the name of the performing artist, song title, and names of production team members.

12. Graphics and music should fade together at the end of the music selection.

13. Students should be reminded to video insert the graphics, just as they did the other images on the video. If the graphics are assemble edited at the end of the video, the control track will be broken and the end of the song selection will be erased.

STORAGE AND VIEWING

14. Edit all of the completed videos on a master tape for viewing and rebroadcast. These videos make excellent ending credit footage for the school news show. Make sure a tape log is completed for the master tape so you can quickly and accurately locate each selection.

Lesson 4: Composing Graphics

EQUIPMENT

1. The graphics project can be completed using the following equipment:

   a. CG

   b. VCR

   c. monitor

   d. switcher (used for keying effect and fades)

2. Sections of this project can be removed or modified for completion on your school's television equipment. Some functions may not be available on your character generator.

3. Graphic #3 requires the use of a switcher to key graphics over a video picture. The key effect may be eliminated to conform to your program's equipment limitations.

4. Graphic #4 requires students to compose and record a rolled graphics page. If your CG is unable to roll graphics, this portion of the project can be deleted or adapted to match your CG functions.

5. Additional graphic attributes such as size, letter color, background color, shadow or border edging, or letter styles can be added to each of the graphic pages to allow students to use these functions on your character generator.

GROUPS

6. Students can work individually or in pairs to complete this project. If students are working in pairs, each student should type half of each graphic page.

7. Schedule students for 20- to 25-minute intervals to complete this assignment.

FORMAT

8. Students should complete and record each page of graphics on their videotape. Each page should be recorded for 15 seconds. Fade in and fade out of each page.

9. After all four graphics have been recorded, they should be turned in for grading.

10. A grading scale is located on the assignment sheet.

Lesson 5: The Switcher

EQUIPMENT

1. Each activity is designed to use a switcher for producing several video effects.

2. Activity #1 requires the following equipment:

   a. 2 cameras

   b. switcher

   c. VCR

3. Activity #2 requires the use of a switcher/DVE to produce some digital video effects. Delete any effects that are unavailable to your students using your school's television production equipment.

4. Activity #3 is designed to use a switcher in a videotaping activity involving several production crew members. The equipment necessary to complete this activity includes:

    a. two cameras

    b. switcher

    c. CG

    d. two VCRs (one for playback, one for recording)

GROUPS

5. Activities #1 and #2 can be completed individually, one student at a time. Activity #3 requires at least four students working together as a production team.

6. Students can be assigned to groups of four for activity #3, and students can select their jobs within each group.

SCHEDULING

7. It is easier to schedule students and manage equipment if all of the students complete activity #1 before moving on to activity #2. Once the equipment has been set up, several students can complete an activity each day. Once all of the students have completed activities #1 and #2, you can assign groups and begin working on activity #3.

GRADING

8. A grading sheet has been included in this lesson.

Lesson 6: ENG Reporting with On-Camera Comments

PROJECT FORMAT

1. The purpose of this project is to familiarize students with the format and content of a typical ENG news report. Comments and statements recorded on-camera expressing the opinions and ideas of individuals concerned with the topic are used to show both sides of an issue.

2. Students may choose to use a stand-up for the lead-in or the summary, but only one stand-up can be used in this project.

3. Use of a 1-shot is required for recording on-camera statements.

4. Project length (45 to 90 seconds) should be strictly adhered to for this project.

5. Students may benefit from critically watching some local or national ENG news reports to observe project format.

TOPIC SELECTION

6. Encourage students to select a topic that can offer various possible opinions, ideas, and conclusions. Topic ideas could include:

   a. How do students and teachers feel about the school's homework policy?

   b. Can students effectively balance schoolwork and a job?

   c. Should attendance be required?

   d. Is an open lunch policy a safe choice?

   e. Should there be a minimum grade point average for sports participation?

   f. Why do we have to pay to get into school athletic events?

7. All topics need to be approved before groups begin production.

GROUPS

8. Groups should be limited to two or three members. These include a reporter, videographer, and a director. Some groups may choose not to use a director position.

SUGGESTIONS

9. Each project should contain a beginning, a middle, and an end. For example:

   Beginning: "Many students are concerned that...."

   Middle: "We discussed this issue with students and here's what they had to say...."

   End: "As you can see by the opinions expressed in this report, both students and teachers feel...."

10. If possible, encourage students to use graphics to identify people giving statements on-camera:

    John Smith
    Student

11. Encourage students to use split-line editing for the narrative sound track.

12. Edited comments should be made where a natural break occurs during the statement. Discourage chopping a statement in the middle of a sentence or phrase.

GRADING

13. A grading sheet is included.

Lesson 7: Floor Director's Cues

GROUPS

1. Students will work in groups of two to complete this project. One student will appear on-camera performing the cues given by the other student, who will be operating the recording equipment. They will switch roles after the first student has completed all of the cues.

SCHEDULING

2. Each group (two students) should take about 15 minutes to complete this assignment. Most class schedules permit scheduling three to four groups per day.

EQUIPMENT

3. Students will be recording these cues on camera. The equipment needed to complete this assignment is:

    a. camera/deck or camcorder

    b. two-way communication system (optional)

4. If your program does not use a two-way communication system, cues can be given verbally by the camera operator.

PROCEDURES

5. Each student should record their cues on their own videotape.

6. Students should cue up the tape and turn it in along with the floor director's project sheet.

SUGGESTIONS

7. Demonstrate the appropriate way to give each cue prior to students videotaping their cues.

8. Students should spend at least one class period practicing their cues prior to taping.

Lesson 7: Teen Conflicts and Social Issues

OBJECTIVE

1. This project is designed to encourage students to seriously explore topics and issues that affect their lives. Students should be presenting information and ideas about topics that interest them and that are often discussed by students and peers.

TOPIC SELECTION

2. Topics that are open-ended (have no right or wrong solution) offer the best possibilities for video subjects.

3. Students should be encouraged to develop subject ideas for this video project. Classroom discussion about real-life issues and experiences can be helpful in getting students to identify topics for presentation.

4. Newspapers, magazines, and local news shows can be helpful in identifying some issues facing teenagers today.

5. Topics should be presented fairly and professionally. Reporters must remain unbiased and show both sides of an issue. Allow the viewer to make judgments based on the information available in the project.

GROUPS

6. Group size will vary depending on the format and project ideas of the students. Make sure everyone involved in a group has a job responsibility.

FORMAT

7. Students need to use a wide variety of ways to present information so that the project will be interesting to the viewing audience.

8. Statistical information is important and should be used in this project. Graphics can be used to enhance the statistical information.

9. Professionals involved in the subject area can be a great source of information, and many of them will be glad to appear on camera.

10. Many topics will have information and possible video footage available at the city library or school media center.

11. A short discussion group segment may be included in this project at your discretion.

GRADING

12. A grading sheet is included in the lesson.

Lesson 8: Studio Video

EQUIPMENT

1. This project is designed to use studio-configured equipment. Equipment necessary to complete this project is:

   a. two cameras

   b. switcher

   c. two VCRs (one for recording, one for playing video segments)

   d. CG

   e. audio mixer

   f. microphones

   g. music sources (CD player, tape deck, turntable)

2. Project format can be adapted to meet individual school equipment limitations. For example, if the video segments (opening and prerecorded segments) cannot be rolled in during production due to switcher limitations, they can be edited in during postproduction.

3. Personnel may perform several tasks to meet equipment demands during production. Do not assign personnel superfluous jobs if there is no real equipment for them to operate.

TOPIC SELECTION

4. Students should choose topics that can be adapted to the project format. Selecting a topic is one of the most difficult decisions a producer faces. Allow students to experience this part of the process.

5. Talk shows, discussion groups, and even game shows are some of the program formats that work well with this project. Students should be encouraged to be creative.

PROGRAM FORMAT

6. Each program must contain:

   a. An opening: This 20-second opening must include program title, video footage, and an audio track. This should be produced prior to taping studio content.

   b. Show content: This is videotaped in the television studio. Each show must include a videotaped segment. These segments can be produced prior to taping the show, or they may simply include footage that is overlaid over studio audio. For example, a show about the upcoming World Series may include footage of both teams that is overlaid as the announcers discuss each team's potential.

   c. Graphics: Every show should include ending graphics that list each individual, along with their job description. For example:

   Produced by:
   Joe Lewis

   Ending graphics must include an audio track (music).

7. Storyboards are a necessity. Do not allow students to proceed with studio taping until all storyboards have been approved and duplicated (one set for each production crew member).

GROUPS

8. Students can select groups and jobs, or you may assign them. You can also assign production teams and allow them to select their own positions (jobs) within each team.

9. Some students may work with several groups, performing a different job for each group. For example, a student may choose to be a technical director for one group and talent in another group's project.

SCHEDULING

10. Each producer is responsible for maintaining a production schedule. The teacher needs to check daily with each group to monitor progress and make suggestions.

11. Each group should schedule one day for rehearsals and walk-throughs.

12. Program taping should only require one day of studio use and another day of postproduction.

PRODUCTION

13. Supervise the students, but allow them to coordinate and direct their own activities. This is an integral part of the learning process.

14. Make sure everyone understands their job tasks and has prepared for the taping activities.

GRADING

15. A grading sheet has been included in this lesson.

2 ADVANCED TELEVISION PRODUCTION

Objectives

After successfully completing this unit, you will be able to:

- *list the components of a school news program.*
- *complete a television news format sheet.*
- *identify the personnel needed to produce a school news program.*
- *list the equipment needed to produce a school news program.*

Producing a daily or weekly news show is one of the main reasons school administrators initiate a television production program in their facility. Usually this program is broadcast throughout the school on a closed-circuit television system, taking the place of the mundane "morning announcements" broadcast over the intercom system. In many schools, the responsibility of producing/directing these programs rests on the media specialist, working with a small group of students in the media center. Some programs are coordinated by teachers who volunteer to assist in producing the show during their planning periods or after-school hours. Many high schools now offer a television production curriculum with one or two full-time teachers instructing three to six classes per day. Although the programs differ in their methods and complexity from school to school, their goal of producing a school news show is the same.

This chapter is designed to assist you in planning and producing your school news show. It will identify the personnel and skills needed for production staff, offer suggestions and ideas for show formats, and provide you with information and forms for implementing your school news program.

Planning Your Program

The first step in producing your school news show is to identify the show format, or show components. For instance, you need to decide how your show will begin each day, what types of features it will contain, the number of on-camera talent you will need, how the show will end, and whether to broadcast a live or taped show. These are the kinds of decisions that need to be made as you are planning your program with your staff and personnel.

Opening Your Program

Every television show has an opening, and so should yours. Openings can be as simple as titles and graphics with music or a camera focused on a flag while the National Anthem is played. Sophisticated openings can be produced by students using video footage of an array of school activities edited with graphics, titles, and music. Producing a variety of openings for your program can be a useful project for advanced television students. These openings can be "rolled in" prior to switching to the anchor desk for announcements. Show openings should be relatively short in length so as not to cut into show content. Creativity and innovation can lead to some interesting openings.

Show Format

Consistency will help you develop a program quickly and eliminate a lot of technical mistakes. As you and your staff become more proficient, your show's format can become increasingly complex and creative. Start with a very basic format, keeping camera angles, special switcher effects, as well as show content, simple. Once your technical crew gets accustomed to producing a show each day, you can make your shows more technically challenging to produce. Try adding just one or two new items to your show each time. Don't overwhelm your staff by adding too much too soon.

Always meet as a group just before taping or broadcasting and discuss the show content and format sheet. Duplicate the daily format sheet so that everyone involved in the show has a copy to review. Discuss camera shots and angles, the order of announcements and introductions to features and segments, and any special features or technical areas that might need to be highlighted. It is critical that everyone pays close attention to avoid both technical and on-camera mistakes. The overall quality of your program can be improved tremendously by these preproduction meetings.

Figures 2.1, 2.2, and 2.3 (page II-2-5) illustrate the concept of show formats. Figure 2.2 is a format sheet for a basic school news show. Equipment needed is one video camera and tripod, one desk/boom microphone, and an audiocassette deck.

This very basic format would be typical of a beginning program in an elementary or middle school with limited equipment and staff. Most schools have the equipment necessary to produce this type of show. This program could be broadcast live or pretaped for the next day of school.

Fig. 2.1. School news show format sheet.

Camera # Shot	Talent	Audio/Description	Length
Close-up of flag		Pledge of Allegiance audiocassette	:25
Zoom out 2-shot	Anchors 1 and 2	"Welcome to ______ edition of ______ News"	
Pan to Anchor 1 1-shot	Anchor 1	Read announcements and introduce Anchor 2	
Pan to Anchor 2 1-shot	Anchor 2	Read announcements and "Now back to Anchor 1"	
Zoom out 2-shot Fade to black at closing	Anchors 1 and 2	Closing of show Music/audiocassette	:20

Figure 2.2 is a format sheet for an expanded school news show. Equipment needed is two video cameras and tripods, two VCRs (one play and one record if taped-delay broadcast), one switcher/DVE, two microphones (desk or lavaliere), and an audio mixer.

Fig. 2.2. Expanded news show format sheet.

Camera # Shot	Talent	Audio/Description	Length
VCR 1	Opening	Music/sound on tape (SOT)	:30
Camera 1 2-shot	Anchors 1 and 2	"Welcome to...."	
Camera 2 1-shot	Anchor 1	Read announcements and introduce Anchor 2	
Camera 1 1-shot	Anchor 2	Announcements and introduction to "Science Fair Report"	
VCR 1	Reporter ______	Science Fair Segment/voice on tape (VOT)	1:15
Camera 1 1-shot	Anchor 2	Tag report and close	
Camera 2 2-shot	Anchors 1 and 2	"That's all for today's show...."	
VCR 1	Shots of science fair	Music/audiocassette	:45

In figure 2.2, the show begins with a 30-second prerecorded opening that contains school shots and music. Switch to camera 1 (2-shot) of the anchors. After their welcome statement, switch to camera 2 (1-shot) of Anchor 1. Anchor 1 reads the announcements and introduces Anchor 2. Switch to camera 1 (1-shot) of Anchor 2. Anchor 2 reads any announcements and then introduces a prerecorded feature by a reporter on the Science Fair. Switch to VCR for the 1:15-minute segment. Switch to camera 1 (1-shot) of Anchor 2, who tags the segment and closes. Switch to camera 2 (2-shot) as anchors 1 and 2 close the show. Switch to VCR for second prerecorded segment containing Science Fair shots with music used for 45-second closing.

As you can see, this example uses a more complicated format than that shown in figure 2.1. The use of a switcher for different camera angles, a second VCR for "rolling in" prerecorded segments and features, and the use of an audio mixer for switching sound from two microphones requires the coordinated effort and technical skills of both on-camera talent and technical crew.

Figure 2.3 is a format sheet for an extended school news show. Equipment needed is two cameras and tripods, three VCRs (two play and one record if taped-delay broadcast), one switcher and/or DVE, one character generator, one audio mixer, three microphones (desk or lavaliere), and an audiocassette player.

The extended news show begins with a 30-second prerecorded opening with music. Switch to camera 1 (2-shot) for welcome. During this 2-shot the show title and date are superimposed over the camera shot. Switch to camera 2 (1-shot) and superimpose Anchor 1's name as he or she reads announcements and introduces the reporter segment on Math Fair winners. Switch to VCR 2 with prerecorded audio dub. Switch to camera 2 (2-shot) of Anchors 1 and 2 as they tag the segment and go to Anchor 2. Switch to camera 1 (1-shot) and superimpose name as Anchor 2 reads the announcements and introduces the reporter segment on the Teacher of the Year. Switch to VCR 1 with prerecorded segment. Switch to camera 2 (2-shot) of Anchors 2 and 3 as they tag the segment and introduce sports. Switch to camera 1 (1-shot) and superimpose the sports anchor's name as sports announcements are read and he or she introduces the Basketball Team Victory segment. Switch to the prerecorded segment. Switch to camera 1 (1-shot) as the segment is tagged. Switch to CG as scores are read. Switch to camera 1 (1-shot) as sports anchor closes and goes to Anchor 1. Switch to camera 2 (3-shot) for close. Switch to VCR 1 and super ending credits as music is added.

The extended news show uses several aspects of the production team and facility not required by the formats displayed in figures 2.1 and 2.2. For instance, the CG operator and technical director must be ready to superimpose graphics at the appropriate times throughout the show. The audio engineer has to be alert in order to switch microphone sound from one anchor to another, as well as relaying sound from prerecorded segments and overlaying sound for ending credits. The technical director and producer have to work closely together to achieve smooth transitions from one camera shot to another and to prerecorded segments. The VCR operators need to be alert and ready to roll tape on cue. They also need to call out tape times so that the technical director can be ready to switch from VCR to camera shots as segments end.

Due to its complexity, the extended news show demands teamwork, concentration, and attention to detail from everyone on the production staff.

Fig. 2.3. Extended school news show format sheet.

Camera # Shot	Talent	Audio/Description	Length
VCR 1	Opening	Shots of school/SOT	:35
Camera 1 2-shot Super CG	Anchors 1 and 2	Welcome and intro	
Camera 2 1-shot Super CG	Anchor 1	Announcements and intro to report on Math Fair	
VCR 2	Reporter ______	VOT/Math Fair Winners	:60
Camera 2 2-shot	Anchors 1 and 2	Tag report ... go to Anchor 2	
Camera 1 1-shot Super CG	Anchor 2	Announcements and intro to Teacher of the Year Report	
VCR 1	Reporter ______	Teacher of the Year	:45
Camera 2 2-shot	Anchor 2 Anchor 3	Tag and intro to Sports	
Camera 1 1-shot Super CG	Sports Anchor	Sports announcements and intro to Basketball Team Victory	
VCR 2		Game shots/SOT	:30
Camera 1 1-shot	Sports Anchor	Tag and go to sports board	
Graphics		Anchor voice-over (VO)	
Camera 1 1-shot	Sports Anchor	Close and go to Anchor 1	
Camera 2 3-shot	Anchors 1 and 2, and Sports Anchor	Close show: "We'll leave you with some more action from last night's game."	
VCR 1 Super Ending Credits		Music added/audiocassette	:45

Closing the Program

One of the rewards students obtain from their hard work and effort in producing the show is seeing their names and job titles in the show's ending credits. The recognition from faculty and friends goes a long way in motivating the technical crew day after day. If your facility has a character generator, ending credits can be superimposed over a variety of school footage, or even over the anchor desk as lights dim in the studio. Music can then be added and your show is complete. If your facility has no equipment for producing graphics, they can easily be handwritten on poster board or bulletin board paper and videotaped. You can be really creative and place these credits in unique places around the school to be taped. A simple audio dub will enable you to complete your closing.

News Show Forms

Announcement Forms

Preprinted forms on which faculty and staff members can write announcements are a necessity. You also need to arrange one or more locations where the forms can be picked up. Set a deadline for turning in the announcements to be read on each day's show. Be as considerate as possible, but don't compromise yourself and your technical staff by accepting last-minute announcements. The faculty will learn to plan ahead just as you must do.

Club Activity Forms

Club sponsors or officers can notify your production staff of activities that might be interesting to videotape, report on, or announce in your daily show.

Sporting Events

Upcoming sporting events can be announced, videotaped, and edited for highlights. Completed events can be placed in graphics on a "Scoreboard" feature of your news show. Outstanding athletes and their contributions can be recognized on the air.

Television News Personnel

Depending upon the type of facilities and equipment available, the following positions/jobs will be used in producing your school news show:

- *Producer:* Responsible for coordination of all technical crew. Relays messages to the floor director, calls cues for VCR operators, audio engineers, and the graphics operator. Assists in cueing the technical director, and notes camera angles and positions. The producer is responsible for cutting production when a technical error occurs and for resuming taping once the problem has been corrected. If the show needs editing, it is the producer who supervises the editing and makes critical judgments.
- *TD (Technical director):* Responsible for operating the switcher. Decides on the use of various cuts, wipes, dissolves, and special effects.
- *Floor director:* Cues the talent concerning camera angles, microphone checks, and VCR running times; supervises all activity on the studio floor. Responsible for overall maintenance of studio props and sets.
- *Videographer:* Responsible for turning on and setting up studio cameras. Follows format sheet carefully to obtain the best shot possible for each camera angle. After the show's completion, the videographer carefully returns camera cords, lens caps, and headphones to original positions.
- *Graphics operator:* Types in and stores graphics for each day's show, making changes as needed. Works closely with the producer and technical director during taping to ensure that graphics are superimposed when needed.
- *Audio engineer:* Responsible for conducting all microphone checks and adjustments. Switches microphone inputs as needed. Ensures that sound levels are consistent throughout the show's taping and that music selections are cued and ready when needed. Turns off all audio equipment and microphones when taping is completed. Periodically checks mic cables in studio for labeling and readiness.
- *VCR operator:* Cues and times all videotaped segments for the daily show. Calls out cue times as segments are running. Rewinds and replaces tapes in appropriate locations. Makes sure all tapes are properly timed and labeled.
- *Editor:* Edits show to producer's notes and format. Labels and records master tapes for broadcasts.
- *Anchor:* Responsible for obtaining announcements each day and preparing them for broadcast. This may include rewriting or typing announcements. Dresses and acts professionally at all times. Prepares intros for segments on each day's broadcast. Develops good on-camera skills.
- *Reporter:* Responsible for producing ENG reports on various school events and activities. Segments include interviews, taped highlights, previews of upcoming events, and graphics specifying dates and times events were to be held.

Occasionally, due to class size and program limitations, there may be more students enrolled in a class than there are real jobs to perform. Do not assign these extra students frivolous jobs such as "set decorator" (changes bulletin board paper once a month behind the anchor desk), "lighting technician" (no existing set lights, but switches on fluorescent overhead lights), or "prop manager" (no props to manage). These additional students can be used to rotate jobs within your production crew, job shadow existing personnel for training, produce openings/closings for your program, or form a second, completely separate crew to rotate with your primary crew on a daily or weekly basis to produce the news program. Students soon realize when they have been assigned a superfluous job or position and will become disenchanted and uninterested in your program. Make every effort to allow all students enrolled in the class to be major contributors to the program.

Summary

Fig. 2.4. Producing a school news show.

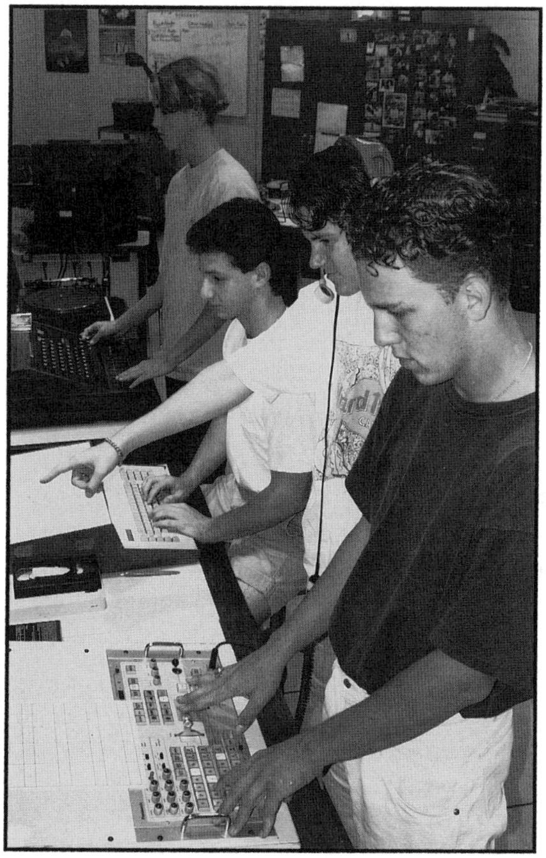

Producing a school news show is an exciting and rewarding experience (figure 2.4). The training and skills students receive will prepare them for entrance into college programs, technical and trade schools, or careers in the community. The teamwork and interaction with their peers develops strong leadership and communication skills that will benefit them throughout their lives.

The school news program provides a vehicle for promoting school spirit and pride; recognition for students, faculty, and staff members; information about school events, classes, and activities; as well as an instructional program for television production students.

Review Questions: Chapter 2

1. Match the television personnel titles with their job descriptions in a through j.

TD	Graphics operator
Floor director	VCR operator
Audio engineer	Editor
Producer/Director	Anchor
Videographer	Reporter

a. Calls out cue times to producer as video segments are playing. [VCR operator]

b. Cues on-camera talent for camera shots and angles. [Floor director]

c. Types in and stores graphics. [Graphics operator]

d. Coordinates all technical crews. [Producer/Director]

e. Follows format sheet to obtain the best shot possible for each camera angle. [Videographer]

f. Conducts all sound checks, cues necessary music material, and adjusts microphone levels. [Audio engineer]

g. Produces ENG reports for later broadcast. [Reporter]

h. Labels and edits master tapes. [Editor]

i. Prepares announcements and introductions to segments and features on the daily newscast. [Anchor]

j. Operates switcher. Performs wipes, fades, dissolves, and creates special effects. [TD]

(Review questions continue on page II-2-10.)

2. Create an example of an extended news show using the following format sheet.

News Format Sheet

Camera # Shot	Talent	Audio/Description	Length

[Student descriptions will vary.]

3. List and describe at least three benefits of having a school news show broadcast daily. (*Answers should include the following.*)
   a. [Provides information to students and faculty.]
   b. [Provides skills and training for television production students.]
   c. [Promotes school spirit/pride.]
   d. [Provides recognition for faculty and students.]
4. List and describe some of the problems and concerns you must address when planning a daily school news show. [Student responses will vary.]

Activities: Chapter 2

1. Write or type a letter to a 4-year university requesting information on programs offered in communications, television broadcasting, or journalism. Submit a copy of the letter to your instructor for approval prior to mailing. Bring materials to share with the class when you receive them.

2. Write or type a letter to a community business involved in some type of video production requesting a brief visit or tour of their facility. Suggested facilities could include television stations, recording studios, film stages and soundstages, postproduction and editing facilities, corporate video facilities, or tape duplication centers. Submit a copy of your letter to your instructor for approval prior to mailing. Follow up your letter with a telephone call approximately 7-10 days after mailing.

   After completing your visit, write a brief summary highlighting key aspects of your visit. Staple a business card or informational literature obtained during your visit to your summary. Present this information to the class in a brief oral presentation.

3. Record two newscasts from different stations aired in your community. Compare and contrast these telecasts in terms of style, technical expertise, content of features, and overall appeal.

4. Record and review a local reporter's feature story aired on your evening news. Write a brief analysis of the feature in the following terms: reporter's intro and summary, overall length, use of interviews and comments from those involved in the story, and overall appeal of the story.

Final Exam: Video Resume

OBJECTIVE

Students will produce a 5- to 10-minute video resume that illustrates their technical, production, and on-camera skills.

FORMAT

1. Title (Graphics)

   These must include the words *Video Resume* and your name. Graphics can be included anywhere during the first 45 seconds of the resume.

2. Opening (Grabber)

   This is one of the most important aspects of your resume. It should grab the viewer's attention. Use your technical and production skills to produce an exciting visual montage of your past video projects in television production. This is sort of a sneak preview of what is included in your resume. The opening should be 30 to 45 seconds in length.

3. Introduction (On camera)

   Introduce yourself and describe some of your skills and abilities. Dress and act professionally!

4. Section 1: Examples of Video Skills

   Edit brief clips that best illustrate some of the video skills you possess. These can be presented in a variety of ways. For example, sports videotaping could include footage of football, basketball, or other sports activities you have taped; ENG reporting could include brief clips from some of your best ENG reports and projects. Editing could feature edited clips that demonstrate your editing abilities. On-camera talent could show some clips that demonstrate your ability to act and perform on-camera. Postproduction skills could be demonstrated with some clips that reflect this skill. In any event, don't include entire projects, but use small segments that illustrate your best work.

   Section 2: News Staff

   Edit brief clips that illustrate some of the positions you have held on your school news show. You can even include video of you performing your job.

Section 3: Equipment Skills

Identify the technical skills and television equipment you can operate. This can be done in a variety of ways, but it must include a listing (graphics) of the major pieces of equipment you can operate. Group equipment into these categories:

Audio Equipment:

Tascam Microphone Mixer
Yamaha M508 8-channel Sound Board

Video Equipment:

Panasonic 5000 ENG Camera
Panasonic 5600 Switcher
Panasonic 6500 1/2" Editing System
Sony 5800 U-Matic Editing System

5. Ending

   End this in a big way. Must include your name, address, and telephone number. Should be 30 to 60 seconds in length.

6. A log sheet for use on this project is on page II-2-14.

Log Sheet

Show #	Description	Counter #	Length
1			
2			
3			
4			
5			
6			
7			
8			
9			
10			
11			
12			
13			
14			
15			
16			
17			
18			
19			
20			

Observation Checklist and Contract Grading Criteria

You may benefit from knowing how you will be evaluated in television production. The observation checklist (page II-2-16) gives you a chance to see the types of things your teacher will be observing when determining your overall performance and grade for the course. The sample contract grading criteria (page II-2-17) is a tip-off on what you have to do to earn a grade of *C* or better. **Note:** Find out whether your teacher will be using these or other criteria when determining your grade.

Observation Checklist

NAME ______________________________ Date ______________

Job Description ______________________________

Ratings: S=Superior E=Excellent G=Good F=Fair U=Unsatisfactory

1. Attendance S E G F U
   ______ Attends class daily
   ______ Gives notice of absences
   ______ Arrives for class on time

2. Job Performance S E G F U
   ______ Routinely does job effectively
   ______ Overcomes problems
   ______ Assists others
   ______ Acts professionally

3. Preparedness S E G F U
   ______ Comes prepared to class each day
   ______ Returns equipment to proper positions after use

4. Innovativeness S E G F U
   ______ Seeks new ways to improve show quality or job performance
   ______ Accepts suggestions and implements them in newscasts

5. Attitude S E G F U
   ______ Cheerful
   ______ Encourages others
   ______ Respects the rights of others

6. Cooperation S E G F U
   ______ Works well with staff
   ______ Avoids confrontations
   ______ Assists in correcting technical problems

Teacher's comments:

Overall rating: ______________

Sample Contract Grading Criteria

To Receive a Grade of *A*

1. Perform assigned duties for your staff position in a superior manner. You will be observed and evaluated three times during this grading period.
2. Complete Daily Journal each day. Submit for evaluation once a week.
3. Complete one visitation to a related industry, such as a television station, radio station, or production facility. Must include a written summary of visitation, a business card or informational literature, and an oral presentation to the class.
4. Complete one ENG news report to be broadcast on school news show. Sign up for taping date, tape and report on highlights, edit for newscast.
5. Produce one opening for newscast.

To Receive a Grade of *B*

1. Perform assigned duties for your staff position in an excellent manner. You will be observed and evaluated three times during this grading period.
2. Complete Daily Journal each day. Submit for evaluation once a week.
3. Complete one ENG news report to be broadcast on school news show. Sign up for taping date, tape and report on highlights, edit for newscast.
4. Produce one opening for newscast.

To Receive a Grade of *C*

1. Perform assigned duties for your staff position. You will be observed and evaluated three times during this grading period.
2. Complete Daily Journal each day. Submit for evaluation once a week.
3. Complete one of the following:
   a. ENG news report to be broadcast on school news show.
      Sign up for taping date, tape and report on highlights, edit for newscast.
   b. Produce one opening for newscast.

Note: All criteria for each grade component must be completed to receive that grade.

Notes to the Teacher

Training Television News Personnel

As discussed in the "Television News Personnel" section on page II-2-7, there are several job functions involved in producing a school news show. Students should be allowed to participate in as many of them as possible throughout the school year. Remember, this experience will help to prepare them for future careers in the field of communications, or for entrance into college programs. Allow them to develop talents in several areas, both as on-camera talent and behind the scenes as technical staff. Students will generally choose jobs that most appeal to them. Allow them to pursue their interests, but also select jobs for them that you feel will benefit them in the future.

The best way to train your personnel is to provide hands-on experiences. Before you begin actual production of your program, tape a week or two of practice shows. Fill out your format sheets, conduct preproduction meetings, and then tape and view your shows for critical comment and feedback.

Select your personnel carefully. Establish firm rules for attendance, conduct, responsibility, and job performance.

Once your show is in production, students can "job shadow" each other before assuming another technical position. By doing this, they can observe another student performing the job in a real-life situation and slowly develop their skills before assuming the new position. Students can learn quickly from one another, and job shadowing will enable them to develop teamwork skills as well.

Evaluation

Grading and evaluating your production staff requires going beyond the usual paper-and-pencil tests and quizzes given in most classrooms. The objectives and skills mastered by students in this area are not easily measured by objective tests. Other forms of evaluation are needed to measure and grade the performance of students.

Daily Journals. Evaluation can be done via a *journal.* Each staff member should be required to keep a daily journal of his or her activities and production work. Typical journal entries would include the date of each entry, a summary of show content, a brief description of the tasks completed during the show, and a comment on their own performance for the day. These journals are collected periodically and the teacher may jot down comments for staff to read.

Exams. Semester and final *Exams* are required by some schools. A written exam can be given to the students, but it won't benefit them or your program in the future. Try to pursue the idea of creating a useful production as an exam. For a final exam, have the students produce a video resume. Not only will this enable them to condense a lot of their work into one piece, but it can assist them in the job and college application process.

Observational Checklists. Teacher observation and the use of a *checklist* for periodic evaluation of staff members can be very effective (see page II-2-16). Students will benefit from knowing which types of behaviors and skills will be evaluated. After observation and completion of checklists, a brief informal conference can be held with each student to provide feedback and suggestions.

Contract Grading. At the beginning of each marking period, a handout indicating the criteria for achieving desired grades (*contract grading*) can be distributed and discussed among staff members (see page II-2-17). This type of grading is extremely beneficial to those students engaged in production activities. Naturally, all completed work must meet the quality standards established by the teacher.

As each assignment is completed, the teacher can evaluate and record the completed assignment in his or her grade book. At this level, almost all of your students will establish high goals for themselves. Contract grading enables students to set their own goals, develop independent learning skills, and experience the reality of working for a television station or production company with deadlines and features to complete.

Grading and evaluating student performance is a necessity. Whether you use one method, or a combination of methods, it is your responsibility as a teacher to be accurate, fair, and professional. If you can develop a system of grading, both you and your students will benefit when it comes time for evaluation.

Scheduling News Show Broadcasts

Once your school has decided to initiate a news program, the next logical step is scheduling the method and times of broadcast. If your school has a closed-circuit television system, broadcasting schoolwide is relatively easy. Schools without this system must be more creative in designing and planning their broadcasts.

Most elementary and middle schools broadcast their programs at the beginning of the school day. Their shows usually include the Pledge of Allegiance, some simple announcements, maybe one feature, and the day's lunch fare. Some shows may have a special guest each day. Scheduling these shows is just a matter of implementation.

High school programs, however, are generally more complex and difficult to schedule. The start of the school day is a difficult time slot because it allows the production staff little or no preparation time. Most high school programs feature sports highlights or news features from the previous day. A first-period time slot would make it difficult to edit these pieces in time for the day's show. Also, a first-period slot would put tremendous pressure on the production staff in other ways: Replacing an absent staff member, handling equipment setup or breakdowns, preparing announcement and segment introductions, and creating the graphics would all be difficult to accomplish by the start of the school day. The last period of the day also presents difficulties:

- Students who have questions about any of the teachers' announcements concerning classroom or club activities would not have time to verify the information by the end of the school day.

- Many activities (ticket sales, club events, and fund-raisers) occur during lunch time. By broadcasting at the end of each day, students will have missed the opportunity to obtain information concerning these events.

- Students who leave school early due to work programs, internships, or sporting events will miss the announcements.

Work closely with your school administrators to develop a schedule that will benefit both your program and the student body. Try to position your program during the third or fourth periods. Adjust the bell schedule so that this period is 6 to 10 minutes longer than the other periods; this will eliminate any problems with teachers complaining about shorter class times for those sections. Daily broadcasts during this time slot enable the production staff to prepare a professional show and allow students and teachers the time to benefit from the information presented.

Weekly or monthly broadcasts are less difficult to schedule. Once a week, or once a month, students can go on an "activity period" or homeroom to watch the program or obtain information about school events and activities. These types of shows are generally longer than the daily broadcasts and need to be scheduled accordingly.

Live or Taped Broadcasts?

Whether to broadcast live or to prerecord a show for later broadcast is a decision most instructors must make when planning and scheduling their news program. Most community television news shows are done as live broadcasts. But you must remember that their staff include trained professionals earning significant amounts of money. Students in a learning environment do not usually possess the maturity and savvy of professional newscasters. There are, however, some significant benefits of producing a live broadcast:

- The character and atmosphere of a live broadcast are exciting for both staff and viewers.
- Live broadcasts eliminate the need to purchase and store large quantities of videotape.
- Technical and on-camera talent will learn and train in a real-life broadcast setting.

Some of the disadvantages of a live broadcast include:

- The use of sophisticated equipment and complex programs tends to produce technical errors and on-camera mistakes for students involved in the program.
- High school students usually are very critical of mistakes and miscues and tend to dwell on them.
- You can never be absolutely sure what a teenager will do or say at any given moment.

Taping your program and broadcasting later in the day eliminates most of the problems that can occur during live broadcasts. Students feel more comfortable and secure knowing that some simple editing will eliminate their miscues and bloopers. Personnel can experiment with new formats, special effects, unique camera angles, and other innovative techniques without the fear of appearing less than perfect in front of their peers. Teachers and staff will be more apt to give up some class time to watch a "professionally produced" program. Taping your newscasts allows the students to critique and evaluate their performances, and to make copies of them for later use in video résumés or portfolios. Encourage the students to duplicate copies of the shows to view with their parents. This is a great public relations tool for your program.

Regularly Scheduled Programming

Producing a regularly scheduled television show can be an exciting challenge or a nightmare. Below are some ideas for making it a success.

Master Tapes

1. Show openings, closings, and any other daily or weekly segments and features should be copied onto master tapes and stored in a convenient location. Log and label each tape as new segments are copied onto the tape. This eliminates a lot of wasted time searching through a student's tapes to locate a particular opening or segment to be used for that day's broadcast. Use a separate tape for each type of feature.

2. In order to retrieve information from your master tapes at a later date, it is important to label each tape with the following information:

   a. Show #, date, and running time

   b. Show content (list each feature/segment)

   c. Special notes, anchor names

   Keep master tapes in a secure, climate-controlled area.

Weekly Program Schedule

3. Organizing each day's show content is essential. In order to help you plan each program, laminate a large poster board to list and organize your weekly show schedule, as illustrated in figure 2.5.

Fig. 2.5. Weekly program schedule.

Content	Monday	Tuesday	Wednesday	Thursday	Friday
Feature Segment	"Teacher of the Year"	Homecoming Pep Rally	Homecoming King and Queen Vote	Students' Homecoming Plans	Tonight's Game
ENG Report	"Prom Plans"	"Math Team"	Float Building		King and Queen Interviews
Sports Feature	Homecoming Game		Football Player Interviews		
Closing	Last Year's Homecoming Dance	Students Making Floats	Pep Rally Highlights	Banners Around School	Football Practice
Other				Tuxedo "Specials"	

News Format Sheets

4. Duplicate 50-75 news format sheets to keep in a file for use as needed (figure 2.6). Fill out and duplicate the completed form the day prior to broadcast.

Announcement Forms

5. Daily announcement forms (figure 2.7, page II-2-24) should be duplicated and placed in several locations around the school campus so they will be convenient for teachers and staff members to find and use. A good feature or segment for your daily news show during the first week would be "How to Get Your Announcement Aired on Our Program."

6. Club activity forms (figure 2.8, page II-2-25) could be given to each club sponsor.

7. Sports activity forms (figure 2.9, page II-2-25) could be given to each coach as their season begins. Your athletic director can also provide you with team schedules and rosters.

(Text continues on page II-2-26.)

Fig. 2.6. News format sheet.

NEWS FORMAT

Director:______________________________ Date:__________________

Camera # Shot	Talent	Audio and Description	Length
VCR			
VCR			
VCR			
VCR			

Fig. 2.7. Daily announcement form.

Daily Announcement Form

Return To: ____________________

Dates Needed To Be Announced: ____________________

Announcement: ____________________

Teacher Signature: ____________________

Daily Announcement Form

Return To: ____________________

Dates Needed To Be Announced: ____________________

Announcement: ____________________

Teacher Signature: ____________________

Daily Announcement Form

Return To: ____________________

Dates Needed To Be Announced: ____________________

Announcement: ____________________

Teacher Signature: ____________________

Fig. 2.8. Club activity form.

CLUB ACTIVITY FORM

Club Name: ______________________________
Date(s) to be announced: ______________________________
Activity: ______________________________

____
____
____
____
____
____
____

Videotaped by: __________ Club Members
__________ News Staff

____
Sponsor Signature

Fig. 2.9. Sports activity form.

SPORTS ACTIVITY FORM

Sport: ______________________________
Date(s) to be announced: ______________________________
Activity: ______________________________

____
____
____
____
____
____
____

Team record Conference: __________ Overall: __________
Next game/event: ______________________________

Grading

8. Design each grading period's contract grading form around the assignments for that period. Encourage students to complete the assignments as soon as possible and avoid waiting until the last minute to turn in projects and assignments. Set a due date for each assignment.

9. If you are planning to use a video resume as a final exam, be sure to pass out and discuss this assignment at least 3 months in advance of the due date. Students will need this time to adequately plan, produce, and edit their final copy. Encourage students to begin work on this project as soon as possible.

3 MOVIE MAGIC

Creating Entertaining Video Shorts

Up to this point, this text has focused on nonfiction television. Producing informative school news programs, video yearbooks, and documentaries is an excellent way to learn the skills of television production. However, creating entertaining fiction video programs can also be educational and fun. This chapter will cover the planning and production of entertaining video shorts.

Many students have the opportunity to enter video contests. Sometimes, the content of the video is dictated by the contest sponsor. But often, the contest only states time limits and very general rules. The rest is up to you! But how are successful projects created? Good fiction television, just like good nonfiction television, is the result of careful planning and detailed production.

Preproduction: Before You Shoot

As you probably know by now, a large portion of the work on any video project is done before the videotape recorder rolls for the first time. Preproduction of a video short involves brainstorming, logistical considerations, scripting, storyboarding, and planning the actual shoot.

Brainstorming

Brainstorming is an excellent way for your class to generate ideas for a video program. Just about everyone has an idea for a comedy or drama. These ideas should be listed on the chalkboard during a class discussion. Some class members will begin to combine and improve upon the submitted ideas. Usually within a few minutes, a topic emerges that combines the most exciting elements of many of the ideas. Here's an example: One idea submitted by a high school student involved a young man visiting New York City and meeting many different types of people. Another student wanted to add a mystical aspect, while still another wanted to parody a Hollywood classic. Many other students wanted to explore the restlessness experienced by many teenagers. After a few minutes of discussion, the group decided to produce a video short about a restless, underachieving high school student who is dissatisfied with his surroundings. Through a freak accident, the young man is magically transported to New York City. He meets many interesting people, confronts a bully, and gains dignity and self-respect. He also learns, like Dorothy in

The Wizard of Oz, that there's no place like home. Any one of the ideas presented by a group member probably would have made a passable project. But a combination of several ideas brings complexity and depth to the video project.

Logistical Considerations

Most high school production teams are limited in their locations and budgets for short fictional video programs. Your group's best idea may be a story of international intrigue set on a navy battleship in the middle of the ocean. However, unless you live near a shipyard and your uncle is one of the Joint Chiefs of Staff, you may have some difficulty with the setting of your video. If you live in Iowa, a program about a surfing championship may be out of reach.

Certainly, careful set building can overcome some logistical problems. But remember, people expect more accuracy and authenticity from television than they do from a play. The musical *Oklahoma!* has been presented by many high school thespian groups. The set usually consists of a makeshift farmhouse facade, a few bales of hay, and perhaps even a few stalks of corn in ceramic pots and a clothesline full of quilts and flannel shirts. The audience is willing to suspend its disbelief, and imagine that they are in nineteenth-century Oklahoma. However, the audience would be much less willing to play along with the same setting on the television screen. Television viewers have come to expect accuracy in location and setting. On the other hand, consider your community's environmental strengths. Are there any interesting architectural designs or natural features in your area? In video production, always play your strengths, not your weaknesses.

Obviously, budget requirements must also be considered in school video productions. Plan early how much money you can spend on this project. You may want to begin your video with an aerial view of a city park. But unless the footage already exists, or a friend runs the local helicopter service, this shot may be financially out of reach. A big budget is not a requirement for a successful program. Once again, take careful stock of the resources that are already available to you, and work to add those extra touches otherwise not available.

Scripting

Once you have fine-tuned the concept of your program and solved any serious logistical problems, you can begin writing the script. You may find it helpful to write a one- or two-page treatment for the script, outlining the characters, the setting, and the plot of the program.

When creating the script, try to write in a conversational style. The spoken word is much different from the written word. Read each line of dialogue aloud after you have written it. Close your eyes and imagine your character saying the line. An escaped convict probably wouldn't use the same words as a college professor. Try to get a feel for the type of language used by each character in your production.

Make sure to include stage directions in your script. Stage directions describe the physical actions of the actors in the program, for example, *Joe walks over to the boat.* Sometimes stage directions convey the emotion intended by the scriptwriter, such as, (*Sobbing*) "How can you leave at a time like this?" Sometimes these directions are crucial to the plot development, for example, *Joe picks up a rusty can and throws it at Fred.* This simple action can set the entire plot in motion. Stage directions act as cues to the director and the actors and serve to maintain the scriptwriter's interpretation of the scene.

Just as you describe the actions of your characters, include basic descriptions of the characters' appearance, especially if their appearance changes in the program. For example, *Fred enters from the left wearing jeans, a varsity letter jacket, and a red baseball cap.* This brief description will help when you begin to collect costumes for the program.

Also include detailed descriptions of the setting in your script. Visit the location and make careful notes for use in the scriptwriting process. For example, *Setting—an inner-city alley. The alley is lined with several garbage cans. Pieces of trash are on the ground. The walls are grimy brick and block. A fire escape ladder hangs into the scene on the left.* (Remember, "left" and "right" refer to the *camera's* left and right.) The setting in the script can also aid in the collection of props to be used in the program.

Storyboarding

A storyboard is a drawing of the shot that you wish to create. Storyboarding a fiction short is somewhat trickier than storyboarding a documentary. Depending on your editing ability, any and all scenes in your program could have many different camera angles. Try to storyboard as many different angle changes as possible without distracting from the script. Let's say that your first scene is a 1-minute conversation between a teenage boy and girl in a high school cafeteria. The entire scene *could* be storyboarded as a single two-shot. But after a few seconds, most viewers would become quite bored with this single angle. Read the script closely, and plan close-ups, reaction shots, two-shots, and over-the-shoulder shots. Each different angle will give the viewer a different perspective of the scene. However, be careful of storyboarding too many different camera angles for a single scene. The more angles in a scene, the more exciting the pace of the program. For our 1-minute conversation, five or six different angles should suffice. For a 1-minute chase or fight scene, you may want to storyboard fifteen or twenty shots. The storyboard is a living document—changeable and adaptable. If you formulate a scene on the spot, don't be afraid to tape it. Just make sure that you storyboard each part of each scene.

Storyboarding is a task performed best by individuals or small groups. Certain scenes should be assigned to individuals or small groups who are interested in storyboarding.

Ideally, all of the storyboarding should be done by one or two people in order to provide continuity between scenes. Whether or not you realize it, you have probably developed a certain visual style in your video production. Do you use a moving camera, or a stationary camera on a tripod? Do you prefer close-ups and extreme close-ups, or bust and medium shots. You can probably imagine what a video short would look like if scene 1 was storyboarded by a student who prefers a moving camera and extreme close-ups and scene 2 was storyboarded by a student who sees the camera as a stationary observer and uses mostly long and medium shots. If several students will be storyboarding the project, agree on a visual style for the program. Decide the activity of the camera, the types of shots to be used, and the approach to action on the set. Establishing these guidelines will help you produce a consistent video project.

Planning the Actual Shoot

Once your script and storyboards have been completed, you are ready to plan the actual videotaping of your scenes.

Times and dates. Establish times and dates that will work best for your project. Make sure to consider continuity of the project, especially if you are shooting in different locations or on different days. For example, let's imagine a video program in which a young man gets off work in the early evening and rides the city bus home. Scene 1 shows the young man packing papers into a briefcase at his office desk and getting on the elevator. Scene 2 shows him exiting a high-rise office building and boarding a city bus on the street corner as dusk gives way to evening. Scene 3 shows the young man disembarking the city bus and walking down the street to his apartment building. If no windows or doors are shown in scene 1 (office interior), it could be shot during just about any time of day. Scene 2 *must* be shot in the early evening and must coincide with the city bus schedule—assuming that city bus rental is not in your budget! Now, when does scene 3 (apartment exterior) need to be scheduled? Of course, in the evening. Shooting scene 3 in the morning would lead the viewer to believe that the young man had ridden the city bus all night!

Of course, this example exposes a strength of manipulating a shooting schedule. Let's re-create the first three scenes of our video program, storyboarding the young man boarding a passenger train instead of a city bus. Now, what would the viewer assume if scene 3 (apartment exterior) was shot in the early morning? He or she would assume that the young man had been riding the train all night and that he must not be going to his own house, but visiting a friend or relative for the weekend. All of this information could be conveyed in less than a minute of edited program with no dialogue spoken!

Once each scene is assigned a time and date, make a list of all of the talent and personnel needed for that particular scene. You may not want to have everyone involved in your video short present for the shooting of every scene. Students can certainly learn from watching each other work, but they can also get in the way. Laminate a large piece of posterboard and use it for a schedule sheet. Re-create the board on a piece of paper and make a copy for each team member. Schedule plenty of time for the shoot. What would happen in our project if the young man missed the bus in scene 2? You might have to wait a half hour or more for the next bus.

Scouting the location. You should never go to a location "cold," with no idea of the layout. There are many factors that need to be considered in choosing and working within a field (out of the studio) location. Those factors have been listed on the "Location Fact Sheet" form (figure 3.1), which should be duplicated and completed for each field location used in your program.

Equipment checklist. Complete an equipment checklist (figure 3.2, page II-3-6) for each location you are using. The list should have three check marks at the end of the day: one check for the planning of the location, one check recorded when the equipment is taken from the school, and a third check when the equipment is returned to its proper place at the school.

Costumes and props. You may choose to make a team member responsible for all costumes and props. But because the costumes will probably come from the actors' closets, it's probably better to let actors gather their own costumes. Obtain a number of large grocery bags and label each bag with the name of the actor, or the character if an actor plays more than one character. Then as the actor gathers his or her costume, he or she can place the clothing in the grocery bag, which is kept in the television studio or the classroom. This way, the instructor can double-check the costumes and the actor doesn't forget part of his or her costume. (The latter seems to occur especially at *early morning* shoots.) Props can also be arranged in grocery bags, using scene location instead of character name for the label. It might be helpful to list all of the props needed on the bag and check off each item as it is obtained. For example, a bag could be labeled "coffee shop." The list on the bag would read "coffee cups, napkin holder, ashtray, matches, rubber duck." (This is an avant-garde video project!) Organizing props and costumes can help your video production run smoothly and allow the team members to concentrate on the task at hand.

Expect the unexpected. Part of the excitement of video production is the range of factors that just cannot be controlled. Most things that cannot be controlled *can* be anticipated.

- Make sure to take back-up equipment in case a camera, microphone, or tripod malfunctions.
- Bring extra videotapes in case of tape breakage or other tape damage.
- Plan for extremes in the weather, especially rain. Each team member should carry a folding rain poncho, and plastic bags should be packed for each piece of equipment.
- Plan for substitute team members in case of illness. Your script may have a scene that can only be shot on one specific day. An understudy may have to fill in for a sick actor.
- Make sure that you are able to control your environment to create your scene. One group planned to shoot a scene in which a bully tips over a garbage can in a city park. Everything went fine until the team realized that the garbage cans were bolted to the cement! A team member had to rush to the hardware store and buy a garbage can along with a bag of potting soil. A few of the team members busily dented the shiny garbage can and smeared it with the black dirt, while the other students searched for garbage (hitting pay dirt in their instructor's car!). The lesson from all of this? Don't assume anything!

(Text continues on page II-3-7.)

Fig. 3.1. Location fact sheet.

Location Fact Sheet

PRODUCTION ____________ NO.________ DATE__________

LOCATION NAME	LOCATION	CONTRACT
SCENE NUMBERS	ADDRESS	ADDRESS
No. of Pages / ☐ DAY ☐ INT / ☐ NIGHT ☐ EXT	PHONE	PHONE

AVAILABILITY (times & days)

No. of Days Needed	Date Needed	Date Secured
Prep:		
Shoot:		
Wrap:		

DISTANCE FROM PRODUCTION OFFICE miles minutes

SECURED
- ☐ Contract
- ☐ Copy Filed
- ☐ Insurance
- ☐ Copy Filed
- ☐ Key
- ☐ Extra key

SUPPORT NEEDS
- ☐ Police
- ☐ Fire Department
- ☐ Guards

FACILITIES **LOCATION**
- ☐ Rest Rooms
- ☐ Eating Area
- ☐ Makeup
- ☐ Wardrobe
- ☐ Actor's Area
- ☐ Secure Storage
- ☐ Prod. Staff Area
- ☐ Equipment Area

PARKING **LOCATION**
- ☐ Grip Truck
- ☐ Camera Truck
- ☐ Campers
- ☐ Staff Cars
- ☐ Picture Cars
- ☐ Generator
- ☐ Vans (props, sound, etc.)

DESCRIPTION OF LOCATION

☐ SIZE of ACCESS DOOR:____________ CEILING HT:________
☐ WALL FINISHES:
☐ CEILING:
☐ FLOOR:
☐ NATURAL LIGHT:
☐ PRACTICALS:

ELECTRICAL DISTRIBUTION

☐ BOX AVAILABLE Phase________
Circuits______Amps_____ Volts_____
Distance from set________ft.
☐ METER LOOP NEEDED ☐ INSTALLED
Phase______ Amps_____ Volts______
Distance from set__________ft.
From loop to transformer__________ ft.
☐ Are room outlets grounded? (YES) (NO)

SOUND ENVIRONMENT

WRAP PLANS

SPECIAL PROBLEMS/LIMITATIONS

REQUIRED CONSTRUCTION/SET DRESSING

☐ ROOM PLAN on back Indicate compass LOCATION MANAGER:
☐ ROUTE MAP on back direction on both LOCATION SCOUT:

Fig. 3.2. Equipment checklist.

Program Title ____________________

Scene ____________________ Location ____________________

Item	Needed	Out	Returned
Video Camera/Camcorder	/ /	/ /	/ /
Videotape Recorder	/ /	/ /	/ /
Tripod	/ /	/ /	/ /
Microphone—Hand-held	/ /	/ /	/ /
Microphone—Lavaliere	/ /	/ /	/ /
Microphone—Shotgun	/ /	/ /	/ /
Microphone—__________	/ /	/ /	/ /
Lighting—__________	/ /	/ /	/ /
__________	/ /	/ /	/ /
Monitor(s)—__________	/ /	/ /	/ /
__________	/ /	/ /	/ /
Headphones	/ /	/ /	/ /
Other—__________	/ /	/ /	/ /
__________	/ /	/ /	/ /
__________	/ /	/ /	/ /
__________	/ /	/ /	/ /
__________	/ /	/ /	/ /

Notes:

- Plan healthy snacks for your team members. A box of granola bars and a few jugs of drinking water or juice will be appreciated on long, isolated shoots.

Finally, create plan B and don't be afraid to use it. Your audience won't know that you had originally planned another scene or location, as long as plan B is as good as plan A.

Production

When all of your preproduction activities have been completed, you are ready to begin shooting the scenes for your movie.

Videotaping the Scenes

White balance. Don't forget to white-balance your camera before you roll tape for each scene. One blue or red shot can turn a first-class production into a B-movie. If you're using colored gels to create a mood with lighting, white-balance under white-light situations, then insert your gels. For example, let's say you're videotaping an old man sitting by a campfire in the middle of the night. The campfire light is not enough for your video camera, so you use a portable light with a crinkled amber gel over the light to create the "light" of the fire. If you turn on the amber light, then white-balance, your camera will read the amber light as white, and adjust all other colors based on that reading. In this case, you would remove the amber-colored gel, white-balance, and then re-gel the light and shoot the scene.

Color monitor. While we're on the subject of light, you should bring a color monitor to the shoot, if at all possible (figure 3.3). The color monitor should be connected to the record VCR for use during record *and* playback. Watch the tape after each scene. Sometimes the actual recorded videotape is a little bit different from the image in the camera viewfinder.

Remember to adjust the color monitor for color trueness (brightness, tint, etc.) *before* leaving the school, and don't adjust the knobs during the shoot or playback. If a scene is too dark on the monitor, don't adjust the brightness. Instead, reshoot with more light, and for goodness sake, don't adjust the tint control. Your videographer will be white-balancing, and you'll be telling him or her how bad the colors are!

Fig. 3.3. A color monitor should be used on location to ensure picture quality. (Photo courtesy of Universal Studios, Florida.)

Storyboards. Even though you've been laboring over the project for weeks, don't forget the storyboards! Unless an emergency presents itself, and you have to go to plan B, stick to the storyboards. Load the storyboards into clear plastic sheet protectors and place them in a three-ring binder. The storyboards should be consulted before each camera angle is created.

Safety. Don't sacrifice safety. Make sure to follow established procedures. Don't get caught up in the excitement and forget common sense.

Focus. In this case, focus refers to keeping the group on task, despite the distractions. One school was recently given the opportunity to shoot for a day at a motion picture studio theme-park backlot. You can imagine the distractions. Every member of your team should remember why they've come to the location.

Rest. If you have several scenes to videotape on one day, encourage your fellow team members to rest whenever possible. Movie production is exciting, even on the high school level. Make sure that you're not burned out at 10:00 A.M. during an all-day shoot. Pace yourself, and rest whenever possible.

Work as a team. The day of the shooting is not the time to question the director about the content and technique of the script. If you have carefully scripted and storyboarded your project, you should be prepared for the shoot. There is a thin line between being creative and trying to commandeer the production. Every team member should be "with the program," or "on the same page," or "receiving the same wavelength." Put your ego aside, shelve your personal agenda, and work for the good of the team.

Fig. 3.4. Videotape labels.

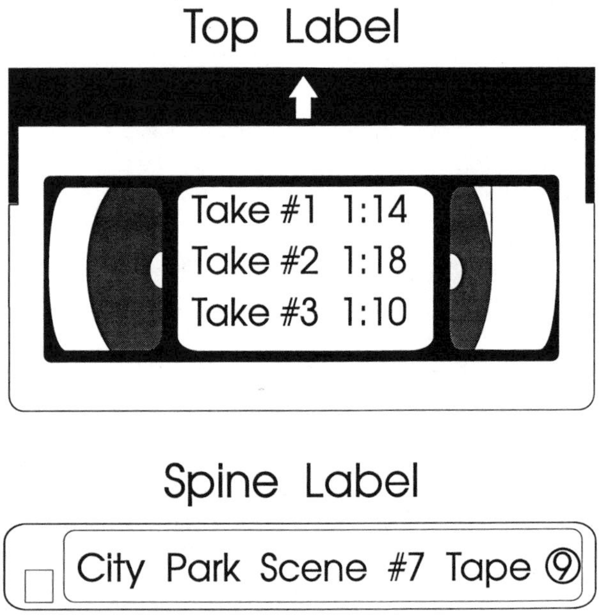

Videotape Labeling and Logging

Even if you shoot the best video footage for your movie, it will be of little use if you cannot find the scenes on the videotape during the editing process. For this reason, you need to carefully label and log each videotape used in your movie production.

Each tape should be labeled on both the top and the spine (figure 3.4). The spine label should include the location, scene number, and tape number. The top label should include the number of takes and the time for each take. This information should also be entered in a separate log for use during editing (figure 3.5). A note can also be affixed to the storyboard page indicating which tape was used for the scene.

Don't forget to pull out the videotape's erase tab to avoid reusing the tape during the shoot.

(Text continues on page II-3-10.)

Fig. 3.5. Video project tape log sheet.

Tape #	Scene #	Scene	Location	Storyboard pages	# Takes
				-	
				-	
				-	
				-	
				-	
				-	
				-	
				-	
				-	
				-	
				-	
				-	
				-	
				-	
				-	
				-	

Postproduction: The Finishing Touch

You can produce a professional video project by employing appropriate audio and video editing techniques. Here are some ideas that should help you with the moviemaking process.

Viewing and Evaluating Raw Footage

Assuming that you viewed the raw footage at the location, viewing and evaluating the raw footage in the studio becomes an exercise in judgment and selection of the best takes. Carefully examine each take to determine which one to use in the finished project. The raw footage should be viewed by many different team members, as each person will see different aspects in the shot. Once your raw footage is evaluated and you have a good idea about the particular shots you'll be using, you're ready to edit.

Videotape Editing

The editing should be completed with the storyboards on hand and should simply combine the shots as described in the storyboard. At the point of editing, the creative process is over. Although editing is creative, it is a reflection of the planning of the project. The editor should craft the raw footage into the complete program, rather than attempt to salvage poorly planned and poorly executed scenes.

Remember the basic concepts of editing. Quick edits can make a scene more exciting and intense. Longer edits of carefully chosen scenes can provoke thought and introspection in your audience. Apply a simple rule to your program pace: Whether the pace is fast or slow, your program should *never* be difficult to watch. Unlike your team, your audience will have no idea of the excitement to come. Your audience lives in the moment of the picture on the screen. The program should be *constantly* captivating. Don't make your audience "wait for the good part." There is no guarantee that the audience will be there when the "good part" finally arrives.

Audio Editing

As described in earlier chapters, music and sound effects can be added to your program; their careful selection can make or break it. When selecting music for your movie, consider using production music to which you own the rights. Production music can offer the specific mood you need, and owning the copyright allows you to duplicate a copy of the tape for each team member. Production music can be purchased from a music company or produced in your school's music lab.

Sound effects are quite effective, especially in comedy videos. In one scene, a young man takes a bite of a sandwich, then faces the camera with a rather unpleasant expression. To magnify his reaction, a team member walked to the orchestra room and recorded a percussionist playing a rising note on a timpani ("boing"). The sound effect was edited into the scene as an audio exclamation point.

One action scene from a student-produced video made good use of creative sound effects. The scene involved a confrontation between a young man and a street bully. The bully extorts money from the young man, who has decided that enough is enough. As the bully walks away laughing, the young man picks up a tin can from the sidewalk and hurls it at the bully, hitting him in the back of the head. A sound effect, the "plunk" of a hollow wood block being struck by a wooden mallet, was added as the can strikes the bully's "hollow" head. As the bully turns to face the attacker, smoke comes from his ears (blown through tubes taped behind his ears) and the sound of a train whistle is added. When the bully charges the young man for revenge, the sound effect of a locomotive accelerating is used. The young man picks up two garbage can lids, and makes a lid/bully sandwich.

Of course, the actor portraying the young man didn't really hit the actor portraying the bully. Two sound effects were used: a cymbal crash, and the actual sound of two garbage can lids being clanked together. The shot then switches to a close-up of the dazed bully in profile, stumbling and falling backwards. The sound effect for this shot is taken from a portable keyboard. A metallic note is played, and modulated using the joystick installed as part of the keyboard, resulting in a "wah-wah" effect. A potentially violent scene, the climax of the movie, is changed to a cartoonlike confrontation using sound effects.

Graphics and Titles

For short movies, the graphics used should be simple, straightforward, and easy to read. Special-effects graphics are nice unless they distract from the actual content of the movie. Remember: The title screen should support the program, not take away from it.

End credits should list all actors and technicians. The credits are important because many students will use the movie for their video resumes. For this reason, no more than one or two team members should be appointed to handle technical tasks. If one technician records all of the location audio, the credit becomes significant to the student. If several names are listed under the "audio" credit, the student will later need to explain which scenes he or she recorded, or be forced to abandon the movie as a resume piece altogether.

Don't forget to thank all of the people who helped you in your project in the credits. Most complex movies will need to borrow several props and set dressings. Most businesses will appreciate a copy of your program as a token "thanks" and will be much more receptive to your future requests.

Opening Night: Screening Your Video

Completion of a "minimovie" is a great accomplishment, and should be celebrated. Plan a big screening party. Obtain the use of equipment such as a big-screen or projection television and an amplified audio system to create a theater atmosphere in a television production studio or classroom. Serve popcorn and sodas, and make sure to invite everyone who has had a part in the production. You may even want to go as far as printing programs and decorating the classroom to look like a theater. Many times the editors are the only team members present when the project is completed. A big premiere party brings all of the team members together and lets everyone know how important their work on the project really is.

Conclusion

Whether for contests, school presentations, or personal enrichment, the production of video movie shorts offers an excellent educational opportunity. Students get the opportunity to work in specific areas of production, such as camera operation, audio recording, and editing. The team members also learn the value of teamwork and the complete production experience—from brainstorming and script development to audio and video postproduction. In the production of video movie shorts students can display their advanced skills in an entertaining and accessible format.

4 YOUR FUTURE IN VIDEO

If you've completed this book, you may be near the end of your high school video experience. But your contact with video production doesn't have to end. There are many opportunities available to continue your training and involvement in television production. They include postsecondary education and training, jobs and internships, and hobby-oriented activities.

Education and Training

As video continues to develop as a dynamic career opportunity, more colleges and vocational schools are offering television production as a course of study. Many colleges award degrees in television broadcasting, film, and communications management. These programs usually involve a theoretical approach to television production and an opportunity to work on college-produced television programs. Many colleges work with local public stations to produce programs for the community. Colleges and universities train students to enter the television production field as working professionals.

Vocational schools also offer programs of study in television production. A vocational approach emphasizes the job skills needed to gain employment in the field. While a university student will probably engage in discussions about the effects of mass media in society, the vocational student will learn how to operate the equipment needed for television production. A successful vocational school graduate can gain entry-level employment as a television videographer or studio technician. Usually, television stations promote employees with vocational skills to supervisory positions in technical areas, while college graduates are assigned as reporters, anchors, and directors.

Selecting a college or vocational school is a very important decision. Here are some things you should consider:

1. Meet with your school guidance counselor before making a final decision. He or she can direct you to valuable resources that can help you choose the best college or vocational school.

2. Visit several schools before making your final decision. Make sure that you evaluate *your* place in the school, not just the record of the football team or the size of the campus.

3. Ask the school for the names of former students working in the industry. Write or call these professionals and ask how their education has helped them.

4. Talk to the school's placement counselor to ask about their services. Once you have graduated, will the school help you find a job?

5. Find out about cooperative education opportunities at each school. Co-op allows students to work in the industry for a semester, often for college credit. Television stations often jump at the chance to hire co-op students who have trained at their stations.

6. Visit a professor or instructor to get a full understanding of the school's curriculum. Compare the department's goals to your career goals.

7. Talk to several students who are currently enrolled in the program. Are they able to use equipment when they need it? Do they feel they are being well prepared for their careers?

8. Make sure to distinguish between private and public schools. Public schools are supported by tax dollars and are able to offer a lower-cost education to students. Private schools rely on student tuition for all of their funding, and may resort to more aggressive marketing techniques to secure your school admission. You may get letters and phone calls from private colleges and vocational schools; you'll probably have to invite yourself to your public college or university. Regardless of how "welcome" a private college may make you feel, make your decision based on the above criteria, not a steak dinner and a free T-shirt. If you choose a private college (especially one that offers a two-year degree program) check the accreditation of the school. Will your private college credits transfer to a public university? Ask the university, not the private college.

9. Compare the television production department's equipment to the equipment that you have used in high school. Will you have the opportunity to learn new items? Does the school plan to update its equipment? Make sure that you don't "move down" to college or vocational school. This is especially important in vocational schools, where equipment operation is the main course of study. Don't be attracted to the familiarity of equipment. If you can already operate each item of equipment that the vocational school owns, then you really don't need to go there!

10. Finally, don't rule out attending a public college *and* a vocational school. In our area, we have a fine community college that has no television production department and a fine vocational school that has a complete video department. Several of our students are taking three or four community college classes during the day and studying video production at the vocational school two or three afternoons a week. This plan keeps the students' video skills sharp until they are ready to attend a university to earn a television production degree.

Jobs and Internships

Some students are able to work part-time while continuing their education. Other students enter the work force immediately after high school. Depending on the size of your community and your local job market, you may be able to use your high school video skills in your first after-high school job.

Make sure to secure a copy of each of your major video projects. Sometimes students edit pieces of these programs into a video portfolio or video resume to present to prospective employers. This video portfolio should include your best work. Make sure to include graphics that indicate your job on the production.

A written resume is always helpful in a job search. If you are interviewing for a video-oriented job, make sure to include your school video experiences. A position of news anchor or technical director on a daily school news program shows responsibility and dedication.

Request letters of recommendation from your teachers *before* you graduate. Teachers are usually happy to write good things about good students. It is embarrassing and often detrimental when a business calls for a reference for a long-forgotten student. A file of four or five recommendation letters from teachers and administrators is impressive to a potential employer. Make several photocopies of each letter to use with different resumes.

Contact local video production services and inquire about job opportunities. Small businesses that videotape weddings, fashion shows, and parties may need extra help. Make sure that you explain that you have had video experience. Mail your resume with a cover letter to the business. If the business expresses an interest, request an interview and bring along your video resume.

Some video-oriented businesses, such as video duplication houses, tape distribution companies, and camera rental businesses, will hire recent high school graduates for entry-level positions. Although these businesses are not directly related to video production, they do offer a chance to gain immediate employment in the industry.

Video as a Hobby

Perhaps you want a career as a business manager, airline pilot, teacher, or engineer. You can still pursue video production as a hobby. Most medium-to-large cities have a video club where other hobbyists meet to share ideas and make amateur productions. Many high schools have community school classes for people interested in creating video projects and learning new skills. Also, a number of video magazines are available that have articles on the latest video equipment. Even if you never plan to use your high school television production education in a career, you can still enjoy the excitement of producing television programs.

Conclusion

Your video experience doesn't have to end just because your high school video class is over. If you plan a career in video, a college, university, or vocational school can give you more education in video production. If you plan to enter the work force immediately after high school, you can possibly get a job in a video-related industry, and even if you have other career plans, you can still pursue video as a hobby.

Part III
SUPPLEMENTARY ACTIVITIES

Enhancing Your Role as Television Production Instructor

1 MAKING MEMORIES

School-Based Video Yearbooks

At the conclusion of your first month of intermediate and advanced video production, you'll be surprised to see just how much great video footage you and your students have accumulated. Some schools decide to combine this footage of the school year into a video yearbook offered for sale to students, staff, and the community. School-based video yearbook production offers a complete video production experience, an excellent historical document of the school year, and a fund-raising opportunity for your television production program. If that sounds interesting to you, read on!

What Is a Video Yearbook?

A video yearbook is a videotape program that chronicles the school year in sound and motion. Video yearbooks are usually one to two hours long, and are sold to the school and community.

Video Yearbooks Versus Print Yearbooks

As you can tell by the definition above, a video yearbook is really not a yearbook at all. There are some major differences between video yearbooks and regular print yearbooks.

Print yearbooks offer two distinct features not available on video yearbooks: a photograph of every student and faculty member, and the ability to collect the signatures of friends. However, while print yearbooks cover the school year until early spring, video yearbooks include the entire school year. Video yearbooks also offer an experience in sight and sound, and every picture on a video yearbook is in full color. Usually, video yearbooks are less expensive than print yearbooks.

So, as you can see, a video yearbook is not really a yearbook at all and shouldn't be considered as a threat or competitor to the print yearbook. The term *video yearbook* is really just a marketing tool to emphasize the comprehensive content of the videotape. In fact, many schools use the terms *video highlights* and *video memories* instead of video yearbook. A television production department should not engage in competition for the yearbook dollar with the sponsor or students producing the print yearbook. Many students will buy both if the price is right and the video yearbook represents a substantial value. The video yearbook should try to carve its own niche in the school market.

School-Based Video Yearbooks Versus Vendor-Based Video Yearbooks

One area of competition that does exist is among the different companies that produce video yearbooks for schools. At the time of this writing, many such companies exist and actively solicit to schools. The typical video yearbook company works like this: The salesperson visits the school and speaks with an administrator about helping the students produce a video yearbook. The salesperson leaves a sample videotape, usually about 60-90 minutes long, that features a successful video yearbook produced by the company. The sample video yearbook contains not only school news but national and world news as well. The tape is often "hosted" by a moderately successful teenage television personality. (This is usually someone who was formerly quite popular, but now hosts infomercials and appears in dinner theaters across the country.)

When the school agrees to work with this company, a faculty member is chosen as the school coordinator, and a group of students is selected to work on the project. The sales representative or another company employee schedules an after-school appointment with the teacher and students. At that time, the school receives on loan from the company one or two camcorders, along with a few hours of training on them; the company usually also provides an armload of blank tape to the school. (The loaned camcorders are often in the Hi-8mm format or S-VHS format. Because a school may not have any other access to these formats, the raw footage shot by the students may be useless to anyone but the video yearbook company, further disenfranchising the students from the actual video yearbook production. For example, a school that makes a weekly news show using the VHS format would not be able to use the Hi-8mm footage that they shoot for the video yearbook company on their news show.) The video yearbook team then videotapes significant events throughout the school year, usually following a checklist of school activities to be videotaped provided by the company. The students also begin taking orders for the video yearbooks. (The money is usually sent directly to the company and the school receives a check from the company for about $5 per tape sold.)

At the conclusion of the school year, all of the raw footage is mailed to the company. Providing a minimum number of video yearbooks have been ordered (usually 50-75), the company edits, duplicates, and delivers the copies, which look remarkably like the video yearbooks produced for every other school the company services. The loaned equipment is returned to the company, and the student group is usually disbanded.

If you have read this book up to this point, you know that this is not the type of activity that we, the authors, deem worthwhile. The students are only marginally involved in the production and have absolutely no input in the postproduction phase. Basically, the company is hiring the students (very cheaply!) to videotape school activities and then selling the students' work back to them.

This is not to say that these companies should be avoided at all costs. We have spoken to many teachers who have been totally satisfied with the finished product. For schools with very little television production experience and almost no video equipment, this may be the only opportunity they will have to produce a video yearbook. We just don't happen to see much educational value in the process, and we hate to see that much money leaving the school. If at all possible, a school-based production should be attempted. It is to the instructors interested in coordinating the school-based video yearbook that the remainder of this chapter is addressed.

Why Have a Video Yearbook?

There are three reasons to consider undertaking the school-based video yearbook project, and they are listed in order of importance.

1. *The school-based video yearbook provides a total video production experience for students.* This is the most important reason to have a video yearbook. Students will become involved in every phase of production: They will plan the program, order blank tape, select a tape duplicator, take orders, and deliver the product. The students will also learn about copyright law, bookkeeping, and working as a team. This top-to-bottom experience closely emulates the real world of video production.

2. *The school-based video yearbook provides a historical record of the school year.* A good video yearbook is basically a two-hour documentary of the school year. Twenty years from now, the video yearbook will truly represent high school life in the nineties.

3. *The school-based video yearbook can make a profit for your program.* Notice that this is the last, and therefore the least important, reason to produce a video yearbook. Video yearbook production is a labor of love and should not be considered solely as a fund-raiser. However, many schools make a substantial profit for their programs while reaping the first two benefits.

Getting Started

An outstanding video yearbook is the result of careful planning. Before announcing the project to your advanced class, consider the following questions:

Do I have access to all of the equipment that I need? You will probably need to perform at least basic edits in your video yearbook. Do you have access to an editing system? Will you use electronic character generation, or will you find a creative way to make graphics without the CG? Do your students have access to cameras/camcorders? Before beginning the video yearbook production, make sure that you have access to the necessary equipment.

Do my students have the skills to produce the video yearbook? Video yearbook production needs to begin the first day of school, as students start the new school year. If this is your first year of offering television production as a class, you may want to provide some extra training to students who will videotape and edit the first segments. As stated in the introduction to this text (page Intro-4), start with small projects and progress. The video yearbook is definitely *not* a small project. You, the instructor, may have to do most of the work for the first few weeks. On the other hand, if your school offers three or four years of television production instruction, you probably have a loyal crew of veterans. They can begin planning the next year's video yearbook before the school year ends.

Do I have the video production skills needed for this project? Ideally, the instructor should be able to produce the video yearbook alone, with the students learning from the instructor. If you are new to television production, you may want to hone your production skills before attempting a project of this nature. Very few video novices could successfully produce a good video yearbook. Shoot the raw footage throughout the year. Make your decision halfway through the school year. Practice will improve your skills.

Once you have decided to undertake the video yearbook project, form a student steering committee to help plan the production. Show the students examples of video yearbooks produced in previous years or by other schools. Discuss the philosophy behind the video yearbook and the objectives mentioned above. Educate the students on copyright law as it applies to music (see page III-1-5) and recorded video clips. After your group has learned about the video yearbook concept, brainstorm possible contents, and make a rough draft of a time budget—a table of contents for the video yearbook (see page III-1-7). Reserve the right to make final decisions. The steering committee will need your maturity and judgment to produce a successful project that will appeal to your audience.

Professional Contacts Necessary for a Successful Product

Just as any professional video production company needs professional contacts to do business, you need to establish professional relationships for your video yearbook production.

Blank-Tape Dealer

If you are running a television production program in your school, you should be buying your blank tape from a wholesale dealer, not a retail establishment. Blank-tape dealers are usually mail-order companies that sell large lots of blank tape at greatly reduced prices. These dealers buy blank videotape—usually professional quality—on huge reels purchased directly from the manufacturer and load the tape into videocassettes. Consequently, a customer can order blank videotape of various lengths. Purchase a number of 5-, 10-, 20-, and 30-minute tapes for video yearbook production. The shorter loads allow you to record a single segment on a videotape. For example, a 4-minute segment of volleyball highlights for the video yearbook can be edited onto a 5-minute videotape. The 5-minute tape can then be stored in a cabinet until it is needed for the video yearbook. The short tape removes the temptation of continuing to use the tape throughout the school year, risking tape damage, theft, or loss. And as you've probably imagined, a short blank videotape is much less expensive than the 2-hour version. If you haven't been contacted by one of these blank-tape dealers, contact your school district office, another school involved in video production, or a local videotape duplicator for a recommendation. If all else fails, check the back of your professional video periodicals or go to the library and check the yellow pages of a big-city telephone book. Purchasing videotape from a blank-tape dealer will save you money while allowing you to purchase videotape that meets the needs of your program.

Industrial Video Sales, Rental, and Service

This is a contact that you've probably already made, but it continues to be important in this phase of production. Your vendor should be factory-authorized to repair all of the equipment that you use. The company should also be willing to make quick repairs to your essential equipment. A good industrial vendor should also serve as an educational resource for new equipment and technology. Many industrial vendors also rent equipment to schools at rates much lower than their standard fee. Finally, your vendor should be friendly, helpful, and ready to serve. If a vendor gives you the "bum's rush," then rush, with broken equipment in hand and dignity intact, to a more responsive video business.

Professional Videotape Duplicator

You should never, never, *never* duplicate more than one or two copies of a videotape on your school equipment. Video equipment is very expensive to repair. Valuable equipment and hours should be used for editing, not duplicating. School videotape duplication becomes more ridiculous considering the reasonable rates offered by most tape duplicators. A copy of a two-hour video yearbook is usually less than $10. This includes the blank tape, the case, the label, and the shrink-wrap.

Most professional duplication businesses have a large number—as many as 200—record VCRs connected to a single-play VCR. In other words, 200 copies can be made in a single pass. All copies are made from the original, and because the VCRs are professional "duplicators," the copies look almost as good as the original. Because of the large number of slave (record) VCRs, duplication can often be completed in one day. Professional duplicators can also assist in packaging decisions and a cover design. Professional tape duplicators are located in most large cities. Even if you're 100 miles from a professional duplicator, make the 2-hour drive. If you schedule a duplication time with the duplicator, you may be able to return that evening with your finished video yearbooks. (Needless to say, this is also a great field trip for your students!)

The Legal Use of Music in Video Yearbooks

With the daily news reports frequently featuring stories related to copyright violation cases, many television production instructors have become hesitant to use *any* music in their video yearbooks. Others throw caution to the wind and adopt the "So, sue me!" attitude. Neither approach is appropriate for video yearbook production, and the latter can land the teacher in jail!

There are legal and acceptable ways to use music in a video yearbook production. They include "production music" (designed for copyright purchase) and original music.

Production Music

Many companies are in the business of providing music for video productions, commercials, and news programs. These companies usually have an extensive collection of songs available for use—for a price. This music, called production music, is usually available on cassette and compact disc; all of the companies provide free demonstration tapes and discs as sales tools. You will probably be surprised when you hear this production music. Some of the music will surprise you with its full orchestration and film-score arrangement. Other music will sound like it should be played on popular radio stations. Unfortunately, you will also be surprised by the low quality of many of the companies' offerings. Some selections are boring, repetitive, and sound like they're being played by a precocious 12-year-old on a mini-keyboard. Others are blatant rip-offs of popular songs, with only one or two notes changed to tease the copyright law.

This music is usually offered for purchase through three methods: the buyout, the lease, and the needle drop.

Buyout music. Once the last refuge of low-quality production music, the buyout system is now the dominant method of purchasing production music. The customer is charged a flat fee for the unlimited rights to the music. While each company varies in specifically assigning those rights, most buyouts include playing the music for an audience and duplicating the music on a videotape program (like a video yearbook). Of course, you need to examine the purchasing agreement for yourself. Duplication is usually the *last* right to be relinquished. A buyout compact disc with eight or ten selections usually costs about $50. One or two of these discs will usually meet the needs of your program. Many companies offer educational discounts and substantial discounts on "last-year's" music. Make the best deal that you can, but make sure that you're buying all of the rights that you need.

Leased music. Unlike the buyout, which gives the purchaser the rights into eternity, the lease program offers the music for a certain amount of time, usually one year. Leased music is practical for television news shows or commercial production houses who will use the music for a brief period of time. Leases are usually only available on large music collections (20 to 30 compact discs) and can be quite expensive, and unlike buyout music, many lease agreements do *not* include duplication rights.

Needle-drop music. For companies that use music only once or twice a year, and don't intend to duplicate the program, needle-drop music is a reasonable alternative to music purchase or lease. The production music company loans the customer a library of production music. When the customer uses the music, he or she completes a brief report form and mails it to the music company. The company then periodically bills the customer for the music use at a preestablished rate. Duplication and broadcast rates are available for needle-drop music, but those rates are much higher than the rate for a single use. Why would a person ever use needle drop? Here's an example. Let's say that you are the owner of a large manufacturing company, and you host annual meetings for your sales staff. You like to play background music while you show slides of your factory employees making the product. As you may know from your copyright studies, playing this music constitutes a public performance and is a violation of copyright law. Your option is to pay the needle-drop fee on a music selection available from the music company. (This example is actually based on a real court case—except the company used a theme from a popular movie and was sued by the copyright owners. The out-of-court settlement was in the million-dollar range!) Because of the paperwork involved, many music companies have "dropped" the needle-drop method of payment in favor of buyouts and leases.

If you have a question about the use of copyrighted music that you intend to purchase or lease, ask the questions before you spend the money. Unfortunately, copyright law is open to various interpretations. Contact the AIME Copyright Hot Line (see page App-A-4) with your specific questions. Encourage your district to purchase buyout music with the stipulation that all schools within the district can use the music. Production music companies are in the business of selling music. They are usually willing to work with schools on special educational packages. They often appreciate the fact that you plan to abide by the law, rather than rip off the copyright owner and claim ignorance later.

Production music is reasonable and affordable for most schools producing video yearbooks. Budget a certain amount of money for music purchase, and make sure you know exactly what you're buying before you place the order.

Original Music

Another source for video yearbook music may be right under your nose. Your school could provide a fountain of original music that will give your production a truly unique approach. Here are some possible sources for original music.

School music labs. Many schools are now offering music composition and electronic music classes. The music created in these classes can be adapted and designed for video yearbook use.

Student band/music groups. If you scratch the surface, you'll probably discover that there are a few bands or other musical groups at your school. If these "garage bands" have original songs, they can be used in your video yearbook. One school used a rap about the school in its video yearbook.

Drum cadences. High school marching bands often write their own drum cadences, which can be used effectively in sports segments. Students proficient at insert editing will enjoy editing to the beats.

Local professional bands. Touring nightclub bands trying to break into the big time are often looking for any free publicity that they can get. Most of these bands perform original songs and have demo tapes and discs for promotional use. You may be able to persuade these groups to let you use their music in exchange for a mention in the credits. At one high school, students phoned a local radio station to request a song by an undiscovered band that they had heard on their video yearbook.

Remember: You must obtain all of the rights for the music that you use. These copyright holders include the songwriter, the arranger, the publishing company, and the performers. For high school students and local bands, this could be a simple process.

Do I Really Need Music?

After reading this section, you may get the impression that a video yearbook is just one big music video. This is not true. Because no other aspect of video production has such a great potential for legal action against a school, an explanation of the use of music is necessary. However, many sections of your video yearbook will have no music at all. The sound recorded at athletic events can certainly add impact to your video yearbook. And you wouldn't want to audio-dub over a pep rally or commencement exercises. Often the best sound is the natural sound recorded with the video.

Don't rely on the music to sell your video yearbook. Violating copyright law to include the most popular songs of the year probably won't sell more tapes, and is certainly not worth the risk. The selling point of your video yearbook should be the sights and sounds of the school, not a jukebox assortment of music.

Possible Contents for Your Video Yearbook

Each school is unique, and one school's video yearbook may be completely different from another. Still, there are some school events that you probably don't want to omit.

- Sports highlights
- Pep rallies
- Homecoming activities
- Dances, especially prom
- Faculty members/Teacher of the Year
- Student performance highlights
- Student interviews—how they feel about current events
- Awards assembly
- Favorite school news show segments
- Individual success stories
- Senior section
- Clubs and class officers
- A collage of school scenes

To Host or Not to Host

Some schools select a popular, verbose student to introduce each segment on camera and serve as a host for the video yearbook. There are certainly advantages and disadvantages to this option. A good host can serve as a continuity point for the video yearbook. The problem lies in the selection of the host. You may be able to find a natural, unassuming host for your video yearbook. But many students would not want to see the student body president or the head cheerleader get more special treatment. Gone are the days when an entire school could unanimously select a representative. Choosing one or two people to personify the video yearbook may alienate more potential customers than it attracts, and you always run the risk of selecting a student who is intelligent and talkative—*before* he or she gets in front of the camera. The effects of a nervous host could be a frustrating shooting session and a lessening of the video yearbook's overall quality.

In our opinion, the video yearbook belongs to everyone in the school. It is a production that strives to feature and represent every segment of the student body, not just the smartest, best dressed, and most popular. If you decide to go with a host, make sure to ask a large and representative sample of your student body whom *they* would like to see hosting their video yearbook. If no general consensus is reached, reconsider your decision.

Tips and Suggestions

Here are a few more points of information that may make the video yearbook production process easier.

- Present a positive image of your school. Remember, you are chronicling the school year on videotape. Don't grind personal axes.

- Remember your audience. Most of your tapes will be sold to high school students. Don't be patronizing or condescending. This is *their* video yearbook. Make it a tape they will enjoy.

- Start working early. You will probably want to include the first day of school rituals (picking up schedules, greeting old friends, finding new classrooms) on your video yearbook. At the end of the first week of school, edit a 5-minute segment based on the previous week. Continue to produce brief segments, according to your plan, throughout the school year.

- Continue to fine-tune your table of contents. Shoot everything, even if you hadn't originally planned to include it in your video yearbook. Remember: Your table of contents is a "living document." Be prepared to change it if something significant happens at your school that was not included in your early plans. For example, you may have planned to budget one or two minutes to the girls' basketball team. But if they win the state championship, they deserve more time. "A Tribute to the Champs" could become a selling point of your project.

- Follow the one-segment, one-tape rule. Don't crowd five or six video yearbook segments on one tape. At the end of the school year, they can all be combined onto the video yearbook master tape.

- Label the tapes and lock them away (figure 1.1). Tapes on certain topics, especially sports highlights and dance footage, can "walk away" once they are completed. Keep your tape cabinet locked at all times.

- Form follows function. Try to keep most of the tape as "real-world" as possible. You may have a fancy special effects generator you'd like to use. But remember: Most people would rather see the winning touchdown video *without* all of the mosaic, strobe, and paintbox effects.

- Don't play favorites. Your end product should be an accurate account of the school year. Share your table of contents with your administrators and several students and teachers. Strive for balance of presentation.

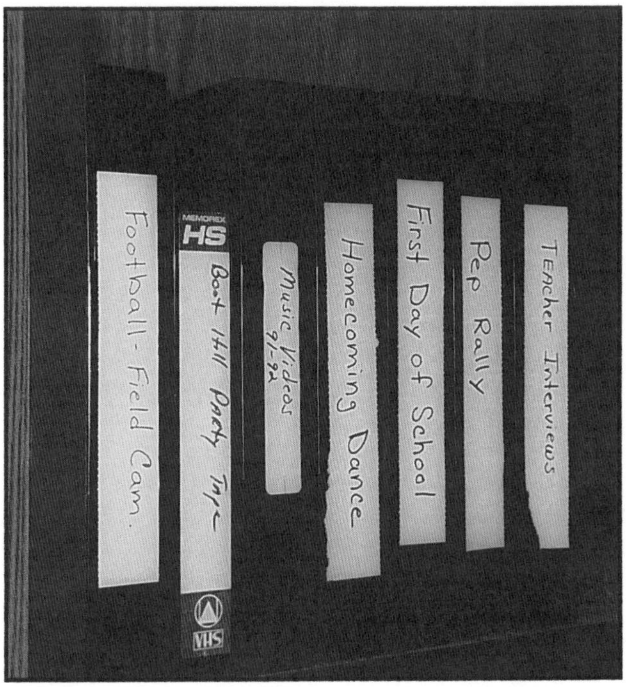

Fig. 1.1. Labeled videotapes.

Editing a Video Yearbook

Once the raw footage has been recorded and most of the segments completed, you are ready to edit your video yearbook. Here are some tips that will maintain the high quality of your project.

- The fewer the generations you use, the better. A copy of an original videotape looks about like the original. A copy of that copy looks a little bit worse. A copy of a copy of a copy (fourth generation) lacks the resolution of the earlier copies. A fifth-generation copy really starts to deteriorate, and a sixth-generation copy is unwatchable. Your video yearbook master tape should be no more than a third generation (a copy of a copy). That means you shoot the original footage (first generation), edit it onto a segment (second generation), and edit the segment onto the master tape (third generation). As you near the end of the school year, you may choose to edit segments (prom, senior activities) directly onto the master tape. While doing this risks tape breakage, it does produce second-generation video of the most-watched part of the tape. The choice is yours. However, your master video yearbook should never contain fourth- or fifth-generation video. A professional duplication company can take your third-generation master and produce copies with very little deterioration.

- Always produce your master tape on the best format available. If you have S-VHS, use it. Your duplicator should be able to accommodate any major format.

- Set deadlines. Don't plan to have each segment completed the last week of school. A major portion of the video yearbook should be completed every three months.

Graduation Ceremonies

Most of your seniors will expect to see their graduation ceremony on their video yearbooks. If you have a small school, you can budget 30 to 45 minutes of your video yearbook for graduation. But graduation for a large high school can take two hours or longer. Here's an easy way to include parts of the graduation for your viewer. It sounds complicated at first, but it's a big video yearbook selling point.

Record graduation ceremonies with two cameras. One camera should remain on a medium shot of the principal and the graduate receiving the diploma. The other camera should record the following: students preparing and anxiously waiting backstage, the processional, the speeches, the singing of the alma mater; and the celebrations at the conclusion of the ceremony. Camera 1 should also record the celebrations.

Assuming that you have chosen not to include the entire ceremony onto your master tape, prepare the following segment: Begin with three or four minutes of the backstage footage. Then edit the processional, complete with music and cheering. Then edit about 15 seconds of black onto the tape. Follow the black with celebrations and hugs. Are you confused yet? Good! You're paying attention. Take the tape, complete with graduation, to the duplicator, and order the number of tapes ordered by your senior students. Ask the duplicator to leave the tapes "tails out," meaning not rewound. When the duplicated copies are delivered, cue each tape to the 15 seconds of black tape. Then record the student's individual graduation (the medium, camera-1 shot) over that black using a video and audio insert (*not* assemble). The results are striking. The viewer will see the pregraduation scenes, the processional, *his or her personalized graduation*, and the celebration. Then, return the video yearbook back to its box, making sure to note the graduate's name on the case.

Questions? Of course. Isn't this a major hassle? Sure it is. Charge an extra $5 for this service. The students will be glad to pay this small amount for a close-up of their personal graduation, and the extra charge is pure profit. This process takes about five minutes per tape. Sixty dollars an hour can help buy equipment for your students to use next year.

How about underclass students who aren't graduating? They get the underclass version of the video yearbook, which does not include the graduation. Those tapes are duplicated with about two weeks left in the school year, and those students can pick up their tapes during the last week of school. The graduation segment just described is edited onto the master tape when it is returned from the first duplication run of video yearbooks for the underclass students.

Remember to be flexible with the graduation section. Twins who will graduate one after another can probably both be edited onto the same tape. And every year, the valedictorians ask if we can edit their speeches onto the end of their video yearbook. We are happy to oblige these simple requests.

Some schools choose to sell the entire graduation ceremonies on a separate videotape. This is certainly a way to raise extra money, but it has two disadvantages: 1) It may cut into your video yearbook sales and 2) it needs to be produced at a very busy time of the year for television production instructors.

The graduation section is an effective way to end the video yearbook, and most students and parents are glad that the service is offered so inexpensively.

Generating Interest in Your Video Yearbook

No matter how spectacular your finished product, you still need to promote the video yearbook in your school. Here are a few ideas that may generate sales.

- Videotape during the print yearbook's club picture day. Announce to clubs that you plan to feature a few seconds/minutes of each club on the video yearbook.
- Conduct a number of person-on-the-street interviews, with questions such as "What is your favorite class?," "What was the best thing about this year?," and "What are your plans after high school?" A person who knows that he or she will be on the video yearbook is more likely to purchase a copy.
- Promote the video yearbook on your school news shows. Show edited clips under the credits of your news show.
- Start a cover contest. Have the students vote on their favorite cover (figure 1.2).
- Roll a VCR and monitor into the cafeteria or commons area and show completed segments at lunchtime.
- Advertise in the parent newsletter. Some parents may want a copy, even if the student is not tremendously interested.
- Make a brief presentation to the PTA, especially if the PTA has donated money to your program. Be prepared to take orders.
- Write a press release for your local newspapers. Make sure to include ordering procedures.

Video Yearbook Sales and Delivery

To many, selling and promoting the video yearbook will be the most exciting aspect of the production. To others, this will be a chore. Here are some strategies that may help you in this area.

- Take orders in early May. Have a cutoff date, but extend it for late orders. Keep selling until the last possible order date.
- Give the lowest price possible. If you are getting your copies for $10, don't go higher than $20 ($25 including the graduation). Most students spend a lot of money at the end of the school year for various school activities. A $40 price tag may make more profit per tape, but fewer people will see the work of your students. Give discounts to faculty and staff and students who worked on the project. The principal, the library media center, and the television production instructor(s) should each get a free copy.

Fig. 1.2. Sample video yearbook cover.

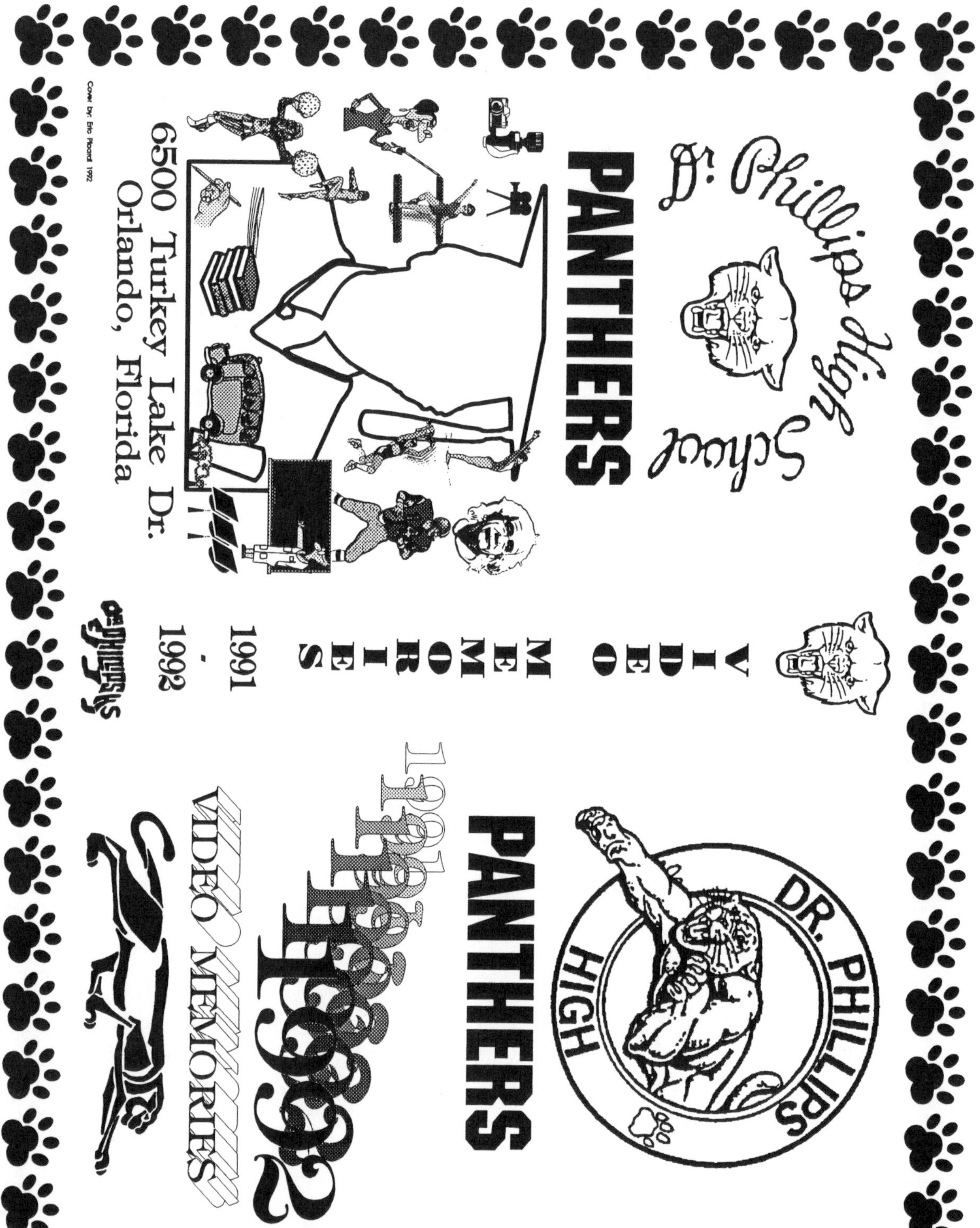

- Collect the money with the orders and deposit the money into the school account daily. Many schools have strict bookkeeping requirements. The school bookkeeper needs to be an ally in this project.

- Use an order form with important information listed. A sample order form is shown in figure 1.3.

- Clip the payment and your copy of the receipt to the order form. This will help with bookkeeping procedures and daily deposits.

- Set up a table at graduation for parents to purchase the video yearbook. Make sure to tell your customers about your plans to include the graduation ceremonies.

- Order 8-10 percent more tapes than you have sold. Many students and parents will want to purchase video yearbooks when they hear about your super product.

- Stock extra tapes at the school store, and make sure the school store gets at least $5 profit on each tape.

- Sell copies of the video yearbook to visiting groups.

- Deliver the underclass video yearbooks during the last few days of school, even if they are duplicated a week before. This will discourage copying.

- Have each student sign his or her order form when accepting delivery of the video yearbook. Each student should also present a photo ID. This way, you will make sure the right customer gets the tape. If he or she can present the sales receipt, that's all the better.

- Mail the senior/graduation video yearbooks. Have the seniors address a large envelope when they order their tapes. When the personalized graduation has been edited onto the student's tape, put the tape directly in the envelope and seal it. The videotapes can be mailed at library rate for less than $1 each.

- Be prepared to replace the occasional defective tape. These tapes should be credited by your duplicator.

Obviously, you will produce an outstanding product. However, one or two customers are bound to complain about the quality of your video yearbook. Like it or not, you have to understand that a very few students will try to return the video yearbook after they have made a copy of it. Generally, we remind the occasional complainer that like the school newspaper, print yearbook, and all other school productions, the video yearbook is produced by students, and students make mistakes. You can't get your money back at a school play if a student misses a line. If the complainer persists, collect his or her receipt (this prevents thieves from trying to cash in on a stolen video yearbook) and write a purchase order for the refund. The refund will be mailed to the student within a week or two. Once again, this will discourage an epidemic of refund-seekers looking for quick cash.

Don't get the wrong impression about this approach to dealing with complaints. Defective products should be replaced immediately with an apology and a smile. However, it must be acknowledged that videotape can be duplicated by connecting two VCRs. Less-than-ethical customers may try to get a free video yearbook with little regard for the finances of your program or the hard work and dedication of your students.

Fig. 1.3. Sample video yearbook order form.

Video Yearbook Order Form

Name________________________________ Phone # __________

Address ____

Homeroom/1st period : teacher__________ room #______

Regular Video Yearbook ($20.00) _____

Senior Video Yearbook (includes graduation) ($25.00)_____

Special Graduation -- If you are not graduating in alphabetical order, check one of the following...

class officer_____ Honor Society _____

other (list) _____

==

>>For office use only<<

Total Paid $______ receipt number ______

cash _____ check #_____

Video Yearbook Order Form

Name________________________________ Phone # __________

Address ____

Homeroom/1st period : teacher__________ room #______

Regular Video Yearbook ($20.00) _____

Senior Video Yearbook (includes graduation) ($25.00)_____

Special Graduation -- If you are not graduating in alphabetical order, check one of the following...

class officer_____ Honor Society _____

other (list) _____

==

>>For office use only<<

Total Paid $______ receipt number ______

cash _____ check #_____

Conclusion

The video yearbook offers a superior production opportunity for high school television production departments. The students get the opportunity to produce a complete, complex video program while providing a valuable service to the school and funding further equipment purchases. With careful planning and meticulous execution, the end product—your school's own video yearbook—will be an outstanding (and fun) contribution to your television production program of instruction.

2 IN-SERVICE FOR FELLOW EDUCATORS

Most schools are equipped with one or more camcorders for teachers' use in their classrooms. These camcorders are usually stored in the school's media center and checked out upon request. The availability of these video cameras, however, does not guarantee their use for educational instruction in the classroom. Because of a lack of training, many teachers are not prepared to use this equipment in the classroom. Training and in-services have either been unavailable or inadequate to meet the needs of classroom teachers in this area.

Some teachers rely on the services of the media specialist to videotape classroom events. In schools where there is a functioning television production class or program, students are often called upon to perform this service. Sometimes these requests place unnecessary demands upon the teacher and students enrolled in the program. Scheduling students and equipment for these requests, along with balancing instructional activities and video projects, add additional burdens to the role of the television production instructor.

The television production teacher can eliminate these problems and provide classroom support for other teachers by conducting in-services and in-school workshops designed to assist classroom teachers in their efforts to use video equipment to facilitate learning.

Scheduling In-Services

First survey the faculty to determine the extent of teacher interest in a workshop or training session at your school. Select a convenient day and time to hold the in-service. Many counties have scheduled days during the semester for workshops and training. Contact your county administrative office for dates and information about conducting workshops in the schools.

Once a date and time have been scheduled, notify the faculty well in advance to allow teachers time to adjust their schedules so they can make definite plans to attend. A written announcement should be placed in every teacher's mailbox. Several interested teachers may not have responded to the initial survey. It's also a good idea to have teachers RSVP if they are planning to attend the training session so you can plan for equipment and information (handouts) needs; schedule a room that is large enough to allow teachers to freely move about and get hands-on experience with the video equipment.

Conducting a Workshop

Conducting a workshop in your school will require some advance preparation. Some of the aspects you will need to address include:

1. *Equipment.* Reserve the necessary equipment needed to conduct the workshop. Equipment needs include an overhead projector, screen, television, VCR, monitor (if available), camcorders, RF cords, RCA patch cords, and adapters (RF to antenna).

2. *Overhead transparencies.* Prepare the overhead transparencies included in this chapter for the workshop.

3. *Handouts.* Teachers rely on easy access to information. It is important to duplicate essential information and to give each teacher present information to take back to class.

4. *Follow-up.* Research has shown that a key element in the success of teacher in-services and workshops has been the use of follow-up sessions for information and feedback. Plan to assist teachers in their initial classroom videotaping efforts and schedule a short follow-up session for the participants a few weeks after the initial training.

An effective workshop provides essential technical information, hands-on activities, suggestions for implementation in the classroom, and a brief time for questions and answers. The following overhead transparencies (figures 2.1, page III-2-5; 2.2, page III-2-7; and 2.3, page III-2-9) and instructional notes will enable you to conduct an effective workshop in your county, school, or both.

Instructional Notes for Overhead #1

[Figure 2.1, page III-2-5]

Equipment: camcorder
television/monitor
overhead projector/transparencies

The initial instruction will be on the operation of the camcorder and its features. Connect the camcorder to a television/monitor so that everyone will be able to see the video picture and how it is affected by the camcorder features.

Depending on the manufacturer and model of the camcorder used in your school, the following camcorder functions should be presented.

Power

Discuss the use of batteries and AC adapters. Demonstrate how to load batteries and check charge indicators in the viewfinder (battery power display). Many classroom situations are best recorded using AC power. Demonstrate how to connect the power supply to the camcorder. Present information about standby functions in camcorders. In some camcorders, the camcorder will automatically switch to standby if the camera is left on for more than a few minutes without recording information.

Focus

Auto-focus cameras have a tendency to blur images when the camcorder is adjusting the focus as the camera is moved from one subject to another. This can easily be demonstrated in the classroom. Show the teachers how to switch the camcorder to manual focus, and demonstrate the technique for manually focusing the camera:

1. Switch to manual focus.
2. Zoom all the way in to the object.
3. Adjust the focus with the focus ring.
4. Zoom out.

Using the manual-focus function of the camera will eliminate some of the problems associated with auto-focus functions.

White Balancing

Describe the use of white balancing to adjust picture color. Most camcorders come with a white-balancing setting for indoor and outdoor taping. If the camera can also be manually white-balanced, demonstrate the procedure:

1. Hold a white index card about 7-10 inches in front of the lens.
2. Press the white-balance set button.
3. Hold the button down until the word "white" ceases to flash in the viewfinder.

If possible, allow teachers to view videotaped material that has been recorded without properly white-balancing the camera. Note the reddish and bluish tint to the pictures.

Iris/Gain

Describe the functions of the iris and gain switches for taping in high/low light conditions. A few camcorders are equipped with manual functions for these features. Demonstrate how to adjust the camcorder to compensate for:

1. Low light conditions
2. High light conditions
3. Backlighting

Zoom

Demonstrate the use of the servo-zoom mechanism. Also illustrate how a manual zoom allows the camera operator to speed up or slow down the zoom.

Camera Trigger

Show the location of the trigger on the camcorder. Describe viewfinder indicators of recording (counter numbers, indicator lights), and standby.

Record/Playback

All camcorders can be used to record information as well as play back the information. Demonstrate how to use the playback function of the camcorder.

Videotape

Emphasize the differences in quality among videotapes. Encourage teachers (pass out a list) to purchase only high-grade videotape to preserve the equipment. Demonstrate the removal of the videotape tab designed to protect the tape from accidental erasure. Stress the importance of properly labeling and storing videotapes.

Once these features have been discussed, teachers should be given a few minutes to handle and practice their skills with the camcorders. Have several camcorders on hand if possible and allow teachers to load videotape and record a few minutes of footage. Monitor their progress and assist as needed.

Fig. 2.1. Overhead #1.

THE CAMCORDER IN THE CLASSROOM

I. Camcorder Features
   A. Power
      1. Battery
      2. AC Adapter
   B. Focus
      1. Manual
      2. Auto
   C. White Balance
      1. Manual
      2. Auto
   D. Iris/Gain
      1. Manual
      2. Auto
   E. Lens
      1. Zoom
      2. Cleaning Care
   F. Trigger
   G. Record/Playback
   H. Videotape
      1. Grades
      2. Tabs
      3. Labeling/Storing

Instructional Notes for Overhead #2

[Figure 2.2]

Equipment: VCR
television
RF cable
VHF antenna adapter

VCRs are often used in the classroom for instructional purposes. Classroom teachers often need assistance in connecting VCRs to televisions.

1. Pass around several sections of RF cable to teachers can examine the connections.

2. Connect one end of the cable to the VCR (labeled "RF Out" or "To TV") and connect the other end to the television ("RF In" or "Cable In"). Older model televisions are not cable-ready, so an adapter must be used to convert the RF cable connector to fit the VHF antenna inputs. Use a screwdriver to loosen the screw labeled "VHF." Connect the adapter to the screws and tighten. Screw the RF cable into the adapter.

3. The television should be tuned to channel 3 to view the videotaped material. Some VCRs have a switch to select channel 3 or 4 for viewing taped material. Make sure the VCR is switched to channel 3. Consult the operator's manual for the VCR if there are any questions.

4. Discuss the use of tracking adjustments to maintain picture quality.

Fig. 2.2. Overhead #2.

CONNECTING TELEVISIONS AND VCRS

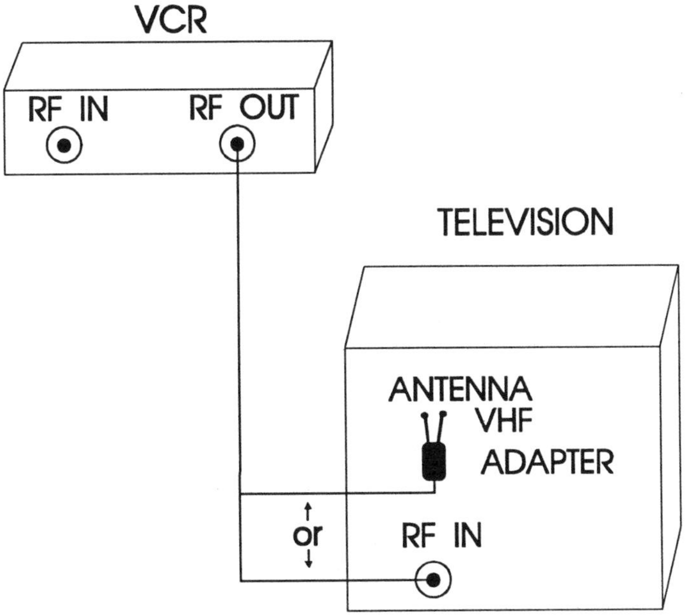

1. Locate the RF Out jack on the back of the VCR. Attach RF cord.

2. Locate the RF In jack on the back of the television. Attach the other end of the RF cord.
* Older televisions may require an RF antenna adapter. Connect to VHF antenna inputs.

3. Turn television to channel 3.

4. Load tape in VCR. Push "Play." Picture should appear on television.

5. Adjust tracking (VCR) if needed.

Instructional Notes for Overhead #3

[Figure 2.3]

Equipment: camcorder
AC adapter
television
monitor
RF cable
RCA patch cord
microphones (lavaliere, dynamic, shotgun)
microphone extension cord
adapter (1/4-inch phone plug to 1/8-inch minijack)
tripod

Microphones

Demonstrate how to connect an external microphone to the camcorder. Most camcorders will come equipped with an 1/8-inch minijack external mic input, so an adapter must be used for microphones with 1/4-inch phone plugs. Some taping situations will require the use of additional microphone cord. Show how easily this can be used to extend the microphone cable.

Discuss classroom activities that are going to be videotaped and how to identify which microphone would be best suited for each type of activity.

Tripods

Tripods are essential for obtaining a steady camera shot throughout the videotaping activity. Demonstrate the use of a quick-release pin for attaching the camcorder to the tripod.

Dollies can be used to assist in moving the tripod about the classroom. Show how to connect the tripod to the dolly. (Note: This should be done prior to attaching the camcorder to the tripod!)

Monitors / Televisions

Explain the difference between a monitor (Audio/Video inputs) and a television (RF inputs). Demonstrate the proper way to connect the camcorder to each piece of equipment. Most camcorders use the AC power adapter for this purpose. Many teachers are unaware of the fact that they can use the camcorder for playback as well as recording events.

Fig. 2.3. Overhead #3.

EXPANDING THE CAMCORDER SYSTEM

I. Microphones
   A. Adapters
   B. Lavaliere
   C. Dynamic
   D. Shotgun

II. Tripods
   A. Release Pins
   B. Dolly

III. Monitors/Televisions
   A. RF (In/Out)
   B. Video/Audio (In/Out)

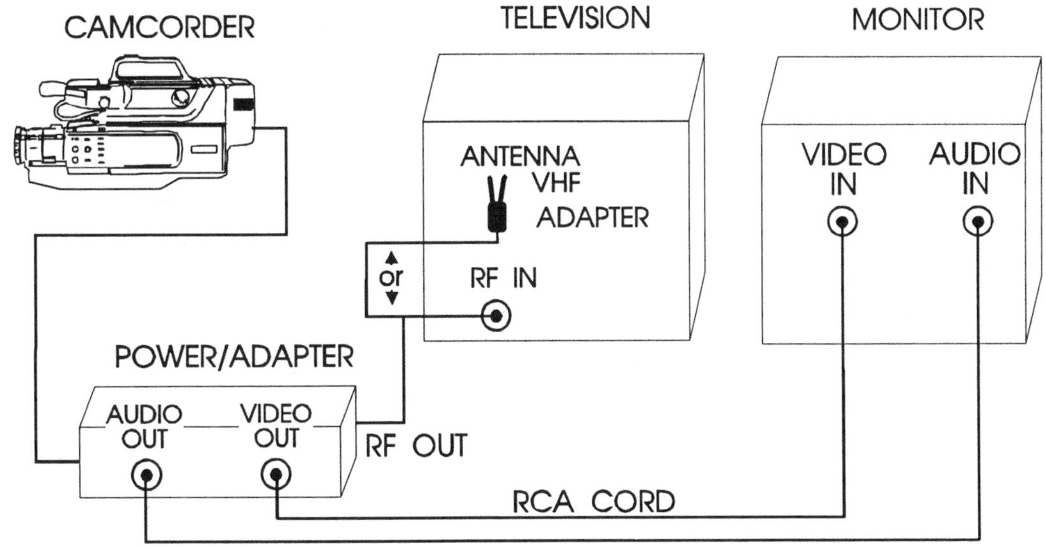

In-Service Follow-Up

The only way to ensure the effectiveness of your workshop is to provide some follow-up activities for the participants. These will enable them to gain confidence in their ability to use video equipment for instruction, as well as assist you in developing more successful workshops in the future. Some follow-up ideas are:

1. Allow a trained television production student to assist teachers in setting up and using video equipment the first few times it is used in the classroom. Caution the student to "assist" the teacher and not perform the setup alone.

2. Review videotaped material with the teachers and discuss techniques for improvement.

3. Conduct a follow-up workshop to answer any questions teachers might have after using the equipment in their classroom.

4. Prepare a follow-up survey to evaluate the effectiveness of the workshop and training.

3 ADULT AND COMMUNITY SCHOOL INSTRUCTIONAL OPPORTUNITIES

Each year, thousands of adults are active in community-based educational opportunities. Some are learning to read and write. Others are reviewing and reviving skills learned years earlier in high school in preparation for a high-school equivalency test. Many are continuing their education by learning a vocational skill, while some are taking courses such as cooking, ceramics, dance, and yes, television production for personal enrichment.

Many high schools across the country remain open in the evening hours and function as centers for adult educational opportunities. These schools are often called "adult schools," "night schools," and "community schools." Some communities even have their own personal enrichment centers, offering classes to members of the community in areas of interest.

The high school television production instructor is often presented with the opportunity to teach members of the community the skills of the trade. Unfortunately, the instructor quickly finds that the lesson plans and techniques used during the day with teenagers do not hold the interest or meet the needs of the adults in the community school class. It is to this need that this chapter is written.

The Adult as a Learner

Many fine books have been written concerning the techniques and strategies used in teaching the adult student. Any television production instructor interested in teaching adults should visit a local library or bookstore to locate such materials. William Draves's book *How to Teach Adults* is quite insightful in its approach to the topic. The section that follows is a combination of the philosophies furthered by Draves and the experiences of the authors of this text. While the list is not intended to substitute for a complete study in the area, it is a primer that can introduce a secondary school teacher to adult education.

Ten Characteristics of the Adult Learner

1. The adult learner is attending class because of a perceived need in his or her life. That need may be recreational, vocational, social, or based on some other motivation.

2. The adult learner has chosen to be in the educational situation. Unlike the high school student, the adult learner has a choice about his or her presence in the educational system.

3. The adult learner may have negative feelings about school. Most instructors love the classroom situation. However, many adults have had bad experiences with education in the past. Those experiences are not easily forgotten.

4. The adult learner may be challenged to define his or her self-image. The adult in your class could be an experienced full-time mother who hasn't been in the classroom or workplace for years, a blue-collar worker who is "testing the education waters," or a retiree who seeks the activity formerly provided by years of diligent work. Your techniques of instruction will influence the self-image of the adult student.

5. The adult learner will have a variety of experiences. Although many high school classes consist of students with largely similar experiences, most community school classes will consist of adults from all walks of life.

6. The adult learner is not a blank slate. All learners are affected by their experiences. If we assume that the adult learner has more life experiences than the typical high school student, then we must also assume that the instruction the adult learner receives in community school will be filtered through an abundance of practical knowledge.

7. The adult learner is more sensitive to physical discomfort. Unlike children, adults are accustomed to being in control of their physical environment. Uncomfortable temperature, seating arrangements, and room lighting can have a negative effect on the adult learner. And when an adult needs to use the rest room, he or she really doesn't want to wait a few minutes.

8. The adult learner is more likely to experience sensory difficulties. As in groups of teenagers, differences exist in hearing and vision. However, the wide range in age usually found in community school classes may magnify these differences.

9. The adult learner is more aware of the value of time. The adult enrolled in community school class is probably surrendering valuable time to be involved in the educational opportunity, time normally used for leisure, recreation, or family activities. Or the adult learner may be sacrificing lucrative job overtime pay to attend community school. Although the teenager may relish classroom "free time," the adult learner will probably become disturbed if the class does not progress at a reasonable pace.

10. The adult learner is task-oriented and prefers a problem-centered approach. "How do we do it?" is more important than "Why do we do it?" to most adult learners. Even though their maturity level may accommodate a lengthy theoretical discussion, the needs of the adult learner lie in the real world, not the abstract realm.

Television Production Course Outline

Perhaps the list above has whetted your appetite to teach television production in community school. Although there are many different strategies for adopting the television production curriculum to an adult audience, a 14-session course outline is provided here. Your adoption of this outline, of course, depends on your personal areas of expertise and the amount of equipment available to the community school class. The activities that you assign your students will also depend on your equipment allotment. Therefore, no specific activities are included in this outline. The outline is divided into two sections: television production equipment instruction and the video project as a vehicle for adult education.

Television Production Equipment Instruction

Equipment operation is a main concern of many community school students. Some students will need basic instruction, while others will want guidance on using the equipment in new, creative ways. Community school instruction also provides vocational training for such tasks as editing and audio mixing. Some community school students enroll for the opportunity to get hands-on experience with many different types of equipment before purchasing equipment for personal and professional use.

The content covered in each lesson can be found in part I, chapters 1 and 2, and in part II, chapters 1 and 2, so it is not repeated here. However, keep in mind the different strategies that you will implement when presenting the material to the adult learner.

LESSON 1: INTRODUCTION TO TELEVISION PRODUCTION

The initial session of many community school classes often includes registration and fee collection. Also, be prepared with name tags and course outlines. Once this process is completed, survey your class members to ascertain their knowledge, level of interest, and needs. The survey may be oral or written (figure 3.1). If a written survey is used, spend a few minutes reading a few responses (anonymously) in front of the class to assure the students that their survey responses will be taken into account in the course and that the course outline is not "written in stone." At this time you may also want to give your students a pretest to further ascertain their level of knowledge. Because some employers will give credit and pay tuition for their employees to take adult/community school courses, many of them require a pretest and a posttest as proof of learning. Figure 3.2 (page III-3-5) provides a quiz that can be used as both a pretest and a posttest.

Next you may want to conduct a question-and-answer session, which will allow you to further gauge your students' level of interest, show your interest in their needs, and establish your own credentials. Be prepared to answer such questions as "How can I make a great wedding video?," "How does a wireless microphone work?," and "How much money should I spend on a camcorder?" Be complete in your answers without getting too detailed. (The material is presented in later class sessions.) Plan to spend about an hour on the survey and the question-and-answer session. The remainder of the first class session should include a presentation and discussion of the basic television production system: camera/deck or camcorder, microphone, tripod, and headphones.

(Text continues on page III-3-6.)

Fig. 3.1. Adult/community school survey/interest inventory.

Adult/Community School
Survey/Interest Inventory

Name ________________________ Daytime Phone (   )________________

Which items of equipment do you feel comfortable operating?

(*please circle*)

home stereo system	microphones	audio equalizer
video camera/deck	video switcher	character generator
audio mixer	camcorder	tripod
home VCR		

Which of the following procedures can you perform?

(*please circle*)

audio dub	video insert
assemble edit	audio insert

= =

Which of the following describes your reason(s) for taking this class?

(*check all that apply*)

_______ hobby/personal knowledge   _______ career interest

_______ teaching career   _______ TV talent career

_______ independent productions (weddings, etc.)   _______ using video in my business

_______ other ______________________________________

____

____

= =

Please list the topics that you would like to cover in this class. Thank you.

Fig. 3.2. Adult/community school TV production pretest/posttest.

Adult/Community School
TV Production Pretest/Posttest

Student ______________________________ Date ______________

1. Name the items needed for a basic video shoot.

2. Name at least five elements in the expanded video-audio production system.

3. List the six personnel positions needed for a two-camera shoot with graphics.

4. Explain the difference between assemble and insert editing.

5. Give three examples—real or fictional—of the use of the chroma key.

6. List three video project ideas for your work site.

Number correct ________ Instructor's initials ________ Date ______________

LESSON 2: THE EXPANDED VIDEO SYSTEM

Introduce the concept of multiple-camera video production. Include a discussion of switchers, video monitors, and record and source VCRs.

LESSON 3: THE EXPANDED AUDIO SYSTEM/ THE EXPANDED LIGHTING SYSTEM

Discuss the integration of audio into the multiple-camera configuration, including the audio mixer, music sources, audio connections, and production music (see part II, chapter 3).

Demonstrate the lighting techniques used in television production. Include studio lights, portable lights, and the use of available light.

LESSON 4: POSTPRODUCTION WORK (Part 1)

Introduce the concepts of audio dubbing and assemble editing. Plan for practice time for the students.

LESSON 5: POSTPRODUCTION WORK (Part 2)

Teach audio and video insert editing.

LESSON 6: FIELD-TRIP POSSIBILITIES

Plan a field trip with the class. Possible destinations include a television production center, television studio, and video duplication center. Remember to ask the students where *they* would like to go.

LESSON 7: POSTPRODUCTION EXTRAS

Demonstrate and allow the students to work with the special features of your studio, including character generation, frame storage, and chroma key.

The Video Project as a Vehicle for Adult Education

If your students have attended class faithfully and absorbed your expert instruction, they should have a good working knowledge of the concepts of television production. You can now guide your students in their first video production.

LESSON 8: TOPIC SELECTION

Decide on a topic for your 5-minute video program. Topic suggestions include your community school, your community, a profile of a community member, and a neighborhood activity. Your topic may be dictated by the time and place of your class sessions.

LESSON 9: SCRIPTWRITING AND STORYBOARDING

Work as a class to outline the script. Then allow small groups to write certain parts of the script. The groups can then begin storyboarding the script.

LESSON 10: CRITIQUING AND REVISING SCRIPT AND STORYBOARD

Make a copy of the script for each student. Revise the script through constructive criticism. Revise the storyboards as needed. Schedule interviews that may be included in the project. Select the music. (Remember to use production music if the program is going to be duplicated.)

LESSON 11: VIDEOGRAPHY ASSIGNMENTS

Divide the storyboard into sections, and assign each section to a camera team. Begin videotaping the program.

LESSON 12: VIDEOTAPING

Continue to videotape in class. View and critique all sections, and re-shoot when necessary.

LESSON 13: POSTPRODUCTION

Edit the project using either the assemble method (edit, then audio-dub) or the insert method (record audiotrack on black, then insert video and interviews).

LESSON 14: VIEWING AND EVALUATING THE FINISHED PROJECT

Watch the finished project and hold a discussion on the good points of the program and the parts that need improvement. Emphasize the positive, and discuss what the group has learned. Make plans to duplicate the tape for those who are interested. Have a party!

This is just one possible outline for a community school class. You could also include talk shows, instructional video programs, and sporting events. The completed student surveys can provide ideas for many more projects.

Conclusion

Television production is a popular topic in adult community schools. Although the curriculum mirrors the content of the high school program, the method of presentation must often be adapted to meet the needs and characteristics of the adult learner. The course content should also reflect the students' interests as determined by a class survey. A good community school class will teach the students 1) how to use television production equipment and 2) how to plan and produce a television production program.

Sources

Draves, William. *How to Teach Adults.* Manhattan, KS: Learning Resources Network, 1984.

Verduin, John R., Jr., Harry G. Miller, and Charles E. Greer. *Adults Teaching Adults: Principles and Strategies.* Austin, TX: Learning Concepts, 1977.

APPENDIXES

[redacted]

QUESTIONS FROM THE FLOOR

A — *Answers to the Most Commonly Asked Questions About Teaching Television Production*

In the following pages, we'll try to answer some of the questions that we've been asked at conventions and seminars and by visitors to our school. Write to us in care of the publisher with your questions or comments.

How can I build a successful television production program of instruction at my school?

Classroom teaching of television production skills is the most important ingredient in your program. Your students need a strong foundation in the skills of videography. After a year or two of dedicated teaching, you will have a group of students with excellent video skills who know exactly what is expected of them. Keep your standards high and don't accept poor productions. But remember, you work at a school, not a professional production center. Your first priority should be teaching your students.

How can I obtain the backing and support of my school's administration?

As business executives have known for years, the best way to gain the support of a boss is to make the boss look better and make his or her job easier. Certainly television production has the capability to do this quite simply. Make a 3-minute school orientation tape with the help of your students. Present this tape to your principal. After he or she has had a chance to view it, ask what services the video department might be able to perform for the school in the future. In short, make yourself an essential member of the faculty. Most principals will respond to this extra effort. Conversely, don't do anything that makes your principal look bad or makes his or her job harder. For example, don't allow your students to jump off the media center roof to simulate skydiving for an action-adventure video. Don't constantly whine about a lack of equipment or overcrowded classes. Instead, show the administration what you can do with your current restraints. Once you have them hooked, tell them what you could do with a little bit more equipment and fewer students per class.

How should I respond to criticism from fellow faculty members?

It really depends on what type of criticism you're receiving. If you're hearing comments like "Why don't you ever feature the math department?" or "You have too much sports coverage!," you probably need to examine your show's content. If the comments are general in nature, speak with the critic and try to get him or her to specify the complaints. Unfortunately, some people complain because they see that as their role in life. They see students in your classes having fun and creating exciting videos. Some "traditionalists" will argue that television production classes have no place in the school. Having to listen to this criticism is part of the job, and shouldn't be taken seriously. These are the same people who didn't want computers or calculators in school, and thought the slide rule was a crutch for poor mathematicians. Remember, to obtain specific criticisms, treat everyone fairly, and ignore petty remarks. If you have a supportive administration, photocopy the critical letter and put it in your principal's mailbox. Advising a supportive administration of criticism gets the situation out in the open and lets the principal know that you plan to correct any perceived problems. The desired result is open communication and an improved program. A person can't talk about you behind your back if you're facing them head-on.

How should I answer the people who say that we should go "back to the basics" in education?

Our reply is fourfold. First, we point out that video production is an excellent way to teach many of the "basics," like reading, composition, science, and math. Second, we state that television production class is just like wood shop and auto body shop classes were 25 years ago. Television production class teaches an important vocational skill. Although it may be a bit more expensive than your standard lecture class, it is worth the extra cost. Third, we ask them to look at the countries that are winning the economic battle. Are these countries turning their backs on technology? Of course not. They recognize the importance of technology, and teach young people how to use it. A "back to the basics" approach will not prepare students for life in the twenty-first century. Finally, we point out that in any emerging technology, if you're not going forward, you're falling behind. Schools teaching television production classes owe it to the students to keep pace with new technologies.

How many students should be in a television production class?

Ideally, a television production class should have no more than 20 students. This number, though, is dependent on the amount of equipment you have at your disposal. If you have a complete studio and five camera setups, you can probably handle 25 or more students. But if you are limited to one or two camcorders, your class size should be limited as well.

Do students have to pay a fee to take television production class?

Many school districts have a policy that allows schools to charge a certain fee to take special elective courses like television production. Other districts prohibit this practice, or collect lab fees only by calling them "program donations." In our program, each student buys a videotape (about $3 from a bulk supplier) and a small earphone or headphone set ($1 and up). While many would argue that the videotape purchase constitutes a lab fee, we see the videotape as a notebook, onto which all of the student's projects are recorded. While we maintain a small supply of headphones, we encourage headphone ownership for the sake of hygiene. We do not recommend collecting lab fees or "donations" to fund equipment purchase or repair.

How do you select the students for your program?

Never one to pass up a straight line, we respond, "very carefully." Actually, we are fortunate to teach in schools that provide a wide variety of interesting electives, so we don't have a long waiting list to get into our beginning television production course. However, we personally interview each student who enters our program. We look for good attendance, good citizenship, and reasonably good grades. A student who misses too much school probably won't finish his or her television projects. Students who are frequently disciplined at school haven't displayed the responsibility and maturity necessary to take television production class, and because all schools offer courses for many different levels of students, As, Bs, and Cs are the norm. In our advanced class last year, we had students who were in the gifted program and students who had learning disabilities. Their academic placement had no effect on their grades in television production class.

Are television production students more mature than other students?

The successful ones are.

Do you ever have students teach each other?

Generally, no. In our program, the students are students and the teachers are teachers. Certainly, the teachers can learn a great deal from the students, and students can learn by watching their classmates. Although students may have the knowledge to teach their classmates, they generally don't have the teaching ability to pull it off. Students-as-teachers tend to overgeneralize a task and forget the step-by-step process involved in their own learning. Student teachers, in the name of success, often perform the task for the learner, instead of helping the learner perform the task for himself or herself. Perhaps you have had success using students as teachers. Ask the students how *they* feel about it. If everybody is happy and learning, you've found a young person who has the gift of teaching. Please encourage that student to consider teaching as a profession!

Do you allow the students to work before and after school?

The studio is open for students to use independently 30 minutes before school and for about an hour after school. When we need to leave "on time" (at the end of the teacher workday) we post a note on the door at the beginning of the day. We don't pull "all-nighters" in the studio. We try to anticipate our needs and plan accordingly.

Do you allow students and faculty members to check out equipment for after-school use?

Our advanced students may check out equipment to work on a television production class project on an overnight basis. The procedure includes a statement of responsibility from the parent and a same-day phone conversation with the parent.

If a student is performing a videotape service for a faculty member (for example, videotaping a volleyball game for the coach to review), the faculty member must check out the equipment after school and return it to school first thing in the morning.

We do not circulate equipment to students or faculty members for personal use. We refer the teachers to the head media specialist. Our media center circulates the consumer-grade camcorders to faculty members on an overnight basis.

How do you handle equipment security?

All ENG equipment is stored in locked cabinets. The studio doors automatically lock. The entire media center is monitored by a sound-sensitive burglar alarm. A single incident of theft can decimate a television production program.

How do you handle your equipment repairs?

We use many different avenues for equipment repair. Our school's advanced electronics class, under the guidance of an excellent instructor, takes care of minor repairs of equipment not under warranty. Our major repairs are done by a factory-authorized business. Repairs are financed by video yearbook sales. We also have a technician from that business come to our studio to test and align all installed equipment each year. We occasionally use our county repair facility.

Do you ever buy used equipment?

Occasionally we purchase used equipment. The used equipment is always purchased from the same vendor that we use for new equipment and repairs. The vendor warranties the equipment for 30 days against defects. We never buy used equipment that is defective, and the price must be *very* good. For example, we recently purchased for the school an industrial-level camera with a 12 x 1 lens and an industrial portable VCR for $1,500. New, the items would cost around $3,000. The equipment was originally purchased from the same vendor and was used three or four times to videotape weddings. The vendor had accepted the equipment in trade on a more sophisticated system. The camera/VCR continues to provide outstanding service a year after the purchase, and we have had no problems.

We don't buy used equipment from newspaper classified advertisements. On several occasions, individuals have called the school and offered equipment for sale, which we courteously decline.

How do you obtain the blank videotape used in your program?

There are several blank videotape vendors in the United States that will ship special orders to schools. Check your telephone directory and professional magazines for the names of these companies.

The blank videotape vendor will offer a superior product at a very reasonable price. When ordering from a tape vendor, you can specify the length of your tape. This allows you to purchase videotapes that are much shorter than the standard 120-minute videotape. These shorter tapes often are called "short loads." For example, our beginning television production students use a 60-minute blank tape. Our media production students, who study video production for nine weeks, use a 20-minute tape. Sixty-minute tapes usually cost about $2.25. A case with label is about $0.25.

The television production department also buys a number of tapes of differing lengths. We purchase about 20 5-minute tapes for storage of brief segments. We also buy quantities of 10-, 60-, and 90-minute tapes.

Purchasing videotape from a tape vendor offers many advantages. The tape loaded into the videocassettes is of professional quality, designed for use at television stations. Your picture response will be better, and the tape will not break or drop particles inside your VCRs. The price is good, and the vendor will ship the tapes to the school and bill an account. Finally, the short loads offer advantages of their own. Students will be less tempted to record a television program or movie on a short tape that won't hold an entire program or movie. With a 2-hour tape, students or teachers may feel obligated to "get their money's worth" by using the entire tape. Editing a segment onto a 5-minute tape eliminates that obligation and protects the tape against accidental loss or erasure. The shorter tape is also less attractive to thieves. Using a 60- or 90-minute tape encourages the student to dedicate that tape to television production class.

What videotaping services do you provide? Do you videotape football games and school assemblies?

This is a tricky question involving many dynamics of your specific school. Unfortunately, many television production instructors have used the promise of supplying videotaping services as leverage for equipment purchase. For those people, the question is moot.

For years, many athletic programs within the school have budgeted money to pay professional videographers and filmmakers to tape/film their games. It is our opinion that this practice should *not* be replaced by school video programs. Videotaping the first few football games might be fun, but the first rainy night can ruin your school's best equipment. Very few instructors are willing to attend so many sporting events, and if you are replacing a professional videographer, the coach will expect professional results, which you and your students may not be able to provide. Videotaping athletic events is certainly good experience for student videographers, and on clear autumn nights, feel free to send a team out to record the game. But replacing professional video services with you and your students distorts the true purpose and objective of your instructional program. And you don't need a coach getting you out of bed at 8:00 A.M. on Saturday morning asking you why the @#!$&* tape is out of focus.

Occasionally, your principal will ask you and your students to videotape school assemblies, plays, etc. Such requests are reasonable, and should be accommodated when possible. A faculty meeting can be videotaped for later viewing by faculty members who were absent that day. The drama director can critique performances on videotape. Parents can check out tapes of the awards assembly or talent show. Many guest speakers will agree to be videotaped. As you can see, these services can be very valuable to the primary mission of your school.

What about copyright?

Copyright is a very serious topic for schools. People who think a copyright holder would never sue a school are wrong! Companies have sued schools *and won*! Most districts have adopted a copyright policy, or are in the process of creating such a policy. Make yourself very familiar with your district's policy. If they don't have one, encourage them to form a committee and volunteer to serve on that committee.

Many schools get in the habit of ignoring copyright law. This is a bad habit and should be broken. Copyright law is firm but fair. Remember, owning two VCRs does not legally permit you to copy everything ever recorded on tape.

Unfortunately, many teachers are uninformed about this body of law. The Association for Information Media and Equipment (AIME) is a valuable resource for those who need to know more about copyright. AIME, a national association of film/video producers and distributors who provide non-theatrical programs to schools and libraries, has made available the Copyright Hot Line (1-800-444-4203) for the purpose of improving the understanding of the copyright law as it relates to film, video, and other electronic media among school personnel and public librarians. Begun in 1989, the hot line has been used by hundreds of schools and libraries for copyright assistance. And the assistance is free!

The Copyright Hot Line may be used for answers and assistance in the following areas: clarification of the copyright law as it relates to film and video use, confidential copyright violation reports, requests for a copyright information packet, orders for a low-cost copyright video, and scheduling of a copyright speaker for your workshops.

AIME also publishes *AIME NEWS*, an informative newsletter available at a moderate cost. The services of AIME are valuable to all instructors and media specialists working with electronic media. Tape the toll-free number beside the telephone, and use it when you need it.

To summarize this long answer: Become familiar with your district's copyright policy, abide by the policy, don't start any bad habits, and use AIME to answer specific questions. Copyright violation is a federal offense.

Is it okay to copy a rented tape for a teacher?

No. You can be sued by about a thousand different people, and you risk losing your job, paying a stiff fine, and going to prison.

Our school recently produced West Side Story. *My students videotaped it for the drama instructor to use for critiquing purposes. Can I make a copy for each student?*

No. The playwrights and musical composers have rights, too. Remember: Copyright law exists to protect creators and provides motivation to keep creating. If you respect the art, then you should respect the artist.

B ORGANIZING A CABLE TV SHOW

Through designated community-access channels, school-produced television programs can be shown to the community. Cable television stations often welcome student-produced programs. Depending on the size of the viewing area and the cable company's schedule, your local cable company may become totally involved in the program production, or simply say "bring us some tape."

Our situation was the latter. Our community cable TV system serves only about 4,000 homes, and was eager to receive any programming produced by the high school.

During one school year, we had a class of fourth-year television production students. There were eight students in the class and they were all interested and proficient in the technical aspects of television production. Because of the orientation of these students and the availability of cable televsion time, we decided to use this class to create a weekly cable television show, "Viewpoint '91."

Preproduction Activities

Creating even the simplest television program is a monumental task. With the school year more than half over, we abandoned any ideas of building complex sets or developing scripts for a drama program. Instead, we decided that we would create a citywide debate tournament for television, a natural choice because two of the instructors in the television production department were former debate coaches.

The initial step in program development was to compose and send a letter to each public and private high school principal in our area. About 20 letters were sent. The letter invited the school to select a student (debate experience optional) to participate in the program. The letter also stated that an orientation session would be scheduled in about two week's time. A return-addressed, stamped postcard RSVP was enclosed, soliciting the name and telephone number of the school, the name of the student participant, and the name of a teacher or other school-authorized adult who would act as a liaison between the student and the television production team. A standard release form was included for completion by the student participant's parent/guardian. The student was advised to bring the completed release form to the orientation meeting.

Back in the studio, the production team created the format, script, and technical aspects of the program. Because several students on the team had previous after-school commitments, it was determined that the program should be taped during the class period and the adjacent lunch period. (We made a note to order pizza on production day!) Because of the shooting time, the debate set had to be simple and portable (the school news show is taped each day about two hours before the debate show was to be taped). Fortunately, the show (now dubbed "Viewpoint '91") was shot only once a week. The students decided to use the existing cyclorama curtain as a backdrop. The two debaters would share a large table, enabling a two-shot of both debaters at the beginning of the program. A lectern was placed beside the debaters' table for the speeches. The judge would have his own table and chair on an adjacent, perpendicular wall; the moderator would stand at a lectern in the corner created by the two walls; and a timekeeper would sit off-camera directly in front of the speaking lectern. The school agriculture department agreed to provide several potted plants to decorate the set. All told, the set could be created in about 10 minutes. Camera angles were mapped on a scenery grid for a two-camera shoot.

Another group of students prepared a format for the show (figure B.1). The cable company requested a 1-hour show with four 4-minute commercial breaks.

Figure B.1. "Viewpoint '91" format.

:00 - :01	opening
:01 - :03	greeting, topic introduction
:03 - :06	ENG segment
:06 - :07	introductions (debaters, judge)
:07 - :11	commercial (black)
:11 - :12	reintroduction, format
:12 - :18	first affirmative speech (6 minutes)
:18 - :21	cross-examination by negative (3 minutes)
:21 - :25	commercial (black)
:25 - :32	first negative speech (7 minutes)
:32 - :35	cross-examination by affirmative (3 minutes)
:35 - :39	commercial (black)
:39 - :43	first affirmative rebuttal (4 minutes)
:43 - :49	negative rebuttal (6 minutes)
:49 - :52	second affirmative rebuttal (3 minutes)
:52 - :56	commercial (black)
:56 - 1:00	winner announced, judge interview, next week, end credits.

Note: This format is based on the Lincoln-Douglas debate format used in debate tournaments across the country, and was familiar to many of the participants.

Because the students were interested in developing their technical skills, the class instructor was chosen to serve as the on-camera debate moderator. A final script was created for the moderator. The script was actually quite short, basically introducing each speaker and welcoming the audience back from commercials. The script was duplicated for each production team member.

As the format reflects, each program included an ENG segment, which explored the topic area and contained "person-on-the-street" responses to the debate topic. The segment was added in the editing process so as not to influence the judge. A student crew of three (reporter, videographer, researcher) was formed and assigned the task of the ENG segment for the duration of the program.

The production team then created a 1-minute opening for the show. They videotaped scenes of students researching topics in the school media center and included several over-the-shoulder shots of students taking notes. They shot the footage in an exciting "music video" style and used a strobe effect and minor posterization to give the introduction an exciting look. Students from the school music lab created an up-tempo instrumental theme song.

RSVP cards began to arrive at the school, and the media center was secured as the orientation meeting site. Each school was telephoned to invite the student and adult sponsor to the orientation meeting. The students were advised to wear nice clothing, as they would be videotaped for promotional purposes. They were also reminded to bring their signed release form.

A six-page orientation packet that gave information about many different areas of the show was created for use in the orientation meeting. The packet included the following:

Time of arrival

Forfeit rule (10 minutes)

Dress code

Topic selection

Ballot type (enclosed in the packet)

Judges

Copyright (retained by the school)

Program format

"Viewpoint '91" press release

Selected bibliography of debate books

Guidelines for each speech in a debate

Each school was given a letter designation (A, B, C, etc.) as its representative arrived. Eight schools decided to send participants. Introductions were made and the orientation packet was discussed. Then the school names were added to a single-elimination tournament schematic that had already been listed A, B, C, etc. This allowed for random assignment of the competitors. Then, topics for the first round were announced. The sides (affirmative/negative) were predetermined by placement on the schematic, and no "switching" was allowed. After a question-and-answer session, the group was escorted into the television studio for a brief tour. Then each student participant was recorded for about one minute on videotape in order to produce a bust shot with the student's name and school listed at the bottom of the screen.

The production team created a commercial for the program using the opening, theme song, participant shots, and a script describing the program. The cable TV station added the time and day of airing to the commercial's end.

Community members served as judges. They included a college professor, a school-board member, and a newspaper editor. One judge was used for each program.

Students were assigned the following jobs on a rotating basis: videographer (2), editor (2), graphics, technical director, audio, floor director, and timekeeper. An instructor served as director for the first few programs, and was replaced by a student after a few shows were produced.

Production Activities

Preproduction is about 75 percent of the job! Videotaping the show was actually quite simple. Each participant (with adult sponsor) and judge arrived prepared and on time. A drama/media instructor applied makeup, and the students were given a few minutes to acclimate themselves to the set. The moderator and debaters were fitted with lavaliere microphones.

Because the show was being edited, several brief "tape stops" were written into the script to minimize movement requirements while tape was rolling. For example, on the format presented in figure B.1 a cross-examination follows each initial speech. After each initial speech, the floor director signaled "cut," and everyone took a deep breath. Then the debaters stood shoulder-to-shoulder for the cross-examination. The next script item was a transition by the moderator. With tape rolling, the moderator made this transition ("Now it's time for a cross examination....") and the switcher cut to the two-shot. Then the cross-examination began. By editing the end of the initial speech to the transition/cross-examination, the editor created the illusion that no time elapsed between the speech and cross-examination.

Graphics were used in the production to announce the topic, the debaters, and the judge. End credits were prepared, listing everyone who worked on the show. Graphics were created in advance and stored on a floppy disk.

The audio technician carefully adjusted microphone levels throughout production. The theme music was also used as a transition as the show went to, and returned from, commercial breaks.

Postproduction Activities

The raw program footage was edited into a program, following the format as closely as possible. The tape began with 10 seconds of tone (100% VU) and color bars, then 20 seconds of silent black. After the black, a 5-second time countdown appeared, followed by the opening. The show was then edited according to format, with silent black used in the commercial breaks. As the moderator announced next week's debaters, their bust shot was video-inserted into the program. The tape ended with two minutes of black.

The television production department purchased trophies for the champion and runner-up, which were presented on the final show. The department also purchased "Viewpoint '91 Crew" T-shirts for each crew member and had a party for the production team.

Conclusion

Producing a cable television show was a rewarding experience for the television production crew, the show participants, and the instructors. The production team members copied several of the programs and used them as part of their video resumes. The school received positive publicity in the media and many nice letters from viewers and school administrators for the endeavor.

Remember: The type of program you produce is not as important as the production experience itself. You may decide to create a talk show, an instructional show, or a ping-pong tournament, complete with expert commentators. Whatever type of program your school produces, your advanced students will learn from the experience of creating a television program for your community.

C ORGANIZING A LIVE BROADCAST

As school populations continue to grow, many schools find that they do not have a facility that will seat the entire student body in an atmosphere that affords the dignity required by an awards assembly. Some schools choose to sacrifice the setting and conduct an awards assembly in the gymnasium or, worse, on the football field. Others use the auditorium and invite only a few students to the assembly.

Our school, with a student and faculty population of more than 4,000, likes to recognize academic achievement. However, like the situation described above, the football stadium is the only facility large enough to hold our entire student/faculty population and still have room left over for parents and friends. And because we live in a state where springtime temperatures often soar to 90 degrees and above, the outdoor setting is not really feasible. So how can we hold an awards assembly that everyone can watch at the same time? Simple. We use our portable EFP system, which is unlike ENG and includes such elements as audio mixing, graphics, and video switching.

Our school auditorium seats about 900 people. The awards committee (a faculty group) reserves about 200 of those seats for parents, community members, and the press. The other 700 seats go to students, regardless of grade level, who have the highest grade point averages in the school. Choosing honor students generally ensures a well-behaved, receptive audience.

Everyone who is scheduled to receive an award (and at our school, that's more than 200 students) sits on the stage. A teacher acts as the master of ceremonies, and the principal distributes the awards and congratulates the recipients. The entire program takes about an hour and a half.

The remainder of the student body and faculty watches the program over closed-circuit television. Our school is wired for closed-circuit, with a television in every classroom. We also have a portable modulator, which allows us to transmit from any TV receptacle in the school. Here's how it works: Our EFP signal (more on that later) is sent through a portable RF modulator to the television RF receptacle in the auditorium. The signal is sent through the school's closed-circuit wiring system to the broadcast control in the media center. The control (also called the "head-end") receives, refines, and remodulates the signal for viewing in classrooms throughout the school.

Equipment

What equipment is needed for all of this? It *could* be done with a camcorder and a tripod, but we choose to make it more professional and, as a result, more complicated. We configure EFP equipment like the "talk show" project discussed and diagrammed in part I, chapter 1, lesson 7. Two cameras are used—one about 8 rows back in the center, and one about 12 rows back on the side. The cameras are connected to a switcher, which allows the technical director to cut and fade from camera 1 to camera 2. The video signal is daisy-chained through a character generator (on transparent background) so that the names of the recipients and their awards can be listed. The video signal comes out of the character generator and is sent to the record VCR so that a copy can be made for posterity. Finally, the signal is sent to the portable RF modulator and begins the trip throughout the school as described above.

Microphones are placed on the stage—one at the master of ceremonies' lectern and the other facing the audience to record applause. A third microphone is used by a television reporter—one of our best students—who does a brief introduction and conclusion on-camera for our "viewing audience." All microphones are connected to the portable audio mixer.

You may want to include music at the beginning and the end of the show. The music sources (cassette, CD) should be connected to the audio mixer. Then the combined audio signal is sent directly to the VCR for recording and processing. The VCR audio signal is then sent to the RF modulator, paired with the video signal, and sent on its way.

Production Guidelines

As you can tell, this is not a tremendously difficult production for advanced students with training in video production. However, the "live" aspect of the show leaves no room for mistakes! Here are some tips to help make your show *almost* mistake-proof.

- About a week before the program, make a list of *all* of the items that you will need to complete the production. Make sure to include all monitors and cords.
- Plan for your electrical needs. You will probably need AC for more than a dozen pieces of equipment. Check with your school maintenance department to make sure that you won't overload any circuits already strained by the lights of the auditorium.
- Plan an intercom system for your director and camera operators. A wired or wireless system can be used.
- Choose your crew very carefully. The students need to be professional, responsible, and mature.
- If you decide to have a reporter introduce the show for your television audience, make sure that the talent is well prepared. In a live show, there is no "take two."
- Give yourself plenty of time to set up your equipment in the auditorium. If your awards assembly is Friday morning, start moving equipment Thursday afternoon. Your principal should provide a substitute teacher for you a half day before the show and all day on the day of the show. If you plan to leave the equipment in the auditorium overnight, advise your school vandal-watcher or security guard. The students who will work as technicians should help move and connect the equipment. This will help give them a sense of their place in the overall production. They, too, should be excused from class for a day and a half.
- Test the equipment as soon as it is connected. Any bad connections or equipment problems should be diagnosed the day *before* the show.
- The instructor and the production team should meet with the awards committee the day before the awards assembly to walk through the program to determine camera angles and camera placement. (You wouldn't want to videotape your principal's worst side for two hours!)
- The graphics technician should preload many of the graphics pages before the program begins. Pages such as the title, the name of your reporter, the principal's name, the master of ceremonies' name, and the credits can all be loaded into the character generator's memory

(internal and external) days in advance. If your memory has a few pages left, you can also load the names of the winners and their awards. As any character generator technician can tell you, it is easier to recall graphics than to create them on the spot. Doing this may mean revealing the heretofore secret award winners to the graphics technician. In this case, revealing the secret is justified.

- Your production crew should arrive early to school on the day of the shoot and report directly to the auditorium. Juice and doughnuts, courtesy of the awards committee, should await them.

- After testing the equipment once more, the crew should take a short break and prepare for the long program. At this point, we run the graphic "Stay tuned for the awards assembly" on a blue background with contemporary, unobtrusive music playing in the background. Make sure that all microphone levels are *down* and that all cameras are on standby, so that someone doesn't broadcast his or her personal agenda while the crew is taking their pre-show rest-room break.

- Continuing the philosophy that we have stated or implied throughout this text, require your students to work in a professional, mature manner. Mistakes should not result in yelling or dirty looks. An auxiliary member of your group (perhaps the reporter) who is trained in all aspects of the production should be ready as a substitute for any student who cannot uphold this level of professionalism.

- Students should dress professionally for this assignment (figure C.1). This includes a necktie for men and a dress or skirt and blouse for women. This dress code will help establish an atmosphere of professionalism.

Fig. C.1. Professionally dressed students working on an EFP assignment.

- As the instructor, plan to spend a few minutes warming up the audience. Tell them what to expect from your crew. They can also help your program run smoothly, providing the "studio audience" that your viewing audience will expect. For example, advise them that your reporter will be stationed at the side of the auditorium and that the master of ceremonies will walk onto the stage as soon as the report is finished. When the master of ceremonies enters the stage, the audience should applaud.

- After the program, the production crew should be treated to lunch by the awards committee. We are firm on this requirement because a job well done deserves a reward! Although we don't bribe students to work in video, we do respect and reward superior efforts and significant time donations to the school. This simple reward can build a sense of responsibility and dedication in a student, and students are much more likely to repeat a school service if they are offered even the smallest reward.

- Provided that no copyrighted music was used in the program, make copies of the tape available for purchase by parents and students. As stated in part III, chapter 1, page III-1-5, the tapes can be duplicated inexpensively and quickly by a professional duplication center. Have a brief advertisement printed in the awards assembly program and announce it during your preprogram audience warm-up.

Conclusion

Broadcasting the school awards assembly through your school's closed-circuit system provides a valuable service to your school. It allows all of the students to see their friends and classmates win hard-earned awards and allows your students to experience a live broadcast in a relatively safe environment. You can also use your EFP set up for pep rallies, football games, variety shows, and a number of other projects. Just remember, preparation and professionalism are the keys to a successful program.

D PRODUCING SEGMENTS ON TEACHER AND STUDENT RECOGNITION

Most schools have a method of determining a "teacher of the year" and possibly a "student of the month." But how many times do we remember those award recipients the day after the announcement is made on the intercom? Probably not very many. Television production can help make these presentations exciting and memorable. We'll describe our method for recognizing our school's teacher of the year. The same philosophy can be applied to a student recognition program, too.

Our school has a rather large faculty, so determining the teacher of the year cannot feasibly be accomplished by a show of hands or a faculty discussion. Instead, the faculty votes for the teacher of the year. Each faculty member can nominate a teacher by listing his or her name on a nomination form. All nominees are placed on a preliminary ballot, and each faculty member can vote for one nominee. This presents a cutoff point, at which time the list of candidates is whittled to five or six teachers. The faculty then votes again, with the faculty member getting the most votes named "teacher of the year" at the school.

The television production response to this procedure contains two parts: a brief presentation of the nominees and a "surprise" visit to the new teacher of the year's room to announce his or her award.

For part 1, a student videographer visits each nominee and makes about five minutes of videotape of the nominee teaching class, helping students, etc. A student reporter gathers facts about the nominees (e.g., college, years of experience, philosophy of teaching). The reporter writes a script that includes information about each nominee and records the script with music and a graphics screen onto a videocassette. Another student can then video-insert shots of the nominee over the pertinent audio. A reporter stand-up introduction and conclusion can also be included. The resulting program is as follows: an introduction by a reporter on-camera, a segment about the nominees, and a conclusion by the reporter, which should end with "Now, let's go to ________ [second reporter's name], who is with ________ [principal's name], who is about to announce this year's teacher of the year." The first half of the program is now complete.

The second part of the program features a second reporter interviewing the principal down the hall from the new teacher of the year's classroom. The reporter can ask the principal questions about how the teacher of the year was selected, what awards he or she will receive, and how the teacher of the year can compete for the district award. When that interview is complete, the camera crew should follow the principal—with tape rolling—into the classroom of the new teacher of the year. The camera operator should get shots of the new teacher of the year and his or her students as they congratulate their teacher. Usually, the principal makes a brief presentation. Then the reporter can ask a few questions of the teacher and his or her students and record a brief stand-up conclusion. A second camera could also be used to record the reaction of the students for insert editing.

The "surprise" footage should be taken back immediately to the studio and edited onto the end of the first part of the program. Here's a complete rundown of the teacher of the year program with suggested times in parentheses:

1. Reporter #1 introduction (:00:20)
2. Documentary of each nominee (total :03:00)
3. Reporter #1 conclusion (:00:10)
4. Reporter #2 introduction and principal interview (:01:30)

5. Tape rolling—surprise announcement in classroom; interviews and reactions (:02:00)
6. Conclusion by Reporter #2 (:00:15)

Total time: :07:15

Obviously, this completed segment should be aired on the same day that it is recorded. In this program especially, old news isn't news at all!

INDEX

INDEX